She Wakes the Night

by

Darcy Carson

Dragons Return, Book 3

She Wakes the Night

Contact Information: info@thewildrosepress.com

Cover Art by *Abigail Owen*

The Wild Rose Press, Inc.
PO Box 708
Adams Basin, NY 14410-0708
Visit us at www.thewildrosepress.com

Publishing History
First Fantasy Rose Edition, 2021
Trade Paperback ISBN 978-1-5092-3503-2
Digital ISBN 978-1-5092-3504-9

Dragons Return, Book 3
Published in the United States of America

"But why pickle your food in those stinking ponds?" she asked.

"It is an acquired taste." Torkel narrowed his golden gaze. He hissed, and the glen filled with the dry, acrid smell of acid dripping from his mouth. *"Blame the Guardians."*

"Us?" piped the two who raced Trell to the dragon circle. *"We are falsely accused."*

Trell laughed as a drop of saliva sizzled on the ground. She was unafraid of being burned—long ago her brother had warded her against dragon acid. Thankfully, she was included in the conversation as the tiny dragons darted around Torkel's massive head.

A black mist began to sparkle around the gigantic dragon. A changing mist. Trell stepped back, aware Torkel was about to shapeshift.

Within moments, a tall, muscular man with ebony hair and striking golden eyes stepped out of the fading mist. Torkel, in human form. He straightened, wearing a tunic and leggings once belonging to Cress that converted with him as he eyed the fluttering Guardians.

"You think we enjoyed carrying your slimy food? We did not. Look at us! How could you expect us to deliver a whole carcass? We are strong, but what you suggest was simply impossible. Putrification aided us in delivering the smaller bits. Just wait until you take a mate and have the task of rearing your own young."

Torkel winked at her. "It is not I who complains."

Dedication

To my sister, Bonnie.
Thank you for being such a great supporter.

Chapter 1

The first rock hit Gren Oyg Har square in his back. He gasped as pain exploded like glass shattering in his body. Several more rocks struck him, shredding his threadbare clothing and cutting deep into his skin. He instinctively curled into a ball to protect his head. He'd sat and slept in this tiny corner of Brenalin's bustling marketplace for days without trouble.

A pudgy butcher, waiting for his morning customers, sneered, "Leave! You are not wanted here."

Swallowing, Gren wondered what crime had he committed. Stoning was a common enough punishment executed beyond the city walls. Why were people doing this to him? The filthy red rags he wore proclaimed him as one of the poor afflicted—an Untouchable. It made him immune.

He flinched again when a fist-size rock smashed his elbow. Sticky blood bloomed like a misshapen flower on the spot. An even larger one slammed into his thigh with gut-wrenching pain.

He'd never realized what a painful way to die stoning was and made a mental note that if he survived and succeeded in his quest, he would outlaw the punishment in his homeland.

A nice thought, but no good now.

Untouchables wandered from town to town, calling none their own. Why torture him now? When the dreaded, flesh-eating disease struck, Untouchables lost everything. Marriages were annulled. Children became bastards. Property was forfeited. All rights were stripped from them. They became non-persons. Dead already, though it might take years before the disease claimed their lives.

In each town an Untouchable visited, food and red cloth were freely given. Whether because people feared contracting the disease or the law forbade them from refusing, he could not tell.

"Don't stop!" cried a male voice. "Stone him."

Gren caught his breath. That voice he recognized. It belonged to his brother, Oded. Looking up, Gren saw a massive green jasper pendant dangling from his brother's neck. The gemstone of Kula, a protective stone, it was a blatant reminder of Oded being the acknowledged eldest.

Oded's pale green eyes burned into Gren, although no recognition flickered within their depths. Would his sibling stop the torture if he knew Gren's identity? Likely not.

Gren looked around for Riff, his younger brother. The pair usually traveled together. Like curs, they were a small pack of troublemakers. He spotted Riff at the rear of the crowd, holding the reins to two of their father's best desert-bred mares.

Gren had anticipated his brothers' arrival in Brenalin, the final destination of their quest. Just not under these circumstances.

A large rock delivered a stinging blow to the side of his head. His vision blurred as he grunted, biting his tongue. Coppery- tasting blood trickled down his throat. Fewer rocks flew at him, but they hit with increasing accuracy.

He heard children chortling. At him?

Dare he stand and try to reason with these townspeople? The thought seemed ridiculous. Untouchables were not known for courage. Surely, the townspeople would stop their torment.

Embedded military training took over. A sizzling strength welled up in his chest. He fought the instinct to defend himself until his muscles relaxed. He ignored the hurtful, burning pain.

Another barrage of rocks assaulted him.

His breathing came faster. Dizziness engulfed him. He hated having to submit. Now it was too late. The strength to stand had long passed.

"Please…stop," he heard himself murmur a guttural plea that no one heard, then cursed silently.

****

The sight of a rock whizzing past Trell Langois's head stopped her in her tracks. She had come to the marketplace to check on the herbalist's latest shipment. She wanted a good supply of medicinal herbs for her journey.

Another rock shot in front of her.

She looked around. A heap of red castoffs lay near the butcher's stand. An Untouchable, swaddled in the folds of those rags, curled on the ground. She watched stains darken and increase in size from seeping blood, and empathy rose.

More rocks flew. The pile moaned. What was wrong with the Brenalins? Hadn't the unfortunate suffered enough? A speedy rush of pity skewered Trell.

Disgusted with the cruelty, she shoved forward. "What's going on here?"

3

"An Untouchable," answered the nobleman standing closest to her. "We will rid your fair city of him."

Something flickered in his pale olive eyes, an ember of contempt that made Trell want to argue back. Worse, the man—a stranger to her—had the audacity to tip her chin up with his index finger and give her a smile meant to melt ice on a winter day. Tall and lean, the nobleman was garbed in a rich tunic and leggings of blue and green and wore a large jasper pendant. Dark brown hair, tied back with golden string, hung past his shoulders.

The Untouchable moaned as though attempting to protest the nobleman's presumptuous touch. Trell wrenched her head away, making the tiny silver bells at the end of her multiple braids jingle. She glanced again at the pile of rags. This time a pair of dazzling emerald eyes peeked from deep within the mass of fabric. Sad and pleading, they stared back.

Another rock struck the Untouchable.

The crowd, women as well as men, and children from babes in arms to those nearly grown, increased. She noticed rocks coiled within many fists. It did not bode well for the Untouchable.

Striding forward, Trell planted herself between the throng and the crumpled pile of rags. She raised her arms. "Cease! What right do any of you have to stone this person?"

"Don't care," said the butcher who wore a blood-stained, greasy apron that fell to his knees. "No liking for Untouchables here. We feed 'em. We clothe 'em. What do we get in return? Nothing."

"You shame yourself, Ultar. It is the law to care for

those unable to do for themselves," Trell countered, recognizing the butcher and believing right sided with her.

A scowl formed on his round face. "Easy for you to say, Trell. You live in the castle. No Untouchables go there. A being like him doesn't threaten your livelihood, but he does ours."

"We know you," someone cried out from the back of the crowd. "You're a student at the Halls of Medsin. What do you know? Have you graduated?"

Trell remained silent, debating with herself about what to do, unsure if reason would influence these people.

"He stole from me," Ultar announced when she frowned at him. "I have rights."

Trell bit her lip to keep from accusing him of lying in public.

"I see by your red cloak that you are a new healer, lovely miss. Surely you cannot be siding with that pathetic creature against the righteous citizens here. Untouchables are a burden upon society. They should be banned from our communities." The tall nobleman spoke as though accustomed to being listened to. "They are beyond contempt. Not just in your fair city, but everywhere. We need to rid our world of every last one of them."

A shudder rippled through Trell as she looked from the man's face to the milling crowd. "Then I'll take him to the King's guards. If he is a thief, they can mete out his punishment."

"Why waste their time when we can handle the matter ourselves?" Ultar argued. "He's unclean. No one wants to risk infection. Our children are in danger. He jeopardizes everyone simply by being here."

Several people nodded in agreement.

While nonsensical to brand an Untouchable unclean, Trell decided to use the crowd's fear against them. She pointed to flecks of blood staining the cobblestones. "You claim he is unclean, yet you are willing to spill his blood onto our streets. Who's going to wash it away? Who will remove his body once he's dead?"

The assemblage listened, although she seriously doubted the accord would last. The high-born stranger already whispered to the man next to him. Likely inciting violence. All around her, the people stood like a predator ready to attack, to do his bidding without hesitation.

"No one will suffer if a creature such as this dies," the butcher said.

Trell spun to face Ultar. "The Untouchable might disagree." Her voice quivered as she struggled to remain calm. The wrongness of this crime infuriated her.

"Be on your way," the nobleman ordered in an ugly, threatening tone. "You've given your opinion, now begone."

Whatever nobility she first glimpsed in his features vanished with the speed of a diving hawk. "Or what?" She refused to budge from her stand. "Will you stone me, too? If I go—" She raised her voice for all to hear. "—he goes with me."

The townspeople shuffled before her. Many knew she was Master Wizard Einer's ward, and she hoped that position held some sway over them. Low growls of protests rolled through the crowd as well as whispered caution, though Trell disregarded both. She slipped her hands under the Untouchable's arms and tugged.

People gasped in shock.

The Untouchable tried to pull away. "No, mistress, you mustn't. I'm an Untouchable."

"Would you have me leave you at the mercy of these *good* citizens?" She uttered the reference as a slight as she continued to help him rise. "I have eyes and can see what you are by your rags of courage."

The Untouchable staggered to his feet. Taller than she expected, he was not the sack of bones the layers of rags covering his body suggested. His brilliant emerald eyes flashed at her through the slit in the shroud; then at the stranger and back to her. Skin glowed a healthy pink at his neck where no rags touched and fine lines spread out from the corners of his eyes, proof this man once laughed with ease. Now, a hard glint shone.

"Come," she said in a low voice, praying to Heyln, the god of Healers, the man suffered no broken bones and could walk without aid. This was the closest she'd ever been to one of the afflicted. To her it was a sign from the gods, providing her with an opportunity to study one even before her journey began. "Best we go."

He bowed his head. "I will follow you."

The crowd parted at her first step. Trell didn't know how fast a pace to set. Surely the Untouchable would have limitations. Her concern proved accurate. He limped on his right leg, though she didn't know if it was from the stoning or the ravage of his disease.

They walked away from the market, down the street until they marched slowly under the great arch of Brenalin's main gate. The walls here were ten meters thick and had never been penetrated in the city's long existence.

After a quarter hour, they came abreast of an apul orchard and stopped to rest in the stippled shade of its budding branches. An old orchard, the trees were twisted with age. The lower boughs were thick, the higher ones thin, reminding Trell of gnarled fingers. In early fall, those same limbs would be heavy with sweet, juicy fruit.

She turned to eye the Untouchable. "Let me check your injuries."

He scrambled back. "That won't be necessary."

She frowned. His refusal didn't make any sense to her. "But I can help!"

He held up his hand. "You mustn't touch me."

She was a healer. Whether he approved or not, she had a duty to perform. "Fear naught. I already did so in town. Remember? You could have sustained a broken bone and not even realize it."

Tension in his stance increased. Perhaps it was best to keep her hands to herself. She rummaged in the pouch tied at her waist for a pinch of cat's claw that she'd boiled and pounded into a powder.

"Fine," she said. "If you have no wish for me to examine you, take this powder and make a paste to rub on the worst of your injuries. Trust me. It will soothe your pain and speed the healing."

He accepted her gift with the hint of a smile beneath his rags as they began walking again. "My gratitude, Healer Trell. I'll use it tonight."

"You have heard of me?"

"I heard the butcher call you Trell, and I know you are newly ordained. My eyesight is good. Healers receive a red cloak upon completion of their studies. I

8

see no rips or tears or stain marks on yours, and the smell of new wool lingers in the air around you."

She smiled at his answer. The disease had not yet dimmed his powers of observation.

"Why did you aid me?" the Untouchable asked as they passed a field where cattle grazed.

A fair question.

Trell realized with a jolt that she had increased her pace and the man kept up. Indeed, a healthy firmness showed in his step. "You were in trouble. I couldn't let murder be committed. Moreover, I suspect Ultar is the real criminal, not you."

Deep laughter billowed out of the man like a warm summer breeze. "You are wise beyond your years. I committed no crime. Rather, I saw the butcher tip the scales in his favor on several occasions. When he caught me watching, he grumbled about my presence and compared me to a three-day-old fish."

His laughter and honesty warmed her insides.

"Can you trust this male human?" The question came through mindspeech and did not surprise Trell. She recognized the speaker and glanced skyward. Most people would take the black dot high above for a crow, but she knew otherwise.

It belonged to her dragon friend, Torkel, the first dragon born from a cache of eggs found in The Wilds. She had visited the hatchery the day of his birth, and he had imprinted upon her while emerging from his egg. From that moment, they'd shared an almost magical bond.

"You fret over nothing," she answered in kind, opening her mind to communicate with him. Thank heaven the Guardians had explained that mindspeech

was merely a means of communication. A person's inner thoughts were concealed. No dragon could read humans thoughts. Oh, that didn't mean they didn't try to trick a person into revealing their opinions. *"I've got you for protection."*

"True. If the human does anything wrong, he will become dragon food."

How like a dragon to make a statement and boast at the same time. She grinned at the thought.

The Untouchable quickened his pace to walk beside her. "I've never met anyone like you before, Healer Trell. Few young women would risk death on behalf of a stranger."

"Is compassion so alien in your homeland? Tell me its location so I may avoid the place."

The man turned his face away.

Blessed Heyln! She'd committed a terrible breach inquiring about his background. Untouchables hoarded their privacy as much as dragons did treasure. "Forgive me. I didn't mean to pry."

He shrugged. "No offense taken. But I would like to learn about you."

Would he now? "You do not want to hear me prattle about myself."

"I doubt it would be prattle. The god Heyln himself could not have a touch as gentle nor care as much as you."

"You flatter me." She glanced to the ground to hide her embarrassment.

"Truth is never flattery."

She weighed the merits of sharing. If she spoke of herself, the Untouchable might impart details about himself. In treating the sick, the more information a healer collected about a patient, the better the odds to restore or preserve a person's health. This was her chance to apply that philosophy.

"I was born in Brenalin," she answered.

He glanced at the bells in her braids, then his gaze swept over her robe. "What made you decide to become a healer?"

"It's my turn to ask a question."

A smile lifted the rags covering his face. "Fair enough. Your turn."

"What brought you to Brenalin?" she asked, starting with an innocent question.

The Untouchable stumbled but raised his hand to forestall her assistance. "I followed the road."

A poor answer if ever she heard one. Surely, he came for a cure. Intuition shouted there was more than what he revealed. "I see."

"His heart beats faster," Torkel said. *"He hides something."*

The Untouchable looked down at her. "I doubt it."

"You may tell me when it suits you." Patience was a quality she had plenty in reserve. "However, I am curious about what I should call you?"

"I am known as Gren."

"Gren." She hadn't expected a given name. "I am deeply honored to make your acquaintance. Company on the road is always welcome. I'm going to see my brother, the Wizard Cress.— You may have heard of him."

The Untouchable's eyes widened in surprise. "Indeed, I have. A mighty wizard who lives deep in Demit Woods. I am honored to be in the presence of his sister. Does he have many?"

"I am the only one. After a short visit with him and his wife, I'll be off to find new cures and different ways of treating the ill."

"A worthy cause, but aren't you afraid to travel the roads without protection? Wouldn't it be safer to continue your studies within Brenalin's walls?"

"My schooling is complete, and I vowed to venture out in the world, if the chance materialized." And it had. "I am a trained healer. It's what I do. Now, that's two questions for you."

The Untouchable's mouth twitched beneath his rags. "Then I'll make it three. What makes you so beautiful and so wise?"

The slow burn of embarrassment rolled up her neck to heat the tips of her ears. She wasn't accustomed to praise. "I am neither beautiful nor wise."

"Let me be the judge."

The gentle way he spoke rippled through Trell. She stared briefly at his striking eyes. The gods had stripped him of everything: family, friends, hopes, and dreams. Unimaginable grief must consume him. Yet, he spared time to compliment her.

"I would never have thought a person like…" Her voice faded away.

"An Untouchable? I might have lost everything, but the law cannot steal what it cannot see—my mind."

Trell let the silence build between them. Far too soon they reached a fork in the road. The main road led all the way to Eudes. For now, she planned on taking the narrower, right fork.

"Here I bid you farewell," she said. "We go our separate ways."

****

Praise the Gods of Feldzvelt, Gren couldn't believe his good fortune. Of all the people to come to his aid. The exact person he sought—Healer Trell, sister of Wizard Cress. He'd learned her name only by accident and suspected his brothers had not. Or their actions in town might have been far different. It was obvious they assumed the healer they sought was older, one with experience. Their mistake.

He didn't believe in coincidence—but providence was another matter.

Heaving a large breath, he calmed his thoughts and directed his attention to keeping his shoulders slumped forward. His muscles ached from fighting the unnatural position. He swore bruises sprouted all over his body from the stoning and blood dried to his clothing, sometimes separating with a bite that made him grit his teeth.

Hopefully, the powder Trell gave him would eliminate the worst pain, especially where an exceptionally large rock had struck his right thigh. That one could have broken bone. His limp had been genuine. Once he could check, he'd probably find ugly discolorations snaking down his leg.

He stood for a few moments, staring at the fork in the road. A setting sun turned the sky into a battlefield of reds, pinks, and golds.

"Wait, Healer. Danger abounds on the road. You cannot rely on your robe to save you from brigands," he heard himself babble.

Multiple braids bobbed in a light breeze. "You don't approve of me traveling alone? Most I see would have me aid them, not harm me."

"Still, I insist upon accompanying you."

"I don't need your protection."

Gren wasn't giving up. "You are defenseless, traveling by yourself. Easy pickings. But…but with me at your side, they will be less tempted."

She stood facing him, a puzzled expression pulling sweeping brows downward. "Do you really think a lone man would make a difference?"

He held his arms wide. "Look at me. They'll fear contamination. I owe you a debt of gratitude. Those who'd dare attack you will see me and fear I might fall upon them. We both know people would rather leap off a cliff than touch me or my clothing."

"You're willing to journey with me?"

"Healer Trell, you saved my life. I can do no less."

The healer didn't answer immediately. He held his breath in the wait. He couldn't appear too eager. Her frown deepened, then a smile replaced it on her heart-shaped face. "I plan to visit my brother first. Since you've heard of Cress, I need not tell you how powerful he is. What you may not know is that he values his privacy. You can accompany me to a glen near his cottage, but under no circumstances should you follow me farther. Promise to do as I say. I would have your word."

Gren caught the warning and made a mental note not to arouse her suspicion. "I vow to await your return in the glen. You have my word, a friend's word."

Her stance relaxed. "Enough light remains for us to cover more distance before we must stop for the night. I brought bread and cheese. We can share it."

Gren smiled. She'd given in easily. If he didn't know better, he'd swear her desire to treat him was the swaying factor. He wished things were different. She knew what he was…or thought she did, which meant he wouldn't be much of a protector. The size of her heart impressed him. He wished deception wasn't necessary to gain her cooperation.

Following her striding, red-caped figure along the path that brought them nearer to towering trees, he tripped.

Trell spun around to study him. "Are you hurt? What's wrong?"

Everything. "Nothing. I merely lost my footing."

When they stopped for the night near a crystal-clear stream, they built a fire of dry sticks and windfall. Trell insisted no branches be broken off living trees, which he found strange, but concurred because plenty of fuel littered the ground.

After eating the bounty Trell provided and feeling sated, Gren sat across the campfire from her, admiring the young woman who looked so fresh and eager. Though he suspected they were close in age, gut instinct told him she had been shielded from the harsh realities of life. "You've not experienced much, have you?"

"My studies have taught me all I need," she replied, "but as I go about the land, I hope practice will be my greatest teacher."

"Then it's a good thing we travel together because I have visited many places. I can be your guide and keep food in our bellies."

Her gaze steadied. "A knowledgeable companion is always welcome on the road."

"And I am talented as well," he said. "Do you like music? I play the flute."

He hadn't meant to boast. Yet the way she pursed

her lips to keep from laughing amused him.

"A flute? What a strange choice," she replied.

He watched her add twigs to the fire. "Why is that?"

"A flute is a military tool used for marching or signaling."

She was astute. He didn't know what he expected from the healer, especially one who seemed young and innocent, but she kept surprising him. He'd have to be careful.

Then, feeling guilty about deceiving her, he volunteered, "A friend gifted me with it. It was the only possession I managed to keep." He pulled the slender woodwind from the folds of his rags and put his mouth directly onto the edge to blow.

Raspy, breathy notes emerged from the age-darkened instrument. Taking a deep breath, he delicately softened the pitch. After a while, he picked up the pace with a loud, piercing composition that filled the night with rushes of energy. His playing could either soothe or make people want to leap up and dance.

A whooshing sound came from the sky.

Gren jerked the flute from his mouth. His gaze shot at Trell in time to see the whites of her widened eyes. "Did you hear that?"

"What?"

He searched the star-lit expanse. "I'm not sure. Something gigantic. Large enough to be a dragon. They exist, you know. It is said the creatures are great music lovers."

"Bah!" she answered. "More likely a colony of bats. Many roost in these woods. They swoop between the trees in search of insects."

"So you did hear something."

"All I heard was your flute music and it was beautiful," she answered, awe filling her voice. "I take back what I said about a flute being a military instrument. In your hands, it's an implement of wonder."

"My thanks," he returned, genuinely pleased at her appreciation of his music.

Moments later the healer snuggled into her bedroll and a lump formed in his throat. He hated himself for having to lie. Especially to someone with such a big heart. What choice did he have?

A kingdom was at stake. His to win from his worthless brothers. Neither Oded nor Riff deserved sitting upon the jasper throne. One was greedy and the other spoiled. Kula deserved better. The plight of the people came first. As sure as he was that the sun would rise on the morrow, his brothers would put the populace in chains or reduce them to poverty. That he could not allow.

Picking up his flute again, he played a soft cradlesong, listening for a dragon.

Chapter 2

Trell fought sleep in constant fear that Torkel would reveal himself. Because she knew the ebony dragon flew above them, every swoop and dive he made sounded like thunder. No way could she confess Torkel's enjoyment of the music nearly ruined her own delight until she could not stay awake any longer.

Dawn nosed over the eastern horizon in a palette of gentle violets and pale pinks. Waking, Trell moaned softly. A jagged rock ground into her hip. She pressed her hand into her back as she straightened her legs. Dew clung to her braids and the edge of her blanket. What she wouldn't give for the soft feather ticking of her bed at Abass castle.

As she stretched the kinks out of her body, the aroma of cooking fish teased her nose.

She remembered falling asleep listening to Gren's spellbinding music. He'd been evasive in answering questions, which, despite her desire to treat him, left her wondering about the wisdom of traveling together. She probably was over-thinking the matter. If they continued together on the road, she would acquire plenty of opportunities to study him.

Still, his music was the most beautiful she'd ever heard. No, not beautiful. Magical. The melody had drawn her in, caressing her ears, mind, and heart with fleeting bursts of sad, wild, and proud notes.

"Glad to see you stir from your sleep."

Trell turned stiffly. Gren looked at her, green eyes crinkling at the edges as he beamed a smile. "I'm afraid hardships of the road will take time to get used to," she greeted. "Didn't the stones bother you?"

Soft laughter rippled from him. "I am accustomed to them."

His answer sounded so natural it was easy to believe him. Then reality struck with the horror of a woodman's axe. What kind of healer was she?

Surely, an inferior one.

The first sense an Untouchable lost was touch. He probably slept the same whether on rocks or feathers, unable to distinguish between hardness or softness.

She rolled her blankets, noticing Gren had no bedroll. A twig dangled from a piece of red fabric. She wondered how long his rags lasted. "I wish you would let me examine your bruises. It would allow me to know the extent of damage done by the stoning."

"My gratitude." His grin appeared so natural, like he possessed no worries. "That's unnecessary. I used the powder you gave me after you fell asleep, and it worked wonders."

Trell sighed. Untouchables not only suffered from disfigurement, but depression for being abandoned. No use pushing. Plenty of time for discovery on the journey. First, she'd earn his trust. She inclined her head toward the campfire where fish cooked on sticks. "You have been busy."

He shrugged. "I promised to supply food. There is an abundance of trout in the stream. They'll keep our bellies full while on the road."

She licked her lips. Thirst and hunger gnawed at

her stomach, the bread and cheese from last night just a memory. Gren handed her a full waterskin, and she drank deeply before asking, "How do you know where to fish?"

"Oh, that's simple. First, I find the deep holes. Trout like to hide in them. And, of course, I believe that I'll catch many."

She eyed the man. If what he said was true, he certainly possessed an instinct for fishing like her affinity for plants. "It relieves me to know that I can set aside my fear of starving."

Gren chuckled low and deep, exchanging the waterskin for a whole fish enfolded in fern moss. "Though ill-favored by the gods, I'll do my best to accommodate you and live a long and well-fed life."

She accepted the fish and bit a mouthful. The flakey meat contained a slightly smoky taste which she found appetizing.

They finished their meal, broke camp, and started trekking on a densely shaded path where high banks of ferns covered the ground on both sides. Gaps in the vegetation showed they walked alongside the same stream Gren fished from that morning. Evergreen needles crunched beneath their feet, freeing a heady pine scent. Dallisgrass, sandbur, foxtail, and even mushrooms sprang up with a vengeance, determined to get a jump on other vegetation.

Trell stopped now and then to examine a plant. Coming across white wake-robins, she requested permission from the lily to gather the leaves to dry later for their therapeutic properties. She also picked a few to grace her brother's table with their ruffled petals.

"How soon to our destination?" Gren asked when

she paused to run her fingers through tall goosegrass.

"It's not far. We'll reach the glen before nightfall. In these woods, I am on familiar ground. I am safe; and with me, so are you."

"Caution is always wise, especially in a foreign place, but I'm not afraid. I ask only out of curiosity."

She turned to face him. "Really? That makes you a unique man. People usually fear the unknown."

"After you saved me in the marketplace, I trust you with my life, Healer. You would not lead me astray."

A warm swell of pleasure at his faith in her made its presence known. "I only did what was necessary."

Stands of fir and spruce dominated the forest, mixed with white birch. On less fertile ground, larches grew with trembling aspen. The vastness and variety of trees gave the feeling of being inside a dwelling, yet sunlight danced upon the ground in bright spots. Lichen clung to the trees. Even the air felt calm and thick.

And the smells! She inhaled the rich, earthy aroma of pine, dirt, leaves, and the mold of decomposition infusing the air, along with an airy tang of water splashing against rocks, and the warm, homey fragrance of cedar heated by the sun. She found a ginger plant hugging the ground and stopped to draw in the aroma of its fragrant leaves. She buried a pebble next to the plant in exchange and dug one root to make a powder to reduce nausea, pain, and inflammation.

Birds chirped. Treetops swayed. Trees called in a soft and gentle whisper.

"Friend. Once-an-Ossa. Welcome."

Trell listened, thrilled. Her heart warmed at the sweet words. For a moment, the world of the forest surged around her, and she exulted in the splendor of memory. She'd been trapped in a spell gone awry and turned into a tree for centuries, rooted to one spot for a thousand years.

"Thank you, Mother Tree. How goes your life?"

"My children are well fed," the tree answered. *"The root fungi share their water and minerals."*

"You seem happy in these woods," Gren broke into her reverie.

She smiled at him, surprised he caught her happiness. She did not realize that she was so transparent. "The forest is full of beauty. Beauty without end. Once I spent many years here."

"Tell me more. What did you do?"

Trell paused to peer into the dense woods. Something about the Untouchable appealed to her on a level she couldn't explain. She wondered what it would be like to share a close bond with a man, like her sister-by-marriage, Becca, did with Cress.

"Nothing and everything," she answered ambiguously. "I enjoyed the solitude. You might say I spent my time watching the seasons come and go."

"Sounds lonely. I would have thought someone as friendly and outgoing as you would have been surrounded by people."

"I am never alone in the woods."

Gren frowned. "Is that so?"

Trell suspected he sought clarification, but she only smiled and kept walking. Late in the afternoon, she called a halt in a sunlit glen.

Two Guardians of Secrets, insect-sized dragons with red eyes that people who ventured into the deep woods mistook for iridescent dragonflies, buzzed her head eliciting a smile that barely moved her lips. One was Parr, mate to Torka, queen of the Guardians.

"Who is the male human?" Parr mindspoke to her.

"A companion. He is traveling with me while I search for new treatments," she answered before turning to face the Untouchable. "I leave you here. Wait for me."

"How long will you be gone?" Gren asked.

"A day or two." Her brother wasn't an ogre, but only a few outsiders were welcomed. She reinforced her earlier warning. "Do not venture from this glen. Beyond here, you encroach upon Cress's solitude. I don't mean to alarm you, but he doesn't much care for other people. I cannot vouch for your safety." She took a step, then paused. "I'll leave my bedroll for you. I noticed you had none."

****

Gren's gut tightened as Trell melted into the woods. Her waist-length red cloak acted like a flag, letting his gaze trail her with ease. His nerves jumbled together in a tight knot. He couldn't believe he had agreed to let her go without a protest.

What if she never returned?

Was kidnapped?

What if his brothers found her?

Questions bombarded him until the compulsion to follow Trell built with each passing second. He took a step and stopped. No! She could be watching from the woods, testing to see if he kept his word to remain in the glen. If he didn't, she might run away on her own.

Then what?

She'd never trust him again.

With a sigh, he began digging a shallow pit for a campfire. Might as well set up camp. Nightfall fast approached. He picked up loose branches and deadfall like Trell had insisted on their journey from Brenalin. If she spied on him, at least she'd see that he obeyed her wishes. That should count in his favor.

He spread out the bedroll she left for him. The kindness created a warm tingle inside him.

After a while, the fire crackled, and he squatted to stare into the mesmerizing flames. As sure as he watched the fire in the middle of the great woods, he knew his life was about to change. Whether for good or bad, only time would tell.

He stretched out atop the bedroll and tucked his hands behind his head. The scent of vanilla rose beneath him, the same scent which always surrounded Trell.

The first hint of stars dusted the darkening sky like diamonds. Fireflies flitted in the woods and in the glen, mimicking the stars with their flickering lights. He watched a dozen or so flit quite near before he closed his eyes.

His last thoughts before sleep took him centered on Trell. He had found her first. Not his brothers. Not anyone else. If she escaped him, he would find her again.

****

Once away, Trell's feet moved faster, racing the darting Guardians for the lead.

In no time, she reached the magical circle created by Torkel's ancestors, the first dragons of Feldsvelt. Here time stood still. How those original dragons had created this enchanted place, she knew not. No one did. If the dragons knew, they were not telling.

Over three hundred meters in diameter, the glen

contained a cottage with a thatched roof that looked deceptively small from the outside but proved far larger once inside. She accepted the phenomenon. After all, her brother, a powerful wizard, had built the structure.

Where she had once stood rooted to the ground by another wizard's spell, only a slight indentation remained. Memories quickened in her mind. Denial. Bitterness. Frustration. It had taken decades to accept being a tree. When she did, she found joy, awareness, and satisfaction.

The rush of leathery wings lifted her gaze. Torkel landed in the center of the clearing, sweeping a cloud of dust and pine needles into the air. At five years of age, he was a young dragon. His black scales shimmered like obsidian beneath the gleam of an evening sun. His golden eyes sparkled with life, and his muscles rippled with unparalleled strength. Airborne, he behaved like grace itself, but now he waddled almost clumsily toward her to tower over her by the height of two grown men.

She gazed into an elongated face with skin stretched so tight over the head that it resembled a skull with deep-socketed eyes and broad nasal openings. He lowered his huge head, and she automatically reached up to scratch the bony top, something he thoroughly enjoyed.

"You stink," she spoke aloud, her nose wrinkling in protest. "The least you could do is rinse the stench off in a river after immersing yourself in the closest swamp."

His nostrils flared. *"I must feed. Would you have me starve?"*

She rubbed between the horns which sprouted from

his head in his first year and now curved in a crescent form above his head with a slight *C* shape, reminding her of a wisent's horns. They were dead black the entire length. Smaller horns jutted from his chin and spikes studded his lower jaw.

Her dragon friend raised his chin where a tiny patch of white scales had never darkened. Even stranger, his back paws were white on the bottom, and when born, his middle claws had been white. A fact that always embarrassed the growing dragon.

"But why pickle your food in those stinking ponds?" she asked.

"It is an acquired taste." Torkel narrowed his golden gaze. He hissed, and the glen filled with the dry, acrid smell of acid dripping from his mouth. *"Blame the Guardians."*

"Us?" piped the two who raced Trell to the dragon circle. *"We are falsely accused."*

Trell laughed as a drop of saliva sizzled on the ground. She was unafraid of being burned—long ago her brother had warded her against dragon acid. Thankfully, she was included in the conversation as the tiny dragons darted around Torkel's massive head.

A black mist began to sparkle around the gigantic dragon. A changing mist. Trell stepped back, aware Torkel was about to shapeshift.

Within moments, a tall, muscular man with ebony hair and striking golden eyes stepped out of the fading mist. Torkel, in human form. He straightened, wearing a tunic and leggings once belonging to Cress that converted with him as he eyed the fluttering Guardians.

"You think we enjoyed carrying your slimy food? We did not. Look at us! How could you expect us to

deliver a whole carcass? We are strong, but what you suggest was simply impossible. Putrification aided us in delivering the smaller bits. Just wait until you take a mate and have the task of rearing your own young."

Torkel winked at her. "It is not I who complains."

Glittering like tiny stars, Guardians whizzed around so fast it became nearly impossible to track them. *"Well, excuse us,"* they said, sounding offended and sailed off in a glimmering shimmer.

"I assume you are glad to see me," Torkel said in a kindlier tone to Trell. "It has been many months since you've left Brenalin."

She raced over to hug him. "I cannot argue with you, especially when you are correct. I have missed you, my friend."

"As only long-time friends do."

"Something you are always eager to remind me," she responded.

Torkel lifted his head and sniffed the air.

A shiver of distress sparked in her head. Trell did not hesitate. "What is it?"

"I was thinking. The male human will be alone. I should keep an eye on him. Make sure he doesn't venture where he is unwelcome. And mayhaps he will play his instrument to keep himself company. I did take a fancy to his music."

"Have you no common sense? Stay away from him. Don't force me to mention your interest to the Guardians," she whispered, trying to shield her words from being overheard. Out of sight did not mean the tiny, ancient dragons weren't listening. Extremely nosy, they were prone to eavesdropping. "They would be unhappy to learn you are drawn to him."

"What can they do?"

An edge crept into his voice. Worry? Fear? Both emotions seemed alien for a creature like him. After all, he was a dragon. She glanced at Torkel a second time, reminding herself of his youth. Not much was known about the speed that dragons grew. It was assumed decades would pass before he gained his full dragon powers. His overlapping scales needed to develop into a stronger, protective armor. While powerful, he remained vulnerable at this stage of his life.

"Do not underestimate them. They, of all the dragons, survived the Great Dying. All they've ever done is protect you."

"I am grown now. Even in this weakling human form, I am many times stronger than a normal male. I search for a lair of my own. A task I do not take lightly."

"At the Guardians' request as I recall. You've outgrown the hatchery. They need space for the new hatchlings."

"That one…" Torkel changed the topic and nodded easterly where she'd left Gren. "Danger surrounds him. He reeks of many layers."

She refused to let Torkel's suspicious nature ruin her chance to study Gren. Few afflicted granted healers the opportunity. "And you know this how?"

"I am a dragon. All knowing. My senses are superior to humans. It is in your best interest to heed my warning."

"Am I not listening?"

"I wonder. Did you know I can hear your heart beating? It speeds up when you speak of the Untouchable."

She frowned. His observation made her uneasy. "You exaggerate."

Before Torkel could reply, the door with a prominent red pentagram above it banged open. A brown and white spotted dog with a jagged scar across its muzzle bounded outside. Cress and his wife, Becca, a warrior woman from The Wilds, followed.

"Tulle, my friend," Trell said to the dog who circled Torkel and her. "Greetings, brother. Sister. I bring fond greetings from Einer and Salida. They miss you and promise to visit soon." She dropped the names of Brenalin's Master Wizard and Cress's old housekeeper in hopes of putting her brother in a mellow mood. Once he learned of her journey, she anticipated his displeasure.

Torkel waved to her brother and sister-by-marriage, gave her a hug, then edged backward. The changing mist formed around him. When it cleared, his huge dragon form stood in the dragon circle.

"Farewell," Torkel said through mindspeech to all three before launching himself with a great flap of wings. Twigs, pine needles, and rocks boiled up.

"We're glad to have you with us." Her brother wrapped her in a hug, then released her. "You have not graced us with your presence in ages. What detained you? Einer sent his crow with word you passed all your tests long ago."

Guilt pinched Trell. "I needed to make plans."

Cress's hair, dark brown like her own, hung to his waist and was tied back with a leather thong. It still showed no sign of gray and would remain that way as long as he lived within the dragon circle. "Plans?"

"Come inside. I have food ready to eat," Becca

said, her solitary blonde braid swishing against her back as she latched on to Trell's arm. Dozens of glowing beads of various sizes winked in the thick plait. The decoration held significance to the married couple, but Trell had yet to learn its meaning. Whenever she inquired, the pair merely exchanged love-struck glances at each other.

Becca opened the door, and Tulle rushed inside. He headed right for the hearth to curl in a tight ball.

Inside, the walls shot skyward, competing in height with the behemoth trees in the dragon circle, until they ended in a tower. Crystals scattered throughout the interior glowed with light. Along its wall, a staircase clung to the solid sides. At the very top, arched windows let light shine inward. Somewhere in the bowels of the hut, cranks, gears, and pulleys clanked away.

Becca grabbed earthenware mugs and poured ale, dark and foamy, to overflowing into them.

"Here." The warrior woman indicated a chair for Trell to sit and offered a mug. "Quench your thirst. Even Luna would be pleased with this batch, I think."

Trell laughed, remembering untold burnt meals the warrior woman had served while teaching herself to cook. She handed Becca the stores she'd brought from Brenalin and the flowers she'd picked on the trail. "My thanks. I see you've been practicing your brewing skills." She took a sip. "Hmmm, I can really taste the difference from your last batch." She took another sip and rolled it around in her mouth to savor. "It is the best you have made thus far. I think I can taste malt; however, there's a nutlike flavor."

Becca blushed dark pink from her cheeks to the

tips of her ears. "A good guess. There is no drink equal to this in my homeland. We are limited by the lack of hops. But here I can experiment. I added a dash of flaked wheat to this mixture. It boosted the foam, but keeping it cold is what makes the difference. Cress spelled my shed, so it is always chilly inside." She beamed at her husband in gratitude and love.

He grinned back at his wife. "It was nothing."

The friendly atmosphere convinced Trell to take a chance. "I might as well get this over."

"Get what over?" Cress put his elbows onto the trestle table, then he smiled. "Ahhh, the plans you mentioned."

Becca slipped away to the hearth where a huge kettle hung suspended over glowing coals.

Trell copied her brother's actions and set her elbows on the table where the wood had been worn smooth. "Long ago healers roamed the land, dispensing medicines to the sick and learning new methods of healing to share with others. Those times are returning. At least for me—I wish to follow in their footsteps."

"Trell, you're too young to be gallivanting around the countryside. You—"

She held up her hand. "I beg to differ. My schooling is complete. There is nothing left for me to learn within the Halls of Medsin. Everyone knows medicine is a risky business. Sophisticated medical judgments can mean the difference between life and death. The tomes hint at other methods, but those skills and cures were not recorded. I believe they exist and can be found elsewhere. Oh, Cress, do not frown so. I can see by your expression you don't approve, but will you feel the same when I return with medicines and

Darcy Carson

skills to relieve people's pain and suffering?"

A bit of ale remained in the bottom of her brother's mug. He tilted it up and drained the dregs, clearly using the action as a stall to think. "It's understandable for someone who lived as a tree for as long as you did, forced to remain in one spot, unable to move, to wish to travel. Your objective is commendable, but it simply isn't a good idea. The world has changed. It's dangerous."

Her brother was right about one thing. For a thousand years, she'd been stuck in one spot. While not fond of meeting new people, especially large crowds, nothing Cress said would convince her to change her mind. This journey allowed her to make up for lost time. The thought of staying idle for any length of time almost suffocated her.

"I can't explain it to you, Cress. I want to travel. I need to. And along the way, I hope to find cures that will help the sick. The only way is to meet people and talk to them."

"You don't like strangers."

"True. I'll just have to overcome my fear. I must go. Besides, I won't be alone. Torkel is coming, and he'll protect me if I'm in danger." Her gaze drifted to Becca for support, but her brother's wife remained quiet. The woman had an uncanny knack of knowing when to speak and when not. She'd obviously decided to hold her tongue. "Furthermore, someone else is with me." The instant she spoke, she wanted to snatch back her words.

Cress paused—so long Trell thought he had not heard—then he glanced at her, his dark eyes full of concern. "Who?"

"Of what importance is their identity?"

Cress stilled again. He mumbled under his breath and pulled a pipe from his pocket. "Do you think I care less about your welfare since you've grown older? Indulge me. I am your brother. It is my duty to insist upon knowing these things."

Trell smiled to herself. Whenever her brother fiddled with his pipe, he attempted to postpone the inevitable. "Really, Cress, I am not being evasive. He is no one you know. Gren is an Untouchable. He was being stoned in the marketplace. I couldn't—"

"An Untouchable!" Cress's mouth fell open. He clenched the bowl of his pipe. "Are you daft? What if he infects you?"

"What is an Untouchable?" Becca asked, her gaze switching back and forth between brother and sister.

Cress glanced at his wife with fond indulgence. "I forget The Wilds is isolated. There are many things you are unaware of. They—these Untouchables—have a terrible disease that causes severe, disfiguring skin sores. It ends in a painful death."

Becca's eyes widened with horror. "Nothing helps them?"

Cress shook his head. "Not to my knowledge."

"Another reason I am traveling with Gren is to study him. If I can learn about the disease, mayhaps I can find a cure for him and others who are afflicted," Trell said before her brother could say more. "You tended me while I was trapped in Bonner's spell. I had centuries to consider my options once set free. This journey is something I must do!"

For several long moments, Cress stared at her, inhaling short breaths as though struggling to accept her words. He rose from his chair slowly, and the chair's legs scraped the floor with a grinding effect. "Then I'm coming, too."

Trell glanced at her sister-by-marriage, then back to her brother.

The fire popped, sending a river of sparks up the chimney. A thick, heavy pause filled the room. The thud of wood on cast iron drew her attention back to the fireplace.

Becca tapped a spoon on the kettle's edge and walked over to the table. She stood next to her husband and placed her hands on his shoulder. "Men and their memories! Remember what I told you last night? I'm with child."

Cress winced.

Trell grinned at the news. "Felicitations. That's the best reason I've heard for you to remain here. I have no idea how long my journey will take. As a husband and soon-to-be-father, your duty lies with your family," she told Cress. "I already have two traveling companions. I do not need a third."

Air crackled with her brother's disapproval. Sparks leaped from his fingertips. Because Gren was an Untouchable, or did something else bother Cress? Trell chose not to ask.

"I am a man," her brother huffed. "I know how they think. You can't trust the Untouchable. Promise me that you'll be careful around him."

"The last time I was here you praised me for my level head," she reminded him. "Do you retract your opinion now?"

"Once, you were easier to influence," he answered.

"Don't avoid my question. Do you or don't you?"

Cress turned to his wife. "I could use some help here."

"Leave the girl alone." Becca's eyes danced with merriment. "I will need you in the near future. Within the dragon circle, time stands still. For this pregnancy to come to term, I'll have to live outside the circle. Or our child will never be born."

"I know when I'm outnumbered," Cress began, then looking at Trell, went on. "This probably won't matter, but I'm saying this because I care about you. After all this time, it's difficult to stop worrying."

"I am not asking your permission. As a courtesy, I came to tell you."

"Consider me informed."

Trell chose that moment to add, "And I hoped you could create a spell to keep Torkel's existence hidden from prying eyes."

"Human magic doesn't work on dragons." Cress scratched his head as if the motion would stimulate new ideas, then he smiled. "Mayhaps I can come up with something. Go with my blessings and love."

Her heart melted with his words. Cress's approval meant the world to her. "My thanks. And I'll take whatever you can offer."

Becca took Trell's hands into her own. "You will be a great healer, Trell. Your skill should be shared." She looked at her husband, gave him a gentle smile, and then back at Trell. "If nothing else, your journey should prove interesting. Traveling with one of these Untouchables and a dragon. Very interesting, indeed. I assume you'll keep Torkel's existence a secret."

"Oh, yes," she answered. "I know the rules. Not a word about dragons."

Chapter 3

Fully rested, Trell entered the kitchen the next morning, the bells at the tips of her braids chiming her arrival.

Cress puffed on his pipe, white smoke twisting upward in the shape of a tightly coiled spring. "Sleep well?"

"I did." She draped her short healer's cloak over a chair. This was her last time to sleep upon a normal bed. It could be weeks or months before another chance presented itself. "Thank you for inquiring." Glancing around, she spied a kettle hanging on the fire irons and smelled porridge seasoned with cinnamon. "How many dragon eggs have hatched since my last visit?"

"A set of twin greens, several whites, blues, reds, and blacks. A few metallics. It brings the total to thirty-seven wyrmlings of various ages. Five more to go. More importantly, fourteen of the fifteen female eggs have hatched. They assure the continuation of full-sized dragon bloodlines. The last female egg is a copper. The Guardians fear it may not hatch. They would probably appreciate your advice."

"I shall go immediately. Once I've seen them, I'll return to the glen where I left Gren." She tilted her head to one side, her brow furrowing ever so slightly as she glanced around the hut's interior. "Where is Becca? I would like to bid her farewell."

"She left before dawn to hunt. She supplies the Guardians with fresh meat for the hatchlings. It allows her to maintain her archer's skill, but she left this for you." He handed her a stuffed burlap sack tied shut. "Fresh soda bread. Becca stayed up last night to bake it for you. She also put some goldenrod, ginger, henpit, and chickweed in for cooking. You'd be proud of her. She's gotten quite apt at recognizing the various plants that grow in the woods."

"She didn't have to do that," Trell replied, touched.

"She wanted to. I wish to do something as well. While I can't spell Torkel without his permission, I can weather spell your cloak. Let me do that for you."

"Truly? I would be most appreciative."

Cress set his pipe down, balancing stem and bowl on the worn, smooth table. He raised his hands in a sweeping motion and murmured under his breath. A subtle shift occurred in the air. It rippled with the tingle of live magic. "There, now the fabric will cast off rain and yet keep you cool in the hottest temperatures. But I'm not done. I want you to take this staff as well. Do you know how to use one?" He strode across the room to retrieve a staff of rowan wood the height of a grown man, decorated with long ribbons of red, blue, and yellow.

"What are you worried about? I wouldn't partake this journey without protection. If people see my healer's cape, they won't bother me except to request treatment."

"Not everyone will care that you are a healer. You need some protection."

Trell didn't take offense as he propped the staff against the table. "In my studies, I took basic self-defense and learned where the body is most vulnerable. Besides, I always carry wasp powder. Tossed in someone's face it is most effective."

"Good, good," Cress said, then pointed to the staff. "See the ribbons tied at the top? No matter what the weather they will remain down unless danger approaches. Sometimes a few moments of warning is all one needs to survive."

Trell's vision blurred at the gesture, and she wiped a tear from the corner of her eye. Her heart thudded with gratitude. Leaving proved harder than she imagined. "Thank you, my brother."

Cress whipped around as if embarrassed and went to the kettle. He scooped a hefty serving of porridge into a bowl and returned to the table to place it in front of her. "Eat."

She suspected he still wasn't happy about her traveling with a man he considered a stranger. But this was her life…to live as she saw fit.

At the first bite of spicy cinnamon and sweetened oats, she wondered how Gren fared. She'd left him alone to fend for himself, and, now savoring the delicious flavors, suffered a pang of guilt. After eating, she stood and draped the woolen cloak over her shoulders. It didn't feel any different. "Oh, one more thing…"

Cress cocked a dark brow and narrowed his gaze.

She scoffed at his suspicious look. "Blessed Heyln, it is nothing bad. All I want to know is if you have an extra bedroll. I gave mine to the Untouchable. I cannot very well ask him to return it."

Shaking his head, Cress went toward a domed chest and pulled out a thick blanket tied into a roll.

"Well, I expect mine back."

The gruff tone. The words. Neither fazed Trell. She beamed at Cress, knowing it was his way of telling her to come home. "Agreed."

She gave him a tight hug and spun away before he spied her tears.

At the dragons' nest lair, she knew what to expect. She'd visited several times, but the place always left her in awe. A short distance outside the dragon circle, the Guardians of Secrets, who ranged in size from tiny insects to medium-sized dragonflies, tended the wyrmlings and dragonets. Cress told her once he'd tried tallying the number of Guardians but could never get an accurate count. He swore they kept their numbers a secret.

Her brother had spelled this lair before she'd been freed from Bonner's spell. It met specific conditions for each dragon type: snow and ice for the whites and silvers; open flames for the reds, golds, and brasses; a gigantic tub for a sulfuric chemical bath for the blacks and the two coppers to immerse in. He enchanted another container to simulate tidewaters flowing over it twice a day for the bronzes and greens. The commonest, yet hardest to care for, were the blues. Each day, their massive eggs were rolled and heated for twelve hours and then rolled and cooled for twelve more.

As she approached, chirps and clicks of hungry wyrmlings spilled out of the maw of the cave. Trell did not cross the entrance.

"May I enter?" she bid through mindspeech, leaning her staff against a tree and setting her bedroll on the ground, pleased to offer her assistance.

39

"By all means," came a chorus of replies. *"We welcome your presence."*

She stepped inside, and her breath hitched at the sight greeting her. A silver male the size of a full-grown wren, obviously newly hatched by its sodden appearance, skittered after a centipede across the floor, providing a hunting lesson and its first meal.

Several shiny blacks caught her eye, so like Torkel in color, yet none equaled his size at birth. They were gobbling up pieces of raw turkey with greedy sucking sounds.

A shower of sparks erupted to reveal red and blue dragonets playing with various gemstones. She couldn't help smiling. They were already learning to hoard. A dozen greens swam through a stream that Cress had created near the ceiling of the cave, each with a pearl in their mouths.

And everywhere, specks flickered like gold dust as Guardians flitted about, spinning abruptly in midair to chase an errant wyrmling or drop a bit of food into the gaping mouth of a hungry dragonet. A shimmering ball consisting of hundreds of Guardians united to push a blue egg the size of a water bucket from one spot to another.

Exhaustion seeped into her bones watching the tiny, golden dragons tending their charges. "They're wonderful," she murmured aloud, just as a white wyrmling scurried over the ground to flick its pale tongue at her toes. She giggled, the sensation reminding her of the rough texture of a cat's tongue. Babies, no matter the species, were cute and adorable.

"They ought to be," mindspoke a dozen Guardians. *"Otherwise, our work will not be worth the effort. They*

are the future."

Trell took a moment to admire how well the Guardians handled all the activity. Impressive. Only dedicated caregivers could keep up with the work. She spotted a reflection in the corner and stared at a dragonet the size of a full-grown deer. "Is that a female gold I see?"

"It is. She's a rare one. As are the green twins. She has already selected a name—Kizzire—The Strong One. She refuses to play with the others. Prefers solitude. Nor does she show interest in jewels. Most odd. We'll keep an eye on her."

As an ancient species, all dragons were valued. She didn't wish harm to befall a single one. "Cress said you are concerned that one of the copper females hasn't hatched," she said to a red-eyed Guardian who landed on her shoulder, its tiny claws pricking through her clothing.

She walked over to a rancid-smelling vat of sulfur holding the precious egg.

A half dozen Guardians fluttered in front of her. *"We'll remove the egg. You aren't protected against this type of mixture."*

Nodding, Trell watched as they dove into the huge pot and slowly lifted their treasured cargo. A few drops of liquid splattered, and tiny blisters pock-marked the ground.

She took a cloth to pat the egg dry. Female dragon eggs were usually smaller than males, and copper the smallest of all. This one appeared barely the size of a clenched fist. Almost gingerly she picked up the egg and rolled it in her palm. A slight shifting of the embryonic female curled within could be felt.

"What do you see?" asked the Guardian.

"It looks like the egg suffered a crack. See here."

Guardians fluttered close, and she pointed to a microscopic line that went from widest point to halfway down the side. The reflective shell changed from brown to brick red in her hands. She sniffed the egg. "I don't smell any rotting. The sulfur concoction must have worked as an antiseptic. That's good. However, I worry about a premature birth. Mayhaps Cress can spell the egg."

A dozen voices answered in her head. *"Won't work."*

"What about a paste?"

"The mixture will eat it."

Trell went over various scenarios in her head. She rejected them all until an idea struck. Smiling, she looked at the Guardians who fluttered before her, waiting for her to speak. "Take the egg to the dragon circle every so often. If we can slow the incubation, that might give the wyrmling time to heal herself. I cannot say what damage has been done. There's a good chance her growth will be slow when she emerges."

"But will the wyrmling survive?"

"In all honesty, I do not know." Trell watched several Guardians pick up the egg and gently lower it into the bath. She hoped her return coincided with the hatching. "We will see."

****

Dawn broke, and Gren woke to the chill of hard steel pressed against his neck. Beads of warm blood trickled beneath his ragged clothing. He blinked his eyes open and found that a woman dressed in green leggings and a leather tunic crouched beside him, scowling. He spotted a bow, looped over her shoulder, and arrows protruding from a quiver.

He tried to sit up. The woman leaned forward to push the blade harder against his throat. The flow of blood dribbling down his neck increased. He lay back with a sigh.

"What do you want?" he asked, spying tension in every muscle of the woman's body. A thick braid containing beads glowing with magic dangled over her shoulder, but more importantly, the sharp knife remained steady in her hand, a sure sign she was accustomed to wielding the weapon. "Look at me. I am an Untouchable. I own nothing of value."

"Silence!" she growled. "By Luna, you will listen, not talk. Understand?"

Gren narrowed his eyes ever so slightly. "As you wish, but who are you?"

"My identity is none of your concern. I can tell you, however, that you do not want me as your enemy. And my knife remains at your neck until you vow not a hair on Trell's head is in danger from you."

He did not mask his surprise. "The healer? What is she to you?"

"That, too, is not your concern." The woman's brows lowered over her eyes. "If any harm befalls her, I shall kill you. Do I make myself clear?"

Gren could give any man a decent workout with knife or sword. This was a totally new experience for him. For a woman to catch him unaware seemed impossible. Yet a blade pressed against his throat.

"Have faith, dear lady," he said, hoping a bit of charm would work on her. "She has my loyalty like no other."

"You didn't answer my question. Do you mean her harm?"

He huffed at the insult. "My word is my bond. You misunderstand. I owe the healer my life. I could never endanger her."

A grunt preceded the woman's response. "You will be watched. I am honor-bound, at least, to give you warning."

Watched? By the dragon he assumed she traveled with? Who? If the woman meant herself, it meant another person was aware of the creature's existence.

Gren didn't know this warrior woman, didn't owe her the truth, but meant what he said. "Why demand my vow? And if I give it, will you even believe me?"

"That depends. Do you dare not give it?"

"Very well, then, you have my pledge."

The woman's expression shuttered as she considered Gren. "I will accept your word, for you kept your promise to wait in this glen. That speaks in your favor. Remain on the ground until I am out of sight." She rose from her haunches to back away to the far side of the camp before sheathing her knife. She shot a glance around the camp as if memorizing every item within, then slipped into the woods without snapping a twig.

The moment she was out of sight, he leapt to his feet, debating whether to charge the woman or let her escape. The risk of discovery remained high. He didn't want to break his ruse as an Untouchable, for everyone considered them too weak to defend themselves.

Still, he took a step…

A spotted dog barked. It waited at the forest's edge, teeth bared as a challenge was issued in a low growl.

That wasn't the only sound.

The buzz of an angry hornet sounded, followed by a hard thud right between his legs. An arrow bit the ground, shaft and fletching quivering. His gaze snapped to the woods. The woman had whirled around as if she possessed eyes in the back of her head and fired at him. Already, she nocked another deadly arrow in her bow.

"I told you to stay down." Her arm drew back a fraction, the curve of the bow framing her face. "Disobey me again and die."

He sank to his bedroll. Trell's sweet scent was still trapped within the wool. He'd fallen asleep with her on his mind. A surge of warmth infused his veins at the reminder.

Looking satisfied he wouldn't move again, the woman melted into the forest with the dog on her heels. Various-sized iridescent insects, like the fireflies he watched the night before, fluttered in the air, seemingly following the woman as well.

Seconds later, the jingle of tiny bells drifted on invisible currents in the woods. Trell approached. He sensed a subtle difference in the air. It seemed as if the trees stood straighter, their branches fuller. He couldn't explain the impression.

Trell stepped into the glen. When she stopped in front of him, a scowl twisted her features. "Your neck is bleeding! What happened?"

He touched the wetness he'd forgotten about. No need to mention his visitor. "I must have scratched myself during the night."

Compassion flowered on her face. "Follow me."

Gren sighed when she spun around and headed for the woods again. "Why? Where are we going?"

"Cease questioning me. I'm a healer. Put yourself in my care," she said. "I saw an anthill beyond the clearing."

Amusement laced her tone. He wondered what an anthill had to do with blood. "So?"

"You'll see."

Doubts wormed a path through him.

At the edge of the trees, Trell stopped in front of a ring of blue flowers and a mound constructed of grains of sands, twigs, and leaves that rose to his knees.

Trell tore a narrow strip from the hem of her skirt and tossed the rag on the mound. Gren frowned but held his comments when she used the bottom of her staff to poke the rag.

Suddenly, a black mass of irritated insects swarmed out of the mound to protect their colony. They attacked the cloth with a vengeance as a single unit.

He watched the rag dampened from hundreds, thousands of bites. Finally, curiosity got the better of him. "What are you doing?"

She continued to agitate the relentless ants. "Creating an ant rag. It will keep your wound from festering."

After a while, she lifted the wet rag with her staff and shook off the insects. The few that were injured, he noted, were carried back inside the nest like soldiers did for comrades struck down in battle.

Trell turned to him with her arm out.

He backed away. He'd never heard of this treatment and refused to let himself be experimented on. "You're not putting that on me."

"By Heyln's robe, I am a healer. Have confidence in my skills. I know what I'm doing. Now, cease complaining and stop acting afraid." She continued toward him, arm outstretched. "I'm not putting it on you. You are."

Gren blinked under her gaze. Maybe if he cooperated, she would trust him. "Fine, then, tell me what to do, and I'll do it myself."

She rolled her eyes. "Wrap this tightly against your wound. Make sure it touches your skin."

The indignities he must suffer to keep his charade! *If not for his quest…*

He had done what he needed. He found the healer.

And, in the end, he would find the dragon reported to be her companion.

Chapter 4

Trell glowered at Gren. The idea that he doubted her skills cut to the quick. In frustration, she couldn't stop tapping her foot as he inched the rag into an opening in the fabric wrapped around his neck.

Few people knew ants were vital to the trees. In all stages of their lives, from seedlings, saplings, and trees, they shared a lifelong relationship. Ants brought topsoil with life-nourishing ingredients to the surface faster than any earthworm.

Now, the insects would assist the Untouchable.

"Are you sure this will work?" Gren asked, still holding the rag.

Trell frowned. Talk about procrastinating. He was taking forever. She fought the impulse to snatch the rag from his hands and do it herself. "Just do it."

He did and a hiss rushed between his teeth. "By the Gods! Why didn't you tell me it would sting?"

"And have you refuse treatment?" she answered with a chuckle. "The fire means it's working."

And, even though fully covered, his Untouchable condition wasn't long into being severe.

The fact that he still retained a measure of sensations was a good sign. She doubted he was grossly disfigured by the disease. The insight fashioned an inner smile.

She continued, "It should eliminate any chance of

infection. I swear, men, no matter their age, are harder to tend than frightened children. You squeak and protest as if your very lives are threatened."

Still scowling, Gren held the rag in place and bent over to pluck a bellflower at the base of the ant mount. Trell gasped upon hearing the plant's scream in her head. It happened so fast she had no time to prevent the destruction. She always asked a plant's permission to pick their leaves or blossoms and left a small token in exchange.

He beamed at her, unaware of the distraught his actions caused. "I know you are doing this to help me. Please, accept this flower in gratitude." He handed her a bellflower.

"A flower!" Torkel's deep voice scoffed in mindspeech. *"Doesn't the fool human know jewels or treasure make better gifts?"*

"Silence," she ordered. The fact that she heard the dragon meant he was less than a league away, the distance it took a person to walk in an hour. *"Humans do not covet fortunes like dragons do."*

"Tell that to my ancestors. Oh, wait…they're dead. Killed by your kind for their treasure."

"Go away. I'm trying to carry on a conversation, and you are interfering."

"You're being pursued."

She brushed off Torkel's warning. Instead, she fixed her gaze on Gren. Cress had cautioned her to always question a man's motives. Right now, she had a more immediate problem and dropped to the ground. Maybe the stems were long enough and there were nodes left to save the plant.

She grabbed a stick and started digging near the

bellflowers. "You destroyed it!" she cried as if no time lapsed. "Picking flowers kills them. Why would you do a terrible thing to such a beautiful flower on a whim?"

"You picked the white ones on our way here."

"With their permission. And I left a token of appreciation."

"Sometimes the best medicine is as simple as a flower," he defended his actions, seemingly unfazed. "They're pretty. The sight soothes the soul."

Surprise hit as if a summer rain doused her. Was this how people who didn't share an affinity with nature thought? "Mayhaps it's not too late. The stem might reroot."

Gren shuffled his feet. "I—I beg your forgiveness. I didn't know your feelings. What can I do to help?" Contrition moderated his apology.

"Fetch some water."

When Gren rushed to the creek, his keenness to help eased a tad of the anger rolling inside her. Plus, confession of his error abated her anger. Few people willingly shouldered responsibility without balking. He hadn't realized the consequences of his actions. Ignorance could be corrected.

He returned within moments, water cupped in his hands. He let it drip onto the limp stem.

Gren's attempt to rectify the damage ignited something deep within her. She felt like she'd been split into two people. The outer person was a dedicated healer, a person who'd spent years mastering treatment procedures and all manner of medications and now felt confident to venture out into the world to test her expertise.

But the other Trell, the inner one, was a novice in

the ways of womanhood that no one seemed to see—except Gren. He made her experience emotions that she shouldn't. The last time a man showed her attention had ended in disaster. A lesson she would not forget.

"I doubt it will survive." She rocked back on her heels, saddened by the loss and longing to escape the confusion inside her. "But I have to try."

"I'm sorry I upset you. I vow to never pick another flower without your permission. What matters is remaining in your good favor."

"Careful," Torkel mindspoke.

"Why?" she mindspoke back before answering Gren. She'd never known an Untouchable on a personal level but doubted they accepted their fate as easily as he did. It made him unique. "Why should you? To be honest, you puzzle me."

Mirth and light danced in his crystalline green eyes. "I don't mean to."

"Mayhaps I'm being foolish. There's a mystery about you I can't explain." She stopped. "Do you still hurt?"

His marvelous eyes widened, and he removed the rag from his neck. "I—nay. The burning has stopped."

"Good. The ants did their job."

"Then we can be on our way."

Gren turned and headed for the glen where he'd set up camp. Following, she waited for him to roll his bedding and douse the coals from the previous night with water.

Looking up unexpectedly, he caught her in an intense stare that left her dazed. With a nod, he shouldered her old bedroll, and they retraced their steps to the main road, around old giants that reached for the

Darcy Carson

sky. Many travelers felt an oppressive weight because of the close ranks of trees. Not her. The kinship she shared with the giants meant she would miss them once they thinned out.

****

Gren and Trell trekked along the road for days, always moving northeast toward the great ocean. With each step, she kept alert for plants she'd never seen before, though the chance of discovering a new species between Brenalin and Eudes was slim.

She'd reached the conclusion that it was going to be a challenge treating the Untouchable. While always friendly, he remained defensive about being examined. How could she learn about his illness?

Most nights Gren pulled out his flute to play for an hour or so. During that time, fear of what Torkel might do made it difficult for her to relax until Gren tucked the instrument away for the night.

Thankfully, the subject of dragons never came up again. Once was enough to cause concern for Trell.

On the fourth day of their journey, in the dead of night, the thunder of galloping horses woke her with a jolt. Iron-shod hooves pounded the road, sending rhythmic vibrations into the softer earth. Trell reached out to warn Gren, only to discover his bedroll empty. A momentary sense of loss sped through her at being abandoned.

She fought back the sickening emotion to strain to see by starlight and spotted him crouched behind a tree, a large limb held in both hands as a club. He hadn't left her. Rather, he'd found a weapon to defend them. Endangering himself on her behalf. What if harm befell him instead?

52

He turned his head in her direction and signaled her to lie flat.

Complying, her gaze darted to the enchanted staff Cress gifted her. The ribbons fluttered wildly and then settled down as the riders sped past.

"Who were they?" Trell whispered when Gren dropped onto his bedroll with his makeshift club.

"I know not, but I suspect they were up to no good. No one risks neck or limb to ride a mount at such speed in the dark unless they are being pursued or are in pursuit." He heaved a sigh. "Trell, we need to talk. I—"

"What?" She shouldn't have interrupted.

Starlight showed his expression turn thoughtful. He shrugged. "Never mind. Mayhaps later."

****

The chance to talk never came.

The next morning Trell and Gren came upon a logging camp. Trell's gaze swept the area dotted with canvas tents. Sunlight glinted off metal in several places. Axes! Bright and shiny, their sharpened edges reminded her of teeth ready to chomp through heartwood like a starving beast. She shuddered at the imagery and put aside her anxiety of meeting new people.

This out-of-the-way place might require medical services even more than a village, for most travelers consisted of merchants, eager to trade between the towns.

Oxen were hitched to logging sleds, chains used to drag the downed giants lay outside one of the bigger tents, long saws that took two men to handle were laid across poles, and wooden wedges dotted the ground. Another shudder rippled down her spine as a wave of sadness threatened to engulf her. These men brought death to the forest.

"Leave this place, if it disturbs you," Torkel mindspoke to her.

Trell gave a mental laugh. Brenalin prided itself on how well it managed the harvesting of the forest in order for the woodlands to thrive. They maintained three permanent settlements in Demit Woods along Sparkle River, where they performed selective thinning, controlled squirrel and deer populations, and accelerated the growth rate of trees. In all likelihood, this camp was an outpost of one of those permanent communities. *"I can't. In all fairness, foresters perform a service. Their systematic logging keeps fires from running unhindered through the forest and keeps the spread of insects and disease at a minimum. And besides, the foresters probably need me. Healers do not travel these roads as they once did."*

"You're too kindhearted."

Still, eyeing the downed trees, she mourned the loss of friends.

Her moment of sad reflection ended when the hard-working woodcutters spotted her red cape. They set their tools aside and approached.

"Welcome, Healer," said a man with a full beard, taking charge. He signaled several men to form a line, which they did with the more severely ill or injured first. "Your services are greatly required, but your companion is unwelcome in our camp."

Outraged, Trell stiffened her spine, ready to defend Gren.

Before she could open her mouth to protest, he backed away, saying, "I'll wait for you by the stream."

Frowning at his treatment, she conceded with a nod. He walked the distance that put him outside their camp, yet stayed within sight, which semi-appeased her sense of injustice.

She set a broken arm and stitched up several deep cuts. The tenth or eleventh logger had a splinter imbedded deep in his arm.

"Two riders rode in last night and asked about a man and woman," he began. "Said the woman was the Healer Trell. Knocked Old Timmons around afore they saw the rest of us. Changed their tune then. Though they didn't say anything about an Untouchable."

Trell blinked in surprise at hearing her name. She glanced at Gren before rinsing the wound with water and pulling tweezers from her pouch. The two riders sounded like bullies, and she wanted nothing to do with people who used force to extract information. "Did they say why they sought this healer?"

"Nay. Never volunteered a word of explanation, and we never asked." His tone sounded dismissive.

"This is going to hurt." She handed her patient a strip of rawhide to bite on and inserted the tweezers into the festering wound, gently probing until the bronze prongs contacted something harder than surrounding flesh. The man moaned.

She hated to cause pain. "Sorry."

The man looked at her with tear-filled eyes.

"They just demanded we answer 'em," said the next man in line wearing a sling on his arm. "When that didn't work, they offered gold."

Trell nodded, glad she hadn't volunteered her name. She focused on squeezing the prongs together to draw out a wicked-looking splinter.

The first logger spit out the rawhide. "As if we would tell them after the way they acted. Noblemen by their clothes, but not from Brenalin."

The rest snickered. Clearly, nobility hosted few friends among these hard-working men.

She applied a salve to the open wound and bandaged his arm. The next man stepped forward. Placing her hands into the small of her back, she arched and glanced down the line. Almost at the end.

A quick check on Gren showed him sitting on the ground. Because the camp's hospitality did not extend to him, when finished, she declined to share a midday meal with them. Still, the woodcutters replenished the bread Becca gave her and presented her with a small wheel of tart cheese. One pressed a bracelet of hematite, a silver-gray stone used for protection, into her hands. Was it for her to use against Gren? Or something else? She put it on and walked away.

Gren stood at her approach. "All done?"

She offered up a tired smile. Discrimination fell into the same category as bullies as far as she was concerned. Neither attitude deserved a place in the world. How tragic that Gren must accept rejection as normal. "I apologize for your treatment at the logging camp."

"Do not concern yourself. They are no different than most. I watched while you worked. You have a gift for healing, and your touch appeared gentle."

The compliment warmed her. "Remember those riders who passed us last night?" She tried to keep her voice casual. "They asked for me."

Gren's eyes widened, then glinted with hardness. "Did those in the camp say who they were?"

That was the same question she asked herself and the note in his tone caused her to wonder even more. "Only that they dressed as noblemen."

"Mayhaps your reputation precedes you."

"I doubt that. I'm newly graduated. Insufficient time to generate a reputation for strangers to seek me out. Something tells me the pair are trouble and should be avoided."

"Once again your wisdom amazes me."

That night, a full moon and stars decorated the wide expanse of sky, and though exhausted, Trell wasn't tired enough to sleep.

"We should forego a fire," Gren suggested. "Those men might still be in the area, and the smoke might attract them."

"A good idea. We don't want to draw attention to ourselves."

She wandered around the edges of their camp. In the growing darkness, the trunk of a pine tree seemed to glow—a sad inkling that the tree would become a silver ghost. She approached and touched a deep gash in the bark. Sticky moisture wet her fingertips. Sap, meant to feed and heal, oozed out of the trunk like blood from a cut.

"I die. My children must survive without me."

Trell recognized the source of feathery words in her head—the pine tree. *"I am sorry, my friend. There is nothing I can do to save you. Lightning has struck you."*

"Will dying hurt?"

The voice reminded Trell of a child. *"You will grow tired as though frost touched the land. Your sap will slow, then stop flowing through your mighty trunk.*

57

You will rest the deep sleep. Mayhaps it will give you comfort to know that your sacrifice will renew the life of the forest floor. Seedlings will receive protection from your fallen trunk and grow strong and healthy."

"An honor I gladly accept."

Tears welled in her eyes. Mindful of Gren, she wondered if he noticed she cried over a tree. She dared not linger and quickly dried her face.

She returned to sit on a rock Gren had rolled near her bedroll. They shared the food the foresters provided and the hazelnuts she'd collected and cracked with a rock.

"Are we nearly there?" she asked.

Gren stopped gathering loose twigs around the camp. "Where?"

"Eudes, of course."

A grin slowly pulled the tattered cloth tight across his face. "We have far to go, Trell. You'll smell the sea long before you see it. Are you tired of travel so soon?"

"Look at me. Do I look tired?" she asked. "I'm just anxious to arrive."

"How much time do you plan to dedicate to this journey of yours?"

His question ignited a wave of determination, even as she wondered herself. "As much as it takes."

He turned toward her and then feathered a bandaged finger over her face. The gentle caress made her body feel like a flower following the sun as it cut a path across the sky. A man had never touched her in this way. Not even Bonner, a friend and young wizard, who had accidentally turned her into a tree. And she'd believed herself in love with him.

She wasn't afraid of contracting Gren's disease.

Fear of Untouchables being contagious was erroneous. The malady wasn't spread by touch. Among healers, the majority believed the disease was spread through coughing or fluid from the nose, and then only in the early stages. Untouchables wore their rags to hide their sores and disfigurement from the censuring eyes of the unafflicted.

"I imagine you are aware my motives for traveling with you are not entirely selfless," Gren said, intruding into her reflection.

A shiver rippled through her, unsure about his tone or his touch. "I assume you seek a cure and hope I will find it."

He shook his head. "That would be nice, but more importantly, I seek companionship. The road is a lonely place, and I have traveled for ages…alone. Plus, I want you to trust me."

Her heart skipped. She hadn't expected that response. "Oh, Gren, it takes a long time for trust to build."

"I'll wait," he said after a moment or two. "All I have is time."

****

Time was running out.

Gren had feigned ignorance the night before about the two riders—his worthless brothers. He cursed his ill fortune. He'd hoped for more time with the healer before they learned her identity. They'd scour the land, using bribery, threats, and whatever means at their disposal in their search for her.

Now diligence would be required to escape Oded and Riff.

Trell wasn't like anyone in his family. They were

judgmental. Harsh. If given a choice, they always picked the negative side. From what he observed thus far, the healer possessed a good heart and routinely believed the best in a person. An unwise habit in today's world.

He hated lying to her. She'd not been what he expected.

Perhaps he should be honest with her and disclose his true identity. Confide that his father sought her...and her dragon. She might be receptive to traveling to Kula. Then his gut rolled.

Abruptly he rose, his quick movement causing Trell to frown. He walked over to his travel bag and drew out a goatskin flask. Returning, he sat beside her and uncorked the flask.

"This is *farbrenen vaser*. It is the oldest, most revered drink of my village. Would you care to try it?" At her nod, he handed her the flask. "Be careful. Just a sip. It's fermented and strong."

She lifted it to her lips, swallowed, and gasped. "By all the Gods! Are you trying to punish me for the ant rag?"

The accusation made him smile. "Honestly. I hadn't thought of that." He nodded at the flask she still held as if considering the idea. "Not everyone cares for it."

She poured a small amount into her hand to examine and sniff. "It doesn't really smell, but makes my mouth water. It has the color of rain, yet is as hot inside my mouth as a burning firebrand."

Gren laughed. "You give an apt description. *Farbrenen vaser* means burning water in our ancient tongue. Its warmth is much appreciated in the mountains of my homeland, for at times our winters seem endless."

"The burning has stopped, and now I taste blackberries and cedar. How is this made?"

Questions were good. They usually implied a willingness to exchange information. "It's made from icicle berries, white fruit that turns transparent when wet. I doubt they grow here. Not cold enough. The process involves freezing the alcohol and removing the ice crystals. Our frigid climate allows the method to work well for us."

"My sister-by-marriage should hear about this," she said. "She is into brewing different drinks."

"Someday you can tell her yourself."

Trell shifted on the rock and took another sip. This time, he swore she was prepared for the blend of flavors that made the drink famous.

"Talk to me, Trell." Gren retrieved the *farbrenen vaser* from her shaking hands, lifted the goatskin flask to his mouth, and swallowed a mouthful. He gasped and caught his breath. "If you prefer, I will start. I come from the kingdom of Kula. You've probably never heard of it. It is a poor country, few resources, very mountainous."

Her façade gave nothing away. "I studied maps before setting out on this journey. I've heard of Kula. It's situated deep in the mountains of Demicland. About five years ago, one of their minor lords led an army against Brenalin."

The perfect lead-in. Gren refused to let the opportunity pass. "I heard a red dragon protects Brenalin, but he hasn't been seen since destroying an army. Now it is rumored a black one flies over the town. What do you know of it?"

A pink tongue appeared to moisten her lips. "A silly rumor. Surely a man of your intellect doesn't believe them."

Tension tightened the set of Trell's mouth. It warned him not to push. "I'm of the belief that all rumors are based on truth, but if it makes you uncomfortable to discuss the hypothesis, what about yourself? I am curious about you."

Her hands quivered. "What would you have me say?"

"Start with something simple," he said softly. "You're a healer. What made you chose that for an occupation?"

"I always enjoyed being outdoors, collecting and identifying plants. It seemed natural to learn how they improved or affected our lives."

He nodded. "Like a blacksmith who loves to create tools with his hands. I understand." This was a momentous beginning. "Aren't you curious how or when I contracted this?" He held out his arms.

"Of course, I am. Your affliction is known by all of Feldsvelt, and yet little is known how the disease is contracted or how it progresses. In the Halls of Medsin, only the oldest tomes mention a cure once existed. But they give no clue how. What if I could rediscover it?"

This time Gren scoffed in disbelief. While those afflicted with the dreaded disease had all his sympathy, he doubted a cure ever existed. "You can't always believe what you read in dusty pages. More likely they are tales to pin hopes on for those unfortunates like me. A cure doesn't exist."

Irritation flashed across Trell's face so fast that he

nearly missed it. "I will prove you wrong. Hold still."

He jerked back when she reached for him. "What are you doing?"

"I said don't move. You're breaking my concentration." She ran her hands through the air from the top of his cowl where wisps of sable hair escaped the covering and wiggled in the air. He swore heat rose from his body. Her hands paralleled his shoulders, not touching.

Healers used medicines to cure, as well as intuition. What if she sensed he faked his illness? What then? He leaned back. "Stop this!"

"Cease moving. I can't get a good reading." She skimmed the rags covering his chest, her motion slow and decisive. "I'm searching for body temperature. Heat or coldness. Heat comes from healthy tissues. Coldness is usually where lesions are. This type of healing is magically based. Respect the magic."

"Respect my privacy," he grumbled.

"Just a bit more."

He gathered his feet under him and stood. "I'm done."

"Sit back down," she ordered. "I'm not finished."

A battle of wills resulted. Neither wasted breath to speak. Brown eyes narrowed to stare at him, and emerald ones glared back. Gren had no doubt who would end up the loser—him. He needed to stay in Trell's good graces. At least for a little while longer. He slumped down with a snort.

Trell pulled out a turquoise stone streaked with dark lines running through skyblue and glided it over his body.

"What is that?" he asked, not hiding his skepticism.

"Turquoise is a healing stone. It works as a purifier. It might not heal you with a single pass but can aid in drawing out negative humors from your body. If nothing else, it might slow the disease's progress."

"Well?" he asked when she finished and tucked the stone away.

"At least you're interested in my findings."

"By all means…speak."

"Most people afflicted with a terminal illness tend to have one of two beliefs. Either they're of a mind that they will overcome the disease. Or they submit to the inevitable," she said.

"Which am I? The former or latter?"

"The former, I think. You are strong-willed. There is a vibrancy to your life force that I can't explain. It feels like you're a healthy person, which is very strange. Mayhaps my hypothesis is wrong."

Gren cringed inside. A cold dread filled him. Her diagnosis only proved his assumption of how skillful her healer abilities were. He couldn't let her get close or examine him again. He was a healthy man hiding beneath the rags of the most ill.

Trell eyed him as if she had the power to draw answers from him by merely looking at him. "Are you suffering many lesions? Nodules? Nosebleeds?"

He didn't move.

Trell pursed her lips. "I—I admit I'm confused. I've never come across a patient like you. Few Untouchables seek treatment. Whether it is because they have lost hope, I don't know. Little is known of the disease, but I do not believe, as some do, that it is a curse from the gods for sinful ways. If only you would let me examine your skin. I'm sure I have seen worse at the Halls of Medsin. It would allow me to give you a more detailed diagnosis."

Guilt reared its heavy head. The hope glinting in Trell's warm, brown eyes made his decision all the harder.

"I think not," he answered softly, his tone final.

Chapter 5

Rejection cut to the quick. Trell tried to dismiss the hurt but it lingered like a bad odor. One of them would have to relent if they were to continue on this journey.

"Do you hear that?" Trell asked as they traveled the road barely the width of a wagon. "Someone is ahead of us."

Muted hooves and a chorus of tinkling bells signaled travelers on the road before Gren actually saw them. Trell touched the tiny silver bells braided in her hair as if to confirm she still wore hers. Following the direction of her gaze, he viewed compact, spotted horses with thick feathering on their legs along with flowing manes and tails, prancing in tandem. He recognized the flashy animals as Fezner horses. Of course, they pulled rounded wagons painted with bright stripes that reminded him of bows.

At least it wasn't his brothers. He could only assume they'd finally learned Trell's name and realized she'd slipped through their clutches. Now they rushed to capture her.

Well, he found her first, and he'd find her dragon, too. He suspected the mythical creature was the real purpose of the quest.

Loud laughter and merry voices drifted on air currents as painted wagons trundled along the road and broke the peace of the woods. He should have anticipated the possibility of running into the traveling folk at some point. Though forbidden entrance to Kula, they trekked from place to place, living in wagons, trading horses, telling fortunes, tatting lace, and selling trinkets.

"Let's get off the road," Gren said, urging Trell into the woods. He gritted his teeth, feeling a slight resistance, and tugged harder.

She stumbled after him. "Why?"

"Fezners," he said the name as if a curse. Associating with the quick-eared people would cause complications he harbored no desire to deal with. Some claimed the wind spoke to them and revealed people's secrets. Further, the more eyes on him, the greater the risk of being exposed. A chance he wasn't willing to take. "They're nomads who roam from town to town."

She twisted free of his grasp. "I know who Fezners are. They visit Brenalin often where they perform juggling and sleight-of-hand tricks. They're very talented."

Her unbiased opinion meant trouble. He blocked her path when she started forward. "We should stay away from them. They're not trusted among honest people."

"For a man ostracized by society, you're behaving very judgmental."

The truth cut through his heart like a knife. "Am I to have no say in the matter? Is there nothing I can say to dissuade you?"

"If you dislike my rules, you may leave. You have no obligation to travel with me."

"You saved my life."

Compassion sped over Trell's delicate features.

"You owe me nothing. What happened in Brenalin was illegal. We both know that. I merely stopped a wrong-doing. We'll go our separate ways. I must meet new people to find new cures."

A strength existed in the slender healer that many veteran warriors lacked. His ears caught the tinkling of fading bells. The chorus of voices grew distant. Thankfully, the caravan rolled onward, and the last wagon rounded a bend in the road.

"You can relax," Trell said. "They're gone."

The danger of exposure reduced, Gren beamed beneath his mask of rags. "Believe me, it's for the best. They probably want no dealings with me."

For the next several days, he played on Trell's empathy and feigned trouble walking. It brought her to his side, where the sweet scent of vanilla surrounded him and reminded him of the cavernous room where cooks prepared repasts at home. Some of his best memories arose from those times.

Shaking free of the past, Gren's first preference was to trail the Fezners. At times, the merry jingle of bells on horses' harnesses drifted on the wind. When he heard them, he always checked Trell and slowed his pace even more, determined to keep the travelers ahead.

After three nights, they crossed a bridge and found a level spot to set up camp. Kindling turned out plentiful in the area.

"What can you tell me of dragons?" Gren asked as Trell crisscrossed sticks onto the fire. "I haven't pressured you about them in a while."

With a huff, she tossed a bundle of deadwood into the flames and dusted her hands clean of debris. "I thought you gave up on them."

"In my village, the best tales were about mythical creatures." He laced sincerity into his voice. "They were my favorites. I cannot force you to talk about them but hope my charming personality will break through your defenses."

"What defenses? There is nothing to reveal, unless you want to waste time exchanging myths created to scare children."

Gren locked his gaze on her lush lips, wondering how they'd taste if they kissed, sure they would be an elixir equal to the *farbrenen vaser*.

Would she kiss him back?

The wild idea surprised him. He was on a mission for his father. He needed to maintain distance between them. Oh, sure, she'd already informed him she did not fear contracting the Untouchable disease. He worried how she would feel if she discovered his deception and the truth about his mission. Would she denounce him? Attempt to flee?

Shaking the thoughts away, his mind returned to the more pleasant idea of kissing her. He stepped closer, still undecided…

"You avoid us. Why? Who be you?" said a youthful voice from the bower of trees.

Instinct took over. Gren whirled to face the danger only to see a brown-skinned lad emerging from the shadows. He glided into their camp without snapping a single twig. Staring at the boy with a dark bronze complexion, bare feet, stained leggings, and tunic, he knew who he was looking at—a Fezner.

"Who are you?" Trell asked.

Gren swore as she stepped forward.

"I be Dotra. Again, I ask why you avoid us?" He

drew closer.

Gren placed himself between Trell and the newcomer. "You're not afraid of me?"

"Fezners fear nothing." The lad grinned and continued to approach, his gaze focused on Trell. "You wear the red cloak. You be a healer?"

"I am." Trell slipped from behind Gren. She grabbed her travel bag off the ground as though anticipating a request for help. "Do you need my services?"

Gren frowned at the eagerness radiating from Trell in rolling waves. Why did she have to be excited? "Are your wits addled? He's a Fezner."

"All I see is a boy," Trell replied. She shot him a stern look of disapproval. "I don't care if he's a stranger. He's a person, the same as you."

The dark-skinned boy's grin showed all his teeth. "Grandmother Lurri be sick. Will you aid her?"

"Of course, I will. Take me to her."

Gren intercepted her, determined to stop her. He turned his full attention on the boy. "What about your own healer?"

The young Fezner didn't flinch. "Grandmother Lurri be our medicine giver."

"Convenient," Gren muttered. "Why can't she instruct someone to treat her?"

Trell huffed. "I don't know the reason for your lack of compassion and don't care." She clutched her supplies in her hands, her knuckles turning white. "You can remain in camp or follow. Your choice."

"Trell," Gren tried to explain. "It's unwise to traipse off with him. Townspeople will frown upon asking for your services if you treat traveling folk."

"I'm sure you're merely being protective. This is my duty. You fret too much."

"All right, then, I am coming, too."

Trell pinched her lips together as if drawing patience from a deep well within her core. "Put out the fire," she instructed, her voice calm. "I don't want a spark to catch the woods on fire."

Gren doused the flames with a bucket of water and stirred the ashes to guarantee no embers remained. When he looked at her, she nodded for Dotra to lead the way.

With boyish enthusiasm, the lad hollered in triumph and leapt into the road. Every once in a while, he dashed off the edge, grabbed a sapling with both hands, and shook it.

After the third time, Trell's curiosity got the better of her. "Why are you doing that?"

Dotra stopped to stare at her, dark eyes wide with amazement. "Be you ignorant of Fezner traditions?"

She glanced at Gren. Shrugging, he was determined to remain distant until she realized the futility of associating with the Fezners.

"I'm afraid so," she answered the boy. "You're the first I've actually spoken to. Those I saw in the marketplace were busy with their clients. I had no wish to interfere while they plied their trade."

The boy nodded as though he approved of her actions. "Grandmother Lurri has a fever and cannot rise from her bed. If I shake a young tree, I be attempting to transfer the fever from her to the tree."

"Has it worked in the past?" she asked.

Gren wondered why she was curious.

The boy shrugged.

Darcy Carson

Not exactly an answer. Still, she smiled in return. "Well, I look forward to meeting your people."

He studied her, wordless, then very deliberately said, "You be an odd outsider, but I like you."

"Thank you, I think."

With a boyish laugh, Dotra urged them to hurry. At a clearing, painted wagons formed a circle. He stopped to turn to them. "Wait here."

A drizzle began to fall.

Gren and she stood obediently beneath the boughs of an evergreen to watch the boy race toward the wagons. He leapt with the grace of a deer over a wooden hitch.

Cooking fires spit and sizzled against the rain throughout the camp.

Some dark faces aimed scowls in their direction, but the majority appeared content to ignore them. Or, at least, pretend to.

Goats scattered and dogs barked as Dotra darted past them.

A woman in a long, swaying skirt and tunic approached with an oversized trencher of aromatic stew, two spoons, and a jug that smelled of warm milk. "Be welcome, strangers," she greeted cheerfully. "Eat. Drink."

As they stood sharing the meal, a contingent of children paying no heed to the rain cascaded from wagons to surround them, pressing against their sides. Small hands grabbed at Trell's cloak and Gren's rags as they tried to tug them from the protective canopy.

"Off with you." The woman shooed the children away. "Or I'll call upon the Winged Man to swoop down and steal you away."

Children shrieked in fear, fleeing from the threat.

"Forgive them," the woman said. "They be young and know not it be rude to overwhelm strangers."

"No harm done," Trell volunteered, smiling.

"Check your pouches," Gren muttered, hungrier than willing to admit. "They can pluck a bird's feather without garnering a single squawk."

"Gren! That is no way to act after receiving a friendly welcome and food. You should be the last person to harbor bias against another."

"We do not allow Fezners to visit in my village. Too many items go missing whenever they are in the vicinity."

Trell turned to the Fezner woman. "I'm so sorry. Forgive my companion's rudeness."

"It be unimportant," she replied, her smile brighter than before. "He speaks true. Fezners have nimble fingers, although none here would dare break the hospitality code and steal from a guest, and guests you be."

Dotra returned just as they finished eating. "Grandmother Lurri be ready for you."

He led them to a green wagon with yellow and darker green trim, where he halted, climbed the steps, and rapped on the door.

"Don't stand outside and be waiting for me to rise from my sickbed to open the door for you," called a voice. "Come in, gal."

Trell swallowed hard.

Dotra offered a meek smile as he backed away to give Trell access. Irritability often was the first sign of illness. Or maybe her patient was just a cranky old lady. Whatever the reason, Trell steeled herself for the worst.

She leaned her staff against the wagon and took her herb pouch. Climbing up, her weight gently rocked the wagon, but she clung to the handle strap, opened the door, and entered.

Two steps inside revealed a decorative and intricately carved interior that momentarily stunned her. The workmanship exceeded anything she had ever seen. A master woodcrafter created this work of art.

She nearly missed a woman of an indeterminate age, anywhere between forty and eighty, staring at her from a bed at the back of the dimly lit space. Her hair was feathered with gray around the face, and a dull crown of silver curls hung around her shoulders.

Trell made a quick mental diagnosis; the dry condition of the woman's hair signaled malnutrition, although a thorough examination was required before she made a final evaluation. The woman's skin appeared slightly flushed, doubtless from fever. Some holly tea would induce sweating and relieve her fever. From what Trell saw of her form beneath the pile of quilted bedding, the woman would only reach her chin if she stood on her toes.

When the quick assessment finished, Trell stared into dark eyes full of intelligence. "Grandmother Lurri?"

"You know who I be," the elderly woman said in a wheezing breath. Golden bangles on her wrists jingled as she pointed. "Who be you?"

"My name is Trell Langois, and I am a traveling healer."

"You think me dense? Your red cloak reveals that." The woman scooted higher in bed. "Well, Healer Trell, what drab will you use to treat me?"

"Drab?"

Grandmother Lurri sent her a fleeting smile of triumph. "Herbs, gal. I sense a powerful magic be around you—tree magic, but you know nothing about Fezner healing."

Trell dampened her astonishment at the revelation. The woman did not sound conceited and had spoken with calm assurance. "I am sorry. Your word drab is unknown to me. First, I must learn what ails you. May I examine you?"

"You'll not touch me nor treat me until you answer to my satisfaction." Grandmother Lurri poked Trell in the stomach when she drew nearer. "What kind of healer be you?"

"A careful one. I would think you would appreciate that." Trell had encountered difficult patients in the past, but an inner voice warned this woman might be her worst. "Can you describe your symptoms?"

Grandmother Lurri scowled and snorted at the same time. "A high fever, cough, sore throat, runny nose, and a soreness throughout my body."

"It's not isolated in one particular area?"

The older woman shook her head. "Nay."

"How long have you been feeling ill?"

"Over a week."

An idea formed. "Has anyone else come down with the same symptoms?"

"None that I'm aware of."

"That's good to hear."

Grandmother Lurri huffed. "You not be the one who is sick."

Trell smiled at the retort. She touched the woman's brow. Warm, but not sweaty. "I'm sure you're

75

uncomfortable. For that, you have my deepest condolences. But taking to your bed probably kept the spread of illness to a minimum."

"All healers be aware of the value of maintaining a physical distance and avoiding direct contact when ill."

"For my patients' sake," Trell began, "I like to err on the side of safety. I have no wish to give you the wrong medicine."

A decreased pinkness in the woman's lips and nailbeds added to Trell's supposition that the woman's diet lacked balance. She envisioned herbs to increase appetite—dandelion and thistle topped the list and were plentiful in the area.

Grandmother Lurri poked Trell in the stomach a second time. "When the situation be hopeless, false hope be unnecessary."

Every healer bore the weight of responsibility when lives were placed in their hands. Not an easy task and Trell was no exception. "You'll not die if I have anything to say about the matter."

"I not be imagining the heaviness in my chest or this hacking cough. I be old and dying. No cure for that."

"Everyone is dying. Have you been drinking warm liquids to ease the congestion?"

"Of course. I know the standard treatments." Grandmother Lurri's demeanor shifted a hair. A glint appeared in her dark eyes, and a rosy color deepened on her cheeks. "What will this cost me?"

"Recover first."

"Nay, first we agree upon a trade."

"Trade?" Trell repeated, surprised the woman wanted to dicker at such a time.

"Fezners be proud folk. We accept no handouts, and I'll not be indebted to you, Healer. I sense a desire to learn in you. Fezners have different—even better—remedies than those learned in your fancy school."

Trell couldn't believe her ears. This was the very reason she began her adventure. "I don't mean to sound ungrateful, but can you give me an example?"

Grandmother Lurri coughed a dry chuckle. "Fair enough. If a patient tells you he cannot sleep, tell him to put his pillow at the foot of his bed and turn his covers around. He'll nod off immediately."

Regret washed over Trell in an unsettling wave. So much for discovering an unknown remedy to a serious illness. "That's superstition, not a cure."

"You not be the person who cannot fall asleep," the old woman replied with amusement. "Here be another…for the hot-cold sickness, the powder of three-horned frogs in spirits will relieve the misery."

Trell had her doubts but kept her opinion to herself. "Ague. I know it."

"As a Fezner healer, there be many things I know. But more will cost you."

A test.

Trell accepted the challenge because she'd passed hundreds to become a healer. "I thought we were trading for my services."

After a moment, Grandmother Lurri coughed, wheezing. "We be, though I not be cured yet."

"Does your throat hurt?"

"Only when I swallow," the old woman replied.

"I'll fetch some pine gum for you to chew. It will relieve the scratchiness."

****

What was taking so long to examine the sick woman?

Rain poured, drenching Gren. He had no intention of stranding Trell with these people. Occasionally, the green wagon rocked from side to side as movement occurred inside. He thought he heard a muffled word or two from the women, although their voices were never clear enough to decipher an entire sentence. Aware of Trell's desire to find new cures, he hoped they discussed or traded symptoms and cures enough that she would be willing to leave.

So far his disguise held. Maybe the Fezners' reputation for being eagle-eyed was an exaggeration. He hoped so because as his rags got wetter, they loosened. He couldn't afford to reveal his healthy skin.

His lips quivered from cold seeping into his bones. Fatter raindrops dripping from tree boughs splattered his head and shoulders. The Fezners deserted him to retreat to the warmth and dryness of their own wagons. He didn't blame them—only a fool stayed out in inclement weather.

So what did that make him?

"Ah, there you be, Untouchable. Why stand in the rain?"

Gren whirled toward the voice. *Dotra.* "You walk too quietly for my comfort. If you must know, this is where Trell left me. This is where I'll wait for her return."

"You be welcome in our camp." Boyish curiosity tinged his tone but softened with politeness.

Gren wished the boy would go away, leave him alone. He knew the law regarding Untouchables extended to the Fezners as well. All people were required to give Untouchables food and clothing if asked. He might as well act the part. "Do you have any red clothing to spare?"

Wet curls lay flat on Dotra's forehead. The task seemed to please the boy. "Let me check. While I do, come, sit beneath a wagon."

Gren harrumphed. Feeling rain dribble down his back, the temptation to accept the boy's offer increased tenfold. He'd risk exposure by being closer, but he'd also be closer to Trell.

"My thanks," he said, following the boy. "I didn't think traveling folk allowed outsiders amidst their camps."

"Outsiders come for the festivities to leave their coin, which we gladly accept. Not to spend the night. Untouchables be outcasts, the same as us, and be welcome."

Gren mulled over this tidbit. It sounded like Fezner society had rules, the same as any town or village. "Which wagon do you suggest we sneak under?"

"Grandmother Lurri's. She really be my grandmother." The boy splashed through the puddles and dove under the colorful wagon with extra-large wheels.

Gren tailed him and crawled under. A tarp covered the ground and kept the place surprisingly dry. The underside of the wagon was stained black with soot.

"I be right back," Dotra said, disappearing faster than Gren could blink.

He had just started getting comfortable when the boy returned. He tossed a bundle beneath the wagon and joined Gren. "I found these."

Gren picked up a threadbare woman's skirt and a

child's tunic. One scarlet and one faded to burgundy, but still in the acceptable palette for an Untouchable. He started shredding the skirt into narrow strips and tying them to the rope belt at his waist and the one circling his neck. "Thank the people who shared," he said.

Dotra took the child's tunic and began tearing it into strips. "Be you still hungry?"

"Nay," he said, disliking being obligated more than necessary. "You have shared enough for one day."

Dotra's smile widened. "We can acquire more."

"No doubt you can."

The boy finished shredding first. He laid the small strips alongside Gren.

Gren continued working while Dotra ignited tinder in a small pit, then added shiny black rocks to the pile.

Gren looked on in amazement when black smoke rose and the rocks put out heat with a golden glow. "What are those things?"

"That should be obvious." Dotra bent over and blew on the black stones. "They be firestones. They burn hotter than wood and be easier to collect, too."

Gren furrowed his brow. "Where did you get them?"

"Here and there."

An evasive answer. Gren stopped his task to pick up a piece to inspect. A dusty, sulfur smell stung his nose and left a greasy, black stain in the center of his palm. "I've heard rumors of magical stones that burn. These look familiar to me."

Dotra raised velvety dark eyes to stare hard at him. "They are rare, difficult to come by. Where have you seen them?"

Maybe he said too much.

He frowned and let the firestone tumble off his fingers. Black flakes that smelled like dirt dusted his palms. Even the odor seemed familiar.

He met the boy's gaze, fully aware he would be gauged by his answer—as if he would allow curiosity to ruin his quest. "One of many places."

Chapter 6

Trell descended the wagon's steps, drawing in gulps of moist air. Rain clung to tree branches and dribbled to the ground. Puddles formed around the camp. Sporadic moonlight showered the site with an eerie silver glow. The effect didn't last long. Clouds scudded across the night sky to cloak the moon.

Being outside reminded her of being an Ossa. She always felt rejuvenated, connected to the earth. Nighttime was when a tree's pulse beat the loudest, when its branches drooped because it slept.

She'd stayed in Grandmother Lurri's wagon longer than planned. The Fezner woman had been an absolute delight with her gruff revelation of cures and promise of more remedies. In some ways, she reminded Trell of Wizard Einer, which brought a smile to her lips. She missed the old wizard after spending five years as his ward.

She hoped Gren had found a place to settle.

As if thinking about him made him appear, Gren crawled from beneath the green wagon on his hands and knees. "Are you looking for me? We've been given shelter from the rain under here." He waved at the ground. "Take a look."

Dotra crawled out after Gren.

"What changed your mind? I thought you wanted nothing to do with these people?" At his shrug, she tucked her braids back to avoid the muddy ground and ducked underneath. She sat, knees folded. Wagon parts slung under the wagon bed, the bottoms of water and grease buckets.

Most importantly, the space provided a place out of the inclement weather.

Gren followed. "One night won't hurt. We'll stay dry, and Dotra gave me a couple extra blankets for a softer bedding. Tonight you'll enjoy a restful sleep. We must take comfort where we can find it."

"This will do just fine. My thanks, Dotra," she said to the boy, then looked at Gren. "Before I can rest, I must find some pine gum for Grandmother Lurri to chew, then brew her holly tea."

Gren crawled closer. "I'll accompany you."

"That's unnecessary. I won't be gone long."

He took a deep breath, as if he needed courage to speak. "I'll play my flute to pass the time while you are away."

"Let him," Torkel mindspoke. *"I fancy his music."*

The mindspeech startled her. Torkel had pouted since she'd forbidden Gren to play his flute while those two riders haunted the area. No fires. No music. Ever since, the dragon declined to communicate with her. She avoided looking at the night sky to give away his presence. Gren was too quick, too observant.

And now other gazes joined his.

For a split second, she refused to speak to dragon or human.

She visualized the massive black dragon. His teeth were sharp as knives, his claws like steel blades, his wings capable of delivering hammer-like blows, with a tail holding the power of a battering ram within its length and a barbed tip. Torkel could defend himself in spite of his youth. Her real concern stemmed from an accidental sighting. His presence would be difficult to explain, and she had vowed to keep his existence a secret at all cost.

"There are many people here," she answered the dragon first. *"You should have stayed with the Guardians. The more eyes there are, the easier it is for them to spot you. You'll be discovered."*

"I shall be extremely vigilant. A whisper calls to my blood like the human male's music."

"What?"

"I know not. This is the first time I've ever heard it."

"Be careful." She kept her tone neutral, forcing her body to relax.

"If I am too far away, I cannot enjoy the music."

She shook her head. *"I wasn't referring to the music."*

"I know."

She gave up and crept from beneath the wagon. She swept her braids back and sprang to her feet. A small lantern sat on the steps of the wagon. She latched onto it before turning to Gren. "Play your flute. Music is said to soothe."

"My gratitude," Torkel mindspoke.

She strained her ears. If she concentrated, the flap of leathery wings echoed in the night. She prayed others believed the rain created the noise.

Within a few steps, she entered the forest.

"Once-an-Ossa, welcome to our land," the trees whispered to her. *"We are pleased to see you with the Walking Ones."*

"I am honored to be among you," she answered back.

No one knew trees and plants spoke to her, not her brother nor the Guardians. Not even Torkel. She trekked through the forest as trees bent their branches to brush her shoulders, and she ran her fingers through their emerald boughs. Another deluge of fat raindrops splattered her, only to make her laugh. Receiving permission to collect sticky resin from the trees, she put the secretion in a small container and licked her fingers clean.

"Is there a holly among you?" she asked.

"A vishnberry grows by the creek."

Vishnberry would work. A bush similar to holly, though not as toxic. Raising the lantern, she headed toward the sound of water splashing over rocks. Within moments, she found a four-foot high bush near the riverbank.

"Greetings, Once-an-Ossa," the vishnberry said upon her approach. *"You seek me?"*

Her lantern cast a dim glow to reflect a glossy-leafed bush. She wasn't startled her visit had been expected. News traveled fast among trees. *"I do. A tea from your leaves would be beneficial to a patient. May I pick them? I'll be careful not to hurt you."*

"I would be honored if my leaves restore a Walking One to health."

"My thanks." Trell buried a piece of bread that she'd palmed as an offering and then gently pinched off each leaf. *"All is well with you?"*

"As good as can be expected when birds and deer munch upon my berries throughout winter, but spring will bring an abundance of flowers."

At times like these, alone in the great woods, the pull of being an Ossa hit Trell much harder. Sometimes she missed those days and knew the trees never understood her desire to become human. They considered her decision a death sentence.

Tonight, the weight of boughs ran through her arms, the heavier mass of branches in her legs slowed her steps, and her torso stiffened as if solidifying into a trunk. Hadn't her feet and toes tingled recently as if still roots, eager to wiggle through the ground seeking nourishment?

In reality, people and trees were not so different. All living things were connected more than anyone knew. Trees recorded their age through the rings in their trunks, as humans gained wrinkles as they grew older. At middle age, trees stopped growing taller and thickened around the middle, the same as many humans.

"Many thanks, my friend. I bid you a long growing season."

"And I you," the bush answered.

As Trell neared camp, musical riffs floated through the air like snowflakes. Poignant and untamed, some notes went up, others down. Some trilled, whirling around, while the cadence of others slowed and combined.

The music wove a powerful spell around her, and she wasn't alone.

Rapt Fezners sat on the steps of their wagons or stood beneath trees with their heads cocked, listienng to the music.

And Torkel flew overhead.

She could almost hear a purr of delight emanating

from the dragon through mindspeech.

Farther away, where the Fezner horses were tethered, the animals stomped the ground or whinnied in protest. She held her breath. The horses sensed a predator—Torkel.

"Do not stop him," the dragon mindspoke as if he fathomed her concerns. *"He does not play often enough."*

"How close did you fly?" She held her stomach in dread. *"No, don't answer. I have no wish to know. Fly back to the dragon circle."*

"I cannot. A force calls to me. I can't decide if it is the music or something else."

In spite of her misgivings, Torkel's repentant tone elicited a grin from her. *"I can't stress the danger. Gren already suspects that a dragon is nearby,"* she reminded her friend. *"This is dangerous for you. You're being selfish. If you won't worry about yourself, think about the dragonets. They are too young to protect themselves."*

"See what you have done," he mindspoke back, dodging her protest.

"What?"

"The music. The human stopped playing. 'Tis all your fault."

Trell shook her head. Sometimes… *"Return to the dragon circle, if you dislike my methods."*

"I follow where you go."

She gave up and paused to listen. Sure enough, the sounds returned to normal where people conversed with one another. The stomp of iron hooves striking the ground added a low tremor as they continued to nicker.

Squaring her shoulders, Trell replaced the lantern

to where she found it. She put water on the fire and wiggled under the wagon. Gren sat with his legs crossed, the flute in his lap.

"You must be weary," she said. "I didn't expect you to play while I was away."

"I missed you, and playing allowed the time to pass quicker."

Her heart fluttered at his flowery words. "How do you feel? I've put a kettle on for Grandmother Lurri's tea. I could make you some chamomile as well."

"That's unnecessary," he answered. "My neck is just stiff, is all."

"Allow me to make you feel better while the water heats." She reached for him.

He jerked back. "Touching me is unwise."

"Don't be silly," she said, continuing to scramble over to him. Her fingers brushed over his neck and shoulders. Much to her surprise, his muscles felt like the cords of a warrior, not those of a sick man.

He scrambled away and stretched his arm to prohibit her from getting closer. "Stay back."

That fleeting touch caused a tingle to run up her fingers like warm water. The sensation flowed up her arms, seeping into all her pores until her head spun.

How sick was he? The disease caused a person to lose extremities due to repeated injuries and infection. They had to be amputated. Some people died within five years, others lasted for several decades. No one knew why.

She liked Gren and wanted to help him. Yet she was sure he hid something from her. How sick was he? Or was he sick at all? She hated having doubts. His feelings mattered to her. It wasn't fair such a kind, decent man suffered. She watched him tuck away the flute with care. A task hampered by rags covering his large hands. Yet those same hands created beautiful music.

She eyed him and smiled. "I would say you have magic in your hands."

"What do you mean?" He repeated her earlier words.

"You create powerful music. It brings joy to all who hear."

She examined the back of his head from under her lashes as if her gaze could pierce his ragged cowl. His music tugged at her heart with its appeal, but something deeply earthy pulled her to the man himself.

That was just wrong.

Consequences existed when caring for someone. It usually meant feelings for them and involved ensuring their well-being. No one could fault her for shielding her heart from another man. One mistake had already cost her a lifetime.

Yet Gren radiated a potency she never felt in anyone else. She imagined him holding a position of power over other men. Women acting silly, batting long lashes, and throwing themselves at him. A warm tingle ran through her. It felt…exciting to fantasize about him.

She shook her head as if to rid herself of the crazy thoughts. Frustration brushed over her like an irritating rash. He was her patient. Nothing more. She took her calling and responsibilities seriously.

****

Duty called Gren. In the early light of the next morning, he woke from a restless slumber. Thoughts of home plagued him. Being second born, he had grown up stuck in the middle. No one catered to his needs or saw to his comfort. Oh, he wasn't mistreated, and he had formed lifetime friendships. He'd received a solid education and extensive training in swordsmanship and diplomacy. All the proper instruction to give him skills to survive in a hostile world.

Gren remembered his last time home. He'd been summoned to the great hall crowded with nobles and leading citizens of Kula who pledged their allegiance to his father, Stal Oyg Har.

A stillness hung heavier than the dignitary's jewel-encrusted robes. Only the unintentional shuffle of a booted foot on the stone floor or a muffled cough broke the silence. Then his father, lord of Barg Castle, king of Kula, announced in a booming voice, "To my three sons... Find the Wizard Cress's sister. She who is the healer. She is the key. Find her. Find her dragon. Let the most deserving son succeed and be my heir. He will sit with honor upon Kula's throne."

Oded's face had purpled with rage. His life had been full of pomp and pageantry, and he'd grown up greedy, arrogant, even cruel. As the eldest, he'd expected to inherit the throne, not hear his destiny be undercut in the blink of an eye. "I forbid it."

"On what grounds," his father countered. "You have to be king to issue edicts, and you are not."

Riff, the youngest, had cheered, as if the quest was designed solely for him to achieve the throne. He'd found favor with both his mother and father, until his mother's sudden death. Doted upon, he'd matured into a young lordling who believed himself incapable of executing anything amiss.

Now, Gren suspected a more diabolical purpose

lounged behind the proclamation. Who was this healer who held the fate of so many lives? What was she to his father? And what purpose did a mythical creature—a dragon—play? To distrust his lord and father's motives seemed foreign to him, only he couldn't help himself.

He'd shot a glance at his father, concerned, yet eager to fulfill the quest. Gren didn't rush out of the great hall like his brothers. Instead, he proceeded with caution and spent the balance of the evening poring through ancient texts to learn as much as he could about dragons.

The next day, Gren set forth with the mere beginnings of a plan, his father's words encouraging him that it would be a fair search. While strict and uncompromising, his father had never broken his word.

No affection or partiality arose from his family. His friends were few and far between.

That is until he'd met Trell.

She defended him against the crowd in Brenalin. Refused the woodcutters' hospitality when it didn't include him. And last night, she'd attempted to tend him. Just him. Oh, she'd looked after the ailing Fezner woman. But returned so promptly her primary concern seemed focused on his comfort, an altogether unique and pleasant change for him.

He remembered with astonishing clarity how she looked the night before—dreamlike, the Goddess Yanna come to earth. Alluring and seductive.

For a moment, his mission slipped a notch while yearning filled him. To even think about Trell with tenderness—to harbor any affection toward her whatsoever—was counterproductive.

The creak of a door interrupted his thoughts.

Someone jumped to the ground. Dotra bowed under the wagon.

"You be wanted inside," the boy said to Trell.

Trell sat up instantly. "Has your grandmother taken a turn for the worse? Is she all right?"

"Grandmother Lurri be wanting to see you, Healer," he repeated, adding, "and your traveling companion."

"Me?" His hand flew to his chest. Had his duplicity been discovered? "What can she possibly want from me? Does she possess a cure for my affliction?"

Dotra lifted his hand, palm up. "Go to the source and ask. I be tending the dream inside me head."

"Pardon?"

"The cobs. Our horses," Dotra said as if anyone with a grain of intelligence knew his meaning. Horses neighed for their breakfast. The boy looked toward the picket lines. "They be my pride and joy. They be spooked last night. A predator must have crept close to scout our camp."

Gren mentally compared the hot-blooded horses his father preferred to the sturdy Fezner horses. A draft heritage was clear in their stocky bodies, but he suspected many breeds had been added to their lineage over the ages. The chance to examine them up close was a temptation he couldn't resist. "I'll lend you a hand," he said.

"Afterwards. Grandmother Lurri first."

"Dotra's right." Trell crept out from under the wagon and straightened her skirt. "It's the polite thing to do to offer her your respects. You can look on the horses later."

The boy winked. "Fezner gold does not clink and

glitter. It shines in the sun and neighs in the dark."

Shoulders slumped, Gren lumbered up the steps after Trell. He blinked to let his eyes adjust to the dim interior. The wagon appeared cozier than he expected. Merry yellow and peacock blue hues tinted the walls. A teakettle whistled on a tiny stove. The wagon held a larder, several chests, a great pitcher of water, cooking utensils, and articles of crockery. "Pleasant."

"Aye, it be that," spoke a gray-haired woman, lying abed with the covers pulled up to her chin. "You be the healer's companion. Come closer. Let me look at you. The number of Untouchables roaming the land grows in number every year. A bad sign for things to come, I think. The cards predict the world sits on an edge about to tilt. We must tread carefully. Though you need not fear, you be welcome among us."

He scooted past Trell to approach the bed. "My gratitude for the hospitality, but we wouldn't want to trespass upon it. We won't remain long."

"We be seeing. Whether you admit it or not, you be trapped."

"Trapped?" he repeated, a tightness developing in his chest at the exchange. "You mean because I'm an Untouchable?"

"The cards told me, and my eyesight be clear," she answered, smiling. " 'Sides, I be saying what you want to hear."

Her cryptic words caught him by surprise. He supposed she spoke in riddles to keep the illusion of mystery alive as much as the gold bangles on her bony wrists revealed her wealth. "If I have passed inspection, I'll take my leave. I told Dotra I would help with the horses."

Grandmother Lurri waved her hand in dismissal, bangles clinking. "Go. I have learned what I need."

A flash of worry shivered down his back. Did the woman have the sight? Had a genuine reason existed for requesting his presence? He shot a glance at Trell. She offered him a quick smile of assurance before he departed.

Outside, he studied his surroundings. Everywhere, Fezners broke camp. It wasn't just Dotra harnessing horses. Children of all ages performed the same task. The animals appeared utterly calm. Unflappable. It made sense. Fezners put all their possessions into their colorful wagons. A temperamental horse in their midst that disobeyed commands could destroy all they owned or harm someone.

An uncertainty poked at him. A tightness constricted his throat. Dare Trell and he travel with these sharp-eyed people? Were a few conveniences— better food, a cover over their heads—worth the risk?

He let the thought dissolve, disapproving of the idea less and less. He pinned his hope on Trell agreeing to part from them as soon as possible.

****

A tingle of excitement made Trell's heart beat faster as she entered Grandmother Lurri's wagon. The air in the interior wafted with the hint of vishnberry, pine, and the pungent scent of cloves. The combination triggered Trell to inhale deeply. It reminded her of the great outdoors when she first became an Ossa. She could appreciate the same things as a human as she once did as a tree.

A lump of pine gum lay discarded in a cup. She'd instructed the Fezner woman to chew until the granules broke and to spit out the impurities.

Overnight a healthy color tinted Grandmother Lurri's cheeks, and her eyes blazed bright and clear. Both good signs.

Trell ran her hand over the woman's forehead. "Your fever broke. I am glad you are feeling better."

"I am better because I be blessed with good fortune. In fact, I be well enough to put my clothes on." Grandmother Lurri waved to a long skirt with rows of shimmering satin ribbon and a plain, dark blouse that Trell had ordered her to remove in case she became overheated. "Hand me those, if you please."

Trell balked. "My advice is for you to remain in bed for a day or two longer. I don't want you relapsing."

"What's an old woman to do?" Grandmother Lurri huffed. "Sleep away the rest of her life? I rise when I want."

Trell clamped her hands on her hips. The movement made the tiny silver bells in her hair chime. "You're under my care and can rejoin the others when you are completely well."

The old woman grumbled but wisely made no attempt to reach for her clothes. Instead, she reclined against her pillow with a sour look and folded skinny arms over her chest. "Tell me, you be traveling with your companion long?"

"Why ask that question?" Did her ready defense stem from a growing attachment to Gren? Of course, she cared about her patients. All were important, but he…he was special.

"No need to defend your actions, gal. I tell you this about Fezners, so you can better understand. People hate us. A child sickens. Dies. They blame us. Crops fail. They blame us. If an item goes missing, we stole it."

"Well, I'm not most people. I prefer to judge people by their actions, not what others say."

A snort of disbelief sounded in the tight quarters. "It's easier for people to point the finger at us because we are strangers than at themselves. From the earliest times, they shunned us during the day, but at night they be eager to visit, and drink our spirits, gamble or dance with our womenfolk."

"If you disapprove of outsiders, why allow them into your camp?"

"How else will we survive? We must earn coin." Grandmother Lurri paused, looked around the interior. "Much is said about us, but only a small part be true. In the beginning, the Gods carved a man and woman out of logs and breathed life into them. Later the Gods realized the world was so boring with these two humans and their children that they decided to liven things up. So one night, when the man slept in his cave, the God Koonts took a bit of jawbone from the man and in a twinkling of an eye, a sturdy Fezner came to be, alive and kicking. We be different from others. Which is why your companion be welcome among us. He be different. You, too."

Trell listened, enchanted. She loved stories as much as medicine. "We were fortunate you were traveling the road."

"It be fate."

Puzzled, Trell leaned closer. Her braids tilted forward. "Fate? I am a highly trained healer."

"Your remedies worked well. They share a potency

akin to forest magic," the old woman continued, "I especially liked the pine gum. Sweetest I ever tasted. The trees gave you their best."

Was the woman guessing at her affinity with plants?

"I'm glad you're pleased. A happy patient recovers faster."

The Fezner patted the thick quilt. "Come closer. Sit. We speak more of cures. Aye? This be a favorite among men. It cures baldness."

"Baldness?" Trell blurted out the word. "That's not life-threatening. Only a fool would waste time trying to restore a full head of hair."

"Mayhaps," Grandmother Lurri said with a hint of amusement in her tone, "but hair on a man's head be a badge of honor many men seek. So listen…Take a large piece of pig skin and with the bristle side inward, have the man rub vigorously, applying as much pressure as possible. Then rinse with a mixture of rosemary and borax water."

"That sounds like a trick for gullible men."

"Did you notice the Fezner men? Not a bald head among them."

Trell searched her memory of the men she'd seen in camp. A few had worn hats, but the rest seemed to have full heads of hair. "Can you share something that has merit, something that will aid the sick?"

"I be serious. Contented people be healthy people. Balance exists in this world for every illness. You think the Gods put the bad in this world without cures?" The silver-haired woman shook her head. "Travel with us, gal. We'll talk more later, and you'll learn. Meanwhile, you must attend my peoples' needs if I am forced to abide by your orders. A fair exchange, I think."

"Agreed."

"Now, go. I wish to rest."

Trell didn't mind being ordered about. A vulnerability wrapped around the older woman. Grandmother Lurri probably felt guilty about being unable to care for her people and didn't like to show weakness because she couldn't tend to her clan's needs. That explained her crotchetiness. The obligation to care for people existed in all healers.

Dismissed, Trell left the wagon. An air of expectancy permeated the camp. Campfires were doused and dismantled, some rocks tossed aside in various heaps, while others seemed neatly stacked at the base of trees. She smelled stale ale, probably consumed the previous night. Somewhere a woman sang.

Children stopped their chores to gawk as she passed.

Women nodded at her approach, smiling warmly, a silent welcome.

Men pretended to ignore her, but she sensed their gazes follow in her wake.

Trell searched for Gren. She felt responsible for his welfare and wanted to make sure these people treated him fairly. Thus far, his familiar tattered garments were not among the colorful wagons.

Her search had not gone unnoticed. A shaggy-haired child ran up to her and pointed.

Gren curried the horses' coats glossy with Dotra while the horses finished their oats and hay. They worked together, enjoying an easy camaraderie between boy and man. It seemed so…natural. They worked as a team, and that pleased her.

Gren waved the instant he looked up and saw her.

Dotra led a pair of spotted horses toward Grandmother Lurri's green wagon.

Silent a moment, Trell pondered her thoughts, wondering how to tell Gren her decision. "Grandmother Lurri's recuperative powers are amazing. She already wants out of bed."

"Good news to my ears. That means you and I can go our separate way from these traveling folk."

Trell narrowed her eyes. "Grandmother Lurri invited us to join them, and I mean to stay. She knows remedies and cures no one else does and has offered to teach me. It's why I'm out here. I want you with me, Gren. I value you and your company, but I'll understand if you decide to go your way."

Chapter 7

As if he could ever leave Trell.

A low groan rumbled from Gren to express his disapproval. The idea appalled him. "Can you not give the proper instructions to someone else?"

"What kind of healer would I be if I didn't treat a patient?" Trell answered him.

He glanced at the Fezners. Their dark complexions made them look different at first glance. He'd been a fool to let others' opinions sway him. Deep down the traveling folk possessed the same values as any family—a deep-seated desire to protect their children and to see them grow into healthy, happy adults.

Wetting his lips, he confessed, "Mayhaps I was misinformed about the Fezners."

While admitting his change of heart about the traveling folk, he still hoped to convince Trell to leave. These people's reputation for being sharped-eyed put him in danger of being exposed as a fraud. And it was too early in their journey for him to reveal the truth.

One more try couldn't hurt.

"Trell, their healer is on the mend. You said so yourself. There's no reason for us to remain. I'm your protector."

"Protector? Did I ask for protection? While I appreciate your concern, I have no need for it. As far as traveling with the Fezners, we were invited. Why not stay?"

Every jingle of harnesses, thud of hooves, and motion of the Fezners increased his tension. Several people skimmed them with dark gazes as they passed to go about their chores. Traveling with them would only create problems.

He owed the young healer his life, which caused guilt to arise. He hated manipulating her. Lying to her. He fought against the avalanche of remorse his deception created. Only when he reminded himself of the merits of his cause did his guilt ease.

For the greater good of Kula.

The reminder didn't help. Rather, it raised questions. If he doubted what he'd been taught about the Fezners, what other falsehoods had been imparted to him?

He shook off his misgivings and put on a brave face to try a final time. "Be sensible, Trell. We don't know these Fezners. Even on foot we can outdistance them in their wagons. They'll be stopping at every town or village along the way to ply their trade. It'll slow us down."

"Why are you acting like this? Being so judgmental? They are people, the same as you and I. They bleed like us. They offer us their hospitality. They are worthy of friendship."

"Are you sure I can't talk you out of staying?"

"You have my answer. I am looking for new medicines," she said softly, firmly. Her chest heaved, and from the neck slit of her tunic sweet vanilla scented the air. "Mayhaps I did not make myself clear when we met. It is my hope to find new cures and remedies. These people might possess the first of many. Plus, I

101

have a patient who needs me."

"But—"

She shook her head. "It pains me to say this, Gren, for I have come to enjoy your company and would miss you if you decided to leave, but I am staying. Grandmother Lurri has promised to teach me new healing methods. It's why I began this journey. Do what you must."

The determination in her voice defeated him. "Trell, this humble Untouchable apologizes from the bottom of his diseased heart and begs forgiveness for my forwardness. I spoke only out of concern for your safety. I will not abandon you now…or ever."

"What am I going to do with you?" Shaking her head, she grinned at him.

A tingle swept up the back of his neck. Gren ran through various arguments before giving in. "I don't know. I really don't."

She reached for his hand, but he moved before she touched him. "We'll figure it out. Together."

His charade sickened him. He tried to maintain eye contact but looked away. One thing, for sure, Trell was no fool. Extreme caution would be necessary to keep his identity a secret. He'd never used dubious means to achieve his goals in the past. That was his brothers' style—one used threats, the other weaseled.

An itch bothered him. Gren tried to run a finger under the clothing at his neck where the irritation developed. Ever since dawning the rags, he'd scratched at various spots. He wondered if it stemmed from a guilty conscience.

If they stayed, which seemed the case, he would have to double, triple his efforts to keep Trell from uncovering his masquerade.

He added the Fezners to his list of concerns. If they spotted his deception, what then? He needed to keep alert, to gauge their reaction or fighting abilities. Could he escape or fight them off? It didn't take intellect to discern the Fezners would side with Trell.

He speculated on whether a worse outcome existed and found one—Trell's crushed look of betrayal once she learned his secret. Devastation would rule the day. For her. For him. He would have nothing to offer except a sincere apology, and he fretted that would be insufficient. In just a few days she had grown important to him. Somehow, some way she had crept into his heart and taken up residence.

****

Trell stood outside Grandmother Lurri's wagon and stretched the kinks out of her body from a long night of rest. After only a few days, she cherished traveling with the Fezners. While they faced discrimination and persecution, the deeds of others didn't control them. They laughed with each other, worked in unison to lessen each other's burdens. It amazed her how easily they adapted, traveling from place to place.

One reason might be because of exposure to the different lifestyles and villages, and change seemed a process that they accepted with ease. She tried to wrap her head around their philosophy after spending the majority of her life in one spot and still couldn't grasp it in its entirety.

When she questioned why they refused to settle for one place or to put roots down, several quoted, "change is home." That answer reminded her of migrating birds and fit the nomadic folk.

While she was happy traveling with the Fezners, Gren caused her worry. At first, he'd seemed frustrated not being able to convince her to leave with him. He acted as though he adapted to living with them, but there were days she swore he wanted to move on.

Daily, she made herself ready and available to help the Fezners. She treated a multitude of cuts and bruises, predominantly children who never walked, but leaped and ran throughout the camp. She treated one woman who burned herself in a fire. A man suffered a sprain that required a splint.

Even Gren demonstrated skills that came in handy. A horse threw a shoe, and the little caravan stopped. He assisted the driver to replace the shoe as if he'd done farrier work all his life. She watched the play of his muscles beneath his rags and couldn't help wondering about his trade before disease stole his life away.

Each night the travelers gathered around a large bonfire. The smallest children were tucked in bed. Men sat close to the fire's warmth, many with musical instruments in their deeply tanned hands. Women wove through the groups, pouring ale from jugs into cups. Young couples stood together, hands linked by twined fingers.

A cheer went up when Grandmother Lurri's door opened and she emerged from her wagon, her first appearance since taking ill. Dotra rushed to the petite woman's side to assist her as she stepped down.

The silver-haired woman glanced around at the various smiling faces, nearly every one related to her in one way or another. Her complexion looked clear, a rosy tint on her cheeks in the firelight. She wore a multi-colored skirt and the healthy bounce in her step delighted Trell.

"What you be looking at?" the old woman demanded from the grinning people when her grandson escorted her to a place of honor in front of the fire. "I be alive."

Brisk laughter greeted her remark. Someone strummed a mandolin with an uplifting tune. The music was designed to make feet tap. A second later, the thumping of a drum was added, followed by a zukra bagpipe with its graceful notes and timing.

A woman with large hoop earrings jumped into the circle around the fire. Arms raised, she twirled in double turns and moved her heels in small, quick steps that were near impossible to follow.

Soon a groundswell of claps and cheers from men without instruments combined with those who played. A spontaneous celebration started. Additional women joined the first dancer.

Trell swayed to music that changed in unexpected ways—fast, then slow, then fast again. Gren touched his flute tucked at his belted waist.

"Join them," she encouraged him.

"Nay, tonight I prefer to listen."

With a nod, she left him to walk over to Grandmother Lurri. "How do you feel?"

"I be good." The older woman looked at the people dancing, laughing, enjoying themselves and chuckled. "Do you feel it?"

"What?"

"The music. Do you dance?"

A snort preceded her answer. "I never had time to learn."

"Lessons be not required. Pretend your ankles be hobbled like the cobs, then let your body sway to the melody. Hear it, feel it. Let it overtake you. When desperate to move, toss back your head and laugh aloud. Break free of your hobbles. Leap up and twirl. All it takes is the will to do it."

"The human female is correct. Do as she says. Take a deep breath. Smell the music."

The wispy brush of Torkel's mindspeech enticed Trell. He was close enough to overhear, but nightfall kept him hidden. She allowed herself to breathe in the sweetness of the melody like a drug, let it flow over her, through her veins.

"Nothing be stopping you," Grandmother Lurri went on. "Try it now."

"Do it," Torkel encouraged.

No other encouragement was necessary. Trell closed her eyes to focus on the music. Within seconds, her body swayed with the beat of the melody. Soon she felt caught in a snowstorm, the music became the wind, the dancers' snowflakes swirling around.

Trell leapt in the circle with the other women— spinning and swirling. They laughed with her and inspired her to dance by clapping, cheering her on. A sense of wildness and freedom came over her. Yet, she felt in control.

A wild thought curled in her mind. Did Gren's marvelous emerald eyes watch her? She found it pleasing that they were the most prominent color in nature. She hoped he did and approved of her behavior.

The sensations were as much a part of her as the melodious tune itself. No wonder Fezner women loved to dance. Power flowed in their svelte movements. In all honesty, they maintained a mastery over the spectators who shouted encouragement, not the other way around as Trell first assumed.

After a while she picked out individual voices cheering her on. Grandmother Lurri's high-pitched one. Dotra's. Even Gren's. His, more than anyone else's, rippled through her veins. The deep baritone stroked her in a soft, sensual way as she danced the night away.

"You dance well," Torkel whispered in mindspeech to her. *"I like these people. They enjoy life and focus on the positives, rather than the maelstrom of others. I see special qualities in the boy, Dotra. But your male companion remains a mystery. Why does he insist upon knowing about dragons when most humans believe we vanished long ago? A perverse reason must exist."*

Trell stumbled, her concentration shattered. Then she twirled in the circle, counting her steps. *"I've wondered the same thing myself. Mayhaps I'll ask someday. Meanwhile, let me dance."*

"As you wish," he said. *"However, be aware I would not mind these piddling humans basking in my glory. All will someday. These can be the first."*

"Nay," Trell groaned in mindspeech before trying her attention back to the music.

It was long after star-rise when Trell made her way to her bed. Bone-weary, she slumped onto blankets spread out beneath the wagon. Gren must have lain upon them to heat them with his body, for when she snuggled down a cozy warmth greeted her. He always considered her welfare before his own. His kindheartedness went far toward her favorable opinion of him.

That and the glow in his devilish, expressive eyes. She never tired of watching them sparkle and flash with life. She couldn't keep from imagining his hands caressing her face with tender strokes. The wanton fantasy sent a shiver of anticipation down her spine.

She rolled to her side to catch stars twinkling in the velvet of the night sky. A star streaked downward. Even before the light faded, another took its place. She counted a half dozen in as many minutes.

Conversations ebbed and flowed around her as Fezners retired for the night. At the approach of two individuals, she peeked from under the wagon at two pairs of feet, one bare and the other, rag-wrapped.

"Do you know why we favor spotted horses?" Dotra asked Gren in a low voice.

The man didn't answer immediately. "I never gave their color any thought."

Trell continued to listen, her eyelids drooping as their voices lulled her into slumber.

The boy laughed softly. "Spotted horses be simple to recognize. Nor can they be swapped as easily as solid ones."

"Makes sense." A pause followed before Gren started again. "I didn't play my flute tonight with the others, but we're alone now and I have a favor to ask."

"What be that?"

"Look to the sky while I play. See if you spot anything unusual."

Trell frowned at the request. What was Gren up to?

Dotra tilted his head back. "What I be looking for? I saw an owl earlier tonight."

"A dragon, no less." The trill of Gren's flute broke the silence of the night.

All thoughts of slumber vanished in a heartbeat. Trell's eyes snapped open, and she skittered from under the wagon to raise her finger and point accusingly at the pair.

"For shame! 'Tis late. People have taken to their beds and are trying to sleep and you're talking about playing music." She tried to balance her tone between chastisement and caution in the hope of distracting them. "Put your silly ideas away. Tomorrow will be a long day."

****

Out of spite, Gren blew into his flute, and the musical blast skyrocketed into the air. As if on cue, the cobs squealed, crazy with panic. Snorting, neighing for freedom, and stomping their thick hooves, they yanked on tethers until lines snapped.

No one saw a cause, except Gren guessed at a reason—the healer's dragon was near.

Men poured from wagons in an array of clothes, some with only leggings, others with their long tunics flapping wildly. They raced to picket lines to grab loose ropes as horses galloped helter-skelter down the road or into the woods.

Frightened children cried in their beds. A woman screamed as a cob raced directly toward her. Only the quick action of another saved her from being trampled.

"We need to catch the horses," Trell said.

Gren winced. The responsibility for the mayhem fell upon his shoulders. His music drew the creature out of hiding. He glanced skyward. Beyond the treetops. Higher. He squinted his eyes. Higher still. Somewhere in the inky darkness, a dragon trespassed in the skies of Feldsvelt.

He cursed to himself. He never meant to bring disaster onto these people. The Fezners needed their horses—their livelihoods depended on them.

Thundering steps raced past them as men attempted to catch the horses.

Dotra grabbed Trell's arm as if to stress his point. "The cobs belong to Fezner men. We will gather them."

"You heard him, "Gren said. "Remain here."

"But why? I can help."

"It's where you belong." The minute Gren spoke, he knew he'd made a mistake. The scowl Trell tossed at him said it all. Chills rippled through his bones.

Her sharp gaze swept the camp. "I have nothing to fear in the forest."

Thankfully, Fezner women reignited the fires, set pots of water over the flames, and showed no sign of joining the hunt.

"We be grateful if you help our women or be ready if someone is injured," Dotra said. "We'll know where to bring them."

The boy made sense, and Gren played on that fact. "He's right, Trell. Racing off in the dark could cause accidents. You'll need to stay centrally located if your skills are called upon."

After her resigned nod, he organized a search. Men and older boys lit torches and headed out in teams.

Gren departed with Dotra.

It took the balance of the night to round up the horses. Thrashing in the dark alerted Gren and Dotra to an injured animal. A medium-sized gelding stood on three legs, his sides heaving and a front leg broken, splintered, white bone sticking out.

All my fault.

Gren's conscience twisted at the waste of good horseflesh. His music had brought the dragon. "Fetch Trell and have her bring herbs to ease the gelding's pain. I'll stay and comfort him."

Dotra nodded, then raced off, crashing through the woods.

Easing the horse to the ground, Gren sat and held the gelding's head on his lap, offering soothing murmurs to keep him calm. The moon hadn't even traveled from the top of one tree to the next before voices filtered through the trees.

"Over here," he hollered.

Dotra and Trell emerged from the dark woods.

Trell stepped into the clearing, frowning at him. He watched her size up the situation before kneeling beside him and the horse. Her fingers nimbly examined the injured leg. Sorrow flitted across her face and tears welled in her eyes when she glanced up. "There's nothing I can do for the poor creature. I'm sorry."

Gren scrambled to his feet. His gaze sought Dotra's, fully aware of the boy's bond with his horses. Pain filled his dark eyes. "I'll put him out of his misery, if you'd like."

"The cob be one of mine. He was set for the auction in Eudes. Taking care of him is my responsibility." Heaving a sigh, Dotra pulled a knife from his boot. "You take the healer back to camp. I'll be there in a while."

Gren hated leaving the boy by himself but suspected any offer of sympathy would be taken as a sign of weakness and rejected. The boy was more man than most.

Trell and he arrived at Grandmother Lurri's wagon

just shy of dawn. Bone tired, they crawled beneath the wagon.

Every night Gren slept near Trell, but never near enough. She fell asleep almost instantly. He listened to the gentle rhythm of her breathing, saw the rise and fall of her chest, drew in the comforting scent of vanilla and the forest rising from her multiple braids. It amazed him that the scent always surrounded her, as if an internal part of her. It was a small but unique feature about her. In moments her expression relaxed in sleep.

He mulled over Trell's reaction when he had mentioned dragons to Dotra. Outrage. Denial. Deflection. She didn't fool him. Her behavior mimicked a bear sow protecting a cub. Why? Was she lying to him?

A long, low sigh slipped from his lips. What right did he have to reproach her? He lied to her. Deceit was a form of lying.

"Why would one slight girl—actually woman—be of interest to my father? What makes you so special?" he whispered after he was sure she'd fallen asleep.

She rolled over, bells adding a faint jingle to the air. "Did you say something?"

"Nothing of importance." To himself he added the lie to many others, another mark against him that would require payment in the future.

She wiggled to a sitting position. "Are you sure? Is everything all right?"

Guilt weighed heavily on him, and he didn't need to enhance his burden. He volunteered a half smile.

She returned one back. "May I see your hand?"

"Why?" Dried blood had darkened the red rags on his palm to nearly black. Instinctively, he tucked his hands under his arms. "It's nothing. I tried to examine the gelding's broken leg."

"I smell fresh blood." She pulled powder from her travel pouch, dropped several pinches into a bowl, poured a bit of water, and began mixing it. "You hurt yourself retrieving the horses. From everything I've ever heard about your condition, your skin is very frail. You're vulnerable to injury and infection. This ointment will aid your healing. You really don't want to know the ingredients."

"Will it sting like the ant rag?"

A smile graced her face. "It will ease your pain and fight infection."

Not a direct answer. Even so, her kindness was the hardest to take. "Just give me the ointment, and I'll apply it myself later."

"How will I monitor your healing?"

"We've already discussed this, Trell. I—I don't want you seeing me like this. I—I mean, my skin is hideous."

"You think that matters to me? I've seen wounds so horrible that the strongest man's stomach would roll."

"I would prefer you imagine me as I once was. A man without unsightly skin sores. Why, some even considered me handsome."

Her hands quivered slightly as she handed him the bowl. "You surprise me. I never expected you to be vain about your appearance."

He accepted the bowl and put it down by his side for later. "There is much to learn about me."

"Tell me."

"Not tonight. We are both tired."

Most of what he told Trell were half-truths, but the deceptions were a necessary evil. He needed to maintain his subterfuge. Now, her continual compassion chipped away at him until he felt beholden to her. He clenched his teeth. If she discovered the truth about him…

A niggling sorrow tore at him for his lies.

The reaction surprised him. He had battled feelings of remorse before and hoped someday to beg her forgiveness.

Right now his quest came first.

Kula demanded his loyalty.

Only winning mattered. At least that was what he told himself.

Chapter 8

Trell swore Gren was the stubbornest man she'd ever met. She still hadn't been able to examine him after a week on the road. To say frustration grew was putting it mildly.

Now, Demit Woods gave way to rolling hills. One by one grossly twisted trees replaced the towering ones. The loss of old friends pained Trell worse than she expected. Her chin trembled so hard that she turned away and fixed her gaze on the road ahead.

She suspected they were fast approaching Eudes, the largest port city on the great ocean, by the growing number of tilled fields she'd seen with men bent over the rows. Women worked smaller garden plots. They stopped their labors to stare at the travelers but offered no hospitality, not even water for the horses. As though their parents' silence heralded an indicator, the farmers' children threw sticks and stones to encourage the caravan did not dither near their property.

Trell scowled. Traveling with the Fezners had turned into a godsend, and she couldn't grasp the cruelty of these other people. They made judgments purely on sight, without taking the time to become acquainted with the Fezners.

So unfair.

Two days later, openly nervous, the Fezners, both men and women, readied themselves for Eudes. The men shaved their faces and dusted off their clothing. The women brushed their long hair until it shone. Some added bells to their dark tresses, copying Trell.

The bracing scent of the sea put a tang in the air. Trell inhaled deeply in an attempt to decipher the new scents—fishy with a sulfury smell and a briny finish. In some ways, the smells reminded her of creamed corn and boiled cabbage.

As the wagons drew closer to the ocean, wind hissed through clusters of grass on the dunes below the road. The thunder of waves crashing against the coastline drowned out the steady clop of hooves on the road.

Rain pelted the area the day Eudes came into view. Trell noticed two things as she stood on a hill overlooking the seaport. The town erected no walls against invaders as Brenalin did and nearly every rooftop contained blue tiles that would match the sky on sunny days. A half-dozen piers jutted leagues into the water and a large square in the center of the town held a gigantic statue of a man with a three-pronged spear facing the great ocean.

Gren nudged her shoulder to indicate a castle high above the town.

One road led to Eudes, the other turned left. The traveling folk went left.

Trell turned to Grandmother Lurri.

A twinkle shone in her dark eyes. "There be a place north of town where we will set up camp. Fezners prefer to stay beside themselves."

"Why not closer?"

"No need. We be seen already. By nightfall word will have spread through the rank and file of Eudes."

116

Trell didn't question the older woman's announcement. "After camp has been set up, I'd like to see the ocean close up."

"Dotra will help me. You go, gal, as soon as we stop."

Trell's heart thudded. Though the distance between Eudes and Brenalin was less than three weeks' travel time, this was her first chance to view the great sight. "You're sure?"

Grandmother Lurri waved away the question with her own. "Would I say so if I didn't mean it?"

Trell laughed, a tingle of joy spreading through her because she'd come to expect the crotchety attitude and, even now, found it amusing. She suspected the behavior was more for show. "My gratitude. I'll prepare the evening meal in trade."

"I prefer my own cooking," the older woman said back, dark eyes dancing.

By the time they rolled into a grove surrounded by scrubby bushes, the rain had let up. Trell understood why the traveling folk chose this spot. The bushes provided a barrier against the never-ending wind. As soon as the wagon stopped, she jumped off.

"I'm going to walk on the beach," she told Gren, who lent Dotra a hand unhitching the horses.

"Wait till I'm done. I'll accompany you. It's been years since I've seen the ocean. The tide's going out. Mayhaps we can dig for clams."

Trell smiled at the offer. "Your company will be most welcome."

Bells jingled on harnesses as Dotra lifted a heavy leather collar off one of the lead cobs. "I be fine alone. Go with the healer."

"I'm with you, too," Torkel mindspoke. *"Already I can see to the edge of the world."*

"Just stay out of sight." She covertly glanced upward, swearing that tiny black dot in the sky belonged to him. Hopefully, no one else noticed. *"You should be ashamed of yourself, Torkel. Your last appearance caused the horses to stampede and one was fatally injured. Their horses are important to the Fezners. They need them, and their importance should not be dismissed."*

"What do you expect? I am a dragon. All creatures fear me."

Trell shook her head. *So typical.* Torkel never liked admitting fault. But he wasn't alone. Self-importance was a common dragon trait.

She scaled the dune with Gren, leaning into a wind that whined in her ears. She dug her staff into the soft, sandy earth and checked the sky to make sure the black dragon remained out of sight. She freed a sigh of relief when nothing appeared overhead. At least, this time Torkel heeded her. A small reward. Sighing, she slumped onto the ground to remove her boots and Gren did the same.

"Is it normally this windy?" she asked him, noticing no lesions or nodules on his toes. Maybe his disease hadn't spread that far yet. She could only hope, for his sake.

As they crested the dune, his red rags snapped like the ribbons on her staff when they sensed danger. "Not this severe. A storm is rolling in. It might blow itself out before reaching landfall, but only the Gods know. Weather patterns are very hard to predict this close to the sea."

Dipping down, they left the dune to sink into loose sand that sucked at their bare feet. Trell rather liked the sensation. They trekked past a jumble of logs, some goliaths, others moderate-sized.

"High tides and storms deposit them there," Gren explained when she looked askance at him.

"The waves are retreating."

"Told you."

Trell kept her smile to herself. Nothing wrong with Gren's ego. It reminded her of Torkel's, and she wondered if it was a male trait.

Gulls swooped in the air, their ha-ha-ha cries piercing. Broken bits of shells and debris littered the shoreline. She poked a bulbous green plant with her staff, and it oozed liquid.

Walking became easier on damp sand, and they picked up speed. After a few paces, Gren dropped to his knees.

"Clams." He pointed to an air bubble the size of her thumbnail. He started digging like a madman. "Come on. Help me dig."

Trell planted her staff in the sand next to him. "I'd rather explore the beach. Look how it stretches endlessly."

"Go then. But be careful. Never turn your back to the ocean and don't wade into deep water. See the way the water swirls. There's a strong undertow in these waters."

She took the warning to heart before starting out. Nearly every wave brought ribbons of yellowish foam to the shore. She dipped her feet into the water and gasped at the coldness, but the sensation of sand running through her toes tickled and kept her in the ocean.

At Gren's yell, she glanced over her shoulder. He held an elongated object high in the air. She could imagine his green eyes sparkling with triumph. A smile formed, delighted he took pleasure in trifling things. Little existed in his life to bring him joy.

A wave crashed into her mid-thigh, soaking her skirt. She lost her balance and stumbled into deeper water before recovering.

Gren stood and watched her for a moment. "Come back and help me dig for clams. They're good raw or in a soup."

A memory slipped forward of eating clams in Brenalin and tasting sandy grit in her food. Once was sufficient. "Later. Let me explore for a while."

Surprisingly, the flat shoreline undulated here and there. She came upon a river of sand the width of a wagon flowing toward the ocean. Tiny pebbles were scattered about the surface. Halfway across the area, a rogue wave caught her and knocked her down. She hit her side, hard, and tumbled along with the rolling sand.

Before she could regain her feet, another wave dragged her off the beach. Yelling, she doubted Gren heard her cries over the roar of crashing waves. She tried to stand and couldn't find the bottom. With rasping breaths, she looked around but didn't know which direction land lay. All she saw were endless waves. She told herself not to panic. That everything would turn out all right.

"Do you need me?" Torkel asked.

Trell refused to ask for help, but a squeak escaped when something brushed against her leg. Spotting a dead fish float below the surface alongside her, she relaxed. *"Nay, stay hidden."*

"I need to save you."

No time to answer. Kicking her legs back and forth and thrashing her arms, she did her best to stay calm and keep her head above water. Inhaling, she gurgled a mouthful of salty brine.

Survival instinct kicked in and she screamed. "Help!"

"Hang on, I'm coming," Torkel said.

The black dot she'd noticed earlier grew larger. Trell cringed inside. *"Torkel, I command you to go back. I would rather die than expose you to danger."*

"Stubborn female human, you cannot order me. I am not the one in danger of drowning. You are."

She lost sight of him in the slate gray clouds. When she looked at the shoreline, she swore it was farther away. How would she ever get back?

"Trell! Where are you?"

She spun in the water toward the faint sound of Gren's voice. Thankfully a blur of red racing along the shore was easy to spot. She raised her arm to wave but sank in the water.

"Here, here." She spit out a mouthful of salty water, refusing to let panic overwhelm her. "I'm here."

"I see you. Swim toward the shore. I'll find a long branch. Mayhaps I can reach you with it."

Trell's chin quivered. She would have happily complied if not trying to stay afloat.

Behind her, a voluminous splash tossed water into the air, but she never saw what caused the disturbance.

A second later something wrapped around her waist.

She screamed at the top of her lungs and thrashed

with all her might to escape whatever held her.

Gren splashed into the waves. "I'm coming, Trell."

The hold on her tightened. "Stop struggling," said a familiar voice in Trell's ear. "I've got you."

Shock hit hard. *Torkel!* She had been simultaneously concentrating on Gren's voice and keeping afloat that she totally forgot about him.

"You got me?" She tried to grab at him. Instead, he rolled her on her back. "Who's got you?"

"Cease worrying. Dragons are natural swimmers. In my human form, I am ten times stronger than a normal human," he answered in what sounded like a chuckle. "That said, take deep breaths and swish your arms back and forth. We're going to drift on the waves until we are past the sandbar."

Trell shuddered hearing that, but a sense of security wrapped around her and she did her best to relax. Not an easy task. After a while, Torkel took hold of a fistful of her tunic and began swimming parallel to the shore. After what seemed like forever, he turned toward the beach.

Gren, his face twisted with worry, had waded into the water up to his chest. He reached for her, but Torkel hung on tight. With a man on each side, they escorted her to the shore.

Exhaustion weighed Trell's steps down. Stumbling out of the water, her knees buckled.

Gren knelt beside her. He tilted her chin up to look into her eyes. "What happened? Are you all right?"

"A-a wave hit me and pulled me out to sea."

He heaved a sigh. "But you're safe now." Then his gaze riveted on Torkel like the two were adversaries. "Who are you?"

Taller than Gren by several inches, his black hair was plastered to his chiseled face. "No one you know. I heard her cries and came to investigate. Luckily I swim like a fish."

Trell nearly coughed at the boast, except the answer seemed to satisfy Gren.

He nodded, standing and helping Trell to her feet. "You have my gratitude, sir. I wish I had coin to pay you."

"No need to thank me."

In spite of the exchange of pleasantries, tension vibrated between the two males, one green-eyed and one golden-eyed, it became clear that each man perceived the other as a rival. It wouldn't take much of a slight for trouble to erupt.

"You have my sincere thanks, as well," she said, pretending not to know Torkel.

"Dangers abound," Torkel said with a hint of amusement. "You were caught in one of the rivers of the sea. They can be deadly."

Trell didn't question how Torkel learned that information. He'd told her once that many of his memories included past dragons in his line.

"I didn't know of them. Only warned her of the riptides." Gren took her arm and urged her away. "If the ribbons on your staff hadn't started flapping crazily after the wind died, I wouldn't have become curious about where you went. When I couldn't find you, I suspected the worst." He drew her against him. "I cannot swim. Never learned, but I plan to acquire that skill in the near future. I don't want to be caught off guard or have strangers rescue you."

Being held by Gren felt right. "I'm wet, cold, but

123

alive. You should be happy that fellow saved me."

"I am happy you're alive but wish it had been me who rescued you."

Gren's stiff posture surprised her. His pride had been wounded, she realized. Chewing her inner lip, she wondered why. "I cannot swim either. You did what you could. I'm just sorry you got wet. If you have open lesions, infections could set in. And I imagine saltwater stings."

"I'd suffer much worse for you."

A snort came from Torkel. *"Well, he didn't save you. I did."*

"I know and I appreciate the kindness." She risked a glance over her shoulder where she'd last seen the dragon turned man and realized he'd disappeared. Did Gren notice?

****

Gren's gut rolled. A silent communication passed between Trell and the stranger. A chill raced down his back which had nothing to do with his damp clothes. If Trell had drowned, his mission would have ended in tragedy. He turned away from the thought of losing her.

Why did his father want the healer or her dragon?

The unanswered question left him uneasy because he was fast becoming unprepared or willing to let Trell walk into Barg Castle uninformed of the danger. Dare he trust his father to keep his word? The older Har ruled with a stern hand, saving the strictest treatment for his own family, his actions based on objective decisions. While known as a man of honor, there could always be a first time for the man to break his word.

Gren made a split-second decision to devise a plan...against what he wasn't sure. But all contingencies needed exploration.

What could go wrong?

He almost laughed at himself. A hundred things. In the uncertainties of today's world, anything was possible.

Who was he kidding? Just the fact his father specifically requested Trell raised numerous questions. If his father meant her harm…

Determination hardened inside him. A trait he shared with his father. And not the only one. While he hated to admit it, other characteristics existed between them.

Retrieving Trell's staff and their shoes, they headed to the Fezners. Entering camp, cries of alarm swept through the travelers. People swarmed them. Gren tried his best to keep their hands off him, but everyone wanted to assure themselves the wet pair were unhurt, and touch seemed the only way. These people and their kindness confused him almost as much as the healer. After spending the last week with them, he saw how hard they worked and their close family ties. No different from villagers in Kula.

The Fezners talked at once, shouting questions.

Gren edged away from the assemblage and raised his voice to be heard. "Trell was pulled into the ocean. She's fine now."

"Let me through," demanded the gruff voice of Grandmother Lurri. With deference, the crowd parted for the old woman. She took one look, shook her head as she assessed the situation. "The ocean be a dangerous place for the unwary. You two come with me. The healer needs dry clothes, and yours are full of sand."

Trell stepped forward.

Gren remained in place. He should have been the one to save Trell. Not a stranger. What kind of man was he? Right now, his insides twisted with jealousy of the dark-haired man for doing what he could not. She could have drowned while he watched. Damn, dogs swam better than he did.

"You be listening, Untouchable?"

The question snapped Gren out of his reflection. "These are my only clothes. I will stand before the fire until they dry, then brush the sand off."

"Fool," Grandmother Lurri grumbled.

Trell wrinkled her face. "She's correct. Sand will irritate your skin. It could acerbate your lesions."

"Rinse him off with clean water," the old Fezner woman ordered. "Then send him to my wagon to dry. I won't be participating in the festivities tonight and can use his company."

Grandmother Lurri sent him a glare, daring him to contradict her. He suspected another motive for the offer. In a couple of hours, after the sun set, people from Eudes would start arriving.

Being inside Grandmother Lurri's wagon kept him out of sight. Made sense. Especially since the attitude toward Untouchables had worsened in Brenalin. The same could be happening here as well. Why upset the citizens of Eudes, if avoidable?

Then another reason to stay out of sight popped into Gren's head. His brothers might have hired spies to keep an eye open for him and/or the healer.

He nodded at the older woman.

After being doused with buckets of heated water, Gren headed for the green wagon with yellow and dark green trim. As he approached, the old woman and Trell chatted inside.

Gren backed off. *Let the healer have a few moments of privacy.*

****

Trell sat in the colorful wagon, all the while wanting to check on Gren, but controlled herself. She eyed the elderly woman. "I've never been this far from home in my life and already I've seen so much," she said. "After Eudes, what lies ahead?"

"Not really sure. Mayhaps more villages," Grandmother Lurri answered. "Eudes be our eastern-most stop. Our people travel a circuit of village to village. We stay a few days and then move on."

"Do you stop at all of them?" Trell tried to learn as much as she could without seeming nosy.

Grandmother Lurri handed Trell a cloth to dry herself. "By the Gods, no. Not all be friendly. Some villages we avoid, others we never venture into. Demicland, for one. In that land we be unwelcome. It be dangerous to travel there."

Trell stripped off her wet clothes. Goosebumps pebbled her body but quickly disappeared as she rubbed her skin dry. Her braids, she knew, would tighten because of the salty seawater, which suited her just fine.

Finished, she looked at the Fezner woman for clarification. "Why do they not welcome strangers?"

"My guess is they fear those who are different from themselves. They consider us lawless and without morals while honest folk toil and struggle to earn a living. There be plenty of bandits who inhabit that mountainous land."

"If they knew you as I do…"

127

"We are not reckless or feckless. I doubt enlightenment will come in my lifetime."

"Then that's where I will go when it's time for us to part. I can inform them that their isolation is creating a false view." She paused to take a breath. "And mayhaps exchange new healing methods."

"Be you touched by the Gods? If you travel there, you place yourself in danger." Grandmother Lurri huffed and pressed a bundle of clothes into her hands. "My daughter's. Dotra's mother."

The skirt and tunic appeared well-mended and hinted of warm sun. Trell scrambled into them and to her surprise, they fit well. "Thank you. And I must travel to places few have visited."

"We have a saying, 'Today we feast, tomorrow we starve, and the day after, we feast again.' If you be dead, you can do neither."

The meaning made nil sense to Trell, so she elected not to request clarification. Sometimes less was more. "Are there many Fezners in the world?"

Grandmother Lurri wet her cracked lips. "The world be a big place. We be all over and call no place home. Except this." She patted the peacock-blue wall of her wagon. "Across the great ocean are many different lands. Even a land without water, a desert, called Midber. There be many island nations that dot the great oceans. There are people who live on boats, traveling from island to island. We be everywhere. Other than the tale of our creation, only one exists about our beginnings and that might be false."

"Would you mind telling me?" Trell asked, torn between acquiring new knowledge and worrying about Gren, outdoors, cold, and wet.

"According to legend, one king wanted the poor in his kingdom to enjoy music and asked another ruler to send him music players. When those musicians arrived, the grateful king gave each one an ox, a donkey, and a donkey-load of wheat so they could live on agriculture and play music for the poor. But the musicians ate the oxen and the wheat and came back a year later with their cheeks hollowed by hunger ready to fill their bags on the donkeys' backs. The king, angered that they wasted his gifts, ordered them to pack their bags and wander the world forevermore."

The captivating tale left Trell pondering. She hated to admit how little she knew of the world. "Do you believe it?"

A wry grin passed over Grandmother's Lurri's wrinkled visage. She shrugged her narrow shoulders. "There not be a better explanation for our roaming the world. Tomorrow I'll start showing you a few of our more obscure cures."

Trell's heart skipped a beat, and she smiled at the opportunity. "Why not tonight?"

"First, enjoy the festivities tonight."

"Fair enough. Be aware, though, that I'm eager to learn."

Finally, Trell pulled the door open to find Gren sitting on the bottom step, looking like a drowned puppy, red rags clinging to his body.

"I'm sorry it took so long," she apologized, clearing her throat. "Go inside. Warm up and get dry."

"Good idea. Out of sight, out of mind."

The response made Trell frown, then she glanced at a Fezner man setting boards over barrels to create a make-shift table next to his wagon. A woman she recognized as his wife set dollies, tinctures, and baked goods on the table. Others loaded their tables with merchandise for sale. She cast a questioning glance at Grandmother Lurri standing in the doorway.

"The sun sets," the old woman said. "People come soon."

****

Gren sat on a chair inside Grandmother Lurri's wagon. It didn't take long for the senior woman to lie on her bed and fall asleep, snoring lightly. That left him to listen to the festivities and indulge in fantasies of his own far into the night.

Voices, some loud, some happy—one angry— ebbed and flowed around the wagon. When footfalls approached the steps, he leapt to his feet. A quick search revealed no place to hide in the cramped quarters. Would someone demand to see the Fezner woman? His muscles poised to run, fearing discovery.

"Are you mad? You shouldn't be here?"

Gren froze, recognizing Trell's voice. Irritation laced her tone.

A soft, deep chuckle preceded any words. "I was curious. I'm practicing my skills. Shifting is still new to me."

The instant Trell's companion spoke, Gren knew his identity. He visualized the tall, black-haired man who'd saved her. Gren's hands curled into fists. The man's voice burned into his skull like a brand. What was he doing here? Who was he? And what was shifting? It certainly was an odd thing to say. Gren pressed his ear to the door to better hear.

Another chuckle rumbled near the wagon. "The more I learn about myself, the better protected I am.

Mayhaps, this is the perfect opportunity to mix and mingle with people. The Fezners will assume I'm from Eudes, and the townspeople will believe me a Fezner. And I do love a party."

The odd conversation puzzled Gren and he frowned. He didn't like the stranger anywhere near Trell or the familiarity in his tone. The reaction surprised him. If he didn't know better, he'd swear he acted jealous.

"Your arrogance is showing. It's unsafe." Tension put a sharp edge to Trell's tone. "Keep your voice down. Gren and Grandmother Lurri are inside the wagon."

"That's where the Untouchable is? Will he play his flute tonight? While these people make pleasant music, I prefer his."

How did the stranger know about him?

Gren put his hand on the door handle and inhaled a deep breath. Dare he open the door a crack? By the Gods he wanted to with all his heart. No! He resisted the temptation. He didn't want the pair to know he overheard them.

"Oh well…I'll mingle for a while, then seek food," the man said. "My appetite grows daily. I saw a couple deer grazing in the bushes not far away."

"Stay away from Gren. It's dangerous."

Footsteps faded away. Good riddance. Gren found no legitimate reason to be bothered that someone else had saved the healer.

Didn't he?

Was he jealous? Or his pride piqued? A lot preyed on his mind.

Gren spent the night separating Trell's laughter

from all the others. It pleased him to know she enjoyed herself. He never heard the stranger again. Perhaps he left. The thought let him fall asleep in his chair.

He woke before anyone else and slipped outside. A few campfires smoldered. An empty bottle lay discarded near a wagon wheel. Someone had dropped a shawl on the ground. The woman who first offered them food gathered kindling. Alana was her name. They exchanged nods.

Gren checked on Trell beneath the wagon and found her sleeping peacefully. He didn't have the heart to wake her for she had retired late.

A glance showed Dotra wasn't abed. Gren assumed the boy tended his precious cobs and decided to head toward the string of spotted horses. They looked up from fresh feed when he approached, but no Dotra. The one thing he'd learned since traveling with the Fezners—they weren't any different from other people. Maybe better than some. If he were to guess, Dotra, half boy, half man, had snuck off on some great adventure. Or a clandestine meeting with a girl he fancied. The Fezner was of an age where anything was possible.

The sound of breaking waves drew Gren toward the great ocean. Arriving at the base of the first dune, shouts drowned out the cries of the gulls. Excited shouts, the egging kind that were almost cheers.

A fight.

Before he could investigate, a shrill cry froze him to the spot. The flesh on his spine tingled. He wasn't the only one who'd heard the shouts.

An unnatural stillness settled over the beach—as if the land waited for the danger to pass. Proof others heard as well.

After a few heartbeats, the shouts started again. Gren climbed the dune and went to his belly to scan the beach. Surprise caught him off guard, and he breathed in grains of sand. A group of a dozen town boys formed a circle, taking turns joining the fight. Whoever they surrounded didn't have a chance against the odds.

A sense of injustice rose within him. The sight hit too close to his own childhood. Memories of bloody fistfights with uneven odds between his brothers came flooding to the surface.

A cheer went up. Gren's reflection faded away. When the circle of boys broke apart, his heart stopped cold.

The boy in the center was Dotra.

Leaping to his feet, Gren charged down the dune like a stampeding wisent bull with his arms waving madly, yelling at the top of his lungs, red rags flapping.

One boy looked up, and all color drained from his face. He pointed a shaky finger at Gren.

Good, he thought and hoped his presence scared the piss out of the town boy.

Then one by one the yelling quieted as other gazes followed the direction where the first boy pointed. Gren raced toward them, blood-curdling yells paving the way, like a monster charging them, which was close enough to the truth to suit him. Most people considered Untouchables monstrosities.

A cry of alarm rippled through the town boys. They abandoned their fun, spun on their heels, and raced away.

Gren rushed to where Dotra lay. His lips were a bloody mess and the beginning of a black eye already showed. A beauty by the looks of it. The boy tried to stand, wobbled, and collapsed to the ground.

"What happened? Are you all right?" Gren lifted the boy to his feet.

A wry smile tried to make an appearance on Dotra's battered face. He brushed off sand-coated clothes and shrugged.

Gren met the boy's gaze. He had no right to criticize. He'd been young once and curious himself and experienced similar adventures.

The boy raised his chin. "I wanted to see what Eudes was like."

Gren shook his head. He should have known. Curiosity was dangerous. "And those boys decided to beat you up."

"It be a game of cat and mouse. Guess I be the mouse." The boy puffed out his chest.

"I'm taking you back to camp," he finally said.

"Grandmother Lurri be unhappy now."

Gren cringed at the prospect of facing the old Fezner woman. He could only imagine. "Because I've been exposed."

"That, too." Dotra tried to smile but winced in pain.

They trekked up the dune. As they did, the tip of Gren's boot stubbed on an object buried in the sand. He picked it up, dusted it off. No bigger than his fist, glossy black and triangular in shape, it made him catch his breath.

Could this be what he thought—a dragon scale?

Chapter 9

Where had Gren gone off to?

An inner sense told her he departed at least an hour ago. Lying still, Trell relished the morning's slow start until someone shook her foot. With sore muscles, she sat up begrudgingly to find Gren beaming at her with the innocence of a child.

"Get up, Trell. Come see what I found." Excitement bubbled through his voice. "You won't believe it."

She crawled from beneath the wagon. His tone ignited nerve endings. Something she couldn't put her finger on. "What could be so important that you needed to shake me awake? I was up half the night."

"I beg your forgiveness. I wouldn't have troubled you, but this is important. You've got to see it."

A quick glance around the surrounding area revealed nothing of merit, which only increased her suspicion. "What?"

He held out his arm, uncurled his fingers to reveal a prize nestled in his palm and stretching to his fingertips. "I found a dragon scale. I wanted to share my news with you first thing. I told you they were real."

Multiple shivers raced up Trell's spine. She stared at a flat, thin, semi-rectangular scale with a faintly burnished ebony surface. One large enough to have come off Tokel's back. Gulping, she prayed her voice didn't crack. "What's that?"

"I already told you. A dragon scale. I found it near the beach."

"That looks more like a piece of obsidian to me. Probably brought by the sea on a storm."

Gren stood steadfast. He twisted and flexed the scale between his two hands. "It bends. Stone does not. Furthermore, if it had been in water for any length of time, the edges would be worn smooth. This is sharp."

Nausea rolled in Trell's stomach. Dragons lost their scales when they grew much like a snake shed its skin. It was bad news for the dragon and her. She needed to destroy the evidence before Gren showed it to anyone else. She reached to grab it from him. "Give that to me."

Gren jerked back his hand. "Nay."

She huffed. "Throw it in the fire. It is nothing."

"I'm keeping this as proof of dragons' existence. I swear, Trell, you're more obstinate than a rational person should have to endure."

"Then why stay with me? I have no claim on you."

The scale disappeared into the depths of a leather pouch at his waist. "Because I like you and enjoy your company. Don't be angry with me."

His words startled her. Anger was the least of her worries. Apprehension fit better. Instinct warned her he would never give up his search for dragons. Whatever his reason, Gren sought a dragon…

Her dragon.

She eyed his pouch, wondering how she could retrieve the evidence. Before she could dwell on the problem in search of an answer, she spotted Dotra standing a few feet away. Blood ran down his chin and his clothes hung in tatters in places. "By Heyln's robe, what happened to you?"

"I be in a fight."

Shaking her head, Trell escorted Dotra to his grandmother's wagon with Gren trailing behind. "In you go. You can explain to your grandmother what happened." She waved to the door, and the boy scurried inside.

Grandmother Lurri already heated water and collected rags for cleaning as if informed of the need. Trell didn't question the woman's ability. She nodded her thanks as the Fezner healer shot dark looks at her grandson. Golden bracelets clinked as she moved forward in the wagon to allow all three people to crowd into the cramped space.

Dotra flicked a glance at his white-haired grandmother. "I be in a fight. Nothing else."

"Boy…" Grandmother Lurri's voice scolded with one word.

Dotra tightened his mouth like a willful child.

Grandmother Lurri sat on the bed. "Best you treat him. I might not be gentle. I be tempted to box his ears for disobedience. He be purblind. My guess is he went to town. Again. How many times have I told you to stay away from townsfolk? How'd you get away?"

"Gren saved me."

Still glaring at her grandson, she went on. "You know what this means. We depart after Trell tends your injuries. You be the one to tell the others to hitch their wagons."

Trell's mind spun about Gren's discovery, grateful to be busy washing and cleaning Dotra's split lip. It didn't bode well for Torkel or keeping his presence a secret.

Sighing, she glanced at Gren, then continued her ministrations of Dotra. His velvet brown eyes watched her every move with suspicion. At least stitches weren't necessary. Extracting a half dozen peppercorns from her bag, she crushed the pungent seeds into a fine powder and dabbed it on Dotra's lip.

His eyes widened with surprise. "It doesn't sting."

"Of course not. Pepper stems the flow of blood and fights infection."

"Count yourself fortunate she didn't use an ant rag," Gren said, standing near the door.

"Too bad," Grandmother Lurri grumbled. "Pain be fear trying to get out. Keep going."

Next, Trell studied Dotra's black eye. Treatment would be simple. "A cold compress for a whole day, then a warm one for the next day will eliminate the worst of the swelling. Does your head hurt? Any blurry vision?"

Dotra shook his head.

"Good. I want you to eat bowls of vegetables and find some wild marigolds. Steep the petals, then soak a rag in the solution and place the rag on your eye. Repeat the process several times a day. It'll reduce the inflammation and abet the healing. If you can't find any marigolds this time of year, look for witch hazel."

A chuckle gushed from Grandmother Lurri. "That be the perfect punishment. He hates vegetables. My thanks, gal. Hopefully, Dotra learns from this experience. If he hasn't, a switch to his backside ought to do the trick." She winked at Trell as Dotra left the wagon, then turned to Gren, who'd remained with the women. "My thanks for saving Dotra. I assume those town boys saw you?"

"Afraid so." Gren shifted from side to side. "I suppose that's why you wanted me in your wagon last night, but I couldn't let the boy be beaten."

The old woman shrugged a bony shoulder. "Intelligence be nice to see in a person, especially a man."

Trell tossed the bloody water out the door and picked up the rags used in tending Dotra. If only she could rid herself of her problems with the same ease. While keeping busy, she wondered why people were so cruel. Not showing compassion. Why did one group mistreat another for being different? Acceptance shouldn't be that difficult. It didn't make sense to her.

In the forest, every tree counted. A healthy habitat of woodlands cooled the land, fought flooding, and blocked winds. Even created rain. Their water vapor escaped into the air to saturate it and bring rains. Together, trees were stronger.

Why couldn't people do the same?

Outside, Dotra hollered instructions to break camp. When the boy's voice faded, Grandmother Lurri focused rheumy eyes on Gren. "Best to avoid trouble. Those boys might not realize you came from our camp; however, an adult might connect your appearance to our arrival. We'll depart within the hour."

Trell cast a worried look around the wagon's interior. The colorful palette reminded her of sunshine and had become a second home. "To where?"

"Back toward Brenalin and beyond. Eudes is our eastern-most destination."

Disappointment swelled. The wrong direction for

Trell. She'd hoped to travel up the coast or trek north to the edge of Demicland. The Fezners returning toward Brenalin meant a parting of ways. She would miss these people. Over the last week, she'd come to care for them like family. Her gaze shot to Gren.

He studied the floor a moment before cracking open the door. The sound of people rushing about, rattling harnesses, and neighing horses broke the silence. "I never meant to cause trouble," he said, descending to the first step.

The old Fezner woman smiled. "It not be your fault."

"I'll help Dotra hitch the horses. It's the least I can do."

Trell sank onto the edge of the cot. Her fingers brushed the coarse woolen blanket.

Grandmother Lurri loomed over her, a hard illusion to create since the woman barely reached her shoulders when they stood side by side. "I'll give you a card reading before we go."

Reading?

Trell had a vague inkling what the word implied, but she'd never placed much faith in superstitious nonsense, always placing faith in science. "I've never had cards read for me."

"Then you be in for a treat." Grandmother Lurri pulled a deck from the folds of her striped skirt. Her bracelets jangled in unison as she shuffled the cards with gnarled fingers in slow motion. Seemingly contented, she handed the deck to Trell. "Shuffle until satisfied, then cut the deck toward me."

Trell mixed the cards, set them on the bed, and split the deck in half.

Grandmother Lurri dealt the top three cards in a line, face down. She turned over the left-most one. "The past. This be the Tower, a powerful card. Sudden changes have occurred in the way you have lived your life. A release from something that you were not responsible for, and now the way is open for you to follow your calling."

Trell blinked, trying to hide her surprise. The card showed a decrepit tower. She couldn't tell if the structure would crumble or remain standing. Grandmother Lurri's accuracy certainly fit, yet the Fezner had no knowledge of her past.

Trell remained silent and kept her expression neutral. Let the woman rattle off her forecast.

Painful-looking arthritic fingers turned over the second card. "This be the present. The two of cups. Tension between two forces. The card doesn't say this, but strange companions accompany you. They be loyal and have your welfare in mind. Though that might not be immediately clear."

Another hit.

Again Trell remained silent. But who did the Fezner mean—Torkel and Gren or someone new? All the card revealed were two cups overflowing.

Grandmother Lurri flipped over the final card, golden bracelets rattling. "The future. The four of wands. Most interesting."

Trell's gaze flicked between the card pictured with what looked like four staffs and the Fezner until she couldn't stand the silence any longer. "What?"

Grandmother Lurri tapped the card on the bed with her fingernail. "This card represents good tidings. And soon, in the next few months or less. Possibly love.

Marriage. I would say the fate of your life is bound in a kiss."

Trell sucked in a breath. The prediction couldn't be farther off the mark. She had no intention of falling in love. She'd loved once and been punished for it by spending a thousand years as a tree. One mistake was enough. "Is that so?"

"Indeed. Cards never be wrong."

"I guess only time will tell."

"Oh, gal, you be on a quest of discovery. Many wonderful events lay before you. Some danger. Some hardships. But in the end, a happy future."

"You can't guarantee that."

"The cards be a powerful voice. Best you heed them." Grandmother Lurri sank down beside her and took hold of her hands. "Let me ease one of your concerns. Have you ever wondered why we be unafraid of your companion?"

"I assumed attitude played a part. Gren is unwelcomed and treated with disdain everywhere he goes, similar to how you are in many places."

"Clever, gal, but you be wrong. There be another reason Fezners are unafraid of Untouchables." The wagon rocked as she moved around the tight interior. She pulled a lavender-colored juglet out of a cubbyhole. Liquid sloshed inside. "This cures the disease if used at the start."

Trell's heart rate quickened. Her gaze fixed on the jug as though afraid it would disappear before she learned about it. "What is it? Why has no one heard of this cure before? Where did you get it?"

The questions poured out of her mouth, unable to stop herself. If the medicine inside performed as claimed, it signified the end of a devastating illness. Her heart beat faster at the idea of no one wandering the world in pain or suffering.

"Don't know." Grandmother Lurri settled down next to her. "Very rare, it be. Fezners have possessed this medicine for hundreds of generations."

"Why have you not shared it with the outside?"

"You see how we be treated. People believe we bring bad luck. I already told you townspeople blame us for all the ills that befall them. Take the spread of the disease. Because we travel from place to place, they think we carry illnesses along our migration routes. A falsehood. When one of us sickens, we keep them in their wagons. What others don't know, doesn't hurt us. We accept Untouchables because no one else does. Eons ago we treated them with this, but as time passed, the results be hit or miss."

A flutter started in Trell's belly. An honor was being bestowed upon her. The Fezners had taught her so much about compassion, and now they were trusting her with a longheld secret. "Why tell me now?"

Grandmother Lurri shrugged. "Why not? You have a good heart in here." She tapped Trell's chest.

Warmth scaled her neck and onto her cheeks. The praise embarrassed her. She needed to think like a healer. To stay clear-headed. She had a moral responsibility to provide the best medicines for treating patients. "May I examine it?"

Grandmother Lurri pulled the cork off with a pop. Trell leaned forward to sniff the contents. No recognizable odor tickled her nostrils. What could the mixture be?

"It has a slight bite. Tingles on healthy skin, but no

other side effects. It'll sting on the diseased," the older woman said. "They feel the torture of an inferno."

Trell hesitated, then decided in order to learn she needed to experiment. She dabbed a small drop of semi-opaque liquid with a slight viscous consistency on her finger. "I feel nothing."

"What? That's impossible." Frowning, Grandmother Lurri put a drop on the back of her brown-spotted hand. Several seconds passed. "It tingles on me."

"Perchance I'm immune?"

The Fezner woman replaced the cork into the juglet. "I've never heard of anyone being immune to this medicine."

Nothing is impossible.

Trell stymied her disbelief. "Mayhaps I can recreate it. Name the ingredients."

Grandmother Lurri shrugged. "Those who knew the ingredients are long dead."

Trell stared at the lavender jug, a common container that held miracles. "Will this work on advanced cases?"

"I have no idea. It has never been tried to my knowledge. But I give you this to use on your companion. I can't swear it'll work, but trying can't hurt."

Thrilled wasn't a strong enough word to describe her feelings. "My thanks for the kind offer. I am most appreciative."

Grandmother Lurri held the jug up to eye level. "This be one of our last bottles."

The hope sprouting within Trell died a quick death. "Then I can't accept your medicine. It's too valuable.

You don't have enough to spare a stranger."

A chuckle rumbled out of the older woman's chest. "You take this. Bottles last for centuries. We are all strangers at the beginning. Gren protected Dotra. Now, you save him."

Trell's heart melted with gratitude. "How do I use it? Does he drink it? Or is it a topical?"

"Rub a drop on his skin."

She clutched the jug in her lap. It represented hope. "I can't tell you how much this means to me. I'll never forget your generosity. It's…it's greatly valued. And I'm sure Gren will be pleased, too. It could mean having his life returned to him, to all those afflicted with the disease."

"Save your gratitude. First, see if it works."

****

Gren listened to the order for wagons to roll boom over the camp. At once, the air filled with the clop of hooves trampling sandy ground. With heads high, long manes and tails flowing, the spotted horses surged forward. Wheels squeaked. The colorful wagons inched along in the sandy ground, then the horses found their rhythm and their pace increased. Nickers were exchanged as though the horses were as eager to travel down the road as their owners.

He looked at Trell, then the Fezners. He hadn't wanted to associate with the travelers, yet now considered them good people. "Someday, you'll see them again."

Tears glistened in her eyes. "I hope so. They became friends, and I'll miss them."

Alone once again, Gren fingered the collar of his red rags. A constant itch tormented him. He adjusted his cowl to relieve the irritation. "Shall we push forward to the next village?"

"First, I want to try something on you. Grandmother Lurri shared a medicine which she claims the Fezners use to treat your malady before it becomes chronic."

Gren rolled his eyes and edged backward. "What is it?"

A soft laugh chased after him. "Hopefully a cure. I can't promise if it'll work. She says usually it is applied at the first signs of the disease. I know your illness is farther along. Even so, may I test it on you?"

Refusal would raise suspicion. If the questioning looks Trell sent his way were a clue, she already entertained doubts about him.

Should he throw off his rags? Let Trell see him as he really was—hale and hearty. They'd traveled together long enough to develop trust. A sick feeling tried to surface. He didn't want to consider the repercussions. Better to play it safe.

He held out his hand. "Give it to me. I'll apply it myself."

****

After all this time together and he still didn't trust her. Trell hesitated in complying and grasped the jug to her chest.

"Please."

Gren's soft voice tugged on her heartstrings. She hated putting him on the spot. "If you're worried about being contagious, set your worries aside. In the Halls of Medsin, most do not believe the social stigma attached to it. Extensive contact is necessary for the disease to spread and only at the beginning of the infection. You are beyond that."

His arm dropped to his side. "Then, aye...on one condition. If you can treat me without looking at me."

Emotions erupted in Trell like a storm. Happy. Sad. Thrilled. Standing in the tall, grassy glade evacuated by the Fezner's wagon, she sought the right response, then practicality set in. "Grandmother Lurri said only a drop is necessary for treatment. All I'll need is your arm, but if it bothers you to show me your skin, I promise not to look."

At his nod, she poured a bead of liquid into her palm and averted her gaze. "Push your rags aside and hold them while I apply the medicine."

Clothing rustled. Trell wondered, once again, why he chose to accompany her if he was so averse to her observing his body.

"Ready," Gren said before she found a key to her own curiosity.

The instant her fingers touched his forearm, a smooth warmness nearly triggered her eyes open. Only willpower kept them shut. She'd expected lumpy nodules, and finding whipcord-hard muscles instead was not at all unpleasant. Just the opposite. Still, she wondered how advanced was his condition.

"It tingles."

"That's a good sign. It means healthy skin survives." Her hands continued stroking him. "Is it burning yet?"

"Nay." His tone sounded off.

Trell felt a frown form. Maybe the mixture wasn't working. "We'll give it a couple minutes. In the meantime, we need to discuss which direction to go now the Fezners are gone. Do you have a preference?"

"I once heard of a man in my village who was cured of the disease by a potion. Mayhaps one like this. Some say it was because of a dragon."

Trell cocked her head to the side. He always came back to dragons. "Those poor creatures have been dead for ages. Trying to find a dragon is like chasing smoke."

"Mayhaps, but it is all I have left."

She stopped rubbing his arm and withdrew her hands. "How far is your village?"

"A ways."

The rasp of fabric told her he covered his arm. "Is that where you wish to travel? You were evicted from there once. I have no desire to put you in danger."

"Who will recognize me now? I am covered head to toe in rags. It is a good direction. I—I mean if a cure exists there, why not seek it out."

Says a despairing man.

Sympathy rose. It did so easily for this man. Because of her growing attraction? For a man whose face she'd never seen. Was it empathy? Curiosity? She suspected the cause went much deeper. Gren stirred a primal need in her like no other man. He shouldn't be a temptation, but he was.

An unchecked quiver went through her—like a breeze ruffled the branches of a tree signaling a change in the weather.

She leaned forward and kissed where his mouth should be. For an instant, warmth pressed against hers. The kiss was tender, and very, very sweet. Her blood heated and longing awoke in her.

She wasn't sure what life held but could hardly wait to find out. She exhaled the breath she'd been holding. With her eyes still squeezed closed, she leaned into him. The spark he ignited set her blood on fire—a tree's worst fear—yet she had no intention of fleeing.

She noticed—as if she would miss something so obviously male—his erection pressing against her. It pulsed hot and hard.

****

Gren hated pulling away from Trell. The situation went too far. No question in his mind that he took advantage of the healer's kindness. He winced in shame. To hold her in his arms, even for a split second, fulfilled his fondest dream. He had lost count of the number of nights thoughts of her kept him awake.

When reality struck, he leapt to his feet. He'd committed a serious blunder. Not that he regretted the kiss. No, never. He'd fantasized about it for weeks and it was well worth the gamble.

At what cost?

He stumbled farther back. Guilt exploded in him about bringing her to his father. He risked failure confessing the truth. The closer to Barg Castle, the stronger his sense of dread. Of danger. That thought twisted his insides. "You shouldn't have done that."

"It was nice. I don't regret it."

"It won't happen again."

"What a shame." She lifted her brown eyes to him, neither sad nor happy, just gleaming with curiosity. "Didn't you enjoy it?"

A harsh breath hissed out of him. By the Gods, of course, he liked the kiss. Never had he taste sweeter lips. Never had he wanted a woman more than Trell.

But for the greater good and with a sense of self-perseveration, he must continue his sham. He inhaled

149

sharply. "There's a place I'd like to show you before we cross the border of Demicland. We'll be able to clean up and make ourselves presentable."

"Where is this place?"

"Less than a week's travel. It's on our way."

Trell nodded, and they set out without another word. Later she flicked her gaze at him.

"What?" he asked.

"How do you feel? Is there any change?"

It took all his willpower not to roll his eyes. No cure existed. Especially for someone not afflicted. "Everything feels the same."

Trell's shoulders slumped as disappointment flashed across her face, and Gren vowed to never make her sad again.

Along the way, they elected to bypass the only village they saw and arrived at the foothills of the mountains. Trell never mentioned the man who'd approached her at the Fezners' camp. And Gren didn't ask. Not then. Not now. Oh, he wanted to, but even more, he wanted her to trust him enough to volunteer the information.

At midday, they called a halt. Gren pulled out his flute. He normally played at night and had yet to catch sight of what his music drew, though he established a pretty good idea—the dragon. Daylight might bring him success.

He checked the block at the bridge of the flute. It barely touched the sound hole. Perfect. Though his fingers were wrapped in rags, the fingers of his right hand covered the first three holes and his left the bottom three. He puckered his lips and placed the mouthpiece under his top lip. He started gently, adding force with his breath.

While he played, Trell tended a pot containing their evening meal. Gren relished watching her, never envisaging a woman could combine innocence and wisdom in such a tempting package. Only she accomplished the feat with ease.

Desire stirred within him, and he averted his gaze before his body's reaction became obvious. After their one kiss, he believed the healer was chaste. He shouldn't have let her kiss him. Knew it then. Knew it now. And would berate himself to his dying day, but that didn't tarnish his pleasure.

Or the fact that he'd gladly kiss her again, if given a chance. He swore something in her response thrilled him.

Playing for an hour and not spotting the dragon, he stopped.

That's when Trell approached him. "It's been a few days. If the ointment hasn't shown any improvement, mayhaps you need another treatment."

"As a matter of fact, I do think there's been a change."

Trell's eyes widened, the brown turning golden with big, round, happy tears. "Wonderful. May I see? I should examine your skin."

"Nay, not yet." He backed away. "The place I wanted you to see is about a half day's journey from here," he went on, the pain on her face nearly undoing him. "Higher in the mountains. On a hunting expedition as a boy, I wandered away from the campsite and got lost. That's when I discovered it. Few know of its existence."

At Trell's nod, the tightness in his shoulders eased.

The next day they climbed several leagues. Skinny pole pines became more abundant, as did outcroppings of huge rocks. Upon arrival in a copse of trees, Gren stood quiet, letting Trell take in the scene. He knew exactly what stunned her into silence—two vertical drops of water so thin that they shone like gossamer silver veils plunging into a pool.

"What is this place?" Trell finally asked with an awe-filled voice.

"I call it Snowsquall Falls. If you listen carefully, you can almost hear the chatter of a marketplace full of people."

She cocked her head and smiled. "It's beautiful."

A curl of warmth swirled through his veins. In spite of his mission, over the past three weeks, her approval had come to mean the world to him. "I've always thought one side ought to be for women and one for men. Would you care to use it?"

The biggest, brightest smile answered him. Trell dropped her travel pack, leaned her staff against a tree, and raced to the pool. She dipped a foot into the water.

"Brrrr. It's cold," she said, then laughing dove into the pond and swam to the falls.

When her silhouette stripped off clothes, he splashed to his side of the falls. He disrobed and stood naked. Raising his face to the water, he let it cleanse weeks of road grime off him. Trell stood in the next fall. Naked, too. He couldn't help but feel they shared an intimacy between them.

Gren saw her make her way to the bank and felt desire stir. She cut a fine line through the water. The sight made him aware of the rags he would have to don to maintain his lie.

An ugly necessity.

They built a huge bonfire to dry themselves off and spent the rest of the night camped near the falls. At dawn, rising, they headed out. After a couple hours of hiking, his homeland came into view. Clinging to the mountainside, cottages with smoke rising from chimneys led to a stronghold that was Barg Castle, his home.

He waved his arm. "Behold Kula! Demicland's poorest kingdom."

Chapter 10

Poor, indeed.

Trell had never seen such an impoverished community surrounded by such gorgeous scenery. This kingdom didn't know what they owned.

A mountain range pierced the sky under the glaring midday sun and reminded Trell of a person's spine. Puffy clouds drifted through peaks, shrouding the highest tops from her gaze as though the magnificence was too much to behold. Barren patches of land sported scraggly grasses and bushes with mounds of boulders. But nothing diminished the beauty before Trell. It stole her breath away and brought tears to her eyes in the cool, clear air.

Lowering her gaze to the spindly forest of trees, she froze. Her friends in Demit Woods had whispered of a boreal forest—also called a snow forest because the trees and plants had the ability to survive in snowy or extreme cold conditions—and this was the first she'd actually seen. The trees were nothing like the behemoths of home. Some barely reached her waist, and others were twisted by wind and snow.

"Hello, my friends. Who among you is the Mother Tree?" she mindspoke as she looked over the landscape.

A wavering, breathy voice, ancient even by normal tree standards responded, *"I am she. We have heard of*

*you, Once-an-Ossa. Be welcome to our land but stay
alert among these Walking Ones."*

A statement Trell agreed with. Intuition counseled
this was a harsh land and unforgiving to the weak.
*"Thank you for the warning. The Demic peoples'
reputation is known far and wide. It is said they run
rampant over the countryside murdering, raping, and
pillaging."*

"Some, not all."

Had Gren participated in the raids? Trell shuddered
at the thought and then pushed the query from her head.
In spite of her suspicions, she refused to picture him in
a bad light. He'd already suffered enough. She had no
right to heap blame on him for crimes unknown to her.

She turned to Gren. "Where does Kula fit within
the other Demic kingdoms? From the dilapidated
cottages, the village doesn't appear to sit high in the
pecking order."

"An accurate assessment. My father has plans, but
I am not privy to them."

The information implied he came from a high-
ranking family if his father believed he could improve
conditions. "I see."

On the side nearest the towering mountain, a
mighty stone castle cast a shadow over the land. A
structure clearly built larger and larger over time. An
ancient fire had turned the thick walls black closest to
her. Even from this distance, grotesque dragon-like
figurines decorated spouts to channel rainwater away
from masonry walls. No wonder Gren showed such
interest in dragons. He grew up beneath a castle
adorned with creatures meant to frighten.

"Kula is an inhospitable land," Gren said, as

though he sensed her thoughts centered on him. "It isn't for everyone. Bitter winds batter the mountains much of the time, and during the long winters people swear death howls nightly."

"I believe you. Despite the beauty, it has that feel."

"A bad place," the Mother Tree whispered to her. *"My children cannot grow tall in this land no matter how much nourishment I feed them."*

Trell acknowledged the comment with a nod. Along her journey she had listened to the forests' heartbeat every night when it grew stronger. The closer she approached this land, the rhythmic beat lessened.

"Do you know why?" Gren asked when she didn't immediately respond. "The boulders there... Many are the size of the castle. Unmovable, making farming impossible."

"It's more than that," the Mother Tree spoke. *"Rocks, our roots can grow around. But the soil is contaminated with toxic elements."*

Trell listened to the Mother Tree but answered Gren. "What do villagers do, then?"

"They forage. Hunt. Fish. Our craftsmen sell leather goods and carve knife handles. Trappers sell furs."

Trell suspected they raided for provisions necessary to survive but kept that opinion to herself. There seemed no middle range in the inhospitable land. "Which is your home?"

"The castle." When she stiffened and her hand flew to her chest, he went on. "The ruler of Kula is my father. I am his second son."

Trell's mind reeled. A breathiness threatened to steal the air from her chest. "You're a prince?"

"A poor prince. Since we are having this conversation, I confess he requested your presence."

Qualms she'd tried to ignore resurfaced with a vengeance. "Is he ill? What is the nature of his sickness? What symptoms does he display?"

"I don't know if he is sick or not." Gren waved to a fallen tree. "Come, sit here. We should talk. It's time for the truth. All of it." He sat and she followed his lead.

Blinking rapidly as if the motion would clear her mind, her curiosity was piqued. She leaned her staff against a tree and sat. What else could he possibly wish to tell her?

As if it mattered.

At least, that's what she told herself. It had taken time to admit, but she cared for Gren like she'd never cared for any man. "Best you explain, then."

"My father sent his three sons on a quest. He gave each of us the same clue—that he sought the healer who was sister to Wizard Cress. I asked along the way and learnt your name. A pretty one, I might say. When you found me being stoned in Brenalin, I was stunned that the very person I sought saved me."

Her jaw tightened until it ached. Her stomach twisted into knots, but she feared jumping to assumptions without hearing Gren's whole tale. Everyone deserved the right to explain. "Go on."

"I have an older brother, Oded, and a younger one, Riff. Instead of naming Oded as his heir, Father announced that whichever son brought him the healer would be named his successor. You're the wizard's only sister."

Trell's breath hitched. She absorbed this

information and swallowed deep breaths to stay calm.

It didn't work.

Stinging betrayal raked her core with jagged claws. Gren had lied to her. Misled her. If not outwardly, then by omission. She squeezed her eyes shut for a brief moment. Finally opening them, she grabbed the first thing to enter her mind. "What about your brothers? Where are they?"

Gren dragged his boot toe in the dirt in front of him. "A fair question. And one I have no answer. We were never close and did not exchange plans before setting out. Knowing Oded, he probably marched into the Halls of Medsin and demanded that you be handed over to him. Riff would have followed his lead to avoid trouble. You actually met Oded in Brenalin." He paused when she frowned in bewilderment. "The nobleman who encouraged the crowd to stone me. That was him. No doubt he didn't recognize me.

"And remember the night two riders raced by us? I'm sure that was them. I have no idea what pact they struck with each other during the hunt for you. Neither one will make a proper ruler for the people of Kula. Oded is greedy and cruel. I had hopes for Riff when he was younger. Although, I have my doubts now. I should have taken more time with him, taken him under my wing, or stood up for him. Mayhaps I could have influenced him if I'd spent more time with him."

She couldn't…wouldn't look at Gren. His confession was too much to take in. She willed her heart to slow, for her mind to clear itself of the fog threatening to consume her. How could she have been so naive?

"Want me to answer that?" Torkel mindspoke.

She knew the dragon couldn't read her mind. He must be close enough to see her body tense. *"Not really."*

"Well, I will anyway. Because you chose not to see any wrongdoing. Humans are so blind. You accepted the male human at face value—a sick, diseased man—because you coveted being the healer who found a cure for his disorder."

So much for her wishes. Torkel's description stopped her cold. She wasn't that vain. Was she? *"Fair enough. This is my mess. Let me handle it. It's between Gren and me."* She cut off the mindspeech to glare at Gren. "And you would make a suitable ruler?"

"I'd like to think so. For the greater good. Look at Kula. It's in sorry shape. The villagers need assistance. More than they're currently receiving at any rate. I'm determined to make life better for all the inhabitants, not just a privileged few. If I can complete this task, I'll be in a position to share the wealth with the people. On my travels, I saw a man use a lever that moved boulders. If we could expand our farming, that would increase our ability to provide for ourselves. Any change would be an improvement."

Trell swayed as thoughts raced. "Good intentions do not justify bad actions. If your father needed a healer, why didn't you just approach me and request my services? My oath would have forbidden me from turning you down."

A frown pulled the rags across Gren's face. He hesitated, then straightened. "Trell, no more secrets between us. I can't swear my father needs a healer or not. Or his motivation." He inhaled sharply. "There's more."

"More…?"

"He believes a dragon answers to you, and he seeks the creature. I suspect that's what he really pursues, but why…I have no idea."

A cold shiver raced along Trell's spine as if a freezing wind swept down the mountain. Bile rose. She jumped to her feet. It was one thing to betray her, quite another to hunt Torkel. She couldn't utter a denial—terror overshadowing anger and betrayal.

"Torkel! You heard? You must leave. Immediately. Danger lurks here for you."

"Of course, I heard. Dragons are a superior species. Our hearing is far better than mere humans. Your puny companion doesn't scare me. Someday I shall be king of all the dragons. Black dragons rule the center of the circle and balance all other elements. It makes perfect sense for me to be the first king because I will create something better than the old league of dragons. I am the logical choice and you want me to flee, to postpone my search for a lair from which to rule? Impossible."

Trell glanced at her staff. The ribbons remained limp. Twice it had warned of danger. She put her faith in Cress's magic. *"First there needs to be a dragon society for you to rule. All I'm advising is caution. You should heed my warning."*

"Too late now. We're here. Nor would it have mattered."

Sometimes talking to Torkel drove her insane. If he had knowledge…

She closed her mind to think, then demanded, *"What do you mean? I always take your advice under consideration. Being fully informed might have altered my decision."*

"Did you hear me?" Gren asked, leaning closer, eyes narrowing.

Dragonic laughter boomed. *"Your decision was made long ago."*

"You foolish dragon."

"You foolish human."

The exchange dissolved into name calling, so Trell blocked the mindspeech. She squinted at Gren sitting, waiting for her answer. How should she respond?

She sucked in a deep breath, drawing in courage. Or so she told herself. He'd been dishonest with her—turnabout was only fair.

"I have no dragon," she lied, but the denial rang feeble to her ears.

Gren have must agreed, too. He snorted. "I did some research before setting out. Legend claims music entices the creatures. That's why I played my flute. I swear it drew a dragon out of hiding. I know one flew above us. And don't forget that scale I found on the beach."

"Stupid human," Torkel interjected. *"He never saw me. You are worried about nothing, Trell."*

Not yet anyway. She glanced at the sky. No sign of the dragon. Thank the Gods. She still had time to formulate a plan.

Then a wild idea struck, and she wondered aloud, "Are you even an Untouchable?"

A crystalline green gaze focused on her for a long second. "I thought I could do this, but no more. I promised…no more lies."

The seriousness in Gren's voice made Trell lean backward. Something died inside her as he began unwrapping the shroud covering his face. Healthy skin glistened on his forehead. She swallowed hard, fearing what she would see, knowing her world was crumbling to pieces.

Sweeping sable brows appeared over those amazing eyes. Her heart beat faster. She pursed her lips, afraid to speak.

Streams of fabric dropped away. A full mouth with lines around it implied many smiles, and a heavy stubble covered his jaws. He dropped the rags that had covered his face to the ground.

"As you can see, I am not." A gulf of sadness edged his tone. "My plan was to attract the attention of a certain healer. *You.* Then, lure you to Kula under the pretext of finding a cure for my affliction. In hindsight, the deception was ill-conceived. I didn't think it through or the consequences. I should have done the honorable thing and just approached you and requested your assistance."

Trell leapt up and spun on her heels. She ran blindly through the forest. It didn't matter where she ended up as long as it was away from Gren. From the truth. The betrayal. A stinging pain cut from the inside out. He was nothing what she thought. Nothing like the person she fell in love with.

The thought came out of the blue and made her stumble. She willed herself to remain upright and kept running. It helped that the trees opened a path before her.

"Trell, stop!" Gren yelled.

Crashing steps resounded behind her. The ground vibrated. She pumped her legs faster to increase the distance. One meter. Five meters. Twenty meters.

Curses erupted. Branches snapped, and fresh pine scented the air. Pinecones thudded the ground behind her as if the trees bombarded her pursuer.

Trell's heart raced. Tears blurred her vision. She sensed Gren gaining ground but dared not waste a second to look over her shoulder. Her goal was the thicker forest.

"Fear not, Once-an-Ossa, we will hinder his progress," came the ancient voice of the Mother Tree.

Trell didn't slow. *"My thanks, Mother Tree. Do not let your saplings injure themselves because of me."*

The conversation, though it lasted only seconds, cost her ground. Her arm was grabbed in a vise-like grip. Gren pulled her to a stop.

His entire front was covered in pine needles, and scratches left raw, red lines across his face. "Trell, please, listen to me."

"Why?" Her lungs burned from the exertion. "You lied to me. Deceived me. How can I possibly trust you?"

"Let me explain."

An inner strength like heartwood in a living tree built a wall against emotions swirling inside her. He had lied to her from the very beginning.

And for what?

Not because of a desperate need for a healer. Because he wanted to find Torkel. Protective instincts surged and solidified into an unbreakable armor. No matter what his intention, Gren wouldn't find her friend through her.

She frowned. "Deceit is never the way to start a relationship."

"My deepest apologies. I thought it best to—"

163

"Thought!" This time red hot anger shattered her defenses. "What do you know of thinking? Oh, you profess concern for Kula's villagers, but you expect me to just accept your apology. Are you serious? You lied to me."

"Trell, I beg you. Forgive me. I started this quest with a plan that was wrong. My number one priority is always Kula's people. I truly apologize. I've gotten to know you. I never realized what a kind, decent person you were. I feel awful." He reached for her hands.

She jerked back. A little piece of faith in humanity died inside her.

"I should have been truthful," he went on. "I realize that now, but I'd already devised my scheme." He raked back thick hair. "It was too late to change after you saved me in Brenalin. Several times I wanted to confess to you, I really did.

"Then there were my brothers... This way my identity was hidden from them. It offered a bit of protection. Remember the logging camp? The woodcutters were told to look for a healer and a man traveling together? It confused them that an Untouchable traveled with you." Green eyes pleaded for forgiveness. "I did what I thought was best at the time. I take full responsibility for my actions. I deserve your recriminations. But hear me out...I want us to start over, Trell."

How could she have been so gullible? The urge to whack him senseless with a stick increased with each beat of her heart. Looking down, she saw that branches littered the ground. All she need do was grab one and beat him for being dishonest. For making her care about him.

She stood motionless, trying to decide what to do next.

When he offered her a drink from his water sack, she growled a refusal. She wanted nothing from him. Betrayal stung too deep, was too fresh.

He shrugged and dribbled the remaining contents on a sapling that looked wilted from lack of nourishment.

He didn't know her. Had no idea who she really was. She glanced down to see a beetle scurry in front of her. The insect was just trying to survive day by day. Same as her.

Then out of the blue another thought materialized. Her feelings for Gren were still forming...growing. Even though their relationship started with deception, she declined to toss them aside as if they meant nothing to her.

"A mistake," Torkel mindspoke. *"Let me kill him."*

Trell snapped upright. *"You're still here? I told you to flee."*

"The male human deserves punishment for his deception. I warned you this human had secrets. Now do you believe me?"

"Stop lecturing me." The notion of Gren dying terrified her.

"I didn't come to lecture you. Believe me, I am not the least bit interested in what happens between humans."

"Then what do you want? You're being a pest. I have the situation under control."

A snort signaled his reply. *"You need me. Someone has to watch over you."*

****

Gren realized he cared about Trell and urged her toward their camp. He'd always believed himself above the machinations of his brothers. Yet...yet now... He could lose her over his duplicity. He never realized how much she meant to him until he'd seen how he had crushed her.

He squeezed his eyes shut against the truth. What if she never forgave him? That would destroy him. He reached to caress Trell's cheek with the back of his fingers and savored the sweet scent of vanilla clinging to her braids.

"I'm sorry I tricked you. I had it all planned out—find the healer, present her to my father, and claim the kingdom. It seemed a simple formula when I started out. Now, I have my doubts."

Trell stared at him, brown eyes sad. "You used me. Manipulated me. I owe you no loyalty. What's stopping me from just walking away from you when your back is turned?"

"Nothing. However, be aware that if you leave, expect my brothers to hunt you down and force you to return with them. At least with me, I am the lesser evil." A huge sigh escaped him. "That doesn't excuse my actions. I hurt you. You deserve better."

"On that we agree."

Gren had cleared his conscience. He admired Trell's grit. He'd never met a woman like her before. The way she cared about people, put them before herself. He never dreamed someone was capable of combining innocence and wisdom in such a slender, feminine package. "Now that you know the truth, you have a decision to make."

Rich brown eyes drilled into him, and he didn't

blame her one iota. "What?"

"I'm not going to hold you against your will. You are free to leave." For the life of him, Gren didn't know what induced him to utter the offer. Maybe because he hated what he'd become. His own treachery had derailed him. He'd have to start all over and show her that he was worthy of her trust.

Trell narrowed her eyes. "Really?"

He still believed in honor and refused to break his word. "I promise not to pursue you."

"And your brothers?"

"I can't vouch for them." He scratched the persistent itch at his neck.

"Why do you want me to meet your father? If he's anything like you…"

"We are not alike." He didn't blame Trell for doubting him. "I'll give you some time in private. I buried clothes in the woods and would like to retrieve them to change. I've worn these rags for months and am ready to be rid of them."

Trell looked up at him. "Go, before I have a change of heart."

He prayed to the Gods that Trell was still there upon his return. He'd committed a grievous wrong and it took a big person to forgive him. "Does that mean you'll continue with me?"

She raised her head, the bells jingling in her braids. "I haven't made up my mind."

****

"What will you do?" Torkel mindspoke while the sun crept over the treetops.

"I don't know. I should just slip away. The trees would hide my trail. Bar Gren from following me, if I

Darcy Carson

request it."

"I'm continuing on."

The dragon's words made her jerk with surprise. *"What? Why?"*

"I must. Dragons came to this world at the bequest of gemstones. Before I can become king, I must find a stone or mineral willing to share its secret with me. I seek a black gemstone not among the usual ones. Something in this land calls to me in a seductive whisper. Something, not mineral, but organic. I cannot leave until I find it. To refuse is unimaginable."

"Don't be ridiculous. You can't stay here. Gren has already lied to me. We can't trust him. Or his family."

"I'm sure what I pursue are firestones. They are what draw me."

"It's not safe for you. Gren's father wants you. Not me."

"I'm unafraid. Nor will I let you be harmed. I'll protect you against them."

The dragon's words cemented her decision. No matter the danger. No matter the consequences. *"Then I'm coming with you. I can't let you venture forward without me. Somehow I'll make them obligated to me."*

Detritus crunched beneath booted steps. Trell glanced in the direction of the sound, and her mouth fell open at the change in Gren. He had donned leggings of black, a tan tunic, and a vest. A heavy, fur-trimmed cloak draped his shoulders and was an almost perfect match to his sable hair. His long legs were muscular, and the tunic and vest couldn't hide the firmness of his body. A scabbard with a sword hung at his side. He truly looked like the prince he was.

Her gaze swept his tall frame for a second time. "Oh my."

"If that means you approve, I'm glad."

So like a man to misinterpret her meaning. "I preferred the rags."

Sorrow flashed across Gren's face. "Will you continue on with me?"

"With conditions. I'll meet your father and see what he wants, and if I am able to help. I also want to meet with the local healer to find out what kind of ailments are most pressing hereabouts." Gren started smiling, nodding, but she ignored him to finish her ultimatum. "Lastly, I require your word that I may come and go as I please. Including leaving permanently."

****

A condition he would die to fulfill.

At Barg Castle, sconces with torches stuck on the curtain wall chased away the forthcoming darkness with pale yellow light for several meters. Sentries paced back and forth at their stations. In Demicland, being prepared against invaders was a necessity, and Kula was no exception. A good defense meant the difference between life and death.

Gren kicked pebbles with a boot toe to alert the guards at the main gate of their approach. He didn't want to appear to sneak up on them. At a wagon's length from the outer gate, he hailed them. They responded by snapping to attention upon recognizing his voice.

He stopped in front of them. "Have either of my brothers returned?"

"Aye, my lord. Both. Well over a week ago." The

taller sentry looked at his partner. "They were accompanied by Healer Trell."

The guard's announcement threw ice cold water on Gren. "We'll see about that."

By the time he and Trell arrived at the great hall, he wondered and worried who his brothers found to impersonate Trell. They stepped into the candlelit hall and he recognized four of the five people in the room. An older woman was a stranger. Her frail body was bent with age, and she stood sipping from a mug.

Gren's gut churned, then he fixed his gaze on the man sitting on the high throne. Taking Trell's hand, he gave it a squeeze and led her forward, striding faster, ignoring the gaping stares from those inside.

Oded, bedecked in green tights and a darker green wool robe with sweeping sleeves that reached the floor rushed forward to block their path. The rich finery was his custom. His gaze raked Trell's slender figure. "What's this, brother? Another healer? I didn't think you had the courage to present a fake one at Father's court."

Gren had to remember to keep hold of his temper. "The woman I brought is the genuine Healer Trell, sister to the Wizard Cress. Who is yours?"

Oded fingered his jasper pendant as he shifted from foot to foot. "I, too, have brought the Healer Trell in compliance with father's request. See for yourself." He indicated the elderly woman with gray hair sticking out of an elaborate headdress. By the way she wove, unsteady on her feet, the beverage she held in her clutching hands wasn't her first.

Gren returned his attention to Oded. "Yours is a pretender."

"There cannot be two Healer Trells, sister of Wizard Cress. I succeeded in our mission first and will be named father's successor."

Before Gren answered, Trell beamed at his brother. "A pleasure to see you again, my lord."

For a brief moment confusion lit Oded's pale green eyes, then his gaze narrowed. "I recognize you. You were the meddlesome healer who insisted upon aiding that Untouchable."

"How kind of you to remember me. Although if you had stopped tormenting that poor man, you might have learned my identity much sooner."

A low grumble from Oded reminded Gren of a mountain bear rummaging for food. And, like the bear, Oded's temper could flare at the slightest provocation.

Gren rested his hand on his sword's pommel. Oded's slights boiled up. It took all his will to bury them in the ground where they belonged. "Tread carefully, brother dear. I have no wish for trouble."

Trell put her hand on his arm. Her touch cooled his blood immediately.

"Ignore him," she said softly. "He's trying to intimidate me through insults. They're only given by the weak. He makes himself feel important by ridiculing others."

Gren liked that. "You're right. Weak and stupid."

His brother stiffened and puffed out his chest. Arrogance clung around him like a mantle of fur. "How dare you."

Trell raised her chin higher. Another thing Gren admired about the healer. She was no coward, and he couldn't be prouder as he stood ready to defend her.

"I dare much." She glared at Oded. "You were the

171

rude man who encouraged my people to break the law."

Oded hissed through his teeth, his long face clouding with undisguised anger. "Laws that protect the undeserving do not merit being upheld."

"As a member of the ruling class you should set a better example. Not flout the laws as if immune to them."

A short, balding man with a fringe of gray on his head and a wispy beard flowing to his waist scurried toward them. His golden robe contained swirls of black throughout.

The newcomer's arrival proved a godsend. "A pleasure to see you," Gren said. "Trell, this is Codo, my father's steward. If you need anything, simply ask him."

The older man bowed. "A pleasure to meet you, my lady."

"I'm honored." Trell bobbed a quick curtsey.

When Codo straightened, he turned to Oded. "Step aside, Lord Oded. Let your brother and his guest pass."

A scowl turned Oded's mouth upside down. "This isn't right. The throne belongs to me. I was the first to return with the healer."

The steward stroked his beard in contemplation. "Do tell, my lord."

"This woman is an imposter. Mine is the real Healer Trell."

Bushy eyebrows wiggled. "That is for your father to decide. I'm sure he will have each prove themselves with a test of some sort. And woe to the one who deceives him."

Oded stood straighter. "It won't matter. Father will change his mind. This quest was a whim. You know how fickle he can be. He'll see the error of his way and change his mind."

Gren inched closer to Trell, ever protective. "I'm not worried. This woman is Healer Trell. She is Wizard Cress's sister. She will confirm it."

"We'll see," Oded said with a sly smile.

"Silence your infernal bickering," boomed their father with authority. "Bring the woman before me, Gren. I expected your return much sooner."

Gren turned his attention away from his brother. He shivered. "There were complications," he answered, trying to ignore the fear racing through his veins.

"It's all right," Trell whispered. "I'm not afraid."

"Well, I am."

Her soft laughter wrapped around him to soothe away his worst concerns. Gren hoped with all his heart she was right.

Chapter 11

Trell prayed to Heyln that her assumption proved correct, even as she buried the quiver of alarm nibbling at the edges of her mind. Five people occupied the great hall. All were dressed in fine, dense broadcloth and rich colors of reds, greens, golds, and blues the likes of which she hadn't seen since leaving the castle in Brenalin. Embarrassment tried to rise. Her simple gown and red healer's cape with travel stains appeared shabby in comparison.

No sense letting Gren or anyone see her unease. Her boot heels clicked on the hard surface of the floor. A quick check of the room showed, with the exception of the peoples' clothes, shades of gray and brown coated the long room. With a sigh, she stepped toward the high seat sculpted from a massive piece of jasper with darker green circles and swirls.

The grizzled, middle-aged man lounging in the carved seat appeared as though he maintained not a care in the world. A backdrop of leaded windows lined the wall behind him, making it difficult to get a clear view of his expression in the fading light.

Battling down apprehension, she lifted her chin in a show of bravery and curtsied upon reaching the dais. "Your Majesty."

"Step closer so I may have a better look at you, girl. You don't appear as I expected." He glanced where the imposter stood. "Someone older, with experience."

She followed his gaze to the fake healer. Trell had already taken the older woman's measure. No threat from her. Her rheumy eyes were bloodshot. No true healer overly imbibed. It fogged the brain, hampered decision-making. Foolish woman. Did she drink to bolster her courage? In all likelihood, she'd been promised great riches for her cooperation. And what would befall her if and when the trickery became exposed? Trell couldn't stop the surge of empathy for the woman.

Wedged next to Gren's side, she stole a glance at him. His nod and half smile gave her the courage to inch forward. "I cannot control my age, Your Majesty."

"It is my turn to counsel caution," Torkel mindspoke. *"These people are strangers. I sense great danger. Tread lightly. Summon me if you need assistance, and I will destroy them all."*

She visualized the dragon. He must be less than a league away to reach her with mindspeech. She tried to block the swell of emotions so Torkel wouldn't perceive her fears. Thank the Gods, while mindspeech was a conscious effort to speak with someone, inner thoughts were private and not shared. No matter how much the dragon pretended to know hers. *"You'll do no such thing. Court dynamics are always difficult to maneuver. Especially in a fractious kingdom. But I do agree caution is prudent. Let's hope this tension is simply brotherly jealousy and nothing more. Best you stay away."*

"Always you want to protect me. I am a dragon, the first of my species hatched on this world in a

thousandfold years. When will you accept the fact that I am capable of taking care of myself? And you."

"I have no time to argue with you."

Ever since the dragon had imprinted on her at birth, a mystical connection existed between them. So far Torkel had followed her commands, yet as he grew older, bolder, controlling his impulsive actions became harder. He was developing his own opinions. Soon, her influence would dwindle to nonexistent. Like any parent, she hoped he would value a smidgen of her advice.

She cast a quick glance at her staff. The ribbons fluttered, but the movement could easily have originated from walking forward.

With increased confidence, she focused her attention on the man who beckoned her. Even though he sat, he did not achieve Gren's height. Nor did any soft flab show on his frame. Rather, a cold hardness emanated from him that sent a prickle of anxiety down her spine.

A servant silently went around the great hall lighting candles in the standing holders. As the candles warmed, they brought the sweet smell of pine and the reminder of home. The room brightened enough for her to see Gren had inherited the man's piercing green eyes, and nothing else. While Gren's generous mouth showed smile lines around it, his father's lips were thin, hard.

A lump stuck in her throat. Instinct shouted that her every word, every action would be judged. More anxiety rippled through her. Not even when Bonner's spell swirled around her legs, trapping her, changing her, had she felt such a strong upsurge of trepidation. She always had faith in her brother's ability to break the spell. Even when centuries passed, after accepting her fate, she hadn't been this troubled.

Now, in this harsh land, among strangers, misgivings churned in the back of her mind. All she could do was trust her instincts and tread with care. She stepped onto the dais.

"Father, I would like you to meet the real Healer Trell," Gren said, slightly behind her. "Trell, King Har."

"Your Majesty, I understand you wished to meet me."

"Indeed, I do." The smile that materialized did not reach his eyes. He extended a hand covered in heavy rings. "But it would seem an abundance of Healer Trells exists."

"Then you'll have a decision to make," she answered in a steady voice.

A life and death decision.

His gaze narrowed. This man was no dullard. "Have no fear, I will. Meanwhile, I am glad you accepted my son's invitation to visit Kula. The timing couldn't be more fitting."

Trell raised a brow. Gren claimed his father requested a healer...with a dragon. What little she saw of the man exposed no sign of illness. His coloring appeared good. No sweating, no labored breathing. He spoke without difficulty and heard without trouble. She would have to observe him longer in order to determine his exact condition and concoct the proper course of treatment.

"It is my pleasure. Dismiss these people so we can discuss your symptoms immediately," she answered, offering a timid smile. "Unless, of course, the other

177

healer has already diagnosed your illness and is treating you."

He leaned over to take her hand. "Do I look sick? The villagers require a healer, not me."

A faint odor came from his mouth, but not unduly unpleasant. Not bad breath from food. Something else. Sometimes an odor was the first indication of illness.

She straightened and stared him right in the eyes. "Do they suffer from any particular ailments? What of Kula's healer? I should seek her permission before I start. Most healers disapprove of other healers trespassing on their flocks."

The questions were a stall for her to gather her wits. If she interpreted the situation correctly, from his few words he intended her stay to be permanent. That wasn't part of her plan. She wanted to travel the land and discover new treatments, but common sense warned her not to contradict the king.

Once again, she appreciated her time spent as a tree, for it taught her patience.

"Alas, that won't be possible. I regret that Healer Dori passed in her sleep in the last week. She served the kingdom well for many years."

A gasp came from Gren. Trell peeked sideways to see sadness twist his face with sorrow. This news clearly came as a blow to him.

A totally different expression flashed over the king's face. If she had to name it, she would say smugness. He had requested a healer before the old one died. Coincidence? She couldn't help but wonder.

"You have my condolences," Trell offered, doing her best to maintain composure, positive any hint of weakness would be her downfall.

The king nodded with approval. "Good. Excellent. Empathy in a healer is always a good trait. I'll spread the word that two healers dwell among us. The villagers will be pleased to have choices. In the meantime, let me be your host and provide quarters during your stay."

"That is most kind of you, King Har, but I would not wish to infringe upon your hospitality."

"Nothing would give me greater pleasure."

Trell glanced at Gren. He stood to the side of the quartet—two men near Gren's age, the steward, and fake healer. Red stained the older woman's cheeks as she guzzled her drink freely. "I'm ready to begin right now."

"Rest, first. I'm sure your journey was long and fraught with difficulty."

"Why delay? I am not fatigued. If people require a healer's services, the quicker I see them and they receive treatment, the faster they'll recover from whatever ailment plagues them."

"The sun has set. Tomorrow is soon enough." He waved to Codo. "Escort our two guests to the high tower. Make sure they are settled in their rooms and are made comfortable."

"I'll accompany you," Gren volunteered, stepping closer to Trell.

"Stay," his father said. "You've been absent from court for a long while, and I wish to confer with you and your brothers in private. We have much to discuss."

The steward approached with the swish of fabric brushing the floor.

Trell blinked, then nodded.

"The old one lies," Torkel mindspoke as she stood staring at the king.

"I thought as much."

"I warned you."

No purpose in concurring. Torkel's ego needed no inflating. He accomplished that well enough on his own.

"And I respect your opinion. Would it help if I told you I like Gren, even though he lied to get me here?" she asked, checking where he stood.

"It might."

"Well, I do."

"Good to know, but if I were you, I would keep my tongue still. Gren isn't in charge here."

Two guards that Trell hadn't noticed closed ranks with their swords scraping the floor. They muscled the imposter, her, and Codo away. Trell barely had time to cast a last look over her shoulder at Gren. Her grip tightened on her staff as they passed over slate-floored hallways and climbed stairs as wide as tandem-yoked oxen.

Their pace slowed due to the fake healer's inability to barely stand upright. After several minutes they reached a door at the base of the staircase.

"I wasn't done with my drink," the fake healer said, her headdress flopping side to side. "Have a servant bring another tankard to my quarters."

"I regret your request will not be fulfilled. The servants have retired for the night," Codo said as he nudged her inside and closed the door.

"What kind of backward kingdom is this?" She spewed outrage at the high-handed treatment through the heavy wooden door.

Trell swore Codo locked the door, but with his long sleeves covering his hands, it was difficult to tell.

So much for being an honored guest.

To be on the safe side, Trell counted the number of doors, made a mental note of twists and turns and the rooms she passed until climbing to a sparsely furnished room with a narrow bed against the wall, a table with a candle and writing paraphernalia, and a chair. Warmth heated her insides. The room reminded her of her quarters in Brenalin where she learned her trade.

A shaft of moonlight pierced a tiny leaded window. "Where am I?"

"Why, among friends." The elderly man tendered a polished smile as he signaled a guard to light the candle on the table. "You will want for nothing while His Majesty's guest. Make a list of supplies that you'll require, and I'll see it fulfilled to your satisfaction."

With that Codo bowed out of the room, closing the door behind him. The latch dropped in place with a clink that left a hollow feeling in the pit of Trell's stomach. On impulse, she strode to the door and pulled. *Locked.*

It prickled her temper but didn't surprise her. The treatment stemmed from the distrustful king.

"I will come for you," Torkel mindspoke.

"No, not yet. I want to see what will happen next. Let the king think I am biddable and will go along with his high-handed tactics."

"A bad idea. Mayhaps when you have second thoughts, you'll be more receptive."

Trell sighed. *"You are a dragon. Humans have to tread more carefully."*

"Aye, I am a dragon. A magnificent, unbeatable dragon. It pleases me that you realize the fact, and mayhaps you can tell me why I bother obeying you?"

"If you must ask me that, then you're not ready to go out on your own."

She shoved the chair under the latch as a precaution against unwelcome visitors and sank to the edge of the bed. If she was going to survive this adventure, she needed a plan.

****

Gren imagined Trell being imprisoned and clenched his fists until his knuckles bleached white. The guards who escorted Codo and the two Trells from the great hall returned. His heart had skipped when the real one shot him a final look. The urge to accompany her pulled so hard that he actually took a step.

This fiasco was all his fault. He'd brought Trell to Kula under false pretenses. He fought against worry bombarding him.

If any harm befell her…

He inhaled and caught the scent of pine, reminding him of the forests he and Trell had traveled through. It settled his nerves a bit. Deep down, growing affection for the healer confused him. He unclenched his fists, and a surge of blood raced down his fingers.

He told himself he stayed for the purpose of reconnaissance. He needed to learn his father's plans.

Thinking of which…he directed his attention back to the bear of a man with silvering hair and shoulders starting to bow. Power radiated from him. And would do so for many more years. His green eyes widened as Gren stepped closer.

"I did your bidding," he told the man sitting on the throne. "I expect you to honor your edict."

"And I shall. As soon as it is determined who the real healer is." Stal raised his hand to silence Oded's

182

grumblings and signaled a servant. "Fetch refreshments. We have much to celebrate."

Within moments the servant returned with a tray, mugs, and a pitcher of ale. His father dismissed the man with a wave. He poured generous portions, handing his sons each one before lifting his own.

"A toast," he proclaimed. "To the winner... Whoever that may be!"

Gren took a swallow. Riff raised his mug and drank. Not Oded.

His younger brother walked over to him and slapped Gren on the back hard enough to echo in the room. "It's good to see you, brother. It took us days to learn the healer's name. One rumor claimed she traveled with an Untouchable. You, I assume. A clever disguise."

Gren relaxed with the praise. "Thanks."

"Then Oded found his Healer Trell."

"I—"

"Silence," his father interrupted. "You can swap tales of your escapades later. Tell me about your healer, Gren. Has she mentioned a dragon?"

Gren fingered the solitary scale in his pocket. He wasn't ready to reveal tangible proof of the creature's existence. "Every time I broached the subject, she denied its existence."

"Really? Oded's healer claims the creatures are real."

"Does she now? Well, if my answer displeases you, so be it."

Oded stepped up. "There! By his own admission, he has failed in the quest. We were to fetch the Healer Trell who knew about dragons."

Gren shook his head. "The rationale is flawed. How can we be sure they live? Have you seen one soar in the skies of Kula?" He turned to challenge his father and both his brothers. "Any of you?"

His father grabbed the stone arms of the throne. "You doubt me? A red one protected Brenalin from Genoy. It destroyed his army. If there is one, others abound as well. Rumors say one follows her."

"Hearsay? That's as bad as believing in the ancient tales of the creatures' existence." Gren stared at his father in disbelief. "Why would you place your throne on the line based on a myth?"

"There is always a kernel of truth in those old tales."

An icy tremor bounced along Gren's spine at the passion in his father's voice. Instincts warned him that Stal Og Har was obsessed with the mythical beasts. Again, he asked himself why. "Even if such a creature existed, what is its importance?"

A scowl darkened Stal's face. "You're not king yet. Do you question my actions?"

"Aye, I do."

The answer silenced the room. Tension rose. But Gren didn't care. The father he'd always admired seemed diminished, a figment of his imagination. Strange, he never noticed before.

"Enough. I tire of this discussion," Stal announced. "Onto more pleasant tidings. I asked for one healer and now have two. Which one should I pick?"

Oded stepped closer to the throne. "Mine is the true healer. I was the first to return to Brag Castle, and she admits to the reality of dragons. I should be named the heir."

Ale rose in Gren's stomach. He cast a glance at his brothers. Oded's expression mimicked their father's earlier scowl. Riff grinned, a twinkle shining in his eyes.

Stal took another sip. "Give me some credit. I've watched all three of you over the years. I know each of your faults and strengths better than you think. Oded, you are the eldest and custom favors you, but Gren has worked harder, practiced every skill assigned to him until he mastered it. He always possessed the most potential. My decision will be based on who brought the true Healer Trell."

Ale soured in Gren's stomach. He signaled a servant to take his mug. While he'd never heard praise from his father for his deeds, his anxiety over Trell preceded any accolades heaped upon him. It could be a trick.

Oded clutched his jasper pendant as he stepped forward to confront his father. "Test my healer. She will prove her worth. The throne should be mine."

Danger glinted in Stal's emerald gaze. "Kula isn't a democracy. We are a monarchy. An absolute monarchy. I rule because I conquered this land. Not you. Not Riff. I can pick my successor. For the good of the kingdom, the next ruler will be the fittest."

"What if I challenge Gren?" Oded asked. "The law gives me the right. A fight to the death will settle this once and for all."

The idea of starting his reign with blood on his hands abhorred Gren. But backing down remained out of the question. He turned to his brother. "I am not our father. I will not kill my own blood. There are always options."

Oded narrowed his gaze. "I have no prejudices. My sword will sing your death song."

"If you do this—kill a brother—it will be a wound that will never heal." Gren clenched his fists tighter. "You do not deserve to be ruler of Kula. You have hurt too many people. The helpless are at your mercy."

"You speak of that little serving wench, Shay, who killed herself. It wasn't my fault she became pregnant."

"Not Shay. Actually, I was thinking of the time you demanded the eldest daughter's favor from that trapper who supplied those white ermine pelts. You left neither one a choice."

Riff sucked in a breath. His face turned scarlet, and his lips pinched into a white line. "You bedded Brit?"

Oded slanted a sharp look at Riff. "Of course, I did. Don't wet yourself over it. You were away on a trade mission."

"You knew I was fond of her."

"How very perceptive of me. I did you a favor. You were young and dumb to harbor feelings for the girl."

"I'll kill you." Riff leapt with his hands outstretched.

The soldiers stationed around the room stepped forward, but a wave from the king halted them.

Oded dodged the attack, stuck out his leg, and tripped Riff.

Gren never knew his younger brother harbored affections for the girl. He had seen the pair together, laughing, strolling the inner courtyard. At the time, he had assumed they were friends. Nothing more.

His older brother, however… Gren frowned at the evil Oded had wrought and would persist if he became ruler of Kula.

Oded pointed at Riff. "Stay down, you simpleton. I have no quarrel with you. The girl was a trapper's daughter. Nothing more. You dally with them, not develop affection for them."

Gren held out his hand to help Riff to his feet. Riff didn't say a word, only accepted the offer, scowling hatred at Oded.

"Temper, temper," Oded said. "It never ceases to amaze me how gullible you are."

Riff advanced a step, then stopped. "Caring about someone doesn't make me weak. It means you want to ensure their well-being."

Oded focused on their youngest brother. "You aren't fooling anyone. You'd like nothing better than have Gren and me kill each other, so you could claim the crown for yourself."

The youngest Har inhaled deeply. "That's not a bad idea."

Gren noticed the look of satisfaction on their father's face. Insight struck like a physical blow. Stal enjoyed pitting them against each other, watching them fight. He fueled the friction between them. Had his father always instigated the bickering? The knowledge that he might have sickened Gren.

"I've listened to you long enough. I'm leaving. I will not allow Trell to be imprisoned," he said, spinning on his heels.

Out of the corner of his eye, the king surged to his feet. "Halt!"

Gren slowed his pace to a crawl but didn't stop. He flicked a glance at the soldiers in the great hall. Their only response to the growing tension was to stand at attention. "Not this time, Father. Trell is my guest. I offered her my protection, and she shall have it."

The king snorted. "Go! Comfort your healer. At least she's young and pretty."

Gren scowled at the remark, vowing to never mimic his father's behavior. He marched all the way to the tower, acknowledging a few servants along the way.

A soldier stood at attention in front of the tower door. He waved the man away. His hand clasped the cold metal handle. Locked. The notion of Trell being imprisoned ignited his temper.

Without hesitating, Gren hit the door with his shoulder. It burst open. A chair lay broken on the floor. Trell sat up in the bed, her multiple braids sticking out in every direction, face pale.

"You're not being locked in like a prisoner," he said and settled on the floor to spend the night, guarding her. "I'm staying here to make sure no harm befalls you."

Gren couldn't sleep a wink. All he could do was think about Trell only a few meters from him. He listened to her breathing, watched the blanket rise and fall, and suffered in silence because he wanted to climb into bed with her and cuddle beside her supple body.

****

Trell never regretted Gren's decision to keep her company once during the long night.

Midmorning, she awoke and tiptoed to the window to discover a wintry river far below. She stared down at white rapids cutting a path through the mountains like a knife.

Gren slept on the floor with his back against the wall, his chin resting on his broad chest. She didn't have the heart to wake him.

She'd already decided the window was too small to squeeze through, which meant calling Torkel for a fly-by and dropping onto his back was out of the question. Not to mention his appearance would initiate panic among the villagers. Besides, she couldn't chance archers being stationed on the battlements, which put Torkel in danger.

That left getting the lay of the land for a ground escape before she could find a way out of the quagmire on her own.

In spite of the situation, she did have Torkel. His loyalty meant the world to her.

And a small measure of trust in Gren returned. His willingness to protect her let faith blossom like new growth in the spring.

A light tapping on the door hanging crookedly announced a caller. Gren must have been more awake than she thought for he leapt to his feet. He rubbed his fuzzy face as if unaccustomed to the facial hair.

Codo awaited outside. His eyes widened at the sight of Gren but only bowed his head. "Healer, his lordship is breaking morning fast and has requested your presence in the great hall."

"I'll gather my things."

"You may leave them. They are safe. No one will touch them."

She checked her staff. The ribbons hung limp. No immediate threat. Yet, as a healer, it felt wrong not to wear the red cape signifying her vocation. She swung it over her shoulders and grabbed her staff, thinking better safe than sorry.

Codo, Gren, and she retraced the same steps as the

night before. They stopped at the door where the other healer had entered to have her accompany them. The older woman look peaked with pale cheeks, a red nose, and bloodshot eyes.

"I'll mix you a fennel tea," Trell offered the woman.

The fake healer smiled. "My thanks, but that won't be necessary. I already ordered a servant to boil some cabbage for me. I'll eat it at breakfast."

In the great hall, a long trestle table stood against the wall. Servants bustled, setting down plates, utensils, and goblets. Gren's brothers and father stood near the head of the table. Guards were stationed around the hall like the night before.

"Join us," King Har commanded when he spotted them. "Sit. Eat."

Coming closer to the group, her heart lurched at the comparison of Gren to his family. Tall and straight as a mighty fir tree, he reminded her of her friends growing in the dragon circle. The remembrance ignited a warmth no fire could extinguish...not that she wanted it to.

Oded, on the other hand, prompted her to imagine a tree deformed with burls, a tumor formed by buds that failed to form. Something inside him was twisted.

Riff, the youngest, appeared slender like Gren, only lacked his muscle mass. He shared the same characteristics of a sapling that bent with the wind while reaching for the sun. Trell sensed a goodness in him, though he did his best to keep it hidden. In time, she believed he would mature into a man and be as strong as a mighty oak. So, when he smiled at her behind his brother's back, she returned it.

And last, but not forgotten, was King Har. No tree fit him in her mind. That seemed odd. Like a warning. And sure enough, the long ribbons on her staff gently fluttered.

"Good morning," she greeted the group, parting from Codo.

The fake healer hurried toward Oded.

A whispered, heated discussion ensued between them.

Trell draped her cape on the back of a chair between Gren and his father. Oded sat with his healer on the other side. She imaged two forces with the same goal.

The morning fare equaled any at Abass castle. Soft breads with hard crusts and crackers accompanied small fish eggs and creamed cheese, supplemented with hard-boiled eggs. When Trell couldn't eat another bite, servants tempted her with more cheeses, nuts, and candied fruits.

King Har reached across the table, his bare arm cutting through a candle's flame without flinching. A sweet, putrid smell overlaid the food aromas.

"Your Majesty…" she cautioned, and he jerked his arm back.

He gave an odd laugh, rubbing his skin and grinning like a boy caught stealing one of cook's pies off a windowsill. "That stung."

Trell's empathy rose. "That might blister. Let me tend you. I have salve to ease the sting and stop the itching."

"Not necessary, healer. Kula breeds tough people. A little pain reminds us that we are alive."

"As you wish. In the meantime, I would like to

visit your previous healer's cottage." At the king's frown, she explained, "To save your steward time creating duplicates. Your old healer might have them on hand. And, depending upon where she lived, I would also like to search the woods. Many medicinal plants grow in the forest and she might have planted those she found useful."

"Describe what they look like and I will send someone to search for you."

"That's most kind, King Har, but I insist. Many plants look alike. Some innocent-looking plants are deadly. It takes a trained individual to recognize the difference."

"Well, let me be a bit selfish. I don't want you tiring yourself out. Oded's healer shows no interest in meeting the villagers or Dori's domicile." They both glanced at the woman already sipping on mead.

"I will not tire myself out, Your Majesty," Trell said between bites.

The king snorted. "I'm hosting a banquet in two nights to celebrate your arrival to our kingdom. The lords of Kula will want to make both your acquaintance."

Trell took a deep breath and scraped her chair on the floor as she stood. She had no conception how far to push this king but decided to find out. "I promise to return before the banquet begins. If someone will direct me to where the healer's cottage is, I'll be off."

"I'll do better than that. These lands are dangerous to wander about without proper protection." The king waved to two soldiers standing at attention by the wall. "Escort my guest to Dori's."

Well, that answered her suspicions. She wasn't

being left alone. So much for coming and going at will.

"I'll accompany her, father," Gren said. "I want to check how the villagers fare."

Chapter 12

Gren meant what he said and vowed to keep Trell safe.

But how?

He grimaced as they walked out of Barg castle with two guards on their heels. He didn't know his father's plans and hated being in the dark. Only one certainty remained. No harm would befall Trell. Not if he had anything to say about it.

"We have a ways to trek," he volunteered. "Unless you wish to ride?"

Trell answered him first with a sweet smile. "I like walking. It keeps me in contact with my surroundings."

Gren nodded, pleased with her answer. The circuitous path, once an animal trail, between the castle and the village was well-worn, wide enough for four to walk side by side. He'd become accustomed to walking as an Untouchable and found the activity enjoyable.

To say frustration ate at him about the previous evening was putting it mildly. A long, sleepless night of watching the tantalizing beauty sleep when his body ached to join her...

First though, he had to regain her trust. Her smile might be a beginning. While he doubted harm would befall Trell immediately, he didn't put it past his father to order her seized and detained to extract the coveted information—the whereabouts of the dragon.

Now, ashamed of the vulnerable situation he'd placed her in, Gren refused to leave Trell alone with his father or his soldiers. "I'm sorry," he said. "This isn't the treatment I expected from my father. I want you to know that I disagree with him."

"What did you expect? A gushing welcome…"

The rebuke set him aback. Especially with Trell staring wide-eyed at him, brown eyes bright with admonishment. "Still, my apologies."

Her expression softened. "Your healer… Did you know her well? Last night you seemed surprised at her passing. Was she not elderly?"

Gren's worry flared sharply, fueled by the unsaid accusation in Trell's words. "Dori did her best to care for the villagers. Her actual age was unknown to me. If I had to guess, I would say middle-aged. Her hair had just begun to silver, and her face showed few wrinkles."

"Was she ill?"

"Not that I was aware of." He turned to study Trell. "Why all these questions?"

"Because if she didn't die from sickness or old age, why would she pass in her sleep?"

A frisson of anxiety raced through him. "I asked myself the same question when Father said she'd perished. She was hale and hearty when I departed. The least I can do for her years of service is to initiate an investigation."

In the distance, smoke billowed from chimneys. The village awakened. People went about their morning chores—men split wood, adolescent boys threw scratch to chickens, pubescent girls drew water from a community well, and women tended the fires. Dogs trotted about, sniffing the ground. One woman stopped to wipe tears from a toddler's face with the edge of her apron.

He waited while Trell took in all the activity and he admired her profile.

"You told me yourself that your father sought a dragon," she said, turning to face him. "Could he have sought the healer's counsel, thinking she possessed information about them?"

"It's possible, but I can't swear for sure."

Trell's red healer's cape flapped atop her shoulders as they hurried along. She rolled her eyes to indicate the soldiers following them. "Your father is not about to let me out of his or his soldiers' sight until I prove to him that I have no dragon at my disposal."

Gren didn't care what his father thought. All he knew was his honor was at stake. "I didn't tell him I found a dragon scale."

She tripped as if caught by surprise at his answer. "I should hope not. If you want me to trust you, it would be gone if you had."

A minor rebuke.

The woman confused him. He'd expected his answer to delight her, not raise her ire. "I couldn't…if it put you in danger. Your safety is of the utmost importance to me. We have a saying, 'Haste makes waste.' Before I confide in my father, I need to discover why he is so determined to find the beast."

Trell turned her head slightly. "Mayhaps I misjudged you. If I had a dragon, I would be very appreciative."

He felt the pull of his brow as he frowned. Trell fibbed a little. He knew it, but oddly it didn't bother him. As long as she kept up the pretense of ignorance, she was safe. "Does that mean you trust me?"

"Not yet. You deceived me once. Remember?"

Her answer didn't upset him. She had every right for caution. "Fair enough. Then I'll just have to prove myself to you."

"You can try."

Gren accepted the challenge with a chuckle. He'd created this mess on his own. He should have been honest at the start, not waited until the last minute. Since traveling with Trell, he'd come to know her and how much she valued honesty. He couldn't believe she was giving him a second chance, but he latched onto it willingly.

Before his conscience provided a reason to ease his mind, they reached the outskirts of Kula. "Let's head for the woods."

Several dogs stood to watch them approach.

Trell stiffened and gave him a quizzical look. "Not the village? I thought you wanted to check on the people."

"I prefer your company above all others," he answered, meaning it.

A man, carrying an armload of split wood to his hut, grinned upon recognizing Gren. Several people waved as well. He waved back and silently vowed to improve their plight.

A surge of embarrassment heated his cheeks. This close, the degree of neglect became obvious. Bare patches in the thatched roofs, missing wattle and daub on several huts. His father should build a sawmill for the villagers, so they could cut serviceable lumber to build sturdier huts. Sparkler River began in the mountains and would provide adequate power.

The entire community showed the same disrepair as when he left. No improvements whatsoever. Fences needed mending, the blacksmith shop was missing a door, and a rock foundation crumbled where a church was once planned to stand

A blush tinted Trell's cheeks pink. "In that case, which way? We should find your healer's dwelling first. Replenishing my supplies is high on my list, if I am to treat the villagers."

"This way, then." He headed up the mountain. "Dori's cottage is nearby. She liked people, but not enough to live in the village with them. Privacy ranked several levels above closeness to her patients."

He glanced at the closest villagers. "I'll return when I'm done showing the new healer Dori's home. Tell the others."

They nodded.

One little girl, a strawberry blonde with round blue eyes, peeked from behind her mother's apron. "Lord Gren, wait."

Warmth stroked him. Gren stopped to let the child catch him. She wrapped bony arms around his legs. He smiled and patted her straggly-haired head. This was a game he played with the child. "Do I know you? I had a friend once with hair the color of yours. Mayhaps you know her. She is called Lizzette."

A bright smile glowed on the child's face. "That's me."

"I beg to differ. While I've been absent from the village, you are much taller than she. She could not have grown to your height."

The girl tapped her chest with a dirty fingernail. "It's me. My mother claims spirits come at night and stretch me taller in my sleep."

Gren pretended surprise as he flicked a glance at Trell. "Why, so it is Lizzette. How are you?"

"I'm fine. Did you bring me a treat?"

He rocked back on his heels and scratched his head, stretching out the game. "Hmmm, let me think. A treat, you say?"

"Gren, don't tease the child," Trell reprimanded him. "If you brought her a treat, give it to her."

Chickens clucked and pecked the ground near Lizzette's bare feet. She flashed an appreciative smile at Trell, then turned her attention to him. Demonstrating great fortitude, he dug in his pocket and pulled out an oil-skinned package that fit in the palm of his hand. "Do you think this will satisfy you?"

Lizzette's patience disappeared in a blink of an eye. Little fingers shredded the wrapping. Crumbs fell to the ground and excited the chickens. "An apul tart. My favorite." She stuffed the whole square into her mouth, puffing out cheeks with her prize. A sugary stream dribbled out of her mouth as she chewed.

Gren laughed and took Trell's elbow. He couldn't shake the satisfying sensation of her warm arm as he led her away.

"That was very kind of you," she said.

The praise arrowed straight into his heart. "If I can provide a treat once in a while that makes a child happy, that is all I ask."

They kept walking.

"I noticed everyone seems to have four letters in their name except Lizzette. Why is that?"

"Her name will be shortened to Lizz at her first blooding. Boys' names are changed after their first

199

hunt." Wanting to impress Trell, he didn't have the heart to tell her that the first hunt consisted of raiding other villages for precious supplies.

Trell nodded her head. "Every culture has unique customs. It's why I believe there are cures out in the world yet to be discovered."

Gren paused to stare at her. She consistently amazed him with her sense of adventure and acceptance. "You are very tolerant for one so young."

"Every individual has the right to choose their own path." Trell fingered the branches of a tree, a coy smile lifting the corners of her bow-shaped lips. "Although I am curious what you were called before reaching manhood."

Gren clenched his fists at his sides. "It hasn't been spoken for over a decade. I never cared for the name. Supposedly, it refers to a creature of darkness, a monster."

"You're no monster. My apologies for putting you on the spot."

Her kindness pulverized his willpower. "Nay, you asked, and I wish for you to know. No more secrets between us. My full name is Grendel Ho Har."

"Grendel Ho Har," she repeated, and the name on her lips drew him like a bee to honey. "I like it, but I think Gren suits you better."

Why her approval was important baffled him. Gren shook his head. Her support meant more than the mountains towering above him. "I was a bit of a terror when young."

"That doesn't surprise me."

Her answer elicited a smile. "When we finish at Dori's, if you don't mind a slight detour, I'd like to check the area for firestones. The Fezners used them, and I think Kula might have a supply. If we do and they burn the same, it could provide us with a valuable resource. We can extract them from the ground, sell them, and bring prosperity to Kula."

They trekked about a half league before a small cottage came into view.

****

Trell stopped to study the well-tended structure sitting in the middle of a small glen. The grounds brimmed with greenery. The healer, Dori, had planted gooseberry and lingonberry, and both grew well in the shade. Two dwarf butternut trees stretched their pale gray branches skyward. The nuts would be ready to harvest in late summer, early fall. She made a mental note to remind Gren to return and collect the fallen nuts so they wouldn't go to waste.

An abundance of plants ringed the hut. Trell recognized several for their medicinal value—pinkish bleeding hearts for pain relief, lady ferns that when crushed eased stinging nettle burns and cuts, fragrant lavender for its relaxing effects, multi-colored blood flowers favored as a heart stimulant, and fuzzy sage valued as an anti-inflammatory.

Others, unknown to her, caught her eye. New plants were always worthy of investigation, especially if the flora granted her permission to remove cuttings for analysis. Or perhaps they would volunteer their usage.

In her mind, the trip proved an instant success.

They approached the entrance, and Gren shoved open the door to allow her inside first.

"Water," came a feathery whisper.

From somewhere within the one room hut pleas erupted. *"At last... So thirsty. Hungry. We die."*

"Parched. I will not last much longer. Me first."

Trell gasped, chilled to the bone.

"What's wrong?" Gren asked, his brow furrowing.

She didn't waste a breath explaining. Instead, she stepped inside the hut. Her eyes widened, trying to grasp the grim situation. "Oh, my, look at the waste. Such a shame."

Shelves crowded three-quarters of the room and on each assorted plants were squeezed together. All hung limp and wilted from lack of water. Several had perished, their leaves dried and turned brown, dropping stems and petals to the floor.

"Fetch buckets of water," she ordered. "Now."

Gren spun on his heels. He barked orders for the soldiers to follow. Within minutes, the trio returned, carrying buckets and containers in both hands. Gren handed a full bucket to her.

"Start watering these plants. Go slowly. Too much water after being dehydrated is not good," Trell instructed. "We must save as many as we can."

She grabbed a ladle and dribbled water onto the parched flora. Gren followed her example, but the soldiers simply stood exchanging looks of bewilderment with each other without moving.

When her gaze flicked in their direction, Gren snapped, "You heard the healer. Do as she commands."

They jumped to obey.

"More water."

Trell glanced at several plants in larger containers. "Those pots by the window can use more. Just don't overwater."

The closest soldier nodded and hopped to her bidding.

A pot in front of her, holding an especially dry specimen, said, *"My thanks."*

"Much appreciation, Once-an-Ossa. You saved us," came a chorus of voices, sounding stronger.

Trell blinked in surprise that the flora had heard of her, especially considering she'd never visited this land before. Perhaps the trees told them. She continued watering the houseplants. *"What happened? Why didn't someone come to attend you?"*

"No one cared until you came."

"You poor dears, I'm glad I arrived in time."

Silence permeated the room, except for the occasional thud of a ladle knocking against a bucket or the splash of water. Gren and the soldiers continued their labors.

"The healer was murdered," spoke a nearby pot of mountain mint. *"He killed her."*

"Murdered?" Trell repeated the word in her head as she inhaled a sharp, deep breath. A spicy scent seemed to waft in her direction. *"Who?"*

"He came for treatment. He asked many questions. We never saw him before. The visit was his first."

"A man? You're sure? What did he look like?"

"The Walking One wore a cape and never removed his hood the entire time, but he wore a sword in a fancy scabbard studded with gemstones. He snuck back in the middle of the night and smothered our caregiver with a pillow. We had no way to warn her. She could not hear our cries."

"I am sorry for your loss. Don't be afraid. Stay strong. While you lost a dear friend, I am here to help.

Can you give me any other details to help catch the fiend? How tall was he?

"Slightly shorter than your companion who hovers near you."

She glanced sideways to see Gren checking on her. He remained silent, so she acknowledged him with a nod. *"How old? Young?"*

The mountain mint acted as spokesman for the plants. *"Impossible to tell."*

"What about the scabbard? You said it was encrusted with gemstones. What kind"

"The usual kind that Walking Ones covet."

Not much help. *"Would you recognize the scabbard if you saw it again?"*

"Possibly."

Once the houseplants were sufficiently moistened, she started inspecting them. They appeared quite pleased a visitor communicated with them. The majority were salvageable, but sadly not all. To her all living things held value, and her chin quivered at the loss.

The healer had nurtured common herbs—catnip, basil, lemongrass, mint, thyme, tarragon, chives, and dozens more. Several plants boasted of aiding Dori for generations through clippings. Even ones she didn't recognize were eager to confide their medicinal properties.

One plant looked exactly like a stone. Another had no leaves. Just a stem and a green flower. Another plant surprised her—a Datura, called the devil's weed. It could poison and alter minds. Then Trell spotted a narrow dish of shiny, scarlet seeds—crab's eyes—a highly toxic seed, if consumed.

Trell sensed rather than heard Gren draw near.

"Well." He wiped his brow and smiled as if offering a bond. "You look worried. What's wrong?"

Swallowing, she forced the knowledge of Dori's murder to the back of her mind. Once she had a chance, Trell intended to interrogate the plants further. "I'm going to need to inventory what's here. Since I doubt your father will allow me to make this cottage my home during my stay, can we arrange for a wagon to transport these plants to the castle? All have medicinal value. Those I don't recognize will require additional examination to determine their usage."

He turned to the soldiers. "One of you return to the castle and fetch a wagon. We're going to be busy."

The older soldier started to protest, but then the taller, younger man took off on a run.

"If you don't mind, I'd like to search for firestones in the wait. Would you care to join me? Your company would be most welcome." Gren eyed the veteran soldier who remained near them and leaned closer to whisper, "I really don't want to leave you alone. Come with me."

Warm breath brushed over her cheek, and the enticement of his deep voice proved an irresistible lure. "A break before the hard labor begins is a wonderful idea."

"An excellent ploy," Torkel mindspoke to her. *"You can get the lay of the land before escaping. I am searching for the best trails to guide you away. Meanwhile, I have found a cave of great interest."*

Trell dreaded these unsolicited conversations. Dragons were the most frustrating creatures in existence. She flicked a glance at Gren to make sure he didn't see her reaction. *"What for?"*

"Silly human. For my lair. After I see you safely away, I shall return."

"Is that wise? The king seeks a dragon. Have you learned nothing? Remaining in these lands is dangerous."

"I am unafraid."

Ever the dragon. Always conceited. Brave beyond common sense.

Trell gave up and changed the subject. *"Tell me about this cave."*

"Strange you should ask. I heard this voice... Not a real voice. Not how you and I communicate. I felt a summons in my bones. My chest throbbed with an ache that drew me out of the sky."

Trell frowned. *"Promise me you'll be careful."*

Draconic laughter tickled her mind in response.

Right now, Trell wished she could talk to her brother. Cress had far more experience with dragons, if one counted the Guardians of Secrets. He always offered sound advice. His answers always seemed right.

If not him, who else?

Gren? No. Not yet. In spite of her attraction to him, intuition warned her to tread softly.

No use asking the trees. They'd only tell her she should have stayed an Ossa pine. Though friendly since the transformation, none understood her desire to become human again.

Trell squared her shoulders. That left her to mull over the complications in her life alone.

First, Torkel hearing a voice. Another dragon? Highly unlikely. He was the sole dragon to leave the hatchery. The others were too immature to do so. Maybe the Guardians possessed the answer. When it came to matters concerning dragons, the insect-sized creatures certainly acted all-knowing.

Nor did she forget the king sought a dragon. His purpose remained unknown. Surely a reason existed. She tamped down a rush of concern for Torkel.

And now, a killer was loose in Kula.

That settled it. She needed to craft an escape plan. Sooner, rather than later.

****

Gren saw Trell furrow her brow and wondered what bothered her. No matter the cause, he vowed to protect her. He swore she inched toward trusting him again, then stiffened moments ago, upset at something unseen by him.

He fretted about inquiring, only to decide to give her space. If she wanted to inform him, she would tell him when ready. He could wait.

Meanwhile, he loved being with her. The scent of vanilla and pine surrounded them. The pine came from the forest's spindly trees, but the appealing sweetness of vanilla came from Trell.

"Several places on the mountains grow little vegetation. The soil is nutrient-poor," he explained. The sparse trees substantiated his claim. The wide spaces between them made the trek easy for Trell and him to climb the slope behind the healer's cottage. "There's a bank along a stream where I remember seeing a black seam. It's as good a place to start as any."

"If you do find firestones, you're fortunate they're so high on the mountain."

Bewildered, Gren paused, unable to follow her train of thought. "Explain."

Trell's multiple braids jingled as she shook her

head as though she didn't understand his lack of comprehension. She kicked a cluster of small pinecones with the tip of her boot. "The wagons will travel uphill empty, downhill when full. Much easier for horses or oxen to transport the heavy loads."

Once again, Trell's insights amazed him. His steps lightened as they hiked the animal trail. "Good thinking. I hadn't considered the difficulty or hardships in securing the resource."

She had other traits that he admired as well... No, admired wasn't strong enough. Desired fit much better. She already owned his heart. All he ever fantasized about was drawing her into his arms and kissing her silly.

He stumbled with the reminder and wrenched his thoughts away at the sound of gushing water. His steps quickened. "We're almost there. Just a bit farther."

Trell hurried after him. "I don't mind being in the woods, among the trees, even if some remind me of skinny dwarves compared to those in Demit Woods. They aren't as thick and are far narrower like toothpicks. Still, I find beauty in them and they invigorate me. The woodsy scent and earthy smell of fallen leaves almost makes me homesick."

"Don't be sad."

"I'm not..." She looked around as though taking in her surroundings. "Being in the mountains, I imagine at the autumn equinox, the cold tingles your nose while the semi-warm sun highlights the various colors."

He smiled at her words. Her ability to see beauty in simple things was another trait he admired. "Your descriptions make me appreciate the woods more than ever."

A stream trickled louder. The sound increased his pace, and when they reached the edge, he knelt down to check the water. A blackish color reflected just below the surface, the same as the firestones.

For good reason—a thin, black vein cut along the bank, just below the topsoil.

Gren grabbed a rock and knocked off a chunk that protruded into the water. He stuffed the lustrous material into his pocket. "If this burns like the Fezners' firestones, I'll bring men to excavate."

****

Trell checked the sun's progress in the sky. Being in the unique woods relaxed her, but the short pause with Gren left her with plenty of questions. Kula's healer had been murdered. By whom? Should she inform Gren? She flicked a glance at the soldier who accompanied them. He was close enough to overhear their conversation.

While she debated with herself, Gren stopped to lean a shoulder against a tree. "You still look sad. What's wrong? Do you miss your home much?"

"Not really. These woods make me a tad melancholy is all."

"I will do my best to make your stay pleasant."

Smiling, Trell appreciated the kind thought. "Not being in charge makes that harder."

"True. Just know that I care." Gren straightened. "Meanwhile, we should head back to Dori's. The wagon should be arriving soon."

Sure enough, by the time they returned, a wagon being pulled by two horses slowed to a stop in front of the hut.

Trell spent the balance of the day and the next two

supervising removal of plants and settling them in quarters that King Har provided within the courtyard of the castle. It gave those needing her services easier access.

Or so he said.

And he was proven correct.

Almost immediately a man approached. A gash on his arm bled profusely, requiring stitches. Trell stopped organizing her space to sew the fellow's arm with sinew and wrapped it with bandages to protect it from becoming infected.

Her second patient was a woman who sought a draught for insomnia. She laughed and suggested the woman place her pillow at the foot of her bed. No harm in recommending the Fezner remedy, especially if it worked. As a precaution, she also prescribed chamomile flowers and instructed the woman to brew them into a tea.

The king and Oded showed up close to the end of the third day. "You have made good progress, I see."

She smiled, then frowned when the plants quivered. No breeze entered the room to cause the movement. She remembered they mentioned a bejeweled scabbard. Eyeing both men, she noted each wore a scabbard decorated with gemstones. "I thank you for allowing me to treat people, Your Majesty."

He waved away her appreciation. "Oded's healer has not come to aid you?"

His tone was critical, but she had no wish to cause trouble. "Nay, she was feeling a tad sickly herself. I brought her a cup of ginger tea to settle her stomach."

"She's sickly all right. She swills *farbrenen vaser* too freely. I wager she'll be well enough to attend tonight's festivities."

"I'll speak with her," Oded said. "She'll do her part."

After the two men left, Trell turned to the plants. *"What is it? Did you recognize someone?"*

"I-t, it was he," the mountain mint said with a tremor in its tone.

"Which one?"

"I cannot say. I sense danger. The smell was the same as the night Dori died."

Which man was the culprit—the king or Oded?

Troubled by the plants' allegation, Trell finished her tasks for the day and went to her quarters in the tower. A new door hung on repaired hinges, replaced the next day. She entered her room, and a gown of lace and silk in a rich, metallic brown lay upon her bed.

For her?

Never had she worn such an exquisite piece. She hesitated to don the gown, but when she did, the lush fabric tickled her skin. With a burst of laughter, she spun around the room until winded.

Halting, breathless, she opened her chamber door. A somber-faced guard awaited in the hallway to accompany her to the great room and follow her every step.

She smiled to hide her annoyance and pretended she could come and go as she pleased, even though surrounded by people. That was one of the things she relished being human. Freedom. As a tree she'd been rooted in place.

The guard tipped his head.

The banquet brought the castle to life. Servants scurried down halls with their arms full. Every sconce and candle flickered with golden light, turning night into day.

Hurrying along the passageway, she slowed as she neared the great hall. The loud drone of voices masked the pounding of her heart. Dozens must fill the room.

Nerves rippled down her spine until she squared her shoulders and gulped a deep breath. Chin up, she pushed open thick double doors to the great hall.

Chapter 13

What was taking Trell so long?

The great hall sang with voices as people clustered in boisterous factions. Gren cast curious glances at them as he stood with friends. He recognized most. Some were Demic lords from other kingdoms. Many nobles he recognized were from Kula. The collection of bodies heated the room hotter than the crackling fire in the massive fireplace ever could.

"Stop looking at the entrance. She's a woman. She'll come when she is good and ready," said Crit, a tall nobleman whose razor-thin frame belied a hidden strength within, and one of Gren's oldest friends.

The other couple accompanying him were a husband and wife. Ebba, a petite woman with shiny brown hair and dark eyes that glinted with sharp intelligence, smiled. Her husband, Maxx, a mountain of a man, towered next to her and grinned ear to ear. Even if his size didn't make him stand out, his sandy-colored hair set him apart in a room of mostly brunettes.

"I can't help it." Gren checked the doorway for the hundredth time in anticipation of Trell's arrival. His breath caught when the doors opened at long last, and the beautiful, shimmering vision that he ached to see entered. The bronze gown he'd commissioned for her contrasted with her hair and made the sun-streaked braids shine like gold. "There she is."

Crit whistled low. "Fetch her quickly, before someone else does."

Gren laughed and made his excuses. He wove through the crowd toward Trell. Curious gazes followed his path until he stopped in front of her. "The gown suits you. You look stunning."

"My thanks. I've never worn anything this beautiful." Her smile stiffened when her gaze fell upon his brothers huddled together.

Gren followed the direction of her gaze, took her hand, and squeezed to reassure her. He wanted nothing to mar her experience in Kula. "Don't worry about them. They're my problem, not yours. I just wish I knew what they were planning. I don't trust them."

"It's not your brothers," she answered.

"What then?"

"'Tis a personal thing."

He prayed it wasn't too late to keep Trell safe. "If you prefer, I'll take you back to your room and make your excuses."

It took her a moment to offer him a smile. "Nay, I'll be fine."

"Fear naught. I'll protect you."

"Now you sound like my brother, Cress. I had to explain to him that as a healer, I have my own resources. A pinch of belladonna in tea can sicken a person or kill. And I know where to slip a blade between the ribs to puncture a man to bleed out."

"And here I thought you looked beautiful, as delicate as a flower. I'll keep in mind that you're not helpless and can protect yourself. In the meantime, Oded has issued a challenge for the throne."

She gasped. "Will you fight him?"

An odd note sounded in her voice. Was that worry for him? The notion she might harbor concern for him appealed more than he cared to admit. "If I must. Though I have no wish to spill blood with him."

When he turned to escort Trell through the crowd, he dismissed the soldier following them with a flick of his hand. The man bowed his head and went to stand near the wall. "Before we sit down to dinner, may I introduce you to some friends?"

"Must I? I'm not very good with groups."

His mind scrambled to understand. "I find that hard to believe. You took to the Fezners with ease."

"It was my duty to go with Dotra. He needed a healer."

Voices waxed and waned throughout the great hall. Most guests started arriving for the festivities by midday, and now the profuse consumption of *farbrenen vaser* had put a rosy glow on many a cheek and everyone in a merry mood. For Trell not to share in the celebration seemed wrong. "Is my brave healer afraid of meeting new people?"

"Not that. I've always been shy meeting new people."

Interesting.

"You are planning to travel around discovering unknown medicines and treatments. How will you overcome this timidity?"

"Through sheer willpower. Being shy isn't being a coward."

Gren chuckled as he wove through the crowd. The more he learned about Trell, the more he appreciated her uniqueness. "My apologies. You are a powerful individual in your own right as a healer. People should be respectful. A wise person never knows when they'll require your services."

Trell smiled softly. "As I recall, you hesitated going into the Fezner camp."

"I was in disguise, trying to keep my identity a secret."

"Perchance I'm just a little tired. And nervous."

"Fret naught. I'm here for you." He winked and adjusted his hold to lead her to the group he had just left, whispering as they went, "Once people get to know you, they'll appreciate you like I do."

"In that case, I would be honored to meet your friends. For the people, then." She offered a meek smile.

Gren stifled a laugh. The phrase resounded like the one he repeated when convincing himself his actions aided the people.

He stopped before the trio. "Lord Crit, Lord Maxx, and Lady Ebba, may I introduce Healer Trell. Trell, these three are my oldest, dearest friends. You can trust them with your life."

A wicked twinkle lit Trell's eyes. "You have friends. I'm surprised."

Ebba giggled. "Oh, I like her. You'd better keep her close to your side, Gren. Someone is bound to steal her."

The statement a repeat of Crit's words, even uttered in jest, raised his ire. "She's not a possession."

"Ignore him." Crit bowed over Trell's hand to brush a kiss across the top. "A delight, my dear. You must excuse Ebba. She delights in teasing Gren. She fancied him once, but in the end, chose to wed Maxx."

"And a lucky man I am." Maxx draped a muscular

arm over his wife's shoulder. "Thank the Gods, Gren wasn't a poor loser."

Gren cleared his throat. "While winning is always preferable, in this case, Ebba did right by herself. I would never have suited, and she deserved the best."

The foursome laughed, and Trell stared at them with a puzzled expression.

Ebba stepped closer to Trell. "It's all right, my dear. We have always been open and honest with each other, even when the truth stings."

Gren took a deep breath. "We'd better take our seats. I see Father directing his other guests to sit. I'm sure he wants to officially introduce Trell and Oded's healer to everyone."

People shuffled to the long table. Chairs scraped the floor. Voices waxed and waned as guests settled into their spots.

The king waved Trell and Gren over to his side. He signaled Trell to sit on his left, and the fake healer to his right. Gren sat beside Oded's healer. Codo sat on the opposite side of Trell, giving her a buffer from Oded. Riff sat next to Gren, and Gren was glad to see Maxx and Ebba across the table from him. Crit sat farther down, but still close.

Gren eyed the other guests, young and old, around the table. His friends' status seemed to have risen since his return. Next came lords and ladies favored by his father, even his aunt and cousin, which came as surprise since his father loathed both. At the far end of the table, mixed together, were Oded's and Riff's closest associates. All scowled. Clearly, they found sitting at the lower end of the table distasteful.

His father rose from his chair. "Welcome, friends

217

and neighbors. I invited you here tonight to introduce the newest members of our kingdom—the Healers Trell."

****

Gasps and low murmurs of surprise ascended to the rafters. People shot glances at one another, nervous about how their reactions to the announcement would be perceived.

Upon hearing her name, for a long heartbeat, Trell remained sitting. Being shy didn't impact her healing abilities, but she detested being the center of attention. Gathering her courage, she swallowed the knowledge that the feast would not last forever. It would have to end.

The imposter shot to her feet, weaving off balance, a grin revealing yellow teeth. She lifted her goblet. "Greetings, my lords and ladies."

No mention of aiding villagers.

Trell rose from her chair as though the weight of the world sat on her shoulders. "Thank you for the kind welcome, Your Majesty. I'll tend as many as I can during my stay."

A smile of approval showed on the king's face. "I have been informed that you have already aided several of my subjects. They are pleased with your ministrations."

Warmth heated Trell's cheeks. "I did what I could."

The king waved her to silence. "You'll love living among us. Shall we begin introductions?"

Live among them... No, no.

Trell pursed her lips to keep from contradicting the king before his subjects. She drew on power within her

218

to project a calm exterior. Mentally, she vowed to explain in private that settling in Kula for an extended length of time was not in her plans.

Introductions were made around the table. Names and titles became a blur. Most forgotten instantly. Intentionally. Trell doubted she would meet half of them again.

The king remained standing when she and fake Trell reclaimed their seats. He drew his blade and rapped the hilt against his tankard until everyone focused their attention on him once again. "Your attention, please. As you are aware, I sent my sons on a quest to find Healer Trell. While two healers, both named Trell, were found, I deem Gren the winner."

Oded jumped to his feet, face scarlet. "Father! I should be declared your heir. I returned with mine first."

"And she is a fake. Now, let me finish." The king turned his back on his eldest son. "For his successful accomplishment, I pronounce Gren as my successor upon my death." He puffed up his chest, looked around the table at the spectators, daring any to contradict him. When no objections were voiced, he tapped each side of Gren's shoulders with the flat side of his blade.

Trell beamed at him to show her approval. From the warmth seemingly pouring out of his brilliant green eyes, the honor bestowed upon him meant the world to him.

Cheers went around the table, the loudest from Gren's friends. Applause exploded. The clapping diminished farther down the table.

The king sheathed his sword, settled in his chair, and summoned refreshments. For the next quarter hour,

219

servants delivered tray after tray of venison, various fowls, fish, and other dishes.

Trell leaned closer to Codo sitting beside her, saying, "His Majesty puts on a fine table."

The steward flattened his long white beard and smiled, cloudy eyes crinkling with pleasure. "We haven't had a feast or gathering of this magnitude in some time, Healer. This is all for you. We want you to feel welcome in Kula."

She lifted her mug to sip her ale. As she did, the distinctive odor of burning flesh—nauseating and sweet—pricked her nose. Her gaze sped around the table, searching for the cause. No one seemed to smell what she did. Did her training in the Halls of Medsin heighten her awareness?

Then she found the cause.

King Har's elbow rested on the table, a candle flame greedily licked his bare forearm as he carried on an animated conversation with a couple, an older woman and younger man, seated half-way down the table. The smell of burning flesh fogged the air. Her breath caught in her chest. This had happened not once, but twice.

Her brain reeled for an explanation. An Untouchable lost his sense of touch first. Had the king contracted the dreaded disease? Could this be the reason he ordered his sons to find her...and Torkel?

Ever since Gren informed her his father sought a dragon, Trell had sought a reason for the king to desire one. Only last night in the wee hours before dawn did she recall an old myth claiming a dragon's skin cured the disease.

Ridiculous mythology.

Superstitious nonsense.

Yet her stomach rolled at the thought of sacrificing Torkel's life to save one person. She would die before she would let him be harmed.

Glancing up, she met the king's stare. A cold fire flickered in the green depths. Panic tried to rise within her. She beat it down and averted her gaze. The spoonful of meat she'd just eaten stuck in her throat.

Out of the corner of her eye, the king yanked down his tunic's sleeve. Had he seen her observation?

She yawned as though tired, then blinked rapidly as if bashful. Let him think she witnessed nothing. She doubted anyone else caught his mistake.

Stal Og Har surged to his feet. The quick motion caused the servant stationed behind him to rush forward. The king whispered in the man's ear. Stiffening, the fellow spun on his heels.

People stopped eating to whisper at each other, speculation creating a buzz through the great hall about what was happening.

Everyone watched the servant scurry to a pair of soldiers. He leaned close to speak in a whisper. They straightened to attention and marched to stand behind Trell's chair.

Hair lifted on the back of her neck. Trell kept her gaze forward and saw Ebba chew her bottom lip in concern.

King Har looked at his guests. "I must apologize. It has suddenly occurred to me that we have overwhelmed the newest member of our village. She has spent days retrieving Healer Dori's herbs and medicines and setting up a room to treat patients." He waved soldiers closer. "Escort Healer Trell to her new quarters. We have overtaxed her. She is tired."

Gren leapt to his feet, his chair sailing halfway across the room when the soldiers put their hands on Trell. "Unhand her!"

The command in his voice stopped the soldiers in their tracks.

Tension pulsated in the room like a beating heart. As a tree, in time of danger, Trell could move sap into her roots to keep safe, but not as a human. Try as she might, her heart thumped in her chest so hard she swore the entire room could hear the pounding. She willed her breathing to slow, refusing to panic.

"Stand down, Gren," his father answered. "Can't you see your poor healer is exhausted? I am merely considering her welfare. I should have insisted she rest longer to recoup her strength before presenting her to our friends and neighbors."

Green fire spit from Gren's eyes as he swung the full force of his fury at his father. His hand went to his sword. "If you mean her any harm. You'll regret—"

"Are you threatening me?" the king interrupted.

"You tell me." Gren pulled his sword and charged around the table.

The two soldiers near Trell closed around her. Four others rushed forward to block his path with swords drawn. People leapt from their chairs to avoid the confrontation.

Lords Crit and Maxx rushed to Gren's aid but were routed by even more soldiers.

Gren managed to shove one soldier against the wall, pressing his arm against the man's throat until he slid to the floor. The other soldiers didn't hesitate. They rushed him with swords swinging.

Trell screamed at the clang of metal against metal. She twisted within the iron hold of the men trying to drag her out of the hall. The bells at the ends of her braids clattered, the familiar tinkling almost soothing in the chaos. Curiosity got the better of her soldiers and they halted in midstride to watch the fight.

It wasn't a fair fight. Gren didn't have a chance.

One soldier sneaked behind him and used the hilt of his sword to crash against Gren's skull. Blood gushed, and Gren crumpled.

Trell screamed and struggled even harder to free herself to no avail. Tears filled her eyes and blurred her vision. "They killed him."

The king's complexion blanched. He eyed Gren's still body on the floor and back at her. His voice cracked with authority that came from years of being absolute ruler and expecting utter obedience. He raised his gaze to the soldiers. "You heard my orders. Obey."

****

Gren woke with a pounding headache. All he remembered was intense worry brimming in Trell's brown eyes. Clenching his fists, he glanced around to find himself still in the great hall. People around the table eyed him with different expressions—curiosity, contempt, and compassion.

Where was Trell?

Damn, he should have known better than to trust his father. While the army sided with him against his brothers, being well paid, they remained steadfastly loyal to the older Har. No one disobeyed him. Ever. His father's word was law.

The rustling of silk at his side brought Ebba into his line of sight.

"Thank the Gods. We thought you were dead," she gasped, face pale.

Maxx held her hand to soothe her. "You were out for quite a while."

"Where's Trell? What have they done to her?"

"They took her away," Ebba explained in a low voice. "Don't worry. Crit followed them. He'll find out where they've taken her and report back."

Other lords and ladies reclaimed their seats and acted as if no interruption occurred.

Riff offered him a hand to help him stand. "Next time think before you act."

Gren hissed. His head pounded.

Riff laid a hand on his arm. "Don't get me wrong. Just keep a level head, if you wish to retain yours."

All that mattered at the moment was Trell's well-being. Was this what love felt like? To put someone else's welfare before his own. To care for them above all else. If so, Gren hoped to have time to find out.

With a nod, he stepped toward the long trestle table. "By the Gods," he shouted at his father, "your so-called concern doesn't fool me."

The king glowered. "You misjudge me, Gren. What kind of host am I if a guest collapses from exhaustion while under my roof? Did you not notice the dark circles under her eyes?"

Since when did his father care about another being? Every survival instinct Gren possessed went off at the same time. "I brought the healer to Kula to ply her trade. I'm entitled to know your designs for her. If anything happens to her…"

A blink of sadness came and went on Stal's face. "Careful. I'll only take so much of your mouth. If—"

224

"You can't let him defy you, Father," Oded encouraged when their father seemed to falter. "He's being belligerent. Rebellious. If other Demic lords learn that you let him speak in such a disrespectful manner, they will think you've become weak."

Gren peered at the noblemen sitting at the table. Too late. They witnessed the exchange and would carry the tale far and wide across the land. He scowled at Oded sitting, staring at him with an indolent expression.

While Gren longed to smash his fists into anything, he noticed something odd. Oded no longer wore his prized pendant and as far as Gren knew he never took the jewelry off.

Riff laid a cautionary hand on Gren's arm once again.

Shaking it off, the warning gave him pause. He couldn't help Trell if locked up. Clamping his lips shut, he stomped out of the room, boot heels echoing in the long hall. A door slammed behind him, and running footfalls spun Gren around to confront the person trailing him.

"So, brother, what do you think is really going on?"

Riff's inquiry startled Gren. He never expected his younger brother to possess sympathy for his plight—or Trell's. How much dare he say? "I don't know, but I plan to get to the bottom of this."

A smile materialized on Riff's face. He patted Gren's shoulder. "Glad to hear it. I never really believed in this silly quest."

"Yet you participated."

"Of course, I did. The chance to become the designated heir was a lure even I couldn't resist. Now, it doesn't matter. You won." He glanced around. "If anything goes awry, all you have to do is ask for my help."

"Switching sides?"

A pained expression flashed over Riff's face. "Let's just say I have no wish for Oded to obtain the throne. I'll never forgive him for what he did to Brit.

Gren narrowed his eyes. Revenge? Was it really possible that Riff turned on Oded over a woman? He wanted to trust him, but dare he?

****

"This isn't the way to my quarters. Where are you taking me?" Her leather soles scraped cobbled stones as the soldiers led her away from the noise of the great hall. She swore footfalls thudded behind them but couldn't turn around to see who followed.

The younger man was one who had accompanied Gren and her to the healer's hut. He aimed a solemn face to her. "My apologies, Healer. King Har's orders were to take you to your new quarters. You'll see soon enough."

And she did.

To the dungeon.

Trell passed empty cells before ducking through a door that barely reached her shoulders. The clank of heavy metal dropping into place sent a shiver down her back.

By the strong, pungent smell, the cell had been recently scrubbed with lye, and afterward fresh rushes scattered on the floor. Even a blanket lay folded on the floor. Not exactly how she envisioned a cell to look.

In preparation for her arrival?

Taking a second breath, beneath the lye she caught

a musty odor, and a strange coldness occupied the room while a pale glow from the outer passageway provided a dim light. As she wondered, her teeth chattered. The chill in her cell brought back memories of winter. It felt as though her blood thickened and slowed like sap did during the dormant time.

Then the scurry of tiny feet over the cobblestones beyond her cell elicited a smile. It just proved that even in the bowels of the castle life stirred. The sound reminded her of squirrels racing up her trunk as an Ossa.

Still, she was a prisoner...in a dungeon in a strange land.

And of her own heart. Gren held that!

Except he was dead.

She feared crying, afraid if she started it would never end. Blinking, fighting heartbreak, her eyes adjusted to the darkness as she struggled with the admission. Blessed Heyln! Gren...dead. She'd lost him. *I'll never see him again.* It couldn't be possible. Why was she heartbroken? The man had lied and deceived her. How could she harbor affection for him? Love had no place in her life. Yet she couldn't deny her feelings.

Her only recourse was to reach out to Torkel. *"Torkel, where are you?"*

"A fine mess you got yourself into," mindspoke the dragon as if he read her thoughts. *"Describe where you are."*

"It's dark. I can barely see in front of me."

"Try," Torkel insisted. *"How can I rescue you if I do not know where to find you?"*

"I'm in a dungeon. Below the castle. No windows. The door is solid. There is no way you can reach me

227

without exposing yourself."

A snort echoed in her head. *"Then you'll be surprised when I do."*

"Don't be foolish. You must stay hidden."

"Let me destroy these puny humans. I've honored my word and never used my acid breath against a living thing other than foraging for food. I could have lied, you know. But I didn't."

"And I sincerely appreciate your truthfulness."

"Give me the word, and I'll destroy those who dared to imprison you. Starting with that pompous human who considers himself ruler of this kingdom. I'll leave Gren for last."

Trell groaned. Gren was already dead. Gone. The stark truth was she could not allow harm to befall innocents. And that was exactly what would occur if Torkel started spraying his saliva.

As tempting as the idea for what these people did to Gren, she refused to let anything happen to her friend. *"You'll do no such thing. If they'll murder a prince, imagine what they'd do to you if you reveal yourself."*

"Why do you keep repeating yourself? What if I tell you I have counted ten times that you have said that since we began this journey?"

"Then I'd have to say thank you for keeping track," she mindspoke back, then added, *"By Heyln, Torkel, think!"*

"Save me from taxing myself. Tell me."

Trell ignored the sarcasm. *"If you show yourself, it confirms the reality of dragons. You put your entire species at risk."*

"Let me think."

"Please do.

Torkel didn't respond, which suited her. She needed privacy to think for herself.

Which she tried to do that night. The hours stretched as she huddled on the floor with a thick blanket to cover herself. That was another odd thing. The blanket's quality surpassed anything she would have expected to see in a dungeon.

She stared at four strange holes in the ceiling, fretting about Torkel's whereabouts and hoping he escaped while able.

She had no idea how much time passed. With each breath, hope withered like the plants in Dori's hut. Would someone care for those she'd brought to the castle?

Clenching her fists, she groaned. She had never appreciated the sun's warmth on her face, air flowing over her arms or rain moistening her skin until those simple pleasures were beyond her reach. What she assumed was the next day, she paced off the length and width, counting each step so often she could accomplish it blindfolded.

When would the torturer come? If it weren't for eating twice, she thought she had been forgotten. Waiting was pure agony.

When creaking iron hinges roused her, she rolled over, rushes poking her backside. A sadness seeped into her bones that she credited to the dankness of her cell.

"Trell?" a familiar voice called softly.

Blessed Heyln! Her heart recognized the owner. Her breath caught. She couldn't move a muscle. The pale wash of a candle let a ghost come into view.

"Gren. I thought you were dead. I saw you die."

"It'll take more than a blow to the head to kill me." He cast an assessing gaze around her surroundings, seemingly flummoxed at the cleanliness.

A warm wave of joy spread through her veins. "What are you doing here?"

"Crit followed you and the soldiers. He told me where to find you. I'm so sorry it took me so long to get here."

"You're here now."

She didn't need to hear any more and leapt to hug him. The strong male scent that belonged only to Gren shoved away all her worries. It meant the world to her that he found her.

The solitary candle lit the cell with a soft glow. Gren set it down and stood before her, solid and comforting. A lump swelled near his temple. The flickering light showed regret twisting his features into a tormented mask.

She stared, amazed he made no attempt to hide his emotions. The response tore up her insides. He had deceived her, tricked her into coming to Kula. Yet she couldn't blame him for another's actions. Gren didn't give the command to imprison her. The responsibility lay with his father.

His hands stroked her like a baby, volunteering comfort. "Forgive me. This is all my fault. I brought your healer's cape and staff, though I doubt either will do much good. We've got to break you free of here. My friends will help. Crit volunteered to hide us. So did Ebba and Maxx. All we'll need to do is reach them."

Leaning into him, she selfishly took a few precious moments to soak up his warmth before pushing away. "They're good friends, but you must leave. If your father learns of your visit, he'll throw you in a cell, too."

"My father be damned! This shouldn't have happened," he said between brushing wisps of hair out of her face. When he stopped, he seemed to study her. "I do have a question, though… You saw what happened with the candle? His lack of reaction. That's why he imprisoned you. It has to be the reason. There is no other."

The absurdity of the situation hit her hard, standing in rushes, the light of one tiny candle flickering and being cross-examined. She almost laughed before gathering her composure. She wavered for a moment. "Ah, you speak of the Untouchable illness."

"I am. I saw his arm in the flame. He didn't feel any pain."

"He can't keep his condition a secret forever. The signs are starting to manifest. Someone is bound to notice. We did."

"What about the Fezner medicine?"

Trell shrugged her shoulders. "I've resided at the castle for four days. He and Oded came to the room while I was setting it up for patients and never mentioned treatment."

"You know the law when it comes to Untouchables. It applies to everyone."

"I am a healer first and foremost. My first concern is always my patient. It is not my responsibility to report his condition to the authorities. But it doesn't matter. I am imprisoned."

Gren let go of her to rub his hand over his face. "You're not alone. Never alone. The lack of contact is a ploy to unravel you. It makes prisoners nervous when

231

left alone, adding to their fear that they'll be tortured or simply locked away and forgotten."

His explanation didn't ease her fears. "Those thoughts crossed my mind."

When Gren held out his arms, she stepped into them willingly. "I don't care what he does to me," he said. "You do not deserve being treated like a criminal."

Her heart hammered against his chest. "If you really care about me, leave the door unlocked when you depart. I'll just slip out in the middle of the night."

"You forget the guards. They have standing orders to kill escaping prisoners."

An uncomfortable silence stretched between them.

"He already has killed. I suspect he murdered your old healer."

There... she said it.

****

Gren nodded. As he surveyed the cell's interior, Trell snuggled against him. A sense of right settled over him that made finding her the best thing to ever happen to him. "I was afraid of that. He probably sought Dori to question her about dragons and disliked her responses."

"That poor woman. What now?"

He blew out a harsh breath. The spark usually gleaming in Trell's dark brown eyes had been replaced with exhaustion, and Gren hated seeing it there. She didn't deserve this ill-treatment. She was worth more than a kingdom to him. He loved her. Heart and soul. He wanted to spend the rest of his life with her.

He rested his hands on her shoulders. "You come first. I have no desire to sit on the throne if it means you must suffer."

She tensed at his announcement. "You can't do that, Gren."

"I can and will. Father must feel trapped and desperate to murder an innocent woman. Oded and Riff can fight over the kingdom. I'm returning you to Brenalin. If Father's price is your internment, he asks too much."

"What about the villagers?"

"Kula has firestones. You saw them. The one I tested burns as hot as the Fezners'. They are a resource worth mining. I'll leave Riff a note, explaining how they can improve Kula's welfare. Prosperity will come to the villagers. Everyone."

For a moment, Gren simply stood and studied her. He was attempting to free a prisoner. In his mind that was sedition against his father. A mortal offense. And here they were discussing trading opportunities and who would rule once he left.

The situation was almost humorous.

A sigh gushed from him and he drew her close to his chest. "You are my utmost concern."

"Gren, I can't let you renounce the throne. You'll jeopardize yourself and the villagers. Think of Lizzette. There are probably dozens just like her who will suffer without your protection."

Her concern for the people of Kula made him love her all the more. "I've already made my decision. I pick you. You are—"

"You can't. I won't let you. I'm a healer. I have my oath to uphold. I will try to cure your father, even if he keeps me locked up."

"I've made mistakes, Trell. Terrible ones. But I'm

asking you to trust me, to love me."

Chapter 14

Love me.

Trell already did. Imprisoned in a secret corner of her heart, just like in the dungeon, the truth lay exposed. Gren's vow bestowed her with hope.

When a stillness settled over the cell, her pulse raced and she swore her heart pounded so loudly that the guard outside could hear. She reached to stroke the side of Gren's face to satisfy herself that he wasn't an illusion.

Heat undulated through her body, and she latched her arms around his neck, eager to taste his kisses and return them with the same hunger she sensed building in his muscular frame. Lips met, and they kissed again and again. The kisses tingled, bringing a tantalizing craving to life in her body.

"Lie on your cloak," Gren suggested. "There's room for two."

Trell's mind turned to petrified sap. She'd listened to maids talk about clandestine trysts with suitors, but never grasped their enthusiasm...*until now*.

In unison, they knelt on the woolen cloak overlaying the freshly strewn straw.

Trell twisted to face Gren. "Love me. Love my body all over."

"It will be my honor."

When his hands covered her breasts, a storm of

delights erupted in her belly and lower. Heat, the likes of which she'd never experienced before, set her on fire.

"Oh, Gren." For all her medical training and study of the human body, what she experienced brought such pleasure and satisfaction her mind couldn't process the sensations. While fully cognizant of the mechanics, the proper words, the correct male and female anatomy, she couldn't recall a single instructor or tome mentioning the luscious feelings it created. All she had to go on were the hushed titters of castle maids. "How are…What are you doing to me? I feel hot, tingly. How are you doing this?"

He brushed fine hairs off her face that escaped her braids. "Doing what, love?"

Straw poked her backside, and she didn't care. Gren's caressing touch erased all discomfort. The sizzling between her legs urged her to rub against him, encouraging him to stroke her.

"Making me feel like this. This feels…it feels…amazing. How…how is it happening?"

A low laugh rumbled in his chest and he squeezed her close. "You are a healer. Surely, you know. It's quite natural between two people."

He started to move away…or so she thought. She clutched his shoulders. "What's wrong? Don't leave."

A choking sound of amusement came from him. "I don't intend to…Unless you've changed your mind, I am yours."

"Blessed Heyln." She snuggled against his hard body. "I want to experience all the delights of being a woman. With a man. With you. Show me what happens next."

"With pleasure, my dear," Gren murmured, her soft curves making him throb for her. He drew in the scent of her skin—vanilla with the hint of pine. The delightful fragrance shadowed him in his dreams and caused his heart to beat for her.

She was his.

He was hers.

In the dim light, his hand slid beneath her bodice. Her breasts were small, just the right fit for a man's hand. He rolled a nipple between his thumb and forefinger and felt it bloom like a flower.

"Oh, aye," she whispered. "All the studying in the world never prepared me for the pleasure shared between a man and a woman. I never knew it could feel so good. I thought the maids were being silly, exaggerating. I-I mean this is…I like how you make me feel. I really do."

A thrill shot through him. He wanted her ready. Hot and willing. His mouth came down to claim Trell's and he plunged his tongue to meet hers, then trailed kisses down her neck. His body ached for her so badly, he could hardly stand it.

Trell bucked beneath him. A whimper came from deep in her throat.

Being in a dungeon didn't matter. Only Trell did. This was her first time with a man, and he vowed to make her experience one to treasure. He snuggled closer and began untying her braids.

She reached to still his hands. "What are you doing?"

"Haven't you heard the legend about a man untying all the knots found on his bride on their wedding night?"

Trell touched her braids. The inch-long bells jingled with her movement. "This isn't our wedding night. Nor do I have any intention of wedding soon."

Gren refused to let disappointment dampen his mood. This might not be where he would have chosen to make love to Trell, for she deserved far better, but this place would have to suffice for now. "I wish to marry you."

Trell stilled. "I never thought of marriage."

He wouldn't push her for now. He gave the room a quick examination—wall to wall, ceiling to floor. Smaller than a Fezner's wagon. Not the place for a sincere proposal. He'd figure out a better, more romantic place and time to ask for her hand. Possibly a trip to Snowsquall Falls where they'd stopped on their way. "We can pretend. I've wanted to make love to you for a long time."

Nervous laughter spilled out of Trell. "In that case, is there anything else I should know?"

"Undoubtedly, but the most important thing is being with a man will hurt the first time, but I promise the pain will fade."

"Right now I feel wonderful. Absolutely naughty."

She epitomized innocence wrapped in a feminine package. Breathing heavily and deeply, he raised the silken gown that bunched between her thighs. Her legs were long and slender. In the dim light, her body glowed, flawless. How many nights on the road had he lay awake dreaming of her?

Far too many to count.

He caressed her velvet skin slowly, making his way to the center of her womanhood. Touching her, he found her wet, ready for him. He slipped a finger inside her and felt muscles constrict around it.

Fear jumped that he had pushed her too far, too fast. "Relax, Trell. Have patience. I'm just preparing you for me."

Flickering shadows made it impossible to judge the nuances of her expression. He had to go by the tone of her voice and the way her muscles tensed and relaxed.

She inhaled and blew out a shuddering breath as though making a decision. "For once, I have no patience. Just do it."

She didn't need to ask twice.

"As you wish." He rolled atop and slipped inside her in a single motion. She was tight, hot, and encased him perfectly. Restraining himself from moving inside the velvet sheath, he asked, "Are you all right?"

Unshed tears glistened in the candlelight. "Even forewarned, I wasn't prepared."

He kissed the tip of her nose. "It'll get better from here on out."

And it did.

****

For the next hour, Gren and Trell forgot about the outside world. Their world consisted of each other…until reality shattered their dream-like intimacy.

Gren sat up, regretting his words before he spoke. "I have to leave, Trell," he whispered in her ear.

She wiggled closer to him, sending waves of desire coursing through him. "Why?"

"To prepare for your escape. I'm going to fetch horses and supplies. Be ready when I return." He kissed her eyelids and the tip of her nose.

"I don't want you to leave."

"You know I must." He had to remain strong. Gren

hated leaving Trell in the dungeon and waited until acceptance dawned in her eyes. "I'll return, and we'll escape together."

With heavy steps, he separated himself from Trell's warm side, slipped from her cell, and emerged from a hidden door that led to the main staircase.

"You certainly took your time," his father announced, coming down the stairway, a smile lifting the corners of his mouth. He stopped several steps above him, claiming the high ground, a greater strategical position. "Oh, don't give me that quizzical look, Gren. That's not how a man should appear after bedding an attractive woman. You should feel nothing but satisfaction."

Gren froze even as his stomach lurched. His father had waited to waylay him. Had someone seen him head for the dungeon? Oded? He wouldn't have put it past his brother to run to their father and tattle on him for visiting the prisoner.

Or had it been Riff? He gave little credence to the thought. His younger brother had transferred his loyalty.

If not one of his brothers, who? How did his father know? Something akin to fear chilled him to the bone.

Gren inhaled deeply to steady his resolve. "I don't know what you mean."

"Come now, Gren. That offends me. I know your wits aren't addled. Cease playing an idiot."

Gren refused to give his father leverage. "I have much on my mind. Kula's welfare requires my full attention."

"Oh, really. Not the healer? I would have wagered a fortune that she appreciated your company," Stal countered. "She talks a lot, doesn't she? Personally, since your beloved mother passed, I prefer my women to remain silent while I satisfy myself with them."

Heat burned a path up Gren's neck to the tips of his ears. His father heard their conversation? Their lovemaking? "You're guessing, and I have no wish to banter about your assumptions."

A gloating smile flashed on his father's face. "Your surprise is showing. I'll tell you a secret. Did you notice the holes in the ceiling of her cell?"

Gren visualized the cramped room, recalling the four holes. He'd given them no consideration at the time. Clearly a mistake on his part. Of course, he had something far more pleasant on his mind. Now, he went on the defensive. "I don't know what you're talking about."

Stal chuckled at his bluff. "They're listening holes. Clever, huh? The original builders of Barg castle were aware that many plots are created by desperate people and who is more desperate than a prisoner. They lead directly to a secret chamber where I can hear every word being spoken in the cell. Everything."

An icy chill slithered down Gren's spine. Secret chambers? Listening holes? His mind tried to do an inventory of their conversation as he stared at his father. His gut clenched. Trell and his privacy had been violated by his father eavesdropping on them while they made love.

Was this a trap? A bluff?

Thank the Gods Trell and he hadn't discussed dragons. He could only imagine the consequences if they had. Still, that bit of relief didn't improve Gren's disposition. He remained on guard.

Stal stepped down a tread. "Oded isn't my heir. You are. I conquered this kingdom through sheer will. I would have the best man rule once I am gone."

Gren felt an eyebrow rise as he stared at his father in shock. A compliment? He tried to process the words. His childhood had been harsh, no room for error. At least that was his memory of growing up.

His world shifted beneath his feet. To accept that his father sanctioned him was a huge leap. After all the years of seeking the man's approval, to finally obtain it created an inner turmoil. Was this support enough? Gren didn't think so. While he loved his father, and always would, a chasm still divided them.

Now, Trell's freedom was at stake. He couldn't live with himself if she didn't have her liberty. He had to help her escape from the castle, from Kula.

Gren stepped to the same tread as his father. "And if I say I no longer desire it? Accepting the designation as heir is a decision I regret now."

"Gren, cease this foolishness. No sane man refuses a kingdom. You are the best candidate. Think of your family. Kula. You have always cared for the people. Do the villagers no longer matter to you?"

His loyalty was being stretched in different directions, but only one mattered. "I found something more important. Someone I love. I will not sacrifice Trell. If you don't want Oded or Riff, let Dule become king."

At the mention of his cousin, his father spat on the floor. "That bastard offspring of my sister's. I'll kill him myself before I let the oily scum sit on the throne. You don't have a choice."

"I disagree." Gren straightened, staring his father in

the eye. "You are not the only one who knows secrets. You have contracted the Untouchable disease."

"That's ridiculous!" His father waved his arm even as his gaze swept the area as though checking to see if people were in the vicinity. "Bring me the accuser. Let me face the fiend who would dare bring shame upon me."

Gren shook his head. His father put on a good show. "He's standing before you. Bullying me won't make the disease go away."

Stal leaned closer. A musky, sour odor like old urine came from his father, but not from his body, rather his breath. "You wouldn't dare. You know the consequences of someone being accused of being an Untouchable."

A noise in the passageway above them caused both men to fall silent in case a servant or someone overheard them.

A worried look flashed across his father's face. "Put aside these silly beliefs about me."

Gren chose his words with care. "If you heard everything, you know Trell and I believe it's true. Why deny it?"

Stal's eyes widened. "Because I refuse to acknowledge such a falsehood. Even an untrue rumor could cause us to lose everything. Chaos would reign. Other Demic lords would swarm like hornets in an attempt to conquer Kula." He stopped, swallowed, and checked for eavesdroppers. "What about this medicine I heard you and the healer discuss?"

Gren buried his surprise. Did his father realize by inquiring about the cure, he admitted the reality about his condition? "Ah, the Fezner medicine."

"I don't care who it belongs to. Where is it? Does it work? I want it."

"Release Trell first." If his father had any sense, he'd agree, except Gren doubted the probability of that happening. "I'm sure she'll be more than happy to treat you with it."

"What if it doesn't work? I'll still need her dragon."

Gren froze. What did he see in his father's eyes? Fear? Worry? His strong façade had cracked. Never in a million years did Gren expect to glimpse weakness in the man he'd idolized. "Did we discuss a dragon? I have no memory of such a conversation. How many times must I tell you? She has no dragon."

"So you say. Obviously, loyalty for the healer clouds your mind. That's understandable. She's beautiful, I'll give you that and would wager that she is worthy of loyalty."

Gren listened to his father in disbelief. The man was trying to distract him from the real issue at hand. "You wrongly imprisoned a woman I brought to Kula in good faith in the dungeon. I expected her to be treated with fairness and respect, deserving of her position as a healer. Not a criminal to threaten and mistreat."

"I had my reasons that I am not at liberty to discuss." Stal straightened as if his confidence returned. "Even if you think you have the upper hand, the real question is what will you do with your knowledge?"

Experience over the last few weeks had taught Gren that no one should suffer through no fault of their own. While wearing the rags of an Untouchable he had endured discrimination. It was a torment he wouldn't wish on his worst enemy.

Yet the man standing on the staircase before him was his father.

****

"Torkel." Trell sat on her cloak in the dim space of her cell and mindspoke. *"Can you hear me?"*

No response. Where was he? Had he fled Kula? She prayed he had.

Enough complications existed in her life right now without worrying about an arrogant dragon who acted as if he didn't care about his personal safety. Except she couldn't help herself. *Oh, Torkel...*

With effort, she set aside her apprehension about the dragon and rubbed her arms to warm herself as she went over her options.

Seeing Gren inspired her. He told her to wait. That he would return. Only she refused to let her fate be decided by others. Her life belonged to her. It was her responsibility. A sense of determination welled up. Time to take action.

She went to the door and put her ear to the thick wooden surface to listen. No sound came from the other side. A good sign. Positive no one could hear, she squatted in front of the door and picked up a bell removed from her hair earlier that night. The thick, one-inch bell was strong enough to work. She couldn't remove the clapper, so she pressed it against the silver side with her thumb and began scraping at the hinge.

Rusty flakes chipped away. After an hour she swallowed a scream. Frustration rose. It was taking forever to make progress. She gnashed her teeth until her jaw ached. Maybe she should try calling Torkel, again.

No! She would do this on her own.

Sweat beaded on her brow. Her fingertips cracked and became raw, but she rejected quitting. Finally, a glint showed a tiny gap between the hinge and pin. Progress.

Inhaling a deep breath, she savored the victory. She wedged the bell's silver lip against the underside of the pin and tapped the bell's shoulder with the palm of her hand, trying to keep the noise to a minimum. Nothing happened. She tried again and again.

On the sixth try the pin inched an infinitesimal fraction. Her heart leapt. Her plan was working, making freedom within her grasp.

****

Gren worried about Trell as he remained on the stairs where his father waylaid him when a hand clamped on his shoulder. Iron fingers sank into his muscle. The strength surprised him because it was stronger than Maxx's, and his giant friend had the strongest grip he knew.

Turning around, he came face to face with a black-haired man whose strange golden eyes pierced him with their intensity. "You? How'd you gain access to the castle?"

"That's insignificant. You remember me. Good. That'll save time on explanations."

Gren composed himself. "What do you want? Only because you saved Trell from drowning, I owe you a debt of gratitude."

The man stared at him for several long seconds in silence. "We need to talk. Is there a place where we can do so without being overheard?"

Gren found himself nodding. "My bedchamber.

Follow me." They took the wide staircase, the treads creaking with their weight. "I never learned your name. What is it?"

"Does it matter?"

"It does to me. I'd like to know who I am speaking to."

They hurried down a passageway covered with thick rugs that muted their footfalls.

The golden-eyed man shrugged. "You may call me Torkel."

Gren slowed. "Torkel is an odd name. I've never heard it before."

"I should hope not. It belonged to a great ancestor of mine."

Gren cocked a brow but withheld making a comment. Reaching the door of his bedchamber, he opened it. He nodded for the fellow to enter. Inside, he closed the door and threw the latch to lock it. He pressed his finger to his lips for silence. Then he proceeded to hunt high and low for listening holes.

Being caught off guard once, shame on his father.

Being caught twice, shame on him.

His search produced nothing, and he spared a moment to glance out his window. The first stars of the night decorated the sky with a ghostly light that made him shudder. A whole day wasted without freeing Trell. As he stood trembling, he realized he could wait no longer.

"All clear." Gren stepped toward the man. "Who are you, really?"

A grin lifted to soften the hard planes that shaped the man's features as he sprawled into the nearest chair and made himself at home. His black hair glistened with a sheen of a gemstone. "Oh, I think you know, Human. Let's dispense with these silly questions and get to the matter which consumes both of us—Trell."

Realization hit with the force of a howling blizzard sweeping down the mountainside. Gren blinked in amazement at the creature before him. "You're the dragon. You—you deceived me once. Prove it."

The fellow stuck out his arm. A cloud darker than the darkest night hovered in the air around his hand. It sparkled with the consistency of firestone powder, and a faint odor of brimstone tainted the air. Ever so slowly a long, deadly-looking talon emerged from the glistening mist. It pointed directly at Gren, then wiggled back and forth.

"That's impossible," he gasped, disputing what was before his very eyes.

"You don't believe what you see. Typical of a human." The talon retreated into the cloud and disappeared. The cloud thinned until it evaporated. Torkel scratched his chin with a finger that must have been the talon. "And now your heart is beating faster. I can hear it. Ba-boom, ba-boom." The man slouched in the chair as only someone without a care in the world could. Blue-black brows lowered over golden eyes. "What does Trell see in you? You're weak, thick-headed. Mayhaps it's unimportant. What is, however, is how are we going to save her? After that—"

"I'm working on a plan."

The dragon-man dismissed his claim with a wave. "She doesn't belong here. She's an innocent. A breath of fresh air. Free her. Or I'll rain down a death this kingdom has never seen." A sigh that sounded like it came from a much larger creature echoed in the room.

Gren shuddered at the threat. He hated to admit being a little disorientated, a little in awe. "You wouldn't dare."

"Really? I am a dragon. Who will stop me? You? I doubt that. Unless, of course, your plan to free her is fool-proof."

He needed to stall, to gain time to think. "Do you have a plan?"

An ebony brow arched over chiseled features. "We could storm the dungeon. Brute force has always worked for me."

"It would alert my father's soldiers, Torkel. Several squads are bivouacked within the castle walls. We'd be overrun in minutes."

Those golden eyes narrowed. "What about a sneak attack? We could slip inside, eliminate the guards, grab Trell, and flee."

Gren kept his disappointment to himself. He'd wanted to hear if this Torkel could concoct a better strategy than his. Apparently not. "If escaping Barg's dungeon was easy, more prisoners would have tried. As far as I know, those who have, have never succeeded."

"There is always a first. What's your plan?" Torkel shot back a similar question to the one he had uttered moments ago.

Gren detested being negative, but Trell's life was on the line and he refused to take chances with it. Only one gambit existed for them to succeed.

"Similar to yours. Except, since the guards know me, I thought to subdue them before they could set off the alarm." Gren studied Torkel. Trell was willing to gamble her life to keep the dragon safe. If she trusted Torkel, maybe he should, too. After all, he'd saved

Trell from drowning in the ocean. "Did you bring reinforcements?"

"I am a dragon, fool human. I need help from no one."

****

Sweat dripped down Trell's brow. Moisture made the lace and silk of her bronze gown cling to her skin. She wiped sweat off her brow from the intense labor. Thank heaven the door to her cell had not been higher. It would have been impossible for her to remove the upper hinge. Of course, it made sense to construct it this way. A man would have to duck to enter or exit, putting him at a disadvantage if fighting erupted.

Clearly, the king hadn't given her shorter stature a consideration. A miscalculation to her benefit.

"Torkel," she mindspoke. *"Are you close?"*

"Close enough."

Relief tempered her enthusiasm. *"I'm escaping after the guards fall asleep."*

"Don't do anything rash. Wait for me."

She almost laughed with relief. Now he answered her! And advised her to use caution. That was a first. How the tables had turned.

The scrape of a chair on stone outside the cell caught her attention. Peeking through the keyhole, she watched one guard leave. Her heart pounded while she waited for the older one to close his eyes, for his flabby chin to slump onto his chest. When snores resonated in the open area, she dug her fingertips into the seam between the door and the wall on the hinge side. It took only seconds to loosen the hinge.

"No time. I'm leaving now. Meet me in the woods beyond the village."

Trell tossed her cloak over her shoulders. The red fabric would provide a measure of cover in the dark. Then she snatched her staff. She wasn't leaving it behind. Besides, if necessary, she'd clobber the guard if he started to wake.

Easing into the murky corridor, she sidled along the left side of the wall. A draft swept down the stairs. The air smelled slightly fresher. She could almost differentiate between the staleness and the woods beyond the castle.

Or did hope play tricks on her?

She acted on impulse. One step, then another. She used her fingers to feel along the rough shadows. Her mouth dried. It tasted like she'd eaten dirt. She thanked Heyln that no other prisoners were detained in the cells. They might have alerted the remaining guard.

Halfway to her goal of the stairs, a noise froze her in place. She cocked her head to listen. The clicking of tiny claws racing over the floor sounded like beating drums. Rats. Then slowly knotted muscles eased. The tiny creatures represented no danger.

Chapter 15

Torkel leapt out of his chair in Gren's bedchamber with the agility of a much smaller man. "Dammit! Trell is the most pigheaded human I know."

Gren shot a look at the dragon-man. At Trell's name his heart quickened with fear. He flicked his gaze at the door, at the window where night ruled supreme. "What's happening? Is she hurt? Are the guards bothering her?"

Golden eyes turned cold. "She's attempting to escape."

Gren grabbed Torkel's arm in an iron grip. "What? How can she…?"

"The healer can be stubborn," Torkel said with a smirk.

No question. Gren pictured her slinking through the damp quarters, trying to avoid the guards stationed on the far side of the dungeon. "All I care about is Trell. I thought you were her friend."

"I am, and because of that only she can raise my ire without consequences. I told her to wait, but she didn't heed my advice. She's attempting to free herself."

Odd. Torkel knew Trell's actions. He frowned. How?

Odder still, Gren believed him. Whatever his thoughts about the dragon-man, his gut knew Trell's welfare mattered to the creature and that counted in his favor. "How do you know?"

"I just do." Torkel yanked open the door and sprinted out, his long strides charging down the length of the hallway.

Gren raced behind him. By the way Torkel ran, like a man on a mission, practically flying down the passageway, he knew more than he was telling, and Gren was determined to stay on his heels. Especially if Trell's welfare was in jeopardy.

Servants stopped their tasks to gape at them. When one burly fellow with thick, muscular arms like a blacksmith took a step in their direction as if to stop Torkel, Gren waved the man off, and luckily no others tried to impede their mad race.

Codo came around the corner. His mouth dropped open, and his eyes widened until the whites showed. Gren's heart skipped a beat. The old steward might mention the peculiar behavior to his father. Gren prayed the two wouldn't meet any time soon.

A growing sense of urgency fueled Gren's strength. He couldn't believe Trell would try to flee on her own, but somehow he wasn't surprised. The healer had a mind of her own and this added weight to his conviction.

"Do you even know where we're going?" Gren huffed a step or two behind the dragon-man.

"She's in the dungeon, isn't she?"

Gren spun left at the bottom of the great staircase for a door tucked beneath the stairway. "Then this way. It's quicker."

Torkel twisted in midstep. The way he contorted his body only added proof that the man wasn't human.

Gren clutched the door handle and took a deep,

calming breath before pressing his finger to his lips. He peered into golden flames that practically leapt out of the other man's eyes. His disquiet increased. No one could withstand the fire in that gaze.

Torkel nodded in understanding.

Heedless of the danger, they slipped inside to find themselves at the head of a narrow staircase where the bottom steps disappeared into blackness. No sconces lit their way.

"I'll go first," Gren whispered. "There should be two guards. They know me. If they see you and don't recognize you, they'll become suspicious. They might sound the alarm, and that would cause problems."

Torkel snorted.

Gren crowded closer. He needed to stress the danger upon the dragon-man. "Consider Trell. We don't want to alert the guards or put her in harm's way. And if we can avoid harming them, I would appreciate it."

"Understood," Torkel whispered back.

"Good."

The dragon-man latched onto his arm with a grip that felt like it could crush bone. "I'm not an animal…without feelings. All I want is to free Trell and see her safe."

Gren smelled brimstone when Torkel's breath wafted across his face. "As do I."

The soft scuff of their boots on the stone stairs sounded unnaturally loud in Gren's head, but he decided his imagination played tricks on him. The descent into the bowels of Barg Castle seemed deceptively long. The lower they went, the stronger a damp, moldy stench grew.

At the bottom step, the glow from a candle flickered in the open area. Hot wax dribbled on the floor. The outline of a guard became visible. His chest's rhythmic rising and falling indicated he shirked his duty and was fast asleep.

Gren tried to peer into the dark corners. Where was the other one?

Torkel clamped a hand on his shoulder. "Stop. Someone is moving in the dungeon, coming in our direction."

Gren's heart skipped. He didn't doubt the dragon-man. "Probably the other guard." He'd hoped to avoid a confrontation. That seemed unlikely now. "I'll knock him out. Which direction is he coming from?"

"The right side of the open area. He's in the shadows."

Gren had never met anyone like Torkel. Of course, he'd never met a dragon. Every tome he had read about the creatures stated they were superior beings in all ways. It left him bewildered why they had all died. How could mere humans manage to destroy such magnificent creatures? Did Torkel possess powers like those ancient tomes suggested?

His questions were replaced with worry. If any harm befell Trell, would Torkel take revenge on Kula? The thought sent a chill racing down Gren's back.

****

Trell froze, her senses on high alert. A barely discernable noise and the barest whisper of movement in the air reached her. If correct, something disturbed the space before her. The wind? The guard returning? Scurrying rats?

She angled her head to better see what lay ahead.

255

Insufficient light prohibited her from seeing her staff's ribbons. She slid her hand to the top to check whether or not the ribbons fluttered in warning. They hung limp.

She freed a sigh of relief and gave a cursory glance around. The only light came from the flickering candle nub at the sleeping guard's feet on the far side. It sat in a puddle of melted tallow and sputtered, fighting to remain lit, but would extinguish itself in moments.

Trell waited patiently for that moment, burying her fears so deep that no emotion could escape and expose her position, then slid her foot along the cobblestones. Despite her caution, a second later her head was snared in a headlock. She swung her staff backward. It missed her captor's head.

Intense pressure set off buzzing in her ears. Stars exploded in her vision. Screaming was out of the question. Her head tipped as darkness descended. Whoever held her captive was about to snap her neck.

Her staff tumbled from her fingers but never clanged on the floor. Someone caught it. That meant two people were near her.

"Release her, Human," hissed a voice she instantly recognized.

Freed from the deadly grip, she choked out a whisper. "Torkel?"

"By the Gods, Trell." Gren wrapped his arms around her to cradle her against his side, and she melted into the heat of his body. "The force I was applying was for a man. I could have killed you."

With the pressure gone, she feathered fingertips over her throat. The candle relit, and she stared from one man to the next. These two were the most important men in her life, and somehow they had found each other and formed a bond to rescue her. "But you didn't. Let's get out of here. There's only one guard, but the other is due back any minute."

Turning as one, the trio fled up the stairway and out of the dungeon. They never stopped, just followed Gren's lead.

Trell shut down her emotions once again. Reflection would come later. Freedom came first.

If they escaped...

Flanked by Gren and Torkel, they raced across the bailey. Thank the gods, the late hour saw many inhabitants retired for the night.

The thudding of their footfalls alerted the guards to their approach. The two soldiers straightened to attention.

"Stand down," Gren yelled as they drew near. "All is well."

The guards obeyed, but Trell feared the bite of an arrow in her back as the trio raced through the main gate. They bypassed Kula and headed for the woods. Her lungs burned, muscles ached, but slowing or stopping wasn't an option until they reached the cover of the trees.

Pitch blackness greeted them away from the castle. No moon. No stars. Not a single light.

Both Gren and she sucked in huge breaths before sighing with relief. Torkel's vision was better than theirs, and he broke the trail. He displayed no symptoms of exertion. She gathered wobbly legs under her to wonder how Gren and Torkel had met again. Thank the Gods, dragons couldn't read minds. Oh, that didn't mean they didn't try or act they had the ability. She didn't want hers under Torkel's scrutiny. She hid the turmoil simmering inside her through a rigid posture because Torkel would pick up her thoughts through body language.

And what about Gren? Did he realize the tall, dark-haired man he followed was actually the dragon he sought? They seemed to be working in tandem with each other. She remembered how Gren had done the same with Dotra.

Torkel stood alert, his golden eyes studying the woods as clouds parted and the moon revealed itself like a silvery pearl. The boreal forest would provide minimal cover.

"No one moves among the trees except you and your party," said the Mother Tree.

"My appreciation," Trell responded.

"Safe journey, Once-an-Ossa."

Trell straightened, gasping between breaths. She compiled ideas and rejected them at almost at the same time. "What now?"

Gren wiped his hair back. "We get out of Demicland."

"An excellent idea." She slipped her hand into Gren's. His warmth garnered a smidgen of relief. "Will your father give chase?"

"We haven't been followed thus far, though I'm sure the guards will talk about our mad dash. As far as my father giving chase, I expect so. Besides losing a valuable healer, he is aware of the Fezner cure and wants it."

A shiver skittered down Trell's back. Doubt popped into her head. Had Gren spoken to his father about the Fezner cure? She would ask when more time arose.

"First he has to catch us," Torkel interjected.

Stars twinkled in all their glory. The night sky glistened black with moonlight. Then high mountain peaks trapped the clouds again and plunged the landscape into darkness. The world became a blur of shadows.

An owl gave a short, low-pitched hoot from the trees. She heard the first flap of wings, then nothing. The nighttime predator was on the move.

Gren huffed. "Don't underestimate him, Torkel. That's a common mistake his enemies have made in the past."

"He hasn't met me, yet."

Males! They were all the same. Not one possessed a grain of common sense.

Trell rejected asking the trees for directions. She put a hand on Gren's arm. "Which way? You know this land better than either one of us."

"We could head for Crit's domain. I know a shortcut. We should be able to reach it before dawn. He can hide us until the searchers give up or pass us by. Except there might be a slight problem."

The moon played peek-a-boo with the land and a shiver wracked her body. "Which is what?"

"My father might head there, too. All that matters now is he knows my friends are willing to aid us. He'll seek them out to stop us."

Her stomach rolled. Horror could come later. "Will they be safe?"

He inhaled deeply. "I think so. Crit's family brings vast amounts of revenue into Kula...or more importantly into Father's treasury. Father's not an imbecile. He won't risk antagonizing Crit's family and

259

losing that income. And they keep their methods a secret. Misguided rulers have fallen because they fought with the moneymakers. Father is a fan of history and has studied past leaders. He won't make the same mistake.

"Maxx and Ebba have many allies within the kingdom. Maxx has helped dozens of lords and peasants over the years, and all feel obligated to him. It would not be looked upon too kindly if they were penalized because we escaped."

Clouds passed over the moon again and plummeted the landscape into darkness once more.

Trell hoped Gren was correct. They needed Grandmother Lurri or another fortune-teller to predict the future or the outcome of their actions, and none were in their group. She didn't want the innocent reprimanded. "Dare we go to one of them?"

"I'm hesitant to do so. My father overheard our conversation in your cell."

"Everything…" She swallowed, a blush burning her cheeks even as she recalled the intimacy they had shared. Eavesdropping on a conversation was one thing, but while they made love… "Blessed Heyln! That's what you meant when you said he knew of the Fezner cure?"

A twig snapped as Torkel stepped closer. "Who needs humans? There's my cave."

Trell blinked, surprised. "You found a suitable one?"

"I did, but let me shift back into my natural state. Being human isn't my favorite form. It's too confining for my tastes."

Something big—an owl—flapped silent wings as it

glided above them. The wind that pushed the clouds dipped lower to rustle treetops. It became a cool breeze to stroke Trell's face and made her shiver even within the protective confines of her cloak. The moon peeked through the night, and she caught her friend's grin. Her heart pounded. He was up to something.

Before she could raise an objection, a black mist formed.

****

Gren stared, awestruck. The night around them thickened, blotting out every shadow around Torkel. The forest fell silent sensing a change. A haze formed around the dragon-man the size of a small hut. Gren wrinkled his nose as a foul smell that reminded him of sulfur polluted the air.

When the mist cleared, a glistening black dragon emerged with horns jutting upward. Torkel ambled forward on four legs with sharp talons gouging into soft forest loam. The beast shook its body like a dog after getting wet. When it plodded forward, each step vibrated the ground. His elongated muzzle, studded with ridges, swung in his direction.

A shiver ran down Gren's back. He swore the dragon's mouth lifted at the corners in a semblance of a smile. The only problem, it revealed a mouthful of deadly-looking teeth, each one the size of Gren's hand. The dragon turned huge golden eyes upon him, and Gren's mouth dried in an instant.

For the first time in his life, genuine fear rippled down his spine. A phenomenon he never expected to experience. Still, he stiffened his back and stood his ground. "You are an impressive sight," he said, trying to sound unafraid. "But if you show yourself to others, not only will confusion reign, but fear as well. And you could be attacked."

"I am aware, Human."

The words popped into Gren's head, stunning him. "You can talk? I—I mean in beast form."

Those expressive golden eyes narrowed. *"Are you addle-brained? You're hearing me, aren't you? That should answer your question."*

In an instant, the novelty of a giant dragon towering above him wore off like snow tumbling down the mountainside. Gren had always admired the stories of the creatures but never expected to see a living, breathing one. A true legend come to life. Much less converse mind to mind with one…

Despite his wonder, common sense rose in Gren. "What do…" he mumbled aloud, then stumbled with the new way of communication. "…*do you want from me?*"

"That should be obvious. Keep Trell safe."

Gren's gaze flicked in her direction. "I'd die for her."

Trell's mouth dropped open. "No one is dying for me. I haven't asked for that sacrifice. Nor will I allow anyone to volunteer."

"Bah! Have confidence in me. No one will die."

"What about this cave you mentioned?" Trell asked. "Tell me about it."

The dragon swung his massive ebony head toward her and dipped it lower. It amazed Gren as she stepped forward and scratched the oily-looking scales. He swore the beast started to purr. The pair acted like affectionate siblings, something he regretted never experiencing. He had to shake off his fascination to listen to the conversation inside his head.

"It's higher on the mountain," the dragon answered. *"Follow the animal trail. I will join you shortly. It's been spelled by dragon magic to hide you from keen-sighted eyes."*

"Where are you going?" Trell asked.

Torkel waddled away. *"None of your concern. Go to my cave."*

Trell pinched her lips together for a split second. *"What landmarks should we look for?"*

"Track the river upstream to the mountain ridge. There are some steep slopes, but keep climbing until it levels off to a low point."

Gren had heard enough. *"That description fits Black Mountain."*

Torkel swung his long snout in his direction. *"The name means nothing to me. What I found there is what counts."*

Gren debated asking questions. Time was of the essence. *"I know the general location of where you want us to go. We had better get moving."*

"Agreed. I will meet you there shortly." With that, the dragon flapped thick, leathery wings several times and rose in the air. Bits of debris fluttered in the air. He hovered above them for a few seconds, then flew off.

Gren's mouth fell open in stunned amazement.

A cool hand touched his arm. The sensation snapped him out of the spell. "We'd better move along."

He smiled to himself. While accepting that the relationship between Trell and Torkel as friends, the dragon was entrusting her safety to him. That contented him.

And they both were trusting him with the secret of a living, breathing dragon.

****

It had been over a month since Trell had last seen Torkel. In that time he seemed to have doubled in size. She had watched the dragon stretch his long, sinewy neck. Only a wingspan lacked from him being as tall as one of the taller evergreens. Even though these trees weren't the height as those in Demit Woods, Torkel had grown to an imposing size.

Now he circled in the sky with the snap of his wings and flew away.

Gren's gaze stayed glued on the dark sky. "Why couldn't Torkel fly us to his cave?"

"In spite of his size, I doubt he's strong enough to carry us together or individually. And I wouldn't ask him because the inability would embarrass him."

She spoke truthfully. She would never intentionally hurt someone she cared about and that included Gren. To love a person and fear that love at the same time seemed contradictory, but she knew she had to deny her feelings. If she truly loved Gren, she would have to protect him from herself.

First, though, they had to get away from Gren's father and find Torkel's cave.

Chapter 16

The boreal forest swallowed them.

"Be at peace, Once-an-Ossa. We will hide your tracks."

Trell smiled, grateful for the sense of security her woodland friends provided and actually slowed her pace. *"My thanks, Mother Tree. I am pleased to call you friend."*

That, she thought, and having Gren beside her. His hold slipped to her hand and their fingers entwined. The heat of his touch since making love thrilled her. She would never forget how well their bodies had fit together, or the passion they had shared. It would be a memory to savor for the rest of her days and into the afterlife.

The remembrance was broken by an owl hooting in the distance. She wondered if the creature was the same one that swooped over their heads moments before. Other nighttime predators stalked the woods, but she had no fear of them. Her staff would warn if danger approached.

A bigger concern was the dropping temperature. She pulled her short healer's cloak tighter. She doubted Cress had spelled it for these harsh conditions, never expecting her to journey into snowy mountains, but she would survive.

Gren intruded on her thoughts. "You've been quiet

since we left. Are you worried?"

Stopping to catch her breath, she vowed to never have contact with the king of Kula or his other sons again. They could rot in their own netherworld as far as she was concerned. She buried the twinge of guilt. Now, Gren and she put their hope in a dragon. "Just thinking."

He brushed a hand over the side of her face. "Fear naught. I won't let anything happen to you. I swear."

She leaned into his touch. "I'm not afraid," she said, and meant it. Swallowing, she stared at him. "Do you know where this cave of Torkel's is?"

This time he swiped brownish sable hair off his brow and glanced about as though taking his bearings. "From his description, it's located higher on the mountain than most people venture. Few are willing to scale above the tree line. It's dangerous. A journey not to be taken lightly."

She frowned. How hard could ascending a mountain be? "Why?"

"You have to have strength in your arms and legs to climb higher." He stopped as if debating with himself about how much to tell. "Mountains are dangerous. Lightning strikes can stab out of a clear blue sky or in our case, a night sky. Thunderstorms can form and drench us with rain and sleet. And there's always freezing to death or avalanches."

Her gaze flew to the night sky, never realizing the danger. "That doesn't sound safe."

He cupped her arm and urged her forward. "I painted a bleak picture, but somehow I doubt your dragon friend would advise us to hide in these mountains, if unsafe."

"You have a point." Heaving a sigh of relief, she moved on faster than intended.

Her feet skated on the glacial till, and she tumbled headfirst.

Gren caught her in his embrace. "You all right?"

"Fine. Don't worry about me." Her breath came out in white puffs. She slowed her steps, making sure each one touched solid ground.

Gren kept pace at her side. "If memory serves me correctly, there's an animal trail not far. I haven't followed it over the mountain, but we can use it part of the way. I'm just hoping Torkel's cave is close."

Trell hoped so, too. Three hours had elapsed since their escape. More and more pockets of snow dotted the ground, the largest accumulation in tree wells where the sun never reached. They should be several miles away from Barg Castle, but the arduous travel left her guessing at the actual distance. "Will your father send soldiers after us once he discovers our escape?"

"More than likely, but they won't know where to start. He'll have to divide his forces to comb the kingdom or systematically search each lord's manor one by one. I have no idea which method he'll use. No more worries. Save your energy for the climb."

She almost glanced over her shoulder to check on whether they were being followed, then thought better of it. She was being silly. "How much time do we have?"

"If I were him, I'd send a few men to my friends, then search the village, on the chance that the villagers would hide a healer. After that, I'd spread to the road. He's got desert horses, which are the fleetest mounts. They'll cover far more ground than a person on foot.

Someone will have to suggest looking in the woods or on the mountain."

"That doesn't give us much time."

"Very little. If those first three locations come up empty, they'll set up a grid pattern. Planning, gathering enough soldiers... All that takes time, but one thing my father knows how to do efficiently is plan. It won't take him long."

Trell pursed her lips. The explanation let hope bloom, only to dash it. "Then let's get as far away as we can."

"My thoughts exactly." He caught her hand again and continued trekking upward. "Where do you think Torkel disappeared to?"

The question pulled a frown out of her. Gren had voiced her own concern. "I have no idea," she replied, then in mindspeech asked, *"Torkel, where are you?"*

No answer. A breeze swept down the mountainside to flap her cloak. She pulled it tighter again. Torkel either refused to speak or had flown beyond the distance of mindspeech. It didn't do any good to fret over his whereabouts. He'd let her know soon enough. Bless the Gods being a tree for centuries left her patience in surplus.

The terrain continued to slant upward toward the snow-capped peaks. The trees thinned. Massive boulders jutted out of the ground. She eyed the mountains, remembering Gren's description how they created their own weather and the dangerous, unpredictable variations. The plunging temperature cut into her bones and made her nose run. The liquid froze before it reached her lip. She shivered again.

"Are you all right?" Gren asked.

She leaned on her staff. A quick glance showed the ribbons hanging down. A safe omen. "As well as can be expected under these conditions."

Gren's nose twitched, and he rubbed it. "I doubt we have far to go."

"Why do you say that?"

"I've never climbed this high before, but my nose is burning with a sulfurous odor. The firestone deposit must be huge to smell this strong."

Trell inhaled and wrinkled her nose at a pungent odor wafting in the air that she'd missed before. "Is it safe being close to a large deposit of firestones?"

"I have no idea, but I'll do whatever it takes to protect you."

The declaration melted her insides. She bobbed her head, her multiple braids striking the sides and tinkling with the movement. Plus, Torkel would never lead her into danger. Her trust in him was well-placed.

And thinking of trust, such a little word with big implications. It began with truth. Trust and truth went hand in hand. Should she disclose information about herself? How would Gren react? Would he be appalled? Was it going to be a stretch for him to believe her?

She wanted no more secrets between them. If honesty was going to exist between them, it made sense for her to take the first step.

"Do I appear young to you?" Trell asked between huffs.

Gren slowed his pace to match hers. "I would say young and beautiful. You don't appear over ten and nine."

Her heart skipped before brushing away the compliment. "Add a thousand to your figure, and you'll

269

be much closer."

Gren jerked to a stop, his emerald eyes widening with disbelief. "No one lives that long. Surely you jest!" He peered into the thinning woods as though answers existed within the gnarled, dwarfed trees. "I'm fully aware that I am the last person with the right to ask, but would you care to explain?"

She'd opened this discussion. Not to continue remained out of the question. "Cress really is my brother. He found a place in Demit Woods—a dragon circle—where time slowed so much it seemed to stop. One day while we visited this enchanted circle, I was trapped in an enchantment that turned me into an Ossa pine until he and Becca broke the spell."

Gren's mouth fell open. His face went from surprise to suspicion, and finally acceptance. "Are you going to age now? Or will you stay young forever?"

Relief flooded her. "Nay, silly. Outside the dragon circle, I age like a normal person. As a tree, I grew as tall as the ancient evergreens, but once free of the spell, I returned to the age I was before being enchanted."

He brushed back his hair. "You must have acquired powerful abilities during that time."

Holding back her frown, his response puzzled her. "Why would I? My brother is the wizard. He has magic. I was a tree. They have no special abilities or powers."

This time Gren frowned. "Truly?"

She inhaled a deep breath. Cool mountain air filled her lungs and she shivered. "All I can tell you is my experience left me with more patience than most. Oh, I might have an affinity for how to combine medicines to treat the sick, but I can't swear it was from being a tree or from studying hard at the Halls of Medsin after I was freed. I do know I intensely dislike hot summers that bring droughts and I also have a healthy respect for fire."

Gren stepped closer. "Nothing else?"

Nothing she wanted to discuss.

At least he didn't dismiss her announcement as fabrication. It took an understanding person to accept a unique idea. All she could do was hope Gren would perceive the significance. She focused on him and decided further risk was worth taking. "Just one thing… I have the ability to talk with trees and plants."

He merely stared at her. In the wait, she drew her cloak tighter and mentally asked the trees for aid.

Their reply came as swift as the wind. Trees began to shake and bend, the closest stretching limbs to reach them. A whisper shot through the woods.

Gren jumped back. "By the Gods, what was that?"

"I asked the trees for a demonstration. To move their branches."

"You control them?"

She couldn't resist smiling. His easy acceptance made her love him all the more. "Of course not. They have free will."

****

While Trell's disclosure stunned Gren, he could honestly say he wasn't totally surprised. Ever since meeting her, she'd constantly amazed him. He barely had time to digest being inundated with magical experiences. "That's incredible. It makes me question what other fairytales are true. If dragons are real and people can live as trees, what else could there be?" He stopped and turned to Trell. "However, there's one ability you haven't mentioned."

271

"I've told you everything. What else?"

He loved the wide-eyed innocence she portrayed. "I catch the scent of vanilla whenever I'm around you. Pine trees have a vanilla scent. Your long existence as one must have given you a natural perfume."

Trell sniffed her forearm as if to confirm his statement. "I've been surrounded by it for so long, I must be nose blind."

Gren loved surprising her. "Well, I find it enchanting... Like you."

He swore she blushed, but the dim light of night made certainty impossible. The sight did remind him of his duty. He had accepted the responsibility and dangers of freeing her from the dungeon without hesitation. It meant death, if caught, but he didn't care. She had become the most important person in his life. He brought her to Kula and vowed to save her from whatever scheme his father planned. It was the least he could do for the woman he loved.

"Come now, it can't be much farther." He took hold of her elbow to lead her up the mountain. A bite in the air nipped at his nose and ears. They'd need heavier clothes to climb higher or if they spent much time in the locale.

She tendered him a smile.

"I know you're tired and cold," he said, wishing to offer comfort. "Once we find Torkel's cave, I'll build fire to keep you warm. The trauma you've endured is bound to drain your strength. You can rest shortly."

"I've endured worse."

The denial didn't fool him. She'd suffered a horrible ordeal, and even by occasional starlight exhaustion darkened the skin under her eyes. "If I haven't said it before, I'm sorry for my actions. I thought finding you and your dragon would solve my problems, but I was wrong."

Trell stopped, chest heaving. White puffs escaped from her mouth as she spoke. "You didn't do anything wrong."

He appreciated her willingness to forgive him. All he had to do was forgive himself. "Since we're being honest, I should explain myself. I thought becoming the designated heir would allow me to improve conditions in Kula for everyone. Instead, I put you in danger."

He glanced at the steep terrain before them. Frost crystals glistened on whitened ground under the stars. More snow pockmarked open spots. "Although I cannot promise greedy people like my brothers won't attempt to recapture you, this I swear—as long as I draw a breath, no one will harm you or anything close to you."

"Including dragons?"

A better lead-in would never come again. "Most certainly dragons. Torkel is important to you. Therefore, he's important to me."

"So are you," Trell answered with a smile.

Laughter spilled out of him. He surveyed the shadows, and in the distance, the black maw of a cave came into view. He pointed. "There. I wager we've arrived at our destination."

****

Hope soared in Trell. They scrambled down the ridge and sprinted across a flat area. She hurried inside, looking forward to avoiding the chill, then halted. Little moonlight penetrated. Her nose twitched at an oily smell heavy in the air.

In Demit Woods, she had visited the dragons'

birthing lair many times and was always amazed at its vast size and the uniqueness within. Torkel's cave or lair was cavernous, as black as his scales because the walls consisted of bituminous firestones.

Trell rubbed her hands together and blew on them for warmth. "Let's make a fire."

Gren's expression sank. His hand dropped where he touched the walls. "I know I promised you a warm fire, but that isn't advisable in here. This entire cave consists of firestones. I know of a tragedy where a seam of them ignited, and fire raged beneath the land and spread through mine tunnels. It has smoldered for over a hundred years. Every attempt to put the fire out has failed. People couldn't farm and had to evacuate the area. Smoke continues to waft over the roads from sinkholes even today.

"If I start a fire, it could be dangerous. We might not be able to extinguish it. I doubt Torkel would approve if we destroyed his new lair."

"He would not," answered a deep male voice. Torkel in human form strode into the cave and came to a stop beside Gren. "You are correct, Human."

Joy leapt in Trell's chest at the sight of the ebony-haired man. She stepped back into the line of moonlight to better view the interior.

Gren marched forward and wrapped his arm around her shoulders. "Trell is freezing. She isn't acclimated to the mountains' coldness. She needs to be warmed or will catch a chill and become sick."

Torkel swung his golden gaze on her. "Does he speak true?"

She waved away the account. "He worries overly much. I've got my cape that Cress spelled. It's supposed to keep me warm and dry."

Torkel's chest expanded as he stepped closer. "That isn't what I asked."

Deceit had started this fiasco. Time for honesty. "We're both cold and tired," she answered.

Gren seconded with a nod.

Immediately, a mist glistened and sparkled like black diamonds around Torkel's human body. Gren shot her a questioning look.

"He's shapeshifting into his dragon form," she explained.

Gren rubbed one hand over his face. "This cave certainly looks large enough to hold him and us."

A black muzzle poked out of the mist. *"Of course, it is. I am shifting to keep you warm."*

The mindspeech caught Trell off-guard. *"I do not need your help."*

The mist cleared and Torkel's massive body lumbered over to them, his long talons scraping the hard ground like fingernails on masonry. He plopped down in front of them. *"The male is correct about one thing—you are exhausted. This wintry climate has drained your strength. You need rest. Lie beside me. The male can take the outside. My tail will provide him with sufficient warmth."*

"His name is Gren." Trell wasn't wont to let the opportunity pass. She dropped to the ground and put her back against Torkel's belly. Almost instantly leathery scales heated her, and she sighed with appreciation. "It's all right, Gren. Lie with me. Torkel has kept me warm many times while I traveled between Brenalin and the dragon circle. You can put my cape over your exposed side."

Gren snorted at her command but complied. Torkel bent his tail around Gren.

****

While Gren agreed to the sleeping arrangements, the warmth emanating from the dragon's tail curled up his front came as a pleasant surprise. He'd expected reptilian coldness. His hand patted the overlapping scales that shrank in size until they ended in a six-inch barb. He had no doubt that all it took was a flick of the dragon's massive tail for the barb to pierce skin and bone.

The dragon's purr settled into sonorous breathing. Gren wished he possessed the luxury to fall asleep in mere seconds. How deep did a dragon sleep? How long did the creature need to rest?

Trell snuggled into his backside, and the movement caused him to take several deep breaths before the steady breathing of sleep claimed her. Gren lay wide awake. The soft mounds of her breasts pushing against his back nearly made him moan. He tried to harden his resolve as another part of his body hardened instinctively.

"I am watching you."

The words popped into Gren's head with a start. He tensed and rolled on his side to peer at the dragon in the darkness. So the dragon wasn't sleeping. Golden eyes with vertical elliptical slits for pupils stared back.

"I don't appreciate having my integrity challenged," he hissed low between clenched teeth. "I'm doing my best to keep Trell safe."

"I will not be tricked, Human. We might have freed Trell together, but I am not her and do not bequeath my trust as easily."

Trell twisted and turned. She sat up and looked back and forth from man to dragon, dragon to man. "What is going on? The way your two bodies were tensing and flexing, I couldn't sleep."

"Your friend doesn't trust me." Gren stood to better defend himself, if necessary.

The Trell's eyes rounded in the dim light. "Well, I do, and that's all that counts."

"It isn't. If this human hurts you, I will eat him."

Gren's hand went to the hilt of his sword. "First, you have to kill me."

Torkel hefted his enormous frame to stand on all fours and lowered his long neck. *"I'll have you know I prefer my food warm and wiggling."*

Gren swallowed the lump stuck in his throat. His grip on his sword tightened. The bony ridge on one side of the dragon's head appeared to rise as if cocking an eyebrow. Gren shot a cynical look back as if asking, "Test me."

Trell threw her arms around the dragon's long neck. "I love him, and he loves me. Does that satisfy you?"

"That's all I wanted to know," the dragon answered in both their heads.

Trell yawned. *"Can we go back to sleep?"*

****

The next morning at first light Gren woke to the familiar sounds of troops, horses, and heavy wagons. Commands were shouted and repeated, echoing down the line.

They'd been found.

His father must have offered numerous tributes to Toyt, the god of war and the most venerated god of all

Demicland to find them this quick. It was the only logical reason he could think of.

Rubbing gritty sleep out of his eyes, Gren couldn't believe he'd slept through the commotion of an army arriving and setting up camp. Normally a light sleeper, he couldn't understand why he hadn't awakened. Had he been that exhausted or had the dragon performed magic on him? He edged the dragon's tail off him, slipping from Trell's cape to stand at the cave's opening.

Above the ridge, his father's standard, a white pennant with a black dragon, snapped in the wind before a yellow and white striped tent with scallop trim in the camp's center. His brothers' pennants flew above tents on either side of the king's. The whole family had converged upon them.

He looked over his shoulder at Trell's staff propped against the cave's wall. The ribbons flapped lightly as if a breeze blew through the cave, but Gren felt nothing on his face.

"The humans arrived during the night," Torkel mindspoke to him.

Gren aimed his gaze at the dragon who had raised its mighty head. Already he accepted this strange mind-to-mind communication. Trell remained snuggled against the creature's belly. *"Why didn't you awaken me?"*

"What good would that have done? You both needed rest."

Gren shook his head, disgusted with himself for sleeping. *"We might have been able to slip away under the cover of darkness during the confusion of bivouac. Now we're trapped."*

"Silly human, there is no danger. I explored this cave thoroughly before I deemed it suitable for my own. Another exit exists."

Gratitude swelled. *"How'd they find us so fast?"*

"My fault," Torkel admitted through mindspeech. *"The reason I left you two to climb the mountain alone was because I was curious and flew over the castle. The sentries noticed me and sounded the alarm."*

"There is nothing we can do about it now. Flee. Take Trell and escape. Protect her from danger. I will speak with my father and stall under the guise of negotiating with him."

****

Gren didn't wait for the dragon to answer him. Trell's safety came first. He spun on his heels and marched out of the cave with his arms out to his side.

The morning air contained wood smoke and the hint of snow as he trekked across the open area and climbed the ridge.

"Take me to the king," he demanded of the first soldier he encountered guarding the perimeter.

The man recognized him and gave a curt nod. "Follow me, Your Highness."

Soldiers parted before them without uttering a word.

At the yellow and white tent, they halted. Gren swooped inside without making a sound and stopped at the sight of his father sitting on cushions eating his morning meal. A lushness had been added to the interior since his last visit. Velvet and satin pillows dotted a red and blue carpet. The slanting roof made of oiled cloth was now painted blue to give the illusion of the sky.

279

Ornate lanterns provided light as bright as sunshine. A massive rug in rich, bright colors covered the ground. Finely carved domed chests lined the tent walls. Pillows of various sizes were piled in a huge mound.

For an instant, he studied his sire. His eyes seemed hollow and a pallor Gren had never noted before reflected on his aged face. While no visible sign of the disease showed, the sickness was taking its toll. "Father."

The king jumped up, his earthenware bowl crashing and shattering on the floor. "Gren!"

"None other." Pity tried to rise at the sight of the man, and he forced the emotion to the far corner of his mind.

Not so with his father. A hard expression quickly replaced surprise. Stal Og Har glared at him as he stepped over the mess of broken pottery and ground oats. "You've given me a merry chase. I assume your appearance means you are surrendering."

How like his father to assume that a show of force would coerce him. "You'd be wrong. Rather, I've come to warn you that if you don't want your army destroyed, you'd best depart."

"You threaten me?" His father eyed the sword encased in Gren's scabbard. "With one sword? You're an excellent swordsman, Gren, but I seriously doubt you can withstand the might of my army."

"I don't intend to try. No disrespect intended, but I will accept Oded's challenge to a fair fight. My terms are this... If I win, Trell and her dragon go free. No pursuit. I'll have your word. I've never known you to break it."

His father's eyes bulged at the mention of the dragon. "So the creature lives."

"Aye, and you know it. He was spotted flying over the castle." Gren debated how hard to press, then decided the situation called for all the tact he possessed.

A battle of emotions flashed over the king's face. "Why should I agree to such conditions?"

"Because where Trell and the dragon are is a cave full of firestones. The value of the find is immeasurable. The mountains are full of firestones. It will make Kula rich." He didn't slow, just leapt onto the next subject. "Moreover, Trell agrees with me that you have contracted the Untouchable disease. She—"

"A falsehood!"

"Is it? Don't make me repeat myself. We've already had this discussion. You're sick. It explains your obsession with wanting to find a dragon. You think the beast's hide will cure you."

Stal Og Har whirled around, his royal cape flapping as he spun, but not before Gren saw agony on his father's face. The disease worsened. He could no longer deny it.

A spot of color reddened his father's cheeks when he turned around to face Gren. "If—and I say if what you claim is true, what are you going to do about it?"

This was what Gren wanted. The longer they spoke, the farther Trell and Torkel could travel. "What can I do?"

The glare his father sent his way didn't deter him. "Demicland's laws are clear. Once my illness is discovered, I will be stripped of all my possessions, the title, Barg Castle, everything. That means neither you nor your brothers will inherit the kingdom. An

Untouchable owns nothing, has no rights except to beg for rags and scraps of food."

As if a blast of icy wind invaded the tent, Gren shivered with recognition that his strong father was afraid. He'd never seen this side of the man. Yet he couldn't blame him. Being an Untouchable meant being sentenced to a living death. The weeks disguised as one gave Gren an affinity for the suffering they underwent. He would never forget the sting of being stoned while in Brenalin.

He rubbed the stubble on his jaw, heard the scraping sound. "Abdicate the throne this day. You've already named me heir."

"Nay! There is much I have to do."

Gren didn't really expect his father to agree. "Then let Trell and her dragon leave," he repeated, "and I promise not to say a word about your condition."

"I need the dragon's skin to cure myself."

"Nay, he doesn't."

The voice materialized out of thin air in Gren's head. A cold shiver rippled down his spine. *"Torkel?"*

"Your sire knows nothing of dragons or our powers. My saliva can cure him, not my hide. Dead is dead, and a dead dragon is of no use to anyone."

"Truly?"

"As I grow, my ancestors' memories return. Remember the Fezner's cure? It came from a black dragon, a long-dead predecessor of mine. Their bottles contain diluted saliva."

Gren studied his father, who seemed to stand motionless, waiting for an answer. First, though, he asked, *"And you know this how?"*

"I sniffed the container Trell carries with her. It is

practically useless, so watered down, but with my superior sense of smell I detected the original source."

Gren flicked his gaze to the man who was revealing a softer side than he remembered. "Father, what if I tell you that I know the real cure? Will you listen?"

Something akin to relief flashed over weathered features. "One thing you've never done is lie to me. Speak."

"The cure doesn't rest within the dragon's hide. It's saliva from a live dragon."

Stal froze, body tense. "You know this for fact?"

So much hope was layered in the question that Gren swore he could feel it. "The dragon told me. Let me return to the cave and secure some from him."

"It can speak? Are you sure it's not sorcery?" his father demanded, then seemed to ponder the situation. "How much does it take?"

"A few drops," Torkel mindspoke to Gren. *"All he need do is rub it on his arms and it will cure the whole body."*

Gren listened. "Not much."

His father looked around the tent's interior. "One thing you are not is a liar. And you promise to return with this—this cure."

"I do. Although I still need to face Oded. He won't halt trying to undermine my authority or kill me, while I've given him no cause for his hatred." Gren hadn't voiced his suspicions. Not even to himself, he quickly realized. The admission proved disturbing, but nonetheless, it was somehow comforting to share his burden. He took a deep breath.

"I fear you are correct," his father answered.

"Perchance I can demand a truce between the two of you."

A commotion outside the tent brought Oded charging inside with Riff on his heels. Gren's stomach pitched as he spun to face his opponents.

Chapter 17

Gren's blood drained. It had been hard enough trying to convince his father not to kill Torkel. Now, his brothers would voice their objections.

"I heard Gren's been captured. Is it true?" Oded's pale green gaze centered on his father before scanning the interior of the huge tent. Spotting Gren, he sucked in a breath, then raked him up and down with a cold stare. "Why isn't he in chains?"

So much for a warm welcome. While Oded was outfitted for battle in a polished breastplate and heavy leather leggings, in his mind Gren saw his brother as the boy who taught him how to ride his first horse. He remembered one sunny day in particular when the lesson ended. Oded gave the horse's rump a hard slap, and the animal leapt into a trot, surprising Gren. He jerked on the reins, but they snapped off in his hands. The reins had been cut.

"Nice to see you, too," Gren returned in greeting, trying to keep his emotions hidden. He'd endured insults, beatings, and a harsh childhood, but the thought of Trell being under his brother's control brought a primal fury to the surface.

Stal Og Har squared his shoulders against his oldest son. "Since when do you issue orders? You are not ruler. Sit down and listen. Gren has made an offer that I am tempted to consider."

"What offer? You cannot believe a word he says. He'd lie to protect that healer. She has bewitched him."

Riff acknowledged Gren with a nod and a tentative smile as he edged away from their eldest sibling.

The king huffed. "Do not put practices on Gren that you perform, Oded. Lies trip from your mouth, while I have never caught him in a lie, even when it meant harsh punishment for his deeds. Now sit down and do not interrupt."

No one sat.

Riff leaned toward Gren. "What's happening?"

Gren put his finger to his lips. "Let Father explain."

Bristling, Oded's face reddened. He stomped across the floor, the sleeves of his linen tunic flapping as he moved.

Sadness aged Stal Og Har when his gaze flicked at Gren. "They do not know. I have not confided in them nor have they become suspicious. Mayhaps it is prudent to bring them into my confidences. After all, the tidings affect their futures."

A sneer flashed across Oded's face. "Naught can be so important that you'd forgive Gren's treachery."

Every muscle in Gren's body tensed. He clenched his fists and controlled the impulse to shout at his brother. Gren had tried all his life to find a redeeming quality in his older brother and failed. Like the incident in the stable, Oded sabotaged him all the time.

Stal Og Har stretched to his full height and squared his shoulders. "I have contracted the Untouchable disease."

Oded jumped to his feet. His face bleached white. "The filthy curse! You are doomed." His voice rose to the pole hub that formed a blue prism above their heads.

Scowling, the king took a threatening step. "Keep your damn voice down. The guards will hear."

"Father," Riff said, striding closer, moisture glistening in his eyes. "What do you want us to do? How can I help?"

"There is nil." A slight quiver shook the king's ring-encrusted hand. He raised it toward his youngest son, then let it drop. "While I appreciate your concern, Riff, pity will not cure me."

Oded tripped on the corner of a rug as he stumbled backward. He grabbed the top of an ornate chest to keep from falling. "It's contagious. You certainly weren't thinking of us when you exposed us. What if we've contracted it? Come on, Riff, we'd better gather as much of our wealth as possible and flee Kula before father's condition is discovered."

Selfish coward. Gren tensed. Oded's first thought was for himself. Why should he expect anything else?

Faster than imaginable, Stal shot across the floor and grabbed Oded by the shoulders. "I'm not contagious. The lumps haven't come out yet."

Oded violently jerked out of his father's hold. "I don't care. Don't touch me. Keep your distance."

Gren debated stepping into the fray. More than not naming Oded his heir, this confrontation was a long time coming and took a life-changing disease to bring it to a head.

The king narrowed his gaze. "You stink of fear."

"Better afraid than dead," Oded retorted.

Riff stepped closer to his father and gave the exposed skin a hard examination. "How long have you been ill?"

"For some time, but I am in the early stage." The king pulled back the sleeve of his tunic. If one looked close small pimple-sized spots lighter than his normal skin dotted his arm. "I've lost the sensation of touch over much of my body. The disease can go on for years before anyone notices. The lesions have not raised into lumps yet."

Oded lowered brows over eyes that revealed equal amounts of hate and fear. "There's no hope for you."

Gren's temper got the best of him. He rushed Oded, wanting to smash his fist into his brother's face. "Shut your mouth, or everyone will hear."

Riff put his arm around their father's shoulders and faced his oldest sibling. "I can't believe you, Oded. You're despicable, unworthy of contempt. Where's your loyalty? He's our father and deserves our compassion."

Snarling, Oded struggled within Gren's hold. "Let go of me. You know I'm right."

Gren released Oded with a shove. Off-balance, he stumbled backward. The cowardly behavior sickened Gren. He couldn't believe he stood in a war tent with his brothers arguing over the fate of their father.

In truth, Riff's stand took courage. Only a brave man would break with tradition and rally against persecution and superstition.

"Riff's accurate," Gren said. "Besides, I know a cure."

The assertion forced his brothers to spin in his direction. He waited a long moment to let their curiosity build. One glared at him with hate, the other with hope glimmering in his eyes.

"I am not deceiving you. That's what Father and I

288

were discussing when you entered. In some ways, he was correct in seeking a dragon, just not to kill. The beast's saliva is the cure."

Oded's face twisted with contempt. "Dragon spittle! Don't be ridiculous."

Gren shook his head, weighing whether or not to let his disgust for his brother rule his actions. "One doesn't drink it. It's rubbed on the skin."

Oded issued a huff of disbelief. "Still disgusting. No sane person would rub such repulsive slime on themselves."

"Even if it meant curing themselves?" Gren sighed. Convincing his brother was going to be harder than he imagined. He flicked a glance at his father and Riff. They both leaned forward, revealing a deep curiosity. "The Fezners have hoarded bottles of the cure for eons. They just didn't know what they were using."

Oded scoffed. "How would you know that?"

"I traveled with them."

"Those thieves. They're liars. You can't believe a word they say," Oded scoffed. "You were dressed as an Untouchable. They were trying to sell you a magical elixir. What better way than to boast of a cure to remove a fool's coin?"

His father shook his head at the continued objections. Riff patted his arm.

It did little good to disclose that the Fezners had already given Trell a bottle. Gren grinned at the three men staring at him. "That gives me an idea. Once Father is cured, we can invite the Fezners to Kula and give them fresh medicine to distribute."

"I haven't agreed to share my saliva," mindspoke Torkel.

Gren didn't blink. *"I'm sure Trell will convince you."* He swore a low growl answered him as he continued to stare at his brother. "They roam worldwide in their wagons. People visit them at every town. And more importantly, Untouchables are welcomed among them. It would be the perfect means to spread the cure."

Oded waved his arm in dismissal. "Associate with Fezners? They're beneath us. They steal children from their beds. Why should we listen to you? You're only trying to save your own hide. You've aided a prisoner in escaping. You're a traitor!"

The reminder made Gren pray to Toyt, patron god of war and Demicland, that enough time had passed for them to flee leagues from this location. He had no idea of the distance required before this new way to communicate stopped being viable. He believed himself on the side of right and trusted the dragon to lead Trell to safety, even though he held little luck for his own survival.

Oded spun to Stal. "Father, you can't heed his advice. We can't trust him."

The king scowled as he cleared his throat. "And I should trust you? I think not."

Oded dared to step forward. "If you're referring to that hag I presented as healer, I humbly beg your forgiveness. She duped me, told me her name was Trell, that her brother was the Wizard Cress. It's not my fault that I believed her." A smug look passed over his face. "Fear naught. She has been dispatched."

A twinge of regret coursed through Gren. Cringing, he imagined the imposter Trell had been slain. Distrust for his brother allowed another thought to materialize about another healer. "Did you kill Dori as well?"

The smirk Oded revealed was louder than a denial.

"Why?" Gren asked, sickened at the loss.

"I don't answer to you."

"But you do to me, Oded. You murdered Dori to keep her from exposing your fake healer. I have overlooked your faults long enough. No more." The king frowned, deep creases scoring between his brows. "That is only one of many lies that trip from your lips."

"That's not true. I have always been forthright with you, Father."

Sadness flashed across the king's face as he stared at his eldest son and shook his head. "The worst lies a person can tell are the ones they tell themselves."

Oded straightened. "Then my earlier challenge to Gren stands."

Gren had always assumed the fight would resurface and stepped forward. "I accept."

"I forbid it," the king roared.

"You cannot deny him." Gren shook his head. "A challenge for the throne cannot be ignored. By Demicland laws, a challenge must be accepted or the throne is forfeit."

Stal straightened. "You forget who makes the law—kings. Laws are to control the masses. They can be broken by kings."

Gren shook his head. "Not this time. It is a law that even you must obey."

The king's shoulders slumped. "Then proceed. And may the man who will rule after me win."

Riff lifted the flap on the tent. He shouted to the soldiers milling about the camp, "Clear a circle. A challenge has been issued."

At his brother's words, Gren hoped Trell escaped.

****

Trell woke nestled against the cozy warmth of Torkel's belly. She stretched, mildly surprised at the lack of confinement. During the night she could hardly move, pinned between Torkel and Gren.

Gren! Where was he? She jerked upright, her gaze searching the cave. Sunlight pierced inside for several meters. The walls, ceiling, and floor contained shiny, black firestones. No sign of Gren anywhere. Was he exploring deeper in the cave? With his military background, it made sense for him to conduct a surveillance of the area.

A low rumble caught her attention. It came from beyond the cave. Had Gren heard it and gone to investigate?

Rising, she went to the entrance. Her heart jumped. She reeled.

Outside, an army encamped on the ridge above the cave. Smoke from scattered fires and the murmur of voices mixed and curled in the cool morning air. She eyed the open space and a knoll between the cave and the campsite, about twenty-five meters wide. It was clear. Atop the ridge, perimeter guards patrolled. She counted off their steps, timing the movements so she could sneak in, if necessary.

"Puny humans think to impress by their numbers," Torkel mindspoke behind her. *"I do not fear them."*

Trell disagreed. *"We cannot win against an army. There are too many even for you."*

"Not for me. I can fly high above the reach of their arrows and spray acid upon them. Besides, they cannot see this cave. An ancestor's memory informed me that since I have slept here, it remains invisible unless I

wish for it to be seen."

She recognized stubbornness in his tone. *"I want no bloodshed. We'll wait until nightfall, then I will distract them while you slip out under the cover of darkness."*

"Never!"

Indignation rang clear in the dragon's denial and Trell warmed at the loyalty. *"Listen to me, Torkel. You are the only one who can reach my brother and King Abbas in a short time. The world needs—"*

"I'll not leave you. Or Gren. He is out there talking with his sire, stalling so we can escape."

A jolt of fear shot through Trell. Her gaze snapped to the cave's entrance. She managed to slow her pulse, even as a wave of anxiety swelled within her. Glancing back at her staff, her worry lessened ever so slightly at the sight of the ribbons hanging limp. They warned of danger to her, but what about Gren's well-being? *"I need to find him."*

"Halt! You will not depart. I forbid it. I gave my word to protect you."

"The army only wants to recapture me. It's Gren's brothers who want me dead. I'll be careful."

The black dragon bobbed his long neck. *"Wait! Gren prepares to fight the older one."*

Trell swayed with the news. *"I've got to stop him. I can't let him die for me."*

She grabbed her healer's cape and began smearing firestones all over it, darkening the familiar red to nearly black. Tossing the altered cape over her shoulders, the whiff of oily smelling firestones assaulted her nose. She hoped no one else noticed, then dashed across the open space to throw herself flat upon the bottom of the knoll just as the muted scraping of wooden scabbards bumping against muscled legs sounded. She waited until the tramp of boots faded, then began to claw her way to the top. Pulling her hood to cover her braids and dull the tinkle of bells, she slipped past tethered horses and sneaked closer until she reached where soldiers formed a circle. She shouldered her way to the forefront.

On the far side, the circle opened. Gren marched into view, followed by his older brother. They drew slender, sharply-pointed blades about the length of an arm with protective hilts and approached the center.

Blessed Heyln. Please, please, don't let Gren die.

Trell clutched her fists with such tightness that the blood flow stopped. She tried to picture the outcome and couldn't. Or wouldn't. She wanted to cry out but knew better than to distract Gren or call attention to herself. Rather, she prayed for a miracle to keep him safe.

Gren raised his weapon to face Oded. His gaze never flinched. "We don't have to fight to settle our differences."

"Oh, aye, we do. I never liked you, you know. I was first-born, but when you came along, I sensed a difference in our parents. Almost immediately they favored you over me. I hated that. I hated you."

"It wasn't in my control, but I never hated you."

Trell ached for Gren at those words. She spotted the king and Riff standing shoulder to shoulder with the soldiers. Scowls twisted their faces with worry and anger. Did they wonder what would happen after the fight? If Oded killed Gren, would the father be next? Then Riff? If the thought occurred to her, surely it did to them as well.

Oded snorted. "When Father demanded my jasper pendant before dinner the other night, I guessed his intent to name you heir and hated that you had won."

"I didn't know."

The bright morning sun glinted off Oded's shiny breastplate when he shrugged. "Does it matter?"

The king cleared his throat and raised his arm above his head. "The fight ends at first blood. Is that understood?"

Both men nodded.

The king hand's swished down.

Oded lept forward, slicing the air.

Trell's stomach knotted at the viciousness of the attack, but Gren met the downward stroke. The blow extracted a grunt from him, and a shudder rippled up his arm.

Gren feinted left, only to charge straight ahead, swinging with all his might. Steel slid down steel.

A second later Gren stumbled, grinding firestones underfoot. Trell gasped, then swallowed her fear.

Callous laughter bubbled from Oded. "What's wrong, brother? Do my skills surprise you?"

Gren didn't answer.

Trell bit her lip. A soldier pressed beside her. She pulled her cloak tighter around her shoulders as if to shield herself.

Oded stalked Gren. "You were always a soft-hearted fool. Caring about the villagers more than your own welfare. The strength of my steel will be your downfall."

"Boastful words, Oded. But I would rather live my life caring for others than allow you to rule Kula."

Sunlight reflected off Oded's blade as Gren swung in a shimmering blur. His war-cry sent chills down Trell's spine. His blade sliced down to his brother's pommel with an ear-splitting hiss.

Oded pivoted on the balls of his feet, his sword slashing.

"Duck," Torkel mindspoke.

Oded's blade whistled in the air above Gren. "You're damn lucky, Brother."

Torkel snorted. *"Go left, you fool. Heed me, and you just might survive."*

"Get the hell out of my head! I don't need you telling me what to do," Gren answered.

Trell heard the mindspeech and remained quiet, holding her breath so long that dizziness made her light-headed. When Gren brought his blade around in a swooping arc capable of taking a man's head off in a single blow, she gasped.

This time Oded's smile disappeared in a flash. He took short, shallow breaths as he shifted his weight from side to side, his blade dipping. He might wear the garments of a warrior, but if his expression was any indication, Gren's tactics befuddled him. Again and again, Oded kept his guard up. Metal clanged against metal.

Both men's movements turned sluggish. They grew tired. Oded's sleeves dripped with sweat at the armholes of his breastplate. Streaks of sweat stained Gren's leather tunic down his back and across the front. One-on-one combat was too intense to last long. Sooner or later one man would tire and make a mistake, with a deadly outcome.

Just as the thought occurred, Gren spun and swept

in under Oded's guard. He sliced flesh from bone along Oded's jaw from sideburn to chin and down his arm.

Oded screamed. Blood oozed, tainting the air with the metallic smell of rusting iron. He touched the wound, his fingers bloody. His face turned pasty white. Fury glinted in his pale eyes before he crumbled to his knees.

"Yield," Gren commanded. "And live."

"Mercy." Oded tossed his sword to the ground.

The fight was over. Gren had won.

Trell watched him sheath his sword and approach his brother. He kicked the discarded weapon into the soldiers' feet. "Leave Kula, Oded. You are hereby banished. If you ever set foot here again, you will be killed on sight."

Oded staggered to his feet. Disgust twisted what remained of his face. The wound would leave a horrible scar. "You won't make a good king. Oh, you're a good swordsman. It takes a strong man—a hard man—to rule. You're too kindhearted. That makes you weak."

Gren turned toward the king and Riff. That's when Oded moved. He reached into the upper sleeve of a high leather boot and pulled a weapon.

Trell screamed, "Knife."

Well-tuned instincts had Gren whirling to face the new threat. In a blur of movement, his knife flew straight at Oded and sank into his neck with a squishy thud of metal slicing through flesh and bone.

Surprise silenced the crowd.

Shock filled Oded's face. He clutched his throat as blood dripped between his fingers and he slipped to the ground. He formed a single word. "How?"

Rushing to his brother's side, Gren lifted Oded's

head into his lap. "I'm sorry, Brother. I find no satisfaction in defeating you."

Empathy rose in Trell at the pain Gren suffered. Hatred shown on Oded's face, refusing to accept any kindness even while dying. His knife tumbled from his hand and rattled on firestones. Struggling within Gren's clutches, he tried to free himself as though agitated, a response Trell had documented in many of the sick and dying.

The gurgling of a man drowning in his own blood was the only sound in the hushed circle. Oded's body went limp as the life went out of his pale green eyes. With a sigh full of regret, Gren closed his brother's eyelids for a final time.

Trell remained in place when two men approached the center—the king and Riff. This was not a time for her to intrude. She ducked back a half step into the crowd.

Stal Og Har put his hand on Gren's shoulder and his body seemed to waver. "What have I done? I did not want blood to be shed."

From her vantage point, Trell wondered if the king steadied himself or his son.

Gren rose and searched the circle for a moment before wiping bloody hands on his shirt front. "Nor did I want this outcome."

The king stiffened like a rod forged by a blacksmith. "Oded died with dishonor. He shamed my blood. My only regret is that Riff fell for his deceit."

"Oded might have thought you favored me," Gren said, "but I always believed Riff was your favorite."

"A ploy to throw attention away from you, which failed. I knew from birth that you would be the best choice to rule Kula. I should have realized Oded would become jealous. Forgive me."

The agony on Gren's face drove Trell crazy. She couldn't let him suffer alone. Pushing through the soldiers, she threw herself into his arms and pressed against the heat of his body. "Fool, you could have been killed."

"Nay, I was safe. You were watching my back. I knew you wouldn't stay in the cave." He adjusted his hold, but never let go of her.

Trell's heart thudded. For an astonishing moment she thought Gren was going to kiss her in front of the entire army. His breathing heaved in an uneven hitch.

The king rubbed his face. "Ahh, so this is the way of things. I should have realized. Come. Step into my tent."

"For what?" Gren asked.

Stal turned away as if ashamed to face them. "What do you think? I let my sons fight to the death. I set brother against brother. What kind of father am I?"

Gren's heart raced beneath her hand.

"Father…Father…" He spared a glance at her as if seeking permission, then walked to the older Har's side. "I have never stopped caring for you. I just disagreed with your treatment of Trell and your plans to kill the dragon. If I could have—" He stopped.

Gren's defense of her and Torkel sent curling ribbons of warmth through her veins, even if he had separated the heated hardness of his body from hers.

After a long moment of silence, the king glanced at Oded's corpse. Anguish flashed over his face. "Take his body to Barg Castle. He will be buried in the family crypt. He was still my son. May his soul find peace in death."

Six soldiers jumped to obey. They lift Oded and carried him away.

When the group disappeared, the king continued. "Each son took a different path. One succumbed to what he thought he deserved by birthright, one accepted his fate, and one showed his heart too often. I had hopes for each of you. That you would all do well. It seemed the Gods deemed otherwise."

Riff stood beside the threesome. "I—I thought…" He stopped and took a deep breath. "Oded believed Gren was too kind-hearted, but I presume you considered me the kind-hearted one. Mayhaps I should state my case while we are disclosing our secrets. I followed Oded because he showed interest in me. I admit to feeling honored by his attention. He was the oldest. His cronies were always eager to do his bidding. But since learning of his actions toward Brit, he sickened me. I could never trust him again."

Torn loyalties filled the youngest Har, and Trell felt a kinship with him. She'd been deceived herself and now he appeared as lost as she. She didn't know where she belonged in this unsettled family either. She loved Gren with all her heart, but as heir to Kula he would have to stay and rule once his father passed. His life was set.

The younger Har had more choices. Leave. Stay.

She turned to Riff. "What will you do?"

The youngest Har froze. "Do? Search for Brit. It crushed me that I was not there in her time of need. I loved her and was a fool not to tell her. She needs to know I played no part in her mistreatment. We cared for each other. I—I would have renounced the throne for her."

A knot twisted Trell's belly. She cast a quick glance at Gren. He had tensed at Riff's announcement. What did he think of the confession? Did it give him ideas? She seriously doubted he would renounce the throne for her.

Not when he'd killed for it.

To linger on the uncertainties of the future seemed pointless. Instead, she took charge. "Shall we see about curing you, King Har?"

Chapter 18

It didn't surprise Gren that Trell took control of the situation as the foursome walked to the king's tent. She had a way of looking forward. Another trait he admired about her.

He willed the pounding of his heart to slow. The fire in his blood from the skirmish cooled rapidly. He'd had no desire to fight his brother, much less kill him. Oded's death became a matter of survival.

Still, Gren did his best to temper the grief and guilt threatening to overwhelm him. Only time would heal his loss. He would have to live with the consequences for the rest of his life. A burden he was willing to shoulder, especially if it meant Trell's safety.

Arriving outside the yellow and white tent, a light flared in his father's eyes that set Gren on alert. He tensed and stepped closer to Trell.

Stal Og Har signaled his captain of guard. "All men, including yourself, are to remain one hundred paces from my tent while I discuss family affairs." Then he turned to Trell. "Step into my tent, Healer. We have much to discuss."

Trell's chin rose. Defiant. Stubborn. And adorable. Gren had seen the little motion dozens of times. She might abound with patience, but stubbornness was also a quality she possessed.

Trell's dark brown eyes flashed. "Why not have

our discussion in the open?"

The king glanced around the camp. A few soldiers dispersed to go about their duties. Others visibly eavesdropped. "You know the reason. I require privacy."

Fear brushed Gren's mind like an icy breeze, and he hoped the invitation wasn't a trap. What if the situation became dangerous? He'd guard Trell, naturally. No way would he surrender her to his father's will again.

As a precaution, he rested his hand on his sword's pommel. His father noted the motion but kept silent. If his father made the slightest threat toward Trell, only death would stop him from protecting her. Better prepared, than caught off guard.

Gren eyed his father, yet still empathy rose. The man was sick, dying a slow, agonizing death. He was grasping at straws for a cure. Who wouldn't do the same? Never in his life had Stal let others do for him. Now, he was dependent on Trell's healing skills and wagering on a dragon's saliva would give the cure he desperately needed.

Even a stronger man would falter under the circumstances.

"Let's appease him. After all, he is the king," Gren said, and against his better judgment, cupped Trell's hand—those gentle hands with the power to heal and stoke fires in him like no other woman—to lead her inside the king's tent.

For a second time in less than a day, he ducked into the yellow and white striped tent. This time he checked for exits hidden in the blue interior folds of fabric. In spite of his willingness to listen, he fought against jumping to the wrong conclusions.

His father and Riff stomped behind them.

The king waved to pillows heaped on the floor. "Sit. I had little hope of ever seeing either one of you again."

Trell locked her gaze on the king. "You were chasing us. We had to assume that meant you planned to reimprison us."

"Assumptions can be a bane. Placing you in the dungeon was for your own protection. Someone murdered Dori. I suspect Oded did to keep her from exposing his healer as a fraud, but without proof, I was at a loss. Then this morning when I confronted him he confirmed my suspicion by his own lack of denial." His gaze settled on Gren.

Gren stared ahead, his mind wheeling, accepting the allegation as truth. "Earlier today I accused Oded, and he just sneered at me. I'd seen that look hundreds of times. He never admitted fault, even when caught red-handed."

The king stepped closer. "I was never granted a chance to explain myself for imprisoning the healer. Forgive me for what seemed like harsh treatment."

Gren shuddered. The man speaking stood like a stranger before him.

Trell remained silent.

"Not only are you a skillful as a healer, as witnessed by those who called upon you for treatment," his father continued, "but a woman who inspires loyalty beyond measure. Admirable traits few possess."

"Being honest and forthright is one way to create a bond of trust," she answered without any sign of fright.

Not so with Gren. Qualms fluttered in him on an

invisible breeze. A king wasn't accustomed to being spoken to in such a bold manner, and his father was no exception. How long before the man's temper got the best of him?

The king waved away Trell's retort. "Set aside your concerns. I suspected Oded was the culprit who murdered Dori. I assumed by putting you beyond his reach, you were safe. Now that the threat has been eliminated, you are my guest."

"Is that so? Your previous hospitality left a lot to be desired," she responded just as quickly.

Riff stepped forward. Gren blocked him. This conversation needed to be aired.

The king shook his gray head. "I'm being forthcoming with you. While my intentions were honorable, my earlier actions were indefensible. I humbly beg your forgiveness."

Trell stepped forward. "Accepted."

Stal grinned at the succinct answer. "Shall we start over? The cure Gren spoke of would be a start. Tell me more."

With a calmness that nearly unsettled Gren, Trell smiled and bobbed her head. The silver bells tinkled with the movement. He had come to accept the lyrical chines as an integral part of her as much as the scent of vanilla.

She lowered herself onto a black pillow embroidered with gold thread. "As you wish. It comes from an old legend. And…and Torkel confirmed it."

Narrowed eyes revealed his father's mistrust. "Torkel?"

"A friend who counseled me." Trell patted the pillows around her. "Come now. We have agreed to save your life because you played fair with the fight between Gren and Oded."

Gren took a step forward. This time Riff stopped him with a calming touch on his arm. Though his brother's face remained impassive, a maturity shone in his eyes.

Trell glanced around the tent's interior. "I'll start with dragons, Your Majesty. What do you know of them?"

The subject of dragons forced all three men to sit. Gren sat first beside Trell. His father and brother followed, sitting cross-legged across from them.

His father plucked at a loose strand on his leather vest. "Not enough, it appears. It has been difficult for me to admit ignorance when I believed a dragon's hide would cure my affliction."

"Admitting lack of knowledge is the first step toward an enlightened future," Trell replied without hesitation.

Gren couldn't have been prouder of Trell. Her gaze never wavered, nor her bravery.

It took every bit of control to keep silent. From his pillowed seat, a quick glance at his father showed the man had aged in seconds. Losing one son to another must be the hardest torment for a parent to endure. Still, the man's relaxed posture didn't fool him. The condescending mood could change in the blink of an eye. At least that was his experience from his childhood.

"You have me at an advantage," Stal Og Har said. "You control a dragon, an ancient magical creature, who has the power to heal me."

"That attitude is another mistake. I do not control

the dragon. He is his own individual. If you truly understood the creatures, you would know that they are stubborn, arrogant, and sometimes abrasive. But they are also highly intelligent, with excellent memories when it comes to grievances."

Gren could attest to a dragon's petulant mood. He released the long breath he'd been holding and chuckled, which drew an odd look from his brother. He signaled Riff that it was nothing. His brother's muscles relaxed.

"Father, Trell knows of what she speaks. The dragon is her friend and, I would like to think, mine," Gren said, deciding to interject into the discussion. "Furthermore, she is an excellent healer. Let her examine you. She'll know what step to take next."

"It appears I have little choice."

Trell shook her head. "You always have a choice."

With a sigh, the king leapt to his feet like a man half his age and pushed up the sleeve of his tunic.

Trell rose to stand beside him, clearly trying to hide a smile. "Actually, Your Majesty, I only needed to check your tongue, but your arm is much better."

Riff snorted, and Gren and he exchanged amused glances. A little light-heartedness eased the tension within the tent.

Trell stepped over a pillow to be close to the king. "Please excuse my cold hands."

"The sensation of touch is gone. I cannot feel. Remember?"

"It means your nerves are damaged. Like with the candle flame." She ran her finger over his forearm and bit her bottom lip as if gathering her thoughts. "I can barely feel the lesions. Are you in any pain?"

A sigh preceded the king's answer. "Pain is the least of my worries."

"How is your vision?"

Har snapped a hard look at Trell as if hating to admit a weakness. "It worsens."

"Another indication of the disease's progression. If my assumptions are correct, the symptoms can be reversed with dragon saliva. With your permission, I will leave to collect it. Black dragons' saliva is very corrosive. I'll have to figure out how much to dilute it."

Long seconds stretched. Silence filled the tent.

Gren held his breath, waiting for his father's response. Once cured... What then? Would he grant permission for Trell to leave?

"Father," Gren prompted.

The softly spoken word snapped the man out of his daze. "Aye, make it so. Fetch the ingredients and bring them to my tent. Although be warned, I am accustomed to having people follow my orders, instead of following theirs."

Trell nodded. Before she could take a step, his father grabbed her arm. Gren's stomach clenched into a knot, and he leapt up, the impulse to protect Trell always in the forefront.

Just as quick the king dropped his hand. "I would like to meet your dragon someday."

Gren nearly tripped in his tracks at the request.

A ghost of a smile touched Trell's lips as she picked up a shallow, wooden bowl. "He's not mine. He is an individual like you. That decision is up to him, but I will pass on your request."

****

Trell paused outside the tent to savor the scents

around her—woodsy pine, men, horses, mixed with fresh mountain air. A path through the campsite opened before her. Gazes from all directions bore into her as she headed out. Muffled whispers sounded, but no one attempted to hinder her way.

"Wait, Trell," Gren's deep voice called. "I'm accompanying you. I'm not letting out of my sight."

She waited for him to draw alongside her. "You sound like your father."

"Don't insult me. Though he appears to have changed, and I hope it is permanent, I will never be like him."

Trell nearly apologized. Childhood created memories that were often false. Perception became reality. This could be such a case. "I know. Shall we find Torkel?"

With a nod, both Trell and Gren laughed, causing soldiers to peer at them as if they were touched. One even made the protective sign against a hex. Superstition ran high among the people of Kula, and Trell couldn't help but wonder about their reaction once they actually saw Torkel in the flesh. It could cause panic.

If there was a way to slowly introduce him to the populace…maybe that would be best.

Then an idea struck her. She grabbed Gren's hand. "We'll need to teach the villagers about Torkel, so his presence does not scare them. Mayhaps we can do so through music? He admires yours very much."

"Don't tell me Torkel would do my bidding if I played my flute for him?"

"Impudent, Human. Just try to sway me and see what you receive."

Trell heard the mindspeech along with Gren. She'd been surprised that he hadn't interjected comments during the conversation with the king. Maybe the dragon was learning patience and tact, though she held out little hope.

A smile formed on Gren's lips. "Not the most promising answer."

"He was not amused."

"No insult intended, Torkel," Gren answered in mindspeech.

They dodged soldiers and campfires, and scrambled down the embankment toward the cave. "You should show more respect. Torkel believes he will be dragon king someday. That is a high honor."

"I just can't picture dragons and music together."

"Why not? When we first met, you claimed music drew them. They are creatures who enjoy beautiful things like any human does."

She spotted the cave's entrance without any trouble, which meant the dragon granted them entry. They popped inside, and Trell shivered with the loss of the warm sunshine. She peered into the inky depths. "Torkel, where are you?"

"I'm here. Where else would I go? Should I fly away and allow you to fend for yourself? Hardly."

She waited for her vision to adjust to the dimness before glancing around the cave. Torkel stretched on the floor, his black body nearly invisible against the firestones. "I'm sure you are aware I need a small amount of your spittle."

"If it was up to me, I would gladly give you all your request, though not necessarily in a manner that you would approve of. Still, I must abide by dragon

310

rules."

Of course he wanted to shower the army with his acid spittle. She pulled brows together in a tight frown, then stepped forward without hesitation. "I've never heard of dragon rules. What do you mean?"

"If you receive something from a dragon, then you must gift him something in exchange. Jewels. Gold. A beautiful maiden. I think a token of that ilk would be a fair exchange."

Was Torkel being serious? Or was he being silly?

Trell tried to read the dragon's expression for a clue. With a shake of her head, she gave up. Reading the bony features of a dragon was impossible. "You're making this up."

"It's your word against mine."

An odd note in Torkel's tone shed light on the situation, then an idea came to her. "I doubt it has to be a maiden or gemstones. It could be a toothpick."

Torkel snorted, blowing fine black dust—firestone dust—into the air. *"That might be true, but first I have to accept the token. If you can tell me why I can never get any female to like me, I might be persuaded to cooperate."*

Trell glanced at Gren. By his confused expression, he wasn't being included in the exchange. She put her hands on her hips. "Oh, you poor thing. If you weren't so arrogant, more people would love you. Mayhaps even a maiden."

Torkel had grown up on this journey, coming into his dragon self, and with that, revealing an arrogance only a dragon could exhibit. He was the largest of his kind, none of the other black dragonets matched his size. While each dragon possessed different personality characteristics, she believed Torkel's heart was good. Oh, he could intimidate with his massive head of curving horns and mouth dripping with caustic saliva, but she refused to believe he would destroy innocent lives.

"Are you sure? Humans are fickle creatures. Dragon history is rich with princesses and maidens being sacrificed as easily as treasure. It's a tradition I just might resurrect."

"Blessed Heyln, I forbid it."

Torkel lumbered to his feet. *"You cannot dictate to me."*

She flinched at the authoritarian tone. Had she pushed him too far?

Gren stepped forward. "I don't know what's happening, but cease this bickering. Torkel, can't you see that Trell is tired. Exhausted. All she has ever done is place your welfare before her own. And, Trell, you know in your heart that Torkel would die to keep you safe. Remember he risked exposure to save you from drowning."

Trell caught her breath and blinked at the simple reminder. Torkel sat back down on his haunches. The words soothed both her and the dragon, and she was grateful for Gren's presence even as the sting of tears attacked her eyes.

She stepped forward to rub Torkel's bony snout between sharp horns. "My sincere regrets, my friend."

"Accepted."

"Is an apology sufficient gift for you?" Trell instantly said.

A low rumble came from Torkel. *"You tricked me."*

A shadow crossed Gren's face. "Enough. Now, answer me this... Will you let the villagers mine the firestones?"

Torkel swung his great head. *"Ahh, I hadn't forgotten about them. I wondered who would bring up the matter."*

Trell appreciated the distraction. It gave her time to collect herself.

Gren stood his ground. "If we can provide a product—the firestones—the rest of the world will pay, and pay well for. What if we split that bounty with you? You'll receive gold on a regular basis."

"An interesting proposal. I would be the first dragon to enter into a contract with humans. Proof of my merit to rule other dragons. I must think on it."

"Fine. Meanwhile, we need your spittle." Trell thrust the bowl in front of Torkel and held her breath. "Please, Torkel."

She swore the yawning maw of the dragon's mouth cracked a smile. Saliva pooled around jagged teeth. It began to dribble out. Trell lifted the wooden bowl higher, not wanting to miss a precious drop.

The first drop hit the bowl with a splatter.

"Stay back, Gren," she said. "I am spelled against the corrosiveness. You are not."

He retreated a few meters. "How will you apply it to my father, if it's that dangerous?"

More sputum splashed into the bowl. It wouldn't take long to collect a sufficient amount. She glanced over her shoulder. "Carefully. I wager that full concentration is too strong. My plan is to dilute the sputum and test it on your father. Results should be immediate, if the strength is correct." She directed her

313

attention to Torkel. "Unless you have a suggestion?"

The dragon snapped his mouth shut. *"Must I do everything? How typical of humans to request favors and then expect me to solve their problem without balking!"*

"You know that's not what I meant. If an ancestor's memory provided you with information, I merely seek it."

"Half strength is the proper dosage."

Gren stepped to her side to peer into the bowl. "That's enough, Trell. The bowl is nearly full."

His closeness, once again, caused a myriad of emotions to sweep over Trell. She feared her attraction meant surrendering her freedom.

Standing next to him, his fingers covered with dried blood, his scent bringing the man she adored and loved closer. She wasn't sorry to love him. Not that. Never.

Would it be so bad to stay in Kula? Her heart and mind tore her apart. Gren would never leave Kula, and he would want her to remain at his side while he ruled.

What about her goals?

She had vowed to travel and find new cures. Tears rose in her eyes once again when the two goals collided.

Chapter 19

A conflict of goals.

In the shadows of the cave, Trell used the respite with Torkel to gather her thoughts. She couldn't stay in Kula. Not an easy decision to make. Far from it. She'd made up her mind. Once treatment for the king proved effective, she would leave. She wanted to stay, but also needed to travel the world in her search of finding new cures.

How am I going to tell Gren?

Watching him fight his brother had torn a hole in her heart. The reality that he might have died revealed how deeply her feelings for him were. She'd grown accustomed to seeing his handsome face and amazing crystalline eyes. Talking with him daily had given Trell a true window to his heart.

While he acted like he understood the importance of her goal, did he really mean it? Never in a thousand years had she faced a more difficult situation. Her eyes watered, burned, and tears threatened to fall.

It was worse than the time while an Ossa pine and a beetle infestation threatened to chew a ring around her trunk and into the inner bark and phloem, which would have killed her. Luckily, her brother eradicated the insects before they launched a mass attack. His actions saved her and the other trees of Demit Woods.

No one guarded her now. She was on her own.

First, though, the king. Treating him should take her mind off talking to Gren. "Are you ready to return?" she asked him.

He raked back his hair. "Not really. Stay here. Out of my father's reach. He might appear a new man, but can we be certain? You could give me instructions on how to treat him."

She drew to a stop, feeling a mild sting. "Don't you trust my abilities?"

"It's not your skill I'm worried about. It's my father."

Trell heaved a heavy sigh. Her heart ached for Gren. He had a lot to adjust to as well. "You heard him. He sounded sincere."

"He's always been harsh and unrelenting. Oh, he's a man of his word, but falling victim to the Untouchable disease made him a desperate man. He, himself, reminded me that desperate people make ill-conceived decisions when they are faced with no options."

She eyed her staff. All the ribbons hung down. While Gren's concern warmed her heart, duty came first. "I'm not worried. Let's discuss this later."

Scowling, he clearly disliked her refusal to listen. His chin rose in a stubborn tilt. "What if there isn't an afterwards? We must consider the possibility my father will refuse to allow you to leave."

She inhaled deeply, nerves stretched to their limit. "You just said he was a man of his word. The king is trusting me to cure him of a disease that's supposedly terminal. I must try."

Gren hung his head. "Then we're in this together. No matter the outcome."

Trell heard enough. She turned to Torkel. "And you…" She shifted the bowl with one hand and wiggled an index finger at him. "I don't want any interference from you. Do you understand?"

"I am a mighty and powerful dragon. I do not take orders from you."

"Blessed Heyln, give me strength. On this you will heed me. Or—"

"Or what? You'll tell the Guardians? Go ahead. You think I don't know how your human mind works. They do not frighten me."

Trell wanted to throttle Torkel's thick neck with her bare hands. She knew he couldn't read her mind, no matter how hard he tried to pretend otherwise.

"They might have some influence over you. That's my hope." She stared at the huge creature who'd been her friend since his birth. He'd looked to her for friendship and guidance. But times were changing. He was maturing into his own being. A gentler hand was necessary to soothe his ruffled scales. Rather than order him about, all she could do was make suggestions and hope that he gave them serious consideration. "At least concede that the existence of one dragon is going to throw the world into a tizzy. If people learn others exist, I have no idea how they will react. They could organize hunting parties to destroy them. Stop being selfish. If you won't take your own safety into consideration, think about them. The dragonets are too young to protect themselves."

He lifted his elongated snout and sniffed the air, clearly stalling. Trell tapped her foot in the wait.

Moments passed before the dragon waddled to the center of the cave, his massive weight sending

317

vibrations through the ground as he walked. *"Understood."*

That was quick. Perhaps too quick.

Trell raised her eyebrows. Torkel might have compromised, but worry niggled her. Being a dragon, by nature his unpredictability was notorious. She'd watch him carefully and somehow get word back to Cress and the Guardians to warn them that Torkel was becoming independent.

She gave her staff a final glance. The ribbons remained down. That assuaged the worst of her worries.

Inhaling deeply, she spared a quick glance at Gren. Their gazes locked. The intimacy lasted for the briefest heartbeat. Trell tried to work out the possibilities of enjoying a future with him after curing the king, then rejected the likelihood.

With a sad smile, she nodded toward the cave's entrance and trod out the opening. She carried the bowl as Gren walked alongside her. The viscous, slime-like liquid jiggled along the sides. On the incline, Gren kept a firm hand on her waist to steady her as she held the bowl level and stepped with care, not wanting to lose a precious, single drop.

Soldiers parted as they approached. The noise in the camp seemed to accelerate, then fade as they passed individuals. No sign of spilled blood or evidence of where Oded had fallen lingered. Several men nodded to Gren in greeting, obviously pleased with the outcome of the battle.

At the king's yellow and white tent, Gren lifted the flap and offered her a smile of encouragement.

Nodding, she entered, letting her eyes adjust to the difference in light.

The king and Riff, deep in conversation, stopped and leapt to their feet.

"Your Majesty." She bowed her head. "I brought the medication."

"What do we do now?"

"I was told the solution should be half-strength. We start with that. I assume that once applied, the healing begins."

The king nodded toward a table. "Riff, fetch the healer another bowl."

The youngest Har did as bade. He handed a shallow bowl to Trell.

She nodded her appreciation. "If I could have a pitcher of water and a rag."

This time Gren jumped at her request. "Here," he said, bringing a clay pitcher that sloshed and a square he'd torn off a larger cloth.

She poured half the gooey spittle into one bowl and measured an equal amount of water by eye. Dipping the rag into the solution, she let the mixture soak into the rag, then turned to the king. "Grandmother Lurri, a Fezner healer, told me that just a drop is required to work on those newly affected. I assume it is absorbed through the skin and travels throughout the body. Let me apply this to your arm, then judge if it is enough or not."

The king cocked a brow. "And if it isn't?"

Focusing on the task calmed Trell. "Then we'll try something else. There's no need to overwhelm you with a step-by-step description. Are you ready?"

A stoic expression settled on Stal Og Har's face, and he nodded without hesitation. The man wasn't a coward. She gave him that and draped the moist rag

319

over his forearm.

A loud gasp sounded from the king, followed by a string of curses that Trell remembered once hearing a seaman utter. These expletives would have made the veteran sailor proud.

The reaction, despite the man's suffering, delighted her. "Tell me what you feel."

He regained his composure and eyed Trell beneath lowered brows. "Blessed Toyt, it stings like my arm is being eaten by millions of creatures invisible to the eye."

"Good tidings indeed."

Scowling, the king demanded clarification. "Meaning?"

"Before you couldn't feel a thing."

"I retract my earlier remarks. There is even a sour taste in my mouth. Dragon spittle is powerful."

"I believe what you are experiencing is a reaction of the spittle on living tissue. I assume several applications will be required over the next few days." Trell grabbed a small blanket and began to fan his arm. "Mayhaps a cool breeze will relieve the discomfort. Keep telling me how you feel. You are the first individual in known history to be treated in this manner with the correct dosage. It is of the utmost importance that I am informed of the changes to document them."

"How fortunate for me," he said through gritted teeth.

She smiled at the sarcasm. "I would say it's far better than the alternative."

Before the king answered, the tent flap was thrown back and a tall, ebony-haired man sauntered inside.

Trell's mouth dropped. "Torkel!"

****

Gren's blood went cold. Damn dragon. He was supposed to remain out of sight. Why expose himself to unknown dangers?

Trell stopped fanning his father. "Torkel, you are so predictable. I'm not surprised you didn't heed my warning."

The tall man shrugged, his golden gaze studying the tent's interior with an amused expression on his stern face.

The lack of concern from both Trell and Torkel puzzled Gren. Out of his peripheral vision, he saw Riff frown. His brother hadn't uttered a word since their return. His green eyes simply followed their every movement. Gren could only guess what he thought.

"How'd you get past my sentries?" the king demanded.

Torkel stood with a brazen stance and grinned in defiance. "Easily."

His father's gaze danced between him and Trell, questioning. "Do you know this man? Who gave him permission to enter my tent?"

Gren stepped forward, prepared to accept responsibility, but his unsaid offer was rebuffed.

Torkel waved away the king's response. "I do not need your permission."

"Insolent cur. Guards!" the king hollered.

A sickening feeling churned in Gren's stomach. He had to curb additional outbursts. "No guards. I know this man, and you might like to be introduced, too."

Stal Og Har scowled. "Who is he?"

"Isn't it obvious, Your Majesty?" Seemingly enjoying himself, Torkel bent a leg in the king's direction. "You requested to meet me."

A bewildered expression flashed over the king's face, then recognition lit his eyes. "You're the dragon."

"At your service," Torkel said, undaunted.

Perplexed, the king frowned. "How—how did you… So, it's true. Dragons can shapeshift."

Gren was amazed at how fast his father grasped the situation. He wished he had.

Torkel flaunted another grin that made his odd yellow eyes gleam. "While I am most impressive in my dragon self, sometimes it is easier to walk among humans as one of them. And sometimes I am curious. Is that not normal behavior among your species?"

Stal Og Har sank into the cushions, keeping hold of the moist rag. "Normalcy has been absent from my life for many years."

"How do you feel?" Trell interjected.

The question made Stal frown. As he considered, his frown deepened. "I itch all over."

"The pain is gone?"

"My—my guest distracted me." Squinting at Torkel, the king nodded. "As I recall in the old tomes, dragons can change their shapes. What other beings can you become?"

A good question.

One Gren was eager to hear the answer. He swung his full attention on Torkel.

"King Har, are you friend or foe?" the dragon-man asked.

Stal adjusted his position on the pillows. "I would like to be your friend, not your enemy. The knowledge I possessed about dragons was grievously inaccurate. I take full responsibility for the error. You are an honored guest in my kingdom."

Torkel took his time answering. He glanced around the plush interior, seemingly taking stock of the richness. "The correct answer. Dragons are powerful creatures. Someday I will be king of the dragons. Right now I am the first to roam free on Feldsvelt, but others will follow on the beat of my wings and a wise man chooses his allies with care."

What did the dragon hope to achieve?

Worry beset Gren. This was unknown territory. He had never thoroughly examined the possibility of Torkel being dragon king. In all likelihood, it meant other dragons would visit the place he choose to set up his kingdom. Folding his arms Gren collapsed against the pillows, resolved to pay attention to this discussion.

Evidently he wasn't alone. Trell joined him and soon Riff sat as well. The conversation interested everyone.

The king's eyes widened. "Naturally, any who wish to pay you homage are welcome here."

Gren froze, amazed at the change in his father. Who was this welcoming stranger? Where was the harsh and unforgiving man who raised him?

A long buried anger clawed its ways to the surface. The veins in his neck pulsed as he clenched his fists into balls. Gren had never wanted to rule Kula. All he'd ever cared about were its people.

Now, as the heir apparent, it meant he would sacrifice what he most desired—Trell.

In good conscience, he could not...would not ask her to give up her ambitions. Only one of them should have to surrender their goal, and he would rather it be him than her. She was an excellent healer, and it would be selfish of him to keep her for himself.

He exchanged a look with her, only to discover sympathy reflecting on her face. Did she grasp his struggle?

His concentration broke when his father rose and sighed. "How can I convince you of my sincerity?"

When Torkel flashed a smile, Gren halfway expected to see jagged teeth with spittle dripping to the ground. Instead, a normal smile appeared. "An interesting question. One full of prospects."

"You have an advantage over me," the king replied. "You know what humans are capable of, but I have no idea what prompts a dragon's actions."

"Many things catch our attention and garner our interest. Of course, treasure attracts our notice. Jewels. Gold. We covet those items without question. But if you're asking what each dragon can accomplish, I cannot say. Each dragon is unique, with different powers."

The king nodded as he absorbed the information. "I'm sure you speak true, but I am interested in what you can do... Ah, Torkel, is it?"

"Torkel is my name. And best you be on your finest behavior, for I am gauging your worth for my attention."

Riff gasped beside him. Bracing himself, Gren put his hand out to stop his brother from leaping forward and perpetuating a mindless deed.

Trell's face paled. "You can't judge who is worthy or not."

"She's absolutely correct," Gren said.

Torkel puffed out his chest and peered down his nose at them. "Firestones are not the only item of value in Kula. Creating a dragon society in this kingdom will elevate its status, thus improving its fortune. Isn't that what you always coveted?"

Gren tensed, petrified the dragon's pompous behavior would trigger an explosion from his father. Narrowing his eyes, he studied his father. A jumble of wonder and cunning slid across the aged face. Gren didn't doubt that his father already schemed how the dragon's presence would benefit him.

The earlier tension in Riff's posture relaxed, his disbelief replaced with astonishment.

Gren clasped Trell's hand, hoping the contact brought a measure of well-being.

She gave him a slight squeeze. "For shame, Torkel. Arrogance is unbecoming in a future king."

"Dragons do not abide by human principles. Best you remember that."

The air in the expansive tent grew stuffy. Gren resolved to make the dragon comprehend that he couldn't dictate whims. Others needed to be taken into consideration. "We have a saying in the mountains… honey garners more cooperation than vinegar."

Torkel focused his golden gaze on Gren. "I like honey."

Was the dragon being obtuse?

Gren never expected a sense of humor from Torkel, but perhaps he did. "It was a metaphor. I was referring to cooperating with each other. Unless you have a dragon rule for that."

Torkel scratched his chin. "Not that I know of if the favors are equal in value. It is a matter of what we can do in exchange for each other. Why didn't you say so in the beginning?"

"I thought I was."

"A subject we can set aside for more important ones." Torkel spared a glance around the tent, pausing on each individual until zeroing in on Gren. "Specifically, what are your intentions toward Trell? Do you love her?"

Trell gasped. "What business is it of your's?"

A niggle of worry wormed its way into Gren's heart. What if she didn't feel the same way? What if he offered for her and she rejected his suit? What then?

His mind returned to the first question. It rocked his world and required an answer. He could not take too long and forced himself to sit straighter. "It is private between Trell and me."

A yellow glint hardened the creature's eyes. "I warn you… Your life depends upon your answer."

"Torkel! Stop!" Trell cried.

Gren remembered her wonderful kisses, the lush curve of her hips, and the soft, warm touch of her hands. He climbed to his feet to face Torkel. "Absolutely, I love her. She holds my heart. I would ask for her hand in marriage." He smiled at Trell, releasing the doubt in his heart. "But I will not hinder her happiness because staying in one place is not what she wants."

Chapter 20

Dragon rules. Bah! Torkel had made them up.

Clenching her fists, Trell thought she would die of embarrassment. Torkel invaded her privacy, and that she declined to allow. "Gren, you didn't have to answer him. Torkel had no right to ask you. I would never put your position as future ruler in jeopardy. The villagers need you."

"I need you more."

Heat rose, burning her cheeks. Her world tilted. A sob escaped her lips. "Nay, Gren, you're—"

"I've already asked you to marry me and will keep doing so until you agree. I would have preferred requesting your hand in a romantic setting, but Torkel ruined that opportunity." Gren cast an accusing look at the culprit, then back to her. "Nothing happens by chance, Trell. I love you with all my heart and soul. You are the reason I take a breath in the morning. Ever since you saved me in Brenalin's marketplace, you've become precious to me."

The avowal shattered her heart into a thousand tiny pieces, and she feared she would never be able to put them back together. "Being together won't work. We have conflicting goals. You need to remain here to rule, and I plan to roam the world."

Gren raised his hand to silence her. "I've given our dilemma serious consideration. Once Father is cured, he will live a long, healthy life. Wed me, and we both can have what we want."

She shot a look at the king. By the man's silence, he seemed to agree with Gren. "And when he dies. What then?"

Sadness flashed over his face when he followed the direction of her gaze. "We return to Kula."

Trell paused. Temptation built with an increasing sense of desire. "You know my past, Gren. All of it. Traveling throughout Feldsvelt has been a dream of mine for eons. It's not something I can give up easily."

"I would never suggest that. You can still journey about after I'm anointed king. Here's what I propose..." He took a deep breath and stepped closer. "We wed now and venture out to find different cures. When it comes time for me to be king, we split our time seeking unknown treatments and administering them to the kingdom. We can leave the mountains, most likely during late fall, then return in springtime. With Torkel here, and his aid, no Demic lord would dare usurp Kula, and if Riff is willing to oversee the duties of the kingdom while we are away, we can have the best of both worlds."

The best of both worlds.

Riff grinned, agreeing with a bob of his head. "I'll find Brit and ask her to join me."

A sob of pure joy shook Trell's insides. "You think it's possible?"

"With all my heart." He took hold of her hands and gave each of her knuckles a kiss. "I wasn't honest with you. I feel so ashamed of my actions."

"I had secrets, too."

The warmth pouring out of Gren's eyes was hard to

refute. "Love is never perfect. It is never balanced equally. It is just love. You feel it...or you don't. If you will have me..."

"What woman wouldn't?" Her heart raced.

Gren stopped, blinked. "I wouldn't have suggested it if I hadn't given the matter serious consideration. Our lives and happiness are at stake."

She sneaked a peek around the tent's interior. The trio of spectators were eager to hear her answer as much as Gren by their tense expressions. She'd always suspected Gren possessed a heart of gold. His insight amazed her.

This only proved it.

Gren's emerald eyes shimmered with hope and expectation. Yet, from his expression, he feared a rejection. "You make refusing impossible. I—"

"Don't say another word," Gren interrupted.

She didn't heed him. The need to explain tantamount. "Nay, I want to be open and honest with you. You might change your mind after this... The first thing I want to do is investigate an ancient legend about a graveyard."

Gren dropped her hands as his sable eyebrows shot up. "Graveyard?"

"A healer was buried there, and on her deathbed, she declared the clay that covered her would be able to cure."

"And where would such a magical place be?"

"Far, far away in a grassland that is alkaline. People use the clay to alleviate minor ailments. Rumors say some eat miniscule amounts or smear it on their skin. It's been reported that all plants from the region have special powers." She laid her hand on Gren's arm.

"What if it's true? I need to check into it thoroughly to see if the soil really has the potential to heal. Not to do so would be irresponsible."

Gren leaned forward. "If that's our first destination, so be it. Meanwhile, I wish to marry you as soon as possible."

"A toast," the king proclaimed. "Riff, fetch mugs. A celebration is about to commence."

Trell's head spun with the quickness of events. "Wait! I haven't agreed. Not really…"

"Will you wed me?" Gren asked before she caught a breath.

Torkel stepped into view. The king bent forward. Riff froze with mugs in his hands.

Four pairs of eyes arrowed into her. She tried to tell herself a delay would give her the opportunity to study the Untouchable disease's cure firsthand. But the truth was she loved Gren and didn't want to lose him. "Aye, I will."

With a whoop of joy, Gren grabbed her by the waist and drew her close. "I love you."

"And I love you."

He ran his hand over her braids, making the tiny silver bells jingle. "Would you let the women of Kula prepare you?"

"Prepare me? What do you mean?"

"We have a custom in the mountains which the women participate in. That's about all I can tell you. The actual ritual is kept secret from men. We are not allowed to partake. But we do appreciate the results." His smile started slowly, then turned brighter than the sun.

The chance to partake in a new tradition excited

Trell's fancy. "I'm certain that I will enjoy it."

Gren accepted the mug Riff handed him and turned to his father. "Shall we make haste to Barg Castle? We are going to have a wedding tonight."

The king raised his arm, holding tight to the moist rag. "Frist, let's raise a toast in celebration."

Riff brought a jug and filled each mug.

The king lifted his drink. "To both of you."

Trell drank and tasted the familiar burn of blackberry and cedar as *farbrenen vaser* glided down her throat. Her family had doubled in a matter of minutes, and a warm tingle wormed its way from her toes to the top of her head. She wasn't sure if it was from happiness gushing within her or the potent drink, and she didn't care.

The king tossed his drink down in a single gulp. "I'll send out riders with invitations for the whole kingdom."

Gren and Riff clinked their mugs, then upended their drinks the same as their father.

Torkel huffed. "Will there be music? I insist upon it."

Trell laughed. Even in human form, the dragon dictated his wishes.

****

"You truly fancy Gren?" Torkel asked after pulling her aside in the tent to a private corner. "He is not pressuring you?"

The implication of his questions hung between them. He would put a stop to the proceedings if she so desired.

"Aye, he holds my heart."

"Then I leave you to participate in your upcoming

matrimony." So saying, Torkel strode out of the tent and camp.

A few seconds later, stepping outside with Gren holding her hand, she took a moment to watch the sun inch its way across the sky. She halfway expected to see Torkel's black silhouette soaring in the upslope of the mountain thermals.

As they forged ahead, tree branches brushed against Trell's shoulders.

"Congratulations, Once-an-Ossa. The Walking One has a good heart and is fortunate to have won your affection. The forest is pleased to have you nearby," the Mother Tree said as they walked through the woods.

Trell swayed, almost dancing. *"My thanks, Mother Tree."*

Word spread on the wind of the upcoming nuptials.

After three hours, a crowd awaited at the village.

Village women rushed Trell, smiling and giggling, trying to separate her from Gren. "Come with us."

Trell looked askance at Gren. He shrugged his broad shoulders. By the silly grin on his handsome face, he encouraged her to go and enjoy herself. "Your Majesty, you must apply your medicine when you arrive at the castle."

The king nodded. "I won't forget, soon-to-be daughter-in-law."

A tall woman with reddish highlights in her hair, Lizzette's mother, stepped forward. "Please, Healer. Come with me now."

"Where are we going?"

Gren bent down and kissed Trell's brow. "They'll explain. No harm will come to you. I promise. I'm told it's an experience wives-to-be enjoy. Very relaxing and peaceful."

Lizzette's mother nodded in agreement. "His lordship speaks true. We're off to the bridal hut. It'll take the rest of the day to prepare you for the forthcoming ceremony."

Curiosity swelled, and Trell allowed herself to be led away by the women. "How interesting. This is a bridal custom?"

At that, the other women crowded around the pair and guided her through the village toward a round hut that sat off to the side. White smoke billowed from a chimney, sweet and fragrant. Trell recognized the sharp scent of jasmine and the woodsy scent of sandalwood, both known for their relaxing properties.

An older woman stepped alongside her and took her hand in a soft, plump one. "You are to be hennaed."

Frowning, Trell pondered the significance of these tidings. The plant was familiar to her. Its leaf used to fight infections and skin diseases. Except she wasn't sick. What other use did the plant possess? "You grow henna in the mountains?"

Laughter preceded a response. "We trade with desert folk from Midber. We crush the leaves into a powder and use it as a dye for temporary body paint." The woman indicated the hut.

She dug in her heels, refusing to take another step until she understood. "Body paint?"

A dark-haired woman walked up to Trell. "It is not permanent. Our drawings are designed to awaken an inner light in the wedding bed."

Definitely a novel ritual.

Trell cast a last look over her shoulder as Gren, his brother, and father continued on foot toward the castle.

She almost wished she accompanied them.

A nudge on her back had her entering the hut. In the center of the room, a table draped with a huge throw made of soft bobcat rose to the height of her waist. Chairs lined the walls, and a small fire heated the room to a cozy temperature.

Lizzette's mother followed on her heels. "Every woman in the kingdom enjoys this night. We pamper you. You relax. We call this the Night of the Henna. It heightens the intimacy between couples and strengthens their bond. Please, let us do this for you and Lord Gren."

Women began crowding into the hut, carrying small black-bellied pots which held a slightly glittering black mush.

"Disrobe and climb on the throw," Lizzette's mother said. "It will keep you warm while we work on you."

Too inquisitive to refuse, Trell did as requested.

Women gathered on both sides of the table. They picked up fine-haired brushes and dipped them into the pots. They started applying the mixture at her knees, waist, and breasts. Coldness touched her skin. It tickled, but to her amazement a webwork of intricacy slowly emerged. The black lines created wild vines and roses, lilacs, and trees on her skin. Only a narrow space below her waist and the top of her thighs remained untouched.

The womenfolk continued their work, giggling, comparing their workmanship with each other. Someone pressed a mug of *farbrenen vaser* into Trell's hand. Her second in the day. She understood why the people loved the drink. It pushed back the mountain chilliness. After a couple sips, the tension in her muscles eased.

"How long does this process take?" Trell asked.

"Many hours," Lizzette's mother answered. "Fear not. You'll not miss your own wedding."

She had to lie still until the black mush dried on her front, then she rolled over and the process started over again. Ultimately done, she sat up to discover a few black lines on her front already flaked. Beneath, bits of reddish-brown designs appeared. A complex network of flora and fauna decorated her body.

For the second time in her life, Trell felt like a living tree. The memory formed tears.

One of the closest women noticed. "Do not weep, Healer. Think of your body as a garden that your new husband will have the pleasure of exploring with all its delights."

"You misunderstand," she said. "I am crying for joy."

Her comment made several women titter.

"Drink more," offered the oldest woman of the village. "Time for the final pattern."

Her head spun from the first two mugs. Surely, another would make it impossible for her to walk a straight line. "Is there room? My entire body is covered."

"Right here." Another stepped forward holding a pot of henna to trace Trell's bare skin above her womanhood. "The last pattern is a chain-linked chastity belt around your hips. It is my honor to paint it on you and for Gren to unlock.

Goosebumps formed at the light touch. Her cheeks burned. If these women knew what Gren and she had already shared, would they be so eager to treat her as if this was her first time with a man?

Several hours later, the henna dry, they draped Trell in a wedding costume. The gown, cinched under her breasts, had long flowing sleeves and was constructed of gossamer veils in a palette of colors that surpassed nature. She was covered from head to toe. Only her hands showed a pattern of swirls, dots, and boxes.

The villagers—men, women, and children—set her at the head of the procession to cut a circuitous path to Barg Castle with them following in her wake.

****

Gren gathered a dozen musicians from his father's army. Three with kettle drums, two with trumpets, two with tabors, four with fiddles, and even one with a bagpipe. The theme of a well-known love song spiraled from the walkway along the battlement. Gren joined the musicians with his flute. It was his way of serenading Trell and welcoming her into his family.

A gentle breeze swept down the mountain to carry the music throughout the land. He hoped Torkel was close enough to enjoy it. He wanted the dragon to feel a part of the ceremony.

"This is for you, Torkel," he said in mindspeech.

"I can hear."

"Good. Enjoy."

Stars twinkled in the black sky. If the dragon flew overhead, he was invisible.

The glow of torches alerted Gren to a festival-like parade of villagers approaching the castle. Custom dictated for Trell to lead the way. He encouraged the musicians to play louder when suddenly the tranquility of the night ended with an ear-splitting roar. Torkel flew over rooftops. A real live dragon.

To the villagers' credit, they did not panic or run away. Although, their mouths dropped open and their gazes were glued to a massive black dragon hovering in the air. With each flap of its wings, a sound cracked like sails filling with wind.

Gren leaned over the battlement. "Fear naught. The creature is my friend, Torkel, and he will be yours as well. You know the healer. She raised him from birth."

Trell broke into a run toward the dragon slowly descending in an open spot.

Behind her, Lizzette's small frame raced on her heels. She grabbed Trell's hand. Trell knelt down to the child's level. Whatever she said erased the girl's troubled expression. Lizzette gave a timid wave to the black dragon.

Torkel landed with a thud and blew dust and debris into the air. He stretched his long neck toward Lizzette. The child lifted eyes full of trust to Trell for reassurance and if her smile was any indication, the healer calmed her. Lizzette patted the tip of Torkel's elongated snout. The dragon bent his head and rubbed one of his horns against the child's cheek. A giggle escaped, and Lizzette spun around to race back to her mother's side.

Trell looked up at the battlement and waved.

Gren's heart swelled, and he urged for her to enter the castle.

****

Trell had heard faint musical notes at the outskirts of the village and instantly singled out Gren's flute. She let the serenade wrap around her, infuse her with its magic, and draw her closer...until Torkel announced his presence with a roar.

Torkel.

Her heart had stopped at the sight of the dragon suspended overhead like a giant shadow. How would the villagers react? She watched him descend, mouth drying, lips pinched with fear.

She ran to him, gossamer veils whipping the air, to throw herself between the beast and the villagers, though none had carried weapons to the wedding celebration. Still, she wasn't willing to take chances with his life.

The music stopped. Dead silence shrouded the area.

If Lizzette hadn't followed her...

Thank the Gods, Torkel proved just as curious about the little girl as she was about him.

When a laughing Lizzette raced to her mother, only then did Trell release a sigh of relief. Acceptance by the child seemed to open a path for the rest of the village.

Her gaze met Gren's, pleased to share a moment, making her wonder how long she stood gaping at him. At his signal, she looked at Torkel, then once again at Gren.

"Go, you fool," Torkel told her. *"Unless you've changed your mind."*

"Nay, I haven't. I never realized until this moment how very important being with Gren was to me."

"Then don't waste another precious second."

Trell nodded and quickened her steps toward the castle. A continuous piece of red silk lay unrolled under the massive portcullis at the entrance. It shimmered under the glow of candlelit lanterns. She stopped, unwilling to ruin the expensive material.

"Go, Trell." Lizzette's mother urged her forward.

"Gren awaits you."

"Walk, Healer," a woman in the crowd said. "There cannot be a wedding without the bride."

People laughed. Trell's heart pounded. Butterflies tickled her stomach. Trepidation and happiness nearly swamped her as she looked from side to side at the press of people crowding the inner keep of Barg Castle. This was the beginning of a new adventure in her life. She spotted the man whose arm she stitched up on her first day of moving Dori's supplies. The woman who couldn't sleep waved from the other side.

Stepping onto the silk, the flowing gossamer veils fluttered over her arms, between her legs. Her feet wrinkled the fabric. Behind her, a joyful murmur of approval rose from the villagers as they followed.

The red fabric continued up three steps into the castle, down a passageway, and into the great hall. To her surprise, nobles were bedecked in brightly colored, long-sleeved velvet tunics down to their knees, belts with buckles decorated with gemstones, woolen leggings that matched their tunics or were a completely different color or pattern for the men, and the women in gowns of purple, forest green, and sky blue cinched at their waists with long sleeves that hung to the floor. They stood shoulder to shoulder in the lengthened room. Riders must have ridden like the wind throughout the kingdom to announce the wedding.

The tall, thin Lord Crit grinned and raised a mug in salute upon spying her. Halfway down the aisle, she spotted the giant Lord Maxx standing protectively next to his wife, Lady Ebba. Both beamed at her, their happiness genuine.

The king sat on the jasper throne with Riff on his

Darcy Carson

left. But the only person to matter stood on the king's right—Gren. Her heart thumped so hard she swore everyone in the crowded room could hear it.

"You look beautiful," Gren said upon her arrival at his side. He took her hand and raised it to kiss. His fingers traced the flowing lines decorating her hand. "Are you ready?"

"Aye…nay! I'm not sure what to do. I've never been married before."

"Neither have I. It'll be something we learn together. One of many adventures."

The king rose from the high throne. "Who gives this woman to this man?"

"I do," boomed a voice from the back of the room.

The entire assemblage in the great hall whirled to face the entrance, Trell included, though she had instantly recognized the self-confident voice.

Torkel, in human form, strode into the room, head high, steps bold, completely ignoring the dozens of stares aimed at him on either side of the room. His leggings and tunic appeared fresh. She couldn't have been happier to have him share this wonderful moment in her life.

Smiling, pleased at his appearance, she studied her friend as he ambled down the aisle.

When Torkel reached the dais, he gave her hand a light squeeze, then narrowed his golden eyes. "You'd better never mistreat her," he warned Gren. "Or you'll answer to me. Is that understood?"

Trell cocked a brow at the boast. "You'll not dictate orders. It's interference."

Gren laid a hand on her arm. "Fret not, Trell. Neither you nor Torkel have to worry in that regard."

"I simply wish to make my feelings clear," Torkel said, stepping off to the side. "Proceed."

Trell smiled to herself. How like the dragon to think he controlled the goings-on.

She stood on Gren's left, noticing he wore the jasper pendant once worn by Oded. Turning, she faced the king. "I give myself to Gren."

"And I give myself to Trell," he replied.

The king froze, clearly unaccustomed to a female determining the proceedings, then recovered quickly. "I hereby bless this union of these two people. May they live long and be fruitful, and let the celebration begin."

Cheers erupted in the great hall with the proclamation.

Chapter 21

With the celebration in full swing since before the wedding service, the guests were well into their cups. Gren couldn't wait to slip out fast enough. He wanted Trell all to himself.

"When can we retire, my husband?" Trell asked him in a low voice as if experimenting with his new title.

He smiled down at her. "My darling wife, you're reading my mind. I'm sure we wouldn't be missed."

"Then let us depart." She waved to encompass the great hall. "People are so busy reveling in our union they'd never notice our absence."

He slipped an arm around her and guided her toward the doors. Outside the great hall they clasped hands and sped up the majestic staircase two steps at a time.

"This way," he said, heading toward his bedchamber.

Halfway down the corridor Torkel mindspoke to him. *"Be warned, Gren. Treat her well. She may not be a dragon, but I value her highly."*

"Fear naught. As I've already told you, her wishes will always come first with me."

At his bedchamber, he skidded to a stop and caught his breath. "You ready?"

"Aways, my love."

Laughing, they slipped inside. He'd never given the room any particular notice in the past. With Trell by his side, he tried to view it through her eyes.

The room was nearly square with a solitary window where moonlight cast a silvery stream inside. Closest to them was the chair Torkel had slouched in, next to it his desk cluttered with papers, a tall wardrobe, and last but not least—his bed with an ornately carved headboard and canopy over the top half. A sixth sense told him Trell studied that particular piece of furniture the longest.

"What a fine bed," she said, once finished surveying the room.

He moved closer to touch a red and gold pillow covering. "My mother bequeathed the head sheet to me. Oded received the featherbed and Riff got the feather bolster."

Trell flashed a look at him, and with one mind, they tumbled onto his overstuffed bed.

After kissing for several moments, Gren raised his head to stare at his beautiful bride. No dungeon cell with straw for cushioning her. Never again. He wanted to go slow, make her first time as his wife special. "We do not need our clothes."

"Then undress me."

He didn't need to be asked twice.

When she lay naked before him, he couldn't believe the perfect warm beauty wrapped in henna decorations. She sucked in her breath when his finger traced a flowing vine that went up her arm and over her shoulder. He paused to admire Trell.

"Why'd you stop? You must discover where they go," she teased him.

Delineating the flowers, he uncovered bees in their centers, so expertly illustrated he could hear them buzzing. A bouquet surrounded her nipples that called for him to kiss.

So he did.

Next, his fingers followed a tree up her leg to discover a bird's nest in a branch across her belly. Everywhere new discoveries unfolded just for him.

Rolling her over on her belly, a gasp escaped him. "There's a whole forest over your buttocks and a dragon flying above it. I wonder how the village women knew to put that on you?"

Trell lifted up on an elbow to peer over her shoulder. "Most people are far more informed and keener than others realize."

His attention returned to the warm skin of her leg, delighted in the way curves arose beneath his fingers. "They missed a spot."

"What?"

He touched her ankle. "No henna. It's bare."

Trell wiggled onto her back and held out her arms. "Kiss me. Please."

"With pleasure."

Kissing led to intimate touching. Gren thought he would die of pleasure. He lost track of time as he brought his beautiful wife to the brink. Ready to explode, he waited for her to surge into the abyss. A pulsing constriction rippled down his manhood when Trell climaxed, and he let himself follow her over the edge.

For several long seconds, neither moved, then she draped an arm over his chest. "I feel so good. Contented. Still tingly. Is this how everyone feels after making love?"

"You should always enjoy it. What we shared is something we will treasure for all time."

"That would be nice. Can we do it again?"

Gren laughed, delighted. "Later, I promise."

A look of disappointment raced across Trell's face in the dim light. "I do admit curiosity about how your manhood creates such wondrous sensations. Mayhaps...if I could examine it while erect..." Her voice trailed off.

Gren choked. He'd always known Trell was unique, that she would delight him in numerous ways. The idea of spending the rest of his life with her just increased tenfold.

Trell sat up. "I—I mean I've seen a man's body afore. You, of course. And the body of a deceased man in my schooling. Now you've made me curious how a piece of anatomy can bring so much enjoyment. It deserves my full attention. I really would like to learn how it functions."

Only Trell could delight him with such thoughts. "Not the most romantic small talk."

"Well, I suppose. But I am curious. Purely for educational purposes."

Gren laughed, his life felt complete with the woman beside him. "Life with you will never be dull. I want you for every minute of every day. I love you, sweet Trell. You are the woman for me."

"And you are the only man I love, Gren Og Har."

She smiled and laughed when he gathered her into his arms. Desire erupted inside him, spreading out from his core as she raised her lips for him to kiss. He brushed her delectable mouth with tenderness, aching for a long life to spend with her.

****

Trell woke in the huge featherbed sated, a happily married woman.

"Where are you going?" a groggy male voice asked beside her.

She scooted upright and bent over to place a kiss on Gren's forehead. "I'm sorry. Did I wake you?"

"I've been awake for a while. I had no wish to disturb you."

Slipping from bed, Trell knew the gossamer gown from the previous night wouldn't be appropriate attire for daily wear. She found her own clothes neatly folded on a chest and donned them posthaste. "I'm eager to check on your father's progress. Learning how to properly treat his condition will have to be assessed. He might require another treatment of Torkel's acid. The more I know, the easier it will be to treat the next Untouchable."

"Wait for me to dress. I'll accompany you."

"Hurry, then." Secretly, Trell appreciated watching Gren's naked form exit the bed. He was a magnificent specimen of a man, which made her proud to be his wife. "Once I've determined his status, I can begin preparations for our journey."

Servants were already up and moving about when they left Gren's bedchamber. They were greeted with smiles and nods as they made their way through Barg Castle.

The king and Riff sat at the trestle table in the great hall supping on their morning meal.

Grinning, the king's eyes widened. "I expected the pair of you to stay abed this morning."

Trell's cheeks burned with embarrassment as they took seats side by side. "We retired early."

"Wish I had," Riff spoke, rubbing his temples. "I feel awful."

Treating a patient always took precedence. She shunted aside her own concerns. "What are your symptoms?"

"My head is splitting in two, and my stomach is rolling like I'm on a vessel in a storm. And I'm no sailor with sea legs."

"You probably imbibed too much *farbrenen vaser* and are dehydrated. Have you been urinating more than usual this morn?"

Riff nodded.

"Alcohol is a diuretic. Your body is trying to flush it out. If you're nauseous or vomiting, the alcohol is triggering those symptoms. I'll give you some ginger to chew throughout the day. First though, you should sip on ginger tea." She turned her attention to the king. "More importantly, Your Majesty, how do you feel?"

No clue showed on the man's face to his inner thoughts. "Best you check for yourself." He held out his arm and shoved back his sleeve.

The moment of truth.

Swallowing, Trell stood and came around the table. The few steps to reach his side seemed like a long walk to the gallows. A shiver ran down her spine. Taking his arm in two hands, she raised it to examine. Afterward, her gaze flicked to Stal's face, then back down. "It worked!"

"Aye, it did."

A wide smile spread across the king's face the likes of which she'd never seen before. The upturned mouth

347

and happy eyes with crow's feet at the corners were genuine. The sight made her heart burst with happiness. "How do you feel? Any discomfort?"

"None whatsoever."

Trell ran her fingertips over his forearm. No swelling and the spots she'd first noticed were barely visible. A few remained, but they had faded, less distinguishable. "I'll reapply the mixture, just to make sure."

"You are the healer. I, merely the patient."

Gren barked out a laugh.

His father scowled. "What amuses you?"

Gren's expression sobered. "You. In all my life, I do not recall you ever yielding. This new behavior is going to take getting used to."

The king straightened his shoulders. "For me as well. I have a future now. I have not shared the secret of my illness with another individual for years."

Two things caught Trell's attention. She picked the most obvious question first. "How long were you infected?"

The king looked away, visibly uncomfortable with discussing the subject. "Before my children were born. I—I loved…" He broke off. "I loved my sons' mother with all my heart. I do not wish to malign the dead."

Both Gren and Riff rose, their expressions hardened as they riveted their attention on their father.

"Father, what does Mother have to do with your illness?" Gren asked. "The time for secrets is long past."

Stal rubbed his arms and legs and let a slight smile show. "I suppose it can't hurt now. Your mother and I were childhood sweethearts. We loved each other deeply. No one else mattered in our eyes. What we didn't know, however, is she came to the marriage already afflicted. When her illness was detected, I couldn't condemn her. I kept her secret."

Riff gasped.

Gren collapsed into a chair.

That answered her second question. How he had contracted the disease? Her heart broke for these three men. Clearly, they loved the long-dead woman. "I'm so sorry."

"Do not begrudge me the years we shared," Stal answered. "Our marriage started with love. We had good times and together produced three sons who were her pride and joy."

"What happened to her?" Trell asked.

A long silence ensued. Both Riff and Gren leaned forward. Plainly, this was a tale that they had never heard before, and like children hearing a bedtime story, they were eager to learn the details.

With a heavy sigh, the king spoke. "When her symptoms began to reveal themselves, she took her own life. She didn't want the taint of the disease to touch me or her sons."

Trell squeezed her eyes shut. "Again, you have my utmost sympathies."

"Pity isn't necessary. I have my memories. And they are good ones. My only regret is you weren't here to save her as well."

****

Gren sat at the large table where his parents had held court and digested the information about his mother. While it didn't explain everything about his childhood, it gave him insight into the past.

"I'm sorry, Father," he said.

Stal glanced at him. "Not more than me. You have no idea what misery is like until you lose the love of your life, and I hope neither you nor Riff suffer that fate. The world becomes shades of gray and beige. I cannot tell you how many times during the day did I turn to discuss a matter with her and she wasn't there. I felt all alone. At night, I retired to my chambers, and tears would pour out of me."

For the strong man to confess such a weakness stunned Gren. He reached for Trell's hand, the urge to touch her overwhelming, and he took strength in her close warmth. "Believe me, I understand."

Trell squeezed his hand. "After we eat, shall we gather supplies for our journey?"

"I have set aside two of my best desert horses for your use," the king said. "It's the least I can offer."

"He's not the only one with a gift for you," Torkel mindspoke.

By the surprise on Trell's face, the dragon spoke to both of them at the same time.

"What do you mean?" Trell asked, sitting straighter and taking the lead.

"The firestones granted me the secret of their existence. One that I can share with whomever I wish."

Gren pulled his brows together in confusion. *"What are you talking about?"*

"Silly human. The gemstones of Feldsvelt called the original dragons to this world with the promise of great wealth. Not all was actual treasure, *but knowledge. If a gemstone truly accepts a dragon, it will gift him with the power of themselves."*

Gren's head pounded trying to make sense out of

350

the dragon's conversation. *"Cease talking in riddles, Torkel."*

"But I'm enjoying myself."

"Then do so on your own time. Not mine."

"Does that mean you have no desire for my gift?"

Gren flicked a glance at his father and brother. They had no inkling the dragon tormented him about a magical gift. He leaned forward, eager to hear details, yet fearing if he revealed an overabundance of interest, the dragon would just string them along. "Come, Trell, if Father has no objections, I'd like to see which horses are ours to use."

"If you'll excuse us, Your Majesty." She stood and smiled.

Gren knew her smile stemmed from understanding his ploy with Torkel. She practically giggled when they reached the hallway.

"Have I told you how much I love you lately?" she asked.

"Not that I recall. Tell me."

"I love, love you."

"Cease this silliness. Your behavior does not amuse me," Torkel mindspoke to them. *"Humans are always in such a hurry. They have no patience. Do you or don't you want to know the power I can grant you?"*

Trell winked at him. *"If you insist."*

"Come to my lair. It will be easier to show you."

Gren turned to Trell. "Should we?"

"Dragons are extremely stubborn. We might as well listen to what he has to say."

The trek up the mountain provided just the peaceful excursion they required after the hectic days. They decided to walk instead of riding, aware closeness to the dragon's presence might spook their mounts.

At the cave, Trell asked permission to enter.

Black on black, Torkel lay in his cave of firestones nearly impossible to see. He raised his bony head when they entered. *"Welcome, friends. I'm glad I could tempt you to come."*

Trell strode over to the massive creature and scratched his long snout. *"I would have come no matter what to bid you farewell."*

Torkel adjusted his position, a difficult task considering his ponderous weight. *"Sit, let me explain. I am the first black dragon to fly Feldzvelt's skies in eons. Firestone is a black organic. Black is the darkest color, the result of the absence or complete absorption of visible light. In simple terms… Black hides things."*

An expanding sensation grew in Gren's chest. Curiosity swelled. *"Is there a point to this discussion?"*

"Patience, Gren," Trell advised aloud.

A cloud of firestone powder rose from the ground as the dragon adjusted his position. *"How typical of a human. Always rushing things. All my life, Trell has protected me, advised caution. It is my turn to protect her."*

Gren scowled, taking offense. *"I can keep her safe."*

"Not like I can. I will not be traveling with you or her, but I can bequeath invisibility upon you both. If the pair of you are going to travel this world, it will come to good use if you are able to disappear at will."

Gren froze, stunned by the prospect. Never in his wildest imagination did he expect such a gift. He tried to digest the information.

Trell recovered first. *"Tell me about this power."*

"I can grant it to just you or include your heirs, if you so wish."

Gren recovered from his surprise. *"Having the ability to avoid bandits and the like is a worthwhile talent. However, invisible children might be difficult to rear."*

The dragon chuckled. *"It could be a power that comes upon adulthood."*

"That I approve of," Trell said, smiling.

"Then let it be."

Gren waited to sense a change in himself but felt nothing. *"When will this change happen?"*

"It already has. Think yourself invisible," Torkel instructed. *"Visualize yourself unseen."*

He and Trell practiced winking out of sight at will. While both invisible, they could see each other. If they took turns, the other could not see where the other went.

Afterward, they headed back to the castle. It took three days for him and Trell to depart Kula with great fanfare. The king appeared completely healed, and the entire village came out to see them off.

As they passed through Kula, Gren stopped and scanned the villagers' faces for Lizzette. When the little girl ran across the open center straight for him, he dismounted and knelt down.

"You're leaving, Lord Gren," the girl said, her small chin trembling.

"I am, but I did not forget about you."

Lizzette's eyes widened. "You didn't?"

"This will have to do until I return." He pulled out an oilskin-wrapped treat. "And mayhaps I'll discover in my travels a new treat to bring back for you."

The smile he received lightened his step. Gren

remounted, shared a smile with his lovely wife, and started playing his flute, the music as sweet and fragile as a budding sapling emerging from the ground. He let the notes, some high, some low, all rich and full surround them and their mounts.

A black dot soared in the sky. *"Hurry back. I shall miss your music while you are gone."*

A word about the author...

Award-winning author Darcy Carson grew up reading everything her mother brought home from the library. Reading romances became her favorite topic. Eventually, her love of those novels led her to start writing them.

She resides in a Seattle suburb with her husband and a prince of a toy poodle.